SOMETHING IS
ROTTEN IN FETTIG

A SATIRE

JERE KRAKOFF

ANAPHORA LITERARY PRESS

AUGUSTA, GEORGIA

ANAPHORA LITERARY PRESS
2419 Southdale Drive
Hephzibah, GA 30815
http://anaphoraliterary.com

Book design by Anna Faktorovich, Ph.D.

Caricatures by Jere Krakoff

Cover: Illustration from *Ladies Home Journal,* Sept 1910, of a typical Lower East Side "street scene" (NYPL).

Edited by: Jordan Baker

Published in 2016 by Anaphora Literary Press

Something Is Rotten in Fettig: A Satire
Jere Krakoff—1st edition.

Print ISBN-13: 978-1-68114-197-8
ISBN-10: 1-681141-97-3
EBook ISBN-13: 978-1-68114-198-5
ISBN-10: 1-681141-98-1

Library of Congress Control Number: 2015949531

SOMETHING IS ROTTEN IN FETTIG

JERE KRAKOFF

ACKNOWLEDGMENTS

I thank my wife, Adria, whose ideas, editorial and moral support made this book possible. I also thank my friends, Walt and Dona Groer, who listened to my readings as the novel was evolving and made wonderful suggestions to improve the story arc. Finally, I want to recognize John Stember, a former colleague, for his numerous contributions to the improvement of the manuscript.

CONTENTS

1   Prosecutor General Umberto Malatesta's   9
     Opening Rant
2   Plotkin's Childhood Education   17
3   Plotkin Ventures Out with Ana Bloom   21
4   Bar Mitzvah Rehearsal   25
5   Bar Mitzvah Speech   30
6   Plotkin's Father Migrates to Republic   32
7   Plotkin's Conscription into the Butcher Shop   36
8   Plotkin Covers His Window with Mud   42
9   Malatesta Contacts Bookbinder/Sprem   47
10   High Minister Threadbare Pressures Sprem   50
11   Chicken Plucker Meets Former Curator, A. I.   55
     Gopnik
12   Bookbinder's Speech   62
13   Bookbinder Introduces Anti-Window   68
     Covering Legislation
14   Malatesta Seeks Indictment from Secret Blind   72
     Jury
15   Plotkin's Arrest   76
16   Plotkin's Is Imprisoned in Purgatory   79
17   Chicken Plucker's Letter to Plotkin   85
18   The Society for Apparent Representation of   88
     Indigent Criminal-Types
19   Attorney Felix I. Bleifus Visits Plotkin in   92
     Purgatory
20   Plotkin Seeks Advice from the Lunatic about   97
     Trials
21   Ana Bloom Visits Plotkin in Prison   104
22   Bloom Gets Bernard Talisman to Represent   108
     Plotkin
23   Plotkin Reunites with his Family   114
24   Plotkin Rekindles his Friendship with Ana   116
     Bloom
25   Plotkin Examined by Psychiatrist Seymour   118
     Peltz
26   Plotkin and Chicken Plucker's Trek to   124
     Talisman's Office

27	Plotkin and Chicken Plucker are Exiled	128
28	Plotkin and Chicken Plucker Wait in the Basement	133
29	Plotkin and Chicken Plucker Meet with Talisman	136
30	Talisman Seeks Prime Thinker's Input	140
31	Prikash Locates Precedent	142
32	Gopnik Assesses the Window	146
33	Gopnik Issues Preliminary Findings	149
34	A Walk to Courthouse for Day 1 of Trial	150
35	Justice Wolfgang Stifel to Preside at Trial	154
36	Jury Selection Begins	156
37	Jury Selection Continues	159
38	Jury Empaneled	162
39	Stifel's Opening Sermon	165
40	Talisman's Opening Rant	169
41	Guda Prikash Enlisted	172
42	Prikash Appears in Court	177
43	Chicken Plucker Declared a Hostile Witness	181
44	Chicken Plucker's Direct Testimony	184
45	Golub Called to Re-Hypnotize Prikash	191
46	Chicken Plucker is Cross-Examined	195
47	The Lunatic is Persuaded to Testify	200
48	The Lunatic Testifies	202
49	Art Expert Hippolyte Thwaite Testifies	207
50	Prikash Cross-Examines Thwaite	213
51	Social Scientist Testifies	219
52	Gopnik's Voir Dire to Qualify Him as an Expert	222
53	Gopnik Testifies	226
54	Malatesta Cross-Examines Gopnik	231
55	Prosecution's Closing Diatribe	237
56	Defense's Closing Diatribe	241
57	Justice Stifel's Jury Directions	245
58	Jury Deliberations	248
59	A Verdict is Reached	251
60	Announcement of the Verdict	255
	Epilogue	260

CAST OF CHARACTERS

Primo Astigmatopolous — Leopold Plotkin's chicken plucker and best male friend

Pincus Barrenblat — Lunatic confined in Purgatory with Plotkin

Felix I. Bleifus — Lawyer with Society for Apparent Representation...

Ana Bloom — Leopold Plotkin's only female friend

Cicero Bookbinder — Inner Chamber Leader

The Concierge — Law firm's gatekeeper

Olaf Dybyk — Director of Internalized Security

Hinta Gelb — Head Librarian, National Library of Pedantic Writings

Hans Gogol — Warden of Purgatory House of Detention

A. I. Gopnik — Defense's Art expert and resident of insane asylum

Milos Gorky — Inner Chamber's "Great Dissenter"

Kimmelmen Bros. — Plotkin's Tearoom friends

Magdalena — A brothel employee and the chicken plucker's sweetheart

Umberto Malatesta — Republic's Prosecutor General

Seymour Peltz — A Warehouse psychiatrist

The Plotkins — Leopold (the protagonist); Jacob (father); Emma (mother); Misha and Moishe (deranged uncles)

Guda Prikash — Prime Thinker and one of Leopold Plotkin's defense attorneys

Jean-Pierre Proust — Commandant of the National Constabulary

Mendel Sprem — Cicero Bookbinder's Alter Ego

Wolfgang Stifel — Judge at Plotkin's trial

Steinbloom, Rogoff, Babel — Bernard Talisman's partners

Bernard Talisman — Senior partner in law firm and Plotkin's defense attorney

Emile Threadbare — Republic's High Minister

Kierkegaard Thumbnail — Prosecution's social science expert

Hippolyte Thwaite — Prosecution's art expert

TABLE OF CARICATURES

Leopold Plotkin	9
Hinta Gelb	17
Jacob, Moishe, and Misha Plotkin	25
Primo Astigmatopolous	36
Mendel Sprem	47
Emile Threadbare and Olaf Dybyk	50
A. I. Gopnik	55
Cicero Bookbinder	62
Milos Gorky	68
Umberto Malatesta	72
Jean-Pierre Proust and Aide-de-Camp	76
Hans Gogol	79
Felix I. Bleifus	88
The Lunatic, Pincus Barrenblat	97
Ana Bloom	104
Bernard Talisman	108
Seymour Peltz	118
The Concierge	128
Guda Prikash	133
Wolfgang Stifel	154
The Jury	162
Guda Prikash Repurposed	177
Magdalena	195
Hippolyte Thwaite	207
Kierkegaard Thumbnail	219

Leopold Plotkin

1

L eopold Plotkin, the infamous kosher butcher charged with "heinous crimes" against the Republic, fidgeted anxiously at the Accused's Table while waiting for his trial to begin. As he scanned the crowded room where the long-anticipated drama would soon unfold, his body rebelled. Rivulets of sweat cascaded from his chaotic thicket of hair onto his forehead. His right eyelid involuntarily closed and refused to reopen. Both hands shook uncontrollably.

The meat merchant wasn't alarmed by the aberrations. He had known since early childhood that a pathological aversion to conflict caused his body to react in abnormal ways when facing imminent hostilities. Sometimes the abnormalities took the form of situational blindness or transient hearing loss. Other times they consisted of shallow breathing, pseudo arrhythmia, or infantile drooling. However manifested, the symptoms typically disappeared within a few hours of onset and didn't return during the same conflict.

Bernard Talisman, a prominent attorney who was representing Leopold Plotkin in the Low Court of Criminal Transgressions *pro bono*, was troubled by his client's deterioration. He feared that the Jury would interpret the phenomenon as evidence of a guilty state of mind. In an effort to avoid that possibility, Talisman leaned into Plotkin's ear and advised the angst-ridden pariah to swab the sweat, shutter the functioning eyelid, and hide his hands under the Table. Grateful that his lawyer was taking an active interest in his case, despite not receiving a fee for his services, the butcher thanked Talisman for the advice and immediately complied.

Even with implementation of the recommended remedial measures, Talisman expected Plotkin to be convicted. Virtually every rational adult in the Republic shared that expectation.

In the days leading to trial, there had been subtle signs of growing pessimism within the butcher's small circle of supporters. Plotkin's parents had packed his few personal possessions in anticipation of his consignment to a penitentiary. His uncles had promised to visit him in prison every third weekend if they weren't experiencing florid hallucinations. *The Monthly Contrarian*, a rarely read anti-authority journal that considered Plotkin a hero to the cause, had declared in a front page editorial: "Regrettably, there is no realistic possibility of an acquittal for this courageous little man who stood up to the powers that be despite knowing it was a futile gesture that would end badly for him."

While Plotkin continued his anxious wait for the trial to begin, Prosecutor General Umberto Malatesta calmly conferred at the Prosecution's Table with a cabal of minions. The career bureaucrat was poised to deliver the government's Opening Rant, a trenchant itemization of why Plotkin deserved to be convicted and removed from society. Malatesta was a practicing narcissist with limited litigation skills. As a result, he craved the limelight but was wary of making a fool of himself. Balancing the pros and cons, he only tried cases that captured intense public attention, were likely to enhance his reputation, and seemed impossible to lose. Plotkin's was such a case.

Consistent with standard operating procedure, the minions had prepared the Rant and all questions Malatesta would pose to witnesses. They had also hosted a series of pretrial dress rehearsals to polish his delivery. Although the performances were uniformly uninspiring, the minions felt they were sufficient to secure a conviction. To feed Malatesta's narcissism, they routinely complimented him for parroting their scripts *brilliantly*. Lacking objectivity, he accepted the lies as the truth.

A gavel pounded against the Great Bench, a five-tiered oak

structure occupied by Justice Wolfgang Stifel and a cadre of low-level functionaries. Because the Bench stood at the center of the Courtroom, all sectors of the tribunal heard the thuds. The sounds prompted a chain reaction. Anticipatory murmurs lapped through the Spectator Pews. Reporters stirred in the Journalist Cubicle. Backs arched in the Jury Stall. Umberto Malatesta cleared his throat at the Prosecution's Table. Leopold Plotkin sagged at the Accused's Table. Bernard Talisman pursed his lips at Plotkin's side.

A Bailiff trundled into the Courtroom Well to announce the start of the trial. As rehearsed, Malatesta sprang from his chair and repositioned his litigation wig to a more belligerent location on his head. Looking appropriately ominous, the beetle-browed prosecutor lifted his trial robe off the floor and crossed the grey marble expanse with long theatrical strides before coming to rest at the base of the Great Bench. He craned his neck toward the gilded ceiling to meet the hooded eyes of Justice Stifel who hovered thirty feet above him on the top tier. "May it please the Court," Malatesta intoned confidently while stroking his moustache. "The Prosecution is ready to rant."

The diminutive judge, who was too short to otherwise be seen from most parts of the Courtroom, stood on a stool to increase his height. A vague smile embroidered Stifel's heavily wrinkled face. The limited sign of pleasure reflected ambivalence over the circumstances he found himself in. On one hand, he was elated that *The Republic against Plotkin,* one of the most important trials in his lifetime, was being presented in his domain. Having occupied the Bench for nearly four undistinguished decades, Stifel envisioned the spectacle as an opportunity to cement his legacy as a pro-prosecution zealot, with few ethical constraints, who worked hand-in-glove with the Government to elicit guilty verdicts. On the other hand, he was disappointed that Plotkin had insisted on a jury trial, a decision that robbed him of the honor of being known as the jurist who convicted the pariah. With an affection reserved for prosecutors, Stifel told Umberto Malatesta that the Court was "*extremely* pleased to have the Republic's *esteemed* representative in the Courtroom" and authorized him to proceed with *zeal* in laying-out the government's case.

Feigning respect for the little respected official, Malatesta genuflected in the Justice's general direction. After performing the charade, he waited for Stifel to dismount the stool, ease into the Judicial Chair, and disappear from sight. He then bounded to the Jury Stall to romance the seven men who had been selected to determine

Plotkin's fate. Strategically positioned only inches from the septet, Malatesta opened his mouth and, in a counterfeit baritone suggesting gravitas, asked, "*Who* or, more accurately, *what* is Leopold Plotkin?"

The question's pedantic delivery mesmerized the Jurors. Eager to learn more about the despised butcher than had been luridly reported in newspapers, they leaned forward in their chairs, mouths agape, eyes bulging, brows furrowed, ears aimed at the prosecutor.

"In a word or, perhaps, two sentences," Malatesta proclaimed, "the *despicable* meat merchant seated at the Accused's Table is a socialist masquerading as a capitalist, a nihilist in sheep's clothing, an unapologetic anarchist, and a devout vivisectionist! More to the point, he is a lapsed exhibitionist who, with malice aforethought and no afterthought, has gone to unprecedented, *illegal* lengths to avoid detection, all to the *profound detriment* of this Republic!"

Observing Malatesta's disdainful scowl, Jurors winced in their Stall. Elsewhere in the capacious venue, spectators grimaced, journalists scribbled, and Plotkin lowered his head. Stoical by nature, attorney Bernard Talisman didn't react.

"What this *pervert* has done is shocking even to Umberto Malatesta, the inimitable civil servant who stands before you!" the prosecutor shouted while raising his hands toward the ceiling like a tent revival preacher. "Anybody other than an imbecile who has been living under a rock knows that his acts and omissions have fomented a Crisis of unspeakable dimensions; unspeakable because the extent of the Crisis has yet to be determined!"

Malatesta tilted forward, gripped the banister that defined the Jury Stall, and shook his head vigorously. The sudden movement of a large object in their vicinity prompted several bodies in the Stall's front row to recoil in self-defense. Courtroom artists recorded the bold move for posterity.

"This *rodent* is an enemy of the State!" Malatesta pronounced with bombast after righting his head. "His *heinous* crimes—crimes that are both beneath and above contempt—continue even as Umberto Malatesta speaks. They are damaging the economic, social, and political well-being of the greatest country in the known civilized world! They imperil the capital city of Fettig and all who reside here, causing one to wonder whether it will lose its reputation as the crown jewel of civilization, the place of high culture, the port of entry for even the lowest of immigrants who come in search of truth and wisdom, not to mention prosperity, freedom, and better prisons!"

The prosecutor stopped talking to enable the Jurors to digest his hyperbole. After a moment of silence, he arched his back and asked, "Must Umberto Malatesta say more about this fiend's *diabolical* nature to enable you to come to terms with who, whom, or what you are dealing with?"

Anxious to see how the Jurors would react to the rhetorical question, Leopold Plotkin raised the eyelid that still functioned. Turning to the Jury Stall, he was disappointed to discover all seven Deciders mouthing the word "No." The butcher slouched lower in his chair and closed the lid tightly, not wanting to see more.

"Look at him!" the prosecutor snarled as he glared at the butcher, spittle dripping from his chin onto his robe. "He sits there calmly, eyes closed, not a care in the world! He's unconcerned with the havoc his crime spree has wreaked! Only a person without a conscience can be so aloof. While it pains Umberto Malatesta to say so, this *monster* is human in name only!"

Elated to see several Jurors staring at Plotkin malevolently, Malatesta bellowed, "This once highly regarded merchant's fall has been both swift and steep! It will be incomplete, however, until a guilty verdict! Unless this *animal* is convicted, as day follows night, spring follows whatever, and so forth and so on, the Republic will remain in harm's way, subject to his whims and caprices! To avoid a catastrophe of biblical proportions, you must send a message that his deviant behavior will not be tolerated in a society governed by *The Rules of Law.*"

Heads nodded piously in the Spectator Pews in recognition of the sanctity of *The Rules*, a collection of legislative edicts credited with the Republic's evolution from a brutish state of nature, where people routinely preyed on one another, to a civil society where predation, although still frequent, was better organized. The most pious heads belonged to officials cordoned in the Dignitaries Section who were responsible for most of Plotkin's pretrial suffering: Cicero Bookbinder, Leader of the Inner Chamber, the legislative body that enacted the law the butcher allegedly breached; Mendel Sprem, Bookbinder's Alter Ego and so-called "Brain," who authored the law; Emile Threadbare, the Republic's High Minister, who forced Bookbinder to propose the law; Jean-Pierre Proust, Commandant of the National Constabulary, whose officers arrested Plotkin for ostensibly violating the law; Hans Gogol, Warden of Purgatory House of Detention, the institution where Plotkin languished and suffered systematic abuse following his arrest; and Fettig Mayor Rumpold Snipe, a prominent local demagogue who,

during an eleventh hour press conference timed to influence prospective Jurors, had denounced Plotkin as an enemy of the Republic, the City's most dangerous resident, and a man who repeatedly
defied *The Rules*.

Heads also nodded outside the Dignitaries Section. One rested
on the narrow shoulders of Felix I. Bleifus, a lawyer with The Society for the Apparent Representation of Indigent Criminal-Types, an
organization that pretended to represent impoverished defendants
for free. Another rested on the neck of psychiatrist Seymour Peltz,
the Permanent Acting Director of Admissions and/or Discharges at
the Warehouse for the Purportedly Insane, a facility that specialized in not treating its patients. A third belonged to A. I. Gopnik,
a Warehouse resident who was observing the proceedings under
the supervision of two orderlies. Bleifus, Peltz, and Gopnik had
encounters with Leopold Plotkin prior to the trial that did not sig-
nificantly contribute to his pretrial suffering.

While Jurors listened with the stillness of wax figures in a museum, Malatesta began to weave a narrative of the events that led
to the criminal charges. Interlacing fact with fiction, he pounded
his fist against the Jury Stall railing to punctuate each item, causing some of the Deciders to flinch with each jarring blow. Then,
the prosecutor abruptly dropped his arms to his sides and stopped
speaking to allow Jurors to dwell on everything he had exaggerated
or misrepresented up to that point.

As Malatesta transfixed the Jury with silence, the egoist's minions were astounded by his performance. He had exceeded their
expectations, risen to the occasion, aped their lines to perfection.
They nervously waited for him to stumble. Justice Stifel, hidden
in his Judicial Chair, was also pleasantly surprised. Never, on the
few occasions that Malatesta appeared in his Courtroom, had the
prosecutor's performances been more than mediocre. "Maybe I
misjudged him," the pocket-sized Jurist mumbled.

Plotkin glanced again at Bernard Talisman to ascertain how his
defense attorney was holding up under the pillorying. Talisman's
face was inscrutable. It revealed none of the outrage or empathy
the butcher yearned for. In need of emotional succor, the butcher
turned toward the Spectator Pews, where a small pro-Plotkin contingent was strategically positioned at the far end of the second
row, near an array of stiffly-posed portraits of Justices who had
died during unusually contentious trials.

The first familiar face Plotkin saw belonged to Primo Astigmatopolous, his long-time chicken plucker, intimate confidant,

apostle, and closest male friend. The next was Ana Bloom, a handsome woman with porcelain skin, who was the unrequited love of his loveless life, only female friend, and Talisman's paramour. The third and fourth faces belonged to the Kimmelmen brothers, Jacobi and Arturo, his Tearoom friends. Although each of them smiled at him congenially, Plotkin felt that he needed more succor than they proved capable of giving.

Casting his functioning eye across the Pews, he came to his closest living relatives: Jacob Plotkin, his stern father; Emma Plotkin, his passive mother; and Moishe and Misha Plotkin, his deranged twin uncles. The family elders, dressed in funereal black, silently mouthed his name while grimacing. Slightly buoyed by their displays of support, Plotkin mouthed each of their names in reply.

The butcher turned his attention to a flock of more distant relations, all of whom were also attired in black. Most ignored him. A few met his needy gaze with scowls. They were upset with him for staining the family's previously nondescript reputation.

After exhausting the last of the relatives, Plotkin's eye drifted to Milos Gorky, the Inner Chamber's "Great Dissenter," an anarchist who had voted against enactment of the law he allegedly violated. Philosophically opposed to lawmaking per se, Gorky had publically pledged his unyielding support for Plotkin's anti-authoritarian behavior. To confirm that the support hadn't evaporated, Gorky met Plotkin's stare with a two-thumbs-up gesture. Relieved that the legislative obstructionist was still on his side, Plotkin returned the generosity by raising a single limp thumb.

The butcher continued to scan the Pews. He struggled to recognize the unfamiliar faces of several middle-age women seated in the back row. They were the board members of the Women's Association for the Prevention of Cruelty to the Truly Despised, a charitable organization chaired by attorney Bernard Talisman's half-sister, Myra Rabinowitz-Pritzker. Not knowing who they were and intimidated by their stern facial expressions, Plotkin moved on.

While moving on, he was startled to see Hinta Gelb, the despotic former Head Librarian of the National Library of Pedantic Writings who had mentored him during his years as an intellectual child prodigy. He had not seen her in three decades. Although Gelb's heavy eyelids were closed, she wasn't asleep. Instead, she was recalling Plotkin's unbounded potential and lamenting that he had turned to a life of crime in middle age. Misinterpreting Gelb's sealed eyes as a sign of indifference, Plotkin was disappointed and looked elsewhere for empathy.

Seated two rows behind Gelb was the part-time rabbi of the Tree of Temptation synagogue who presided at his aborted bar mitzvah decades earlier. Plotkin saw the tufts of white hair protruding from under the rabbi's yarmulke as well as the heavily creased skin. He wondered why the ancient cleric came. The bar mitzvah ceremony had ended in humiliation for Plotkin and permanently scarred his psyche. Seeing the man he believed was responsible for the debacle proved a convenient distraction for the butcher. It ignited memories of the religious spectacle as well as other events experienced during a mostly difficult, joyless life. As Umberto Malatesta continued his tirade, images from the past coursed through Plotkin's mind, causing the prosecutor's voice to become progressively fainter until it disappeared from consciousness.

Head Librarian Hinta Gelb

2

At age six, thirty-seven years before Leopold Plotkin was tried for crimes against the Republic, tests administered by Fettig's Department of Learning revealed that he was a borderline genius. As a result, Leopold was assigned to the Lyceum for Cerebral Children, an elite school that specialized in neo-classical studies. His father, a cynic who didn't consider him a near genius, told the Department that it had made a mistake and demanded a retest. The Department refused. "We don't make mistakes," an insulted Department official explained.

Soon after the semester began, Professors noticed that Leopold interacted poorly with peers and rarely laughed at their jokes. Concerned, the school's Headmaster sought help from a large-animal veterinarian who specialized in treating socially withdrawn primates. After a week of observing the child in his natural habitat, the veterinarian reported:

The subject presents as a well-nourished six year old male with highly sophisticated thinking skills, poor eye contact, and a flat affect. He resides in a two-bedroom tenement flat in the Small Business District with an emotionally combustible father, a taciturn mother, and a pair of identically odd uncles. When questioned about his family, he was defensive. After extensive prodding, however, he acknowledged being frustrated by the elders' lack of intellectual curiosity. He described the home environment as chaotic and contentious. This was verified by the assessor's observations of numerous intra-family battles. The subject tries to be elsewhere when his father is home, usually hiding on the tenement's fire escape or roof.

When asked why he hides, the subject described himself as a pacifist who can't tolerate conflict. He claims to be an outsider in the family, ignored unless he is the object of criticism. Occasionally his mother draws on her shallow maternal instincts to show him some kindness.

The subject states that he prefers books to people because "books are more interesting and less hostile." A cluster of irrational fears impairs his social functioning. He admits to fears of the dark, tripping over sharp objects, ridicule, and pogroms. His greatest fear is that he will become an atheist, like his uncles. A self-described agnostic, he finds the Bible preposterous and wonders whether it is possible to be both a Jew and a non-believer.

The subject aspires to be a public intellectual when fully grown. Although this assessor envisions short-term academic success for this gloomy prepubescent, the long-term prognosis is guarded.

Leopold remained socially awkward throughout his years at the Lyceum. His mind, however, expanded at an extraordinary rate. This further alienated him from peers. In the early grades, while other pupils grappled with age appropriate reading and writing, he devoured university-level literature, wrote densely plotted novellas, and authored the first volume of his memoirs. In the mid-level years, as classmates struggled to master nuances of their native tongue, he became fluent in conversational Latinate and ancient Greek. Later, while others wrestled with marginally difficult mathematical and scientific concepts, he formulated elegant proofs for labyrinthine theorems that his teachers were unable to understand.

By age nine, it was clear to Leopold that the Lyceum alone couldn't sate his intellectual curiosity. Searching for more, he began to frequent the National Library of Pedantic Writings. There he immersed himself in the facility's esoteric collections. Head Li-

brarian, Hinta Gelb, first encountered him in the catacombs reading Early Era non-rhyming poetry. A spinster and pedagogic snob
without a discernible neck, Gelb had long sought a brilliant child
prodigy to mentor. She monitored the intellectual neophyte closely to determine whether he seemed to have the mettle. Fascinated
by his somber mien, sophisticated choice of reading material, and
beat-up briefcase, she offered to let him study at her feet. Sensing
from his concerned look that he construed the offer too literally,
Gelb explained that studying at another's feet was merely a peda-
gogical expression; that no learning would actually take place in
the vicinity of her shoes. With that clarification, he accepted.

At the outset, Gelb outlined her vision. "I will introduce your
embryonic mind to the intricacies of psychology, etymology, neu-
rology, theology, archaeology, and myriad other esoteric things,"
she began. "The natural laws of learning require that you reason
to conclusions and not simply regurgitate facts. To arrive at proper
conclusions, you must deduce, infer, surmise, speculate, eliminate,
integrate, conjugate and, most important, percolate. Each category
of learning requires a different kind of intuitive reasoning that can't
be taught. One either has it or doesn't. Do you believe you have
it?"

"I think so," he whispered shyly.

Leopold's muted reply satisfied the doctrinaire pedagogue.
Over time, she exposed him to the full breadth of the Library's rich
collection, including the essays of philosophers Rabinowitz, Fish-
bein, and Pontefiglio; the self-published autobiographies of solip-
sist Uno Borges; and the regulations of government agencies, which
Gelb considered some of the finest prose ever written.

Hinta Gelb never deliberately attempted to terrorize the boy
but often did. Her twice-weekly Socratic interrogations left him
shaken. Her physical presence—the menacingly splayed shoulders, crooked teeth and guttural sounds emitted through chapped
lips—added to his anxiety. At the same time, he was temporarily
mollified by her occasional signs of approval, especially the tepid
pats on his head dispensed as rewards for particularly insightful
answers.

During the third year of the tutelage, eleven-year old Ana
Bloom appeared at the library. The only child of the wealthy owner
of Bloom's Department Store, she was precociously sociable and
interested in learning more than her private school offered. Realizing that Leopold could benefit from peer companionship and impressed by the girl's social maturity, Gelb offered to take Ana under

her wing in exchange for Ana befriending Leopold. Ana enthusiastically agreed to the terms.

When Gelb introduced her protégé to his new studymate, Leopold looked away. "If he weren't so shy, he would tell you he is pleased to meet you," the mentor explained. The comment embarrassed Leopold and caused him to blush.

Displaying a maturity that belied her tender years, Bloom said matter-of-factly, "I understand" and pretended not to have noticed Leopold's awkward behavior.

In the first days of the socialization experiment, Leopold remained anxious. Seated across from Ana while deconstructing essays, he struggled to ignore her. Eventually overcome by curiosity, he furtively looked her way as she read. He was fascinated by her swan-like neck, alabaster skin, alert eyes, and dark wavy hair. Lingering a moment too long, he was discovered in the act of leering. Ana looked up and saw his gaze. Kind by nature, she took no offense and smiled. Flummoxed, the boy nervously returned to his book.

Over the course of several months, Leopold grew less anxious in his study companion's presence. Eventually, he was able to acknowledge her with subtle nods and flashes of intelligible words. Encouraged by his progress, Gelb designed an array of activities to improve Leopold's social skills. She had him read cryptic poems to Ana, then decipher their meanings. The Head Librarian led them in discussions about dense Russian novels and convened two-person chess tournaments, which she refereed. When satisfied that Leopold had sufficient skills to socialize with the girl on his own beyond the Library's walls, Gelb told them to walk the facility's grounds and discuss philosophy. After seeing Leopold's lips occasionally move as they strolled through gardens, she told Ana that it was time for the experiment to move into the larger world.

"Fly like two birds," she mandated.

3

Until Hinta Gelb's edict to fly, Leopold's physical world was narrow. It consisted of the National Library, the Lyceum, and the pavements of the Small Business District, all within walking distance of the tenement where he resided on the fringe of the District's main thoroughfare, Drabble Street.

The Small Business District was a congested amalgam of Jewish-owned and operated stores, pushcarts, sweatshops, tenement buildings, synagogues, settlement houses, and Yiddish theatres, with a few restaurants, tea rooms, and doctors' offices scattered here and there. Populated by people who dressed in Old World clothing and experienced the vicissitudes of life in a language that only they comprehended, it was viewed by outsiders as an exotic, mysterious community, separate and apart from the mainstreams of Fettig and the Republic as a whole.

There were no trees in the district, but many odors. Most of the unpleasant smells came from scraps of spoiled fish, meat, and fruit inadvertently dropped from pushcarts or from an inferior sewage system that deposited waste into the nearby Fettig River. Leopold didn't particularly mind the odors. However, he was alarmed by the shortage of trees. He had read in botanical books that trees were a vital source of oxygen. Armed with this documented proof, he told his father during an evening meal that perhaps the family should consider moving to a place with trees. The patriarch, who had no faith in science, angrily rebuffed the suggestion, telling him that the family had more important things to worry about than a shortage of oxygen. Jacob added that the boy shouldn't believe everything he read in science books "because the idiots who write those books used to claim the earth was flat."

Ana Bloom had intimate knowledge of the attractions Fettig offered as the Republic's capital city. After learning that Leopold had never been to any of the attractions, she made a chart with the names of significant sites listed in alphabetical order. The chart specified whether a given attraction was of intellectual, cultural, or recreational value. When studying the options, Leopold suggested that they avoid recreational places because he suspected that playing games was a waste of time. Believing that Leopold would never fit in unless he learned to play like an ordinary child, she ignored the suggestion.

Their first outing was to Fettig's Cultural District. There, they sniffed flowers at the National Botanical Gardens, bird-watched at the National Aviary, ogled mummies at the National Museum of Stolen Foreign Antiquities, and admired paintings of the Republic's founding father figures at the National Portraiture Gallery. They also studied the classical architecture that decorated the National Center of Performing Arts. Leopold, who had previously only seen photographs of the site, said that he was impressed by the subtlety of the archways and craftsmanship of the window treatments.

Their next trip was to the Large Business District. There, the clusters of tall buildings and wide avenues intimidated Leopold. Sensing from Leopold's heaving chest that her companion was unnerved, Ana held his hand to calm him as they gawked. "None of these things exist where I live," he told her between gasps for air. To avoid seeming like she was showing off, she deliberately avoided her father's department store.

Knowing that Leopold had particular interests in politics as well as the law, Ana's itinerary included a trip to the Government and Justice District, the Republic's center of political and judicial power. There, they toured Gray House (where the High Minister and the High Minister's wife resided), listened to oral arguments at the High Court of Final Supplications (where the most important appeals were heard), and observed a legislative debate in the National Assembly's Inner Chamber (where lawmakers made long-winded speeches and voted). Although Leopold was impressed by the elegance of Gray House and the logic of the legal arguments advanced by counsel at the High Court, he was disturbed by the hostility exhibited by the Inner Chambermen during a debate. Ana noticed his ashen face and told him it was time to return home.

In the ensuing weeks, she took Leopold to several of the public parks that dotted Fettig. All were named for dignitaries whose fame had given way to obscurity with the passage of time. Against his will, Leopold reluctantly swung on swings, flew kites, and played Simon Says. He was surprised to find that he enjoyed the activities and occasionally laughed. Pleased to discover that he was capable of laughing, Ana told him that he should do it more often, that it was good for his mental health. Leopold said he would try but doubted that he was capable of increasing the frequency of laughter to a statistically significant degree.

Pretending to be spies, the companions scrutinized people who frequented the parks. Young mothers pushing baby carriages, middle-age lovers holding hands, old men reading newspapers, older women feeding squirrels, tourists of all ages taking photographs, and businessmen eating lunches on benches came under their watchful gazes. They speculated about what their own lives would be like when they were adults and came to a park.

He said: "I imagine myself reading an existential novel on a bench while eating lunch during intermission of an all-day lecture I am giving to pseudo-intellectuals."

She said: "I see myself as a suffragette, holding a sign at the park entrance demanding the right of all people to vote."

He added: "I'll bring an extra sandwich for you." Too shy to reveal his secret ambition of someday holding hands with her while eating sandwiches together, he didn't say more.

They periodically boarded trolleys to survey random neighborhoods. After sampling several, Leopold discovered that none compared to the Small Business District. Although a few had the District's narrow streets, storefronts with peeling paint, and so forth—not one had many Jews. This shocked him. Having spent his childhood in a neighborhood that was overwhelmingly populated by Jews, he had assumed that Jews lived everywhere in Fettig, in large numbers.

"Where are the Jews?" he asked with consternation.

"Mostly in the Small Business District," Ana disclosed to her perplexed inquisitor.

Two neighborhoods in particular captured Leopold's attention. One was the Bleak District, a region known for its slums, hardscrabble living, and lack of tourism. There, they looked at shabbily dressed people, boarded-up row houses, shuttered businesses, abandoned warehouses, uncollected garbage, and stray dogs. It seemed to him much worse off than the Small Business District, worse than anything he had imagined. The other was the High District, an area known for its elegant brownstones and important residents. There, he saw well-dressed people, opulent houses, no signs of warehouses or uncollected garbage or dogs on leashes, and numerous trees. Ana told him that the High District was inhabited by government officials, politicians, diplomats, financiers, and assorted entrepreneurs. Because she didn't want to appear privileged, she didn't reveal that she lived there. Leopold sniffed and noted that the District lacked bad odors. The lack of smells fascinated him. He was also intrigued by the lack of laundry lines anchored to buildings and wondered how the residents dried their wash.

Leopold and Ana's favorite destination was the National Zoo.

In the primate section, they befriended a docile orangutan who lived in a cage with several energetic members of his species. Ana named the orangutan Bruno, after her grandfather, a docile man with an energetic wife. They fed Bruno grapes. On one trip, while feeding him, Leopold divulged a secret ambition to his friend. "When I become a public intellectual, I'll write a synopsis of all human knowledge," he said.

"That would be a worthwhile project," she said. "When I'm older, I'll travel the world and eliminate illiteracy. Later, I'll be a head librarian at an important library. I'll give your synopsis a prominent place on a book shelf."

"I'll be the first Plotkin to attend college," he revealed.

"We'll always be good friends," she said, apropos of nothing.

Buoyed by the speculation of a lifelong friendship with Ana Bloom, Leopold often thought about her after that. Among other occasions, he thought about her while at the Lyceum, before and after going to bed, when his father and uncles argued, when hiding on the roof or fire escape, at every meal, and between meals. Thinking about her made him feel good, but exhausted.

The evening before his bar mitzvah, Leopold's father slid a handwritten note addressed to Head Librarian, Hinta Gelb, under the Library door. The note read:

As the boss of the Plotkin family, I am informing you that my son, Leopold Plotkin, won't be coming to the Library anymore. He will be assuming his rightful place in the family business. If he disobeys me and shows up, you are to throw him out. Don't tell the girl he reads with where my son lives. She's a bad influence.

As tears streamed down Gelb's cheeks, she crumpled the message and threw it into a wastebasket. The next afternoon, she intercepted Ana at the Library's main entrance. Stone-faced, she informed the girl that her days of tutoring the boy were over. Sensing that the librarian was masking her feelings, Ana wanted to comfort her but knew that any display of affection would make the librarian uncomfortable.

"You can stay if you wish," Gelb said perfunctorily.

"I don't think I can manage that without Leopold," the girl replied sadly.

Ana extended her arm to shake the tutor's trembling hand, thanked Gelb for the tutorials, and privately mourned the loss of her close friend as she turned and walked away.

Jacob, Moishe and Misha Plotkin

4

During a calm interlude in his emotionally turbulent life, Jacob Plotkin drafted his son's bar mitzvah speech on butcher paper. "This is my magnum opus," the patriarch proclaimed when handing Leopold the finished product. "If delivered properly, it will be a speech for the ages. If botched, I'll be discredited. My legacy is in your hands."

The burden of protecting his father's legacy weighed heavily on the thirteen year old boy. As the bar mitzvah approached, he slept fitfully and wet his bed. On the eve of the ceremony, his anxiety spiked when a horde of relatives descended on the Plotkin flat for a rehearsal.

Seated cheek to jowl around a kitchen table designed for six standard-sized adults, fifteen men and women of various dimensions were poised to offer unsparing criticism. Leopold stood at one end, holding the butcher paper in his quivering hands. His father was seated at the other end, bracketed by Moishe and Misha Plotkin, the patriarch's unhinged twin brothers. His mother was filling teacups with water, the only refreshment she was authorized to serve. Jacob played with his beard, pondering whether his son would do justice to his opus. While the patriarch's heavily creased face sagged in anticipation of withering comments by the audience, he sighed deeply and emitted a faint odor of meat.

The guests shifted restlessly as they waited for the speech to begin. Heavy smokers, they puffed impatiently on cigarettes. Their demeanors ranged from grave to stern. In need of moral support, Leopold looked to his mother as she passed by with a teacup in hand. She smiled pleasantly and told him not to worry because he was an *excellent speaker*. Aware that the statement was a lie designed to bolster his confidence, Leopold's spirits remained low.

"We don't have all night!" Jacob Plotkin thundered impatiently to his son. "Begin already!"

The boy opened his mouth to begin. Both eyelids spontaneously closed. His toes lost feeling.

"Stand straight! You're slouching!" the patriarch shouted before Leopold was able to speak. "Nobody will take you seriously if you slouch."

"He's not *slouching*," Mordecai Himmelfarb, Jacob Plotkin's brother-in-law, corrected. "He's *stooping*. There's a difference between a *slouch* and a *stoop*."

"Don't *contradict* me!" Jacob Plotkin shrieked. "You're here to *listen*. If I want your comments, I'll ask!"

Clearing his throat, the offended *paterfamilias* banged the tabletop with his calloused hand, glared at his son, and ordered the boy to stop stooping. "Another stoop and you'll have to start again!" he warned.

As Leopold straightened his posture and reopened his mouth, Rose Keppler, Jacob's third cousin, interrupted. "Wipe that foolish grin off your face, young man. This is a solemn occasion." She turned to the patriarch and asked, "Did you see that grin?"

"As a matter of fact, I *didn't*!" Jacob Plotkin growled emphatically. "The only grin I'm seeing is on your face! You were invited to listen, not to grin like you're having a good time at my expense!"

"Did I grin, Max?" Rose Keppler asked her husband, who had been staring into a teacup filled with water.

"Not in the least," the milquetoast confirmed despite suspecting that his wife had probably grinned. Grinning was part of her nature.

"Please, let the boy talk," said Meyer Mandelbrot, an *ex officio* peacemaker at family gatherings, who was regarded as an obstructionist for his efforts and broadly despised by the family as a whole.

"He'll talk when I tell him to talk!" Jacob Plotkin proclaimed.

"We determine when he talks," Edith Snitzer, another cousin objected. "We're the audience; we decide."

Tears dripped from Leopold's eyes.

"See what we did," said peacemaker Meyer Mandelbrot. "We made the boy cry."

"*Why* are you crying?" Jacob demanded.

"I wasn't crying, papa," Leopold lied. "It's the cigarette smoke."

"I don't believe him," Rose Keppler said accusatorily.

"What do you know about crying," Jacob replied. "You're a grinner!"

"Where is the boy's yarmulke?" Abraham Zitzer, another cousin asked.

"He doesn't need one!" the patriarch exploded. "This is a kitchen, not a schul!"

"A bar mitzvah rehearsal, even in a kitchen, is sacred," Zitzer insisted.

"That's not true!" wailed brother-in-law Mordecai Himmelfarb.

"Please," peacemaker Meyer Mandelbrot interceded. "Let the boy talk."

A brief silence emerged, except for Misha and Moishe Plotkin's coughing, a major component of their hypochondriacal repertoire. Sensing an opening, Leopold began, "My dear parents and others, today I am ____."

"Did I tell you to start?" Jacob Plotkin interrupted, pounding his fist on the table. "Didn't you hear your uncles coughing? Don't you have any respect for your sick elders?"

"You heard your uncles coughing. Show some respect," brother-in-law Mordecai Himmelfarb echoed, in temporary solidarity with his enemy.

"The speech is too long," Frieda Himmelstein, a great aunt complained. "It needs to be shortened and flattened. My mind drifted."

"Yes, much too long," lamented Isaac Fassbinder, Edith Snitzer's former husband, who was invited because of his reputed objectivity. "Particularly the beginning, middle, and end. And like my ex-wife said, it needs to be flattened."

"Nobody's going to flatten it!" Jacob Plotkin proclaimed. "The speech is flat enough! Any flatter, it will be concave!"

"The speech is too short," said Isaac Fassbinder's mistress, an unexpected guest whose presence scandalized Fassbinder's former wife. "Just as it got interesting, it was over. Also, I could hardly hear him. He was mashing the words." Turning to Jacob Plotkin, she asked, "Does your son have a speech defect?"

"Didn't anybody tell you that when you are new to our family you stay in the background and keep quiet until you're spoken to?" Jacob Plotkin said testily. "The newer you are, the less you say and vice versa. Those who are quiet are more likely to be welcomed into the family fold. Those who talk out-of-turn are shunned."

"The boy never mentioned his relatives," said an uninvited fourth cousin nobody recognized. "We were lumped together with 'others,' which was disrespectful to the extended family. Frankly, I was offended by the slight."

"There was no lumping together," Jacob Plotkin corrected. "I deliberately *left* all of you out. For your information, whoever you are, 'others' refers to *acquaintances*, not relatives."

"Besides leaving out his relatives," said the fourth cousin nobody recognized, "the speech had revisionist tendencies, which I know more than a little about, given my profession."

"What profession is that?" asked Jacob Plotkin. "Professional intruder?"

"I stand by what I said," the fourth cousin, an unemployed college professor, said resolutely.

"Does anybody know this man?" the patriarch asked of no one in particular as he dramatically lifted his palms in a questioning manner. Fourteen shrugs suggested that nobody knew.

"So, who the hell are you?" Jacob Plotkin demanded, leaning over the table.

"No comment," said the distant cousin.

"*I* have a comment," said Mordecai Himmelfarb's wife, Bertha Kepletsky, who had allegedly refused to take Himmelfarb's name because it was difficult to spell. "I'm exhausted. The longwinded speech was fatiguing. Who needs sleeping pills with a speech like that?"

Several relatives snickered.

"That's it!" shouted Jacob Plotkin. "I've had enough of your insults. Everybody out! Particularly you," he said, glaring at Bertha Kepletsky. "You wouldn't know a good speech if you heard one."

"I would have lost my dinner if we had had anything but water to eat," said Bertha Kepletsky. She faced Leopold who was shaking, slouching and grinning stupidly. "If I were you, young man, I wouldn't say anything tomorrow. Sometimes, silence is golden."

"Your invitations to the bar mitzvah are revoked!" the patriarch roared.

With that announcement, the relatives departed *en masse.* As they descended five flights of stairs, they debated whether the speech should have included references to pestilence, plagues, and locusts—none of which they recalled hearing.

For the remainder of the evening, the patriarch revised his masterpiece and the son rehearsed the changes. Finally, the mother timidly suggested to her husband that it was important for the boy to get some sleep before the bar mitzvah. Jacob grudgingly agreed. As Leopold rested his head on a pillow, he prayed that his relatives would heed his father's edict and stay home or, failing that, lose their bearings en route to the synagogue.

5

Leopold Plotkin stood stoop-shouldered on the dais of the Tree of Temptation Synagogue, staring at a sparse audience of relatives and strangers. With unsteady hands, he held the butcher paper that harbored his father's speech.

"Today, I am ambivalent about becoming a man," he began mordantly. "Why? Because attainment of Judaic adulthood is, at best, a mixed blessing. On one hand, it brings an end to my onerous Hebrew lessons under an autocratic instructor."

Leopold paused and looked warily at the Tree of Temptation's part-time rabbi who was seated at the far end of the dais reading the Book of Job to see whether the autocrat would react to the criticism of his teaching style. Immersed in Job's travails, the cleric heard nothing. The bar mitzvah candidate was relieved.

"On the other hand," Leopold continued, "manhood ushers in an era of relentless suffering and despair—a long journey that will be littered with dashed hopes, declining health, decrepitude, and death. The ravages of entropy cannot be held back. Before I die, there will be countless illnesses. After I die, there will be nothing; only an open black hole as worms and other flesh-eating insects devour my body. These realities raise a profound philosophical question: Why bother to live?"

Introducing the bleak Plotkinian worldview at the threshold of a speech traditionally dedicated to evoking optimism produced contradictory reactions among attendees. The strangers, unfamiliar with the dismal philosophy embraced by Jacob Plotkin and members of the extended Plotkin family, gasped. The relatives—most of whom were refugees from the truncated rehearsal—found comfort in the morbidity and nodded approvingly. The part-time rabbi, still reading, did not react.

Despite sensing a schism within the audience, Leopold pressed on. "I am the product of five generations of failed kosher butchers," he warbled in his prepubescent adenoidal voice. "Each of the generations lived on the margins of poverty and suffered in its own way. Since the causes and particulars of the suffering are too numerous to enumerate in a fifteen-minute speech, I won't provide the details. It is the future—the misery and oppression that await me, not the history of unhappiness from which I descend—that warrants closer scrutiny in the limited time that remains."

As the boy completed that sobering declamation, strangers cried, "Enough!" Relatives pleaded for more. Afraid to disappoint his father, Leopold pressed on. He mobilized an array of pessimistic metaphors and bleak asides as he portrayed a future of failure, dejection, depression, and angst; a life in which he was doomed to replicate the miserable existences of his ancestors.

Leopold sipped water to irrigate his throat.

"Could my future be any darker?" he asked after sipping. Before he was able to cite evidence to support his father's thesis that his future could and would be darker, strangers in the audience begged him to stop. When he ignored their pleas, the congregation's president implored the part-time rabbi, still lost in the Bible, to intervene, explaining that the speech was too morbid. The plea aroused the cleric. He closed the Bible, strode across the dais, snatched the butcher paper from Leopold's hands, and shredded it. In rich rabbinical tones he declared, "Not another word! This is a day of celebration, not a funeral!" He then seized the traumatized speaker's shoulders and shook.

Incensed that the religious leader had touched his child without his informed consent, Jacob Plotkin mounted the dais. Astride the dais, he denounced the paper shredding as an act of professional jealousy and proclaimed that only *he* had the right to shake his son.

The challenge to his authority enraged the rabbi. Overcome by furor, the cleric abandoned all efforts to salvage the ceremony and ordered Jacob, Emma, and Leopold Plotkin to leave the Tree of Temptation. Viewing an attack on one of their own as an attack against the entire extended family, the relatives coalesced and joined the evictees in a chorus of grievances. This act of defiance prompted a rabbinical edict for all persons of Plotkin lineage to vacate the premises.

The exiles formed a defensive wall around Jacob, Emma, and Leopold. While moving toward the exit, they complained of unfair persecution. Opening the door, the collective marched from the synagogue, boarded a trolley, and repaired to the Plotkin flat. Once safely inside, they collegially conducted a postmortem of the debacle. Later, they resumed their traditional hostilities until Jacob Plotkin ordered everyone, other than his wife, son, and brothers, to leave.

6

Under Plotkinian rules of generational succession, Isaac replaced Abraham, Youssel followed Isaac, Shlomo supplanted Youssel, and Jacob succeeded Shlomo as the proprietor of ABRAHAM PLOTKIN AND OTHERS KOSHER MEAT PRODUCTS. All of this occurred long before the aborted bar mitzvah ceremony, well in advance of Leopold's birth.

The ancestral business originated in the poorest of the Eastern Countries, where too many butchers competed for too few customers and anti-Semitism was in full bloom. Tired of teetering on the brink of destitution, hiding in the shop's cellar during pogroms, and being mocked by non-Jews as clannish, scheming, vulgar, physically inferior parasites, Shlomo and his wife, Hanna, decided to pursue a less volatile existence in the Republic. Told by a cousin, who fled earlier, that the Republic's streets were paved in gold, they embarked for the New World with their eldest son Jacob, age twenty, and twins Moishe and Misha, not yet seventeen, clinging to a hope that their lives would improve.

Carrying a few possessions and tickets purchased with Shlomo's meager life savings, the Plotkin quintet traveled twelve days by steamship. They shared a steerage compartment with scores of other men, women and children, slept fitfully, and frequently vomited. The Plotkins arrived tired and dehydrated at the Port of Entry, in Fettig Harbor.

An officious clerk escorted the Plotkins with a group of approximately thirty other émigrés to a building where their papers were examined. There, they were registered and asked whether they had any current interest in attempting to overthrow the government. All replied that they had given the matter little thought. Once registered, Shlomo was handed off to another official and asked whether he currently harbored any contagious diseases. A lifelong hypochondriac who enjoyed complaining about his health, Shlomo seized the opportunity to expound at length about his imaginary illnesses. Among other things, he claimed to be an asymptomatic carrier of typhoid fever, tuberculosis, and cholera, in addition to several contagions that were still incubating. Due to those revelations, the official saw no need for a medical examination and summarily denied the hypochondriac entry on grounds that he constituted a clear and present danger to the Republic's health. Wanting the best for his children, Shlomo advised them to be less forthcoming when asked about their diseases and to complete the journey without him and their mother. The offspring balked, saying they couldn't abandon the elders with a clear conscious. The family head pointed out that it was his final decision and, therefore, not subject to dispute.

Aware that their father brooked no dissent, the sons relented. The matriarch embraced each of her sons, gently kissed their foreheads, and wailed. In turn, Shlomo, who was not the demonstrative type, kept his reactions to a minimum. He resisted any show of emotion or the love he felt for his sons by shaking their hands and saying sternly, "A new and better ABRAHAM PLOTKIN AND OTHERS will rise on the golden streets while your mother and I starve and hide from anti-Semites in the cellar." Hanna Plotkin implored her sons to write occasionally after they adjusted to their new life and to be good boys. Riddled with guilt and newly orphaned, the dispirited offspring limped toward an uncertain future.

After a week in quarantine, during which they exhibited no symptoms of disease, Jacob, Misha and Moishe were released to the cousin who had lied about the Republic's streets being paved in gold. Once boarded in the kitchen of the cousin's tenement, the brothers received a modest grant from the Jewish Relief Agency, a benevolent society established by successful Jewish businessmen who had come to the Republic during the First Migration. The siblings used the money to purchase food staples, basic clothing, and cots to replace the shallow piles of rags that functioned as beds. Later, they obtained employment in a slaughterhouse where the cousin worked. Laboring twelve hours a day, they earned a few copper coins for each slaughtered cow.

Jacob and his brothers saved money scrupulously. They also borrowed small sums from several distant relatives in an endeavor to accumulate enough capital to fulfill their father's mandate to establish a butcher shop in the New World. At night, they attended school in a settlement house. There, they learned to speak a broken version of the Republic's tongue. Settlement personnel offered them courses in good manners and assimilation techniques. Believing themselves sufficiently well-mannered and having no interest in blending in, they declined the offer.

Once they raised sufficient funds, the Plotkin brothers vacated their deceitful cousin's kitchen, leased a one-bedroom flat in another decrepit tenement building, secured a small retail space on the street level of the tenement, and resurrected ABRAHAM PLOTKIN AND OTHERS KOSHER MEAT PRODUCTS on the fringe of Drabble Street, the Small Business District's main thoroughfare where kosher butcher shops abounded.

Over the next decade, the siblings lived as bachelors and worked in the densely packed aggregation of Jewish-owned and operated enterprises. During business hours, the streets surrounding ABRAHAM PLOTKIN AND OTHERS grew crowded, noisy, and smelly. The butcher shop, although generally foul smelling and sporadically noisy, rarely attracted a crowd. The reason was obvious to all but the brothers. Jacob (who was disputatious) and Misha and Moishe (who were deranged as well as disputatious) lacked the social skills required to build a significant customer base. Their limited clientele consisted of a few loyal people who didn't mind being belittled, or enjoyed arguing, or were new to the community and hadn't yet heard about the Plotkins' mistreatment of customers.

The brothers' nonprofessional lives fared no better. In the winter, they shivered in a cramped apartment that lacked sufficient heat. In the summer, they slept on their building's fire escape to avoid too much heat. They enjoyed none of the things their fellow émigrés found pleasurable: Yiddish plays, klezmer recitals, lectures, socialist political societies, or prayer services. Instead, they stayed in their flat, complaining and arguing.

Desperate to please their father, the siblings wrote weekly letters to him riddled with hyperbole and lies. They claimed to have created a thriving business, and that they were seriously considering opening a second shop to accommodate the demand for their meat. They sent photographs of themselves, standing stiffly in front of the store, pointing to the sign that confirmed the existence of ABRAHAM PLOTKIN AND OTHERS KOSHER MEAT PRODUCTS in the New World. Once a month, they included small sums of money to their parents, always explaining that most of their funds were tied up in business investments. The patriarch replied to the letters with detailed descriptions of his personal suffering. He never acknowledged receipt of the donations or thanked his sons for their generosity. The omissions didn't surprise or deter the brothers from trying to please him.

Jacob Plotkin met Emma Swirsky after ten years of bachelorhood when the much younger woman unwittingly wandered into the butcher shop to purchase chicken fat. Strikingly demure in temperament, her submissive nature instantly attracted him. He asked if he could see her again. She agreed to meet the following week at a performance of the *Merchant of Venice* at a Yiddish theater that produced sanitized adaptations of anti-Semitic plays. With Shylock erased as a character and all references to pounds of flesh and other offensive language redacted from the play, Jacob found the production "sterile, incomprehensible, and poorly written." Emma, who found the language inspiring, withheld all critical commentary because Jacob impressed her as thin-skinned and not open to dissenting opinions.

Emma Swirsky was one of seven daughters sired by a tailor and a seamstress who had migrated to the Republic in pursuit of a better life. Raised in a deeply religious household, she, her parents, and sisters attended a synagogue largely populated by tailors. Despite her deep commitment to religion and Jacob's selective agnosticism that limited his praying to High Holidays, they proved vaguely compatible and soon married.

The three Plotkin brothers leased another apartment in the same tenement building with two bedrooms to accommodate the new addition to the family. Emma became the butcher shop's cashier and bookkeeper. She was also responsible for periodically replacing the dead chickens, salamis, and other items that hung in the store's display window with fresher versions of the products; keeping the cow tongues, livers, and other products properly aligned in the meat case; sweeping the sawdust floor to cover blood splatters; and making sure the CLOSED FOR BUSINESS sign was turned in the proper direction at the end of the work day. Although her amiable presence in the establishment improved customer relations to a degree, the business continued to operate on the margins, barely eking out a profit.

The Chicken Plucker, Primo Astigmatopolous

7

J acob Plotkin withdrew his only heir from the Lyceum for Cerebral Children two days after the bar mitzvah debacle and conscripted him into the ancestral business. This rupture elicited vehement objections from the Lyceum's Headmaster and a mild protest from the boy's reticent mother who noted that her son's dream of becoming a professional intellectual would be quashed. Her muted dissent fell on deaf ears. "Butchering is our destiny," the patriarch declared. "It's who we are."

Over the next several months, a time when Leopold Plotkin would have preferred reading, analyzing, or enjoying Ana Bloom's companionship, he shadowed his father and uncles around the malodorous shop to acquire basic butchering skills. While shadowing, the distraught adolescent mourned his lost dream of becoming a professional intellectual. Through observation and practice, he learned to slaughter cows, harvest edible organs, dissect carcasses into geometrically precise quarter sections, and cleave the sections into marketable items. When not slaughtering or cleaving, he watched the elders argue with customers who abraded their thin skins. Passive by nature, he found their belligerence impossible to emulate, off-putting, and a constant source of anxiety. Jacob made no secret that his son's inability to argue with patrons was the major disappointment of his life, a criticism that wounded the adolescent and left him feeling even more like an outsider in his family than before.

The elders often debated why business was slow. Jacob attributed it to his brothers' periodically imagining that they heard voices and carrying on conversations with nonexistent people in the presence of patrons. Moishe and Misha attributed it to Jacob's penchant for attacking the customers' opinions when they disagreed with him. Emma remained silent.

Although Leopold lacked the Plotkin brothers' lust for conflict, he learned from them how to suffer intensely, brood deeply, and obsess about matters of no concern for normal people. His maturation into Plotkinian adulthood triggered a persistent low-grade depression, a litany of hypochondriacal illnesses, and a consummate inability to enjoy life. Dispirited from working with the dispirited elders, he had only a few intellectual outlets: the weekly meetings of the Talmudic Debating Society, where he argued points convincingly but without rancor, and reading books borrowed from a local library, a small facility whose selections were inferior to those in the National Library of Pedantic Writings but didn't raise the risk of running into Hinta Gelb—an encounter that would have embarrassed him.

As the years passed, Leopold continued to share the cramped tenement with his parents and uncles. Desperate to escape their constant bickering, he dated occasionally but never seriously, attended plays at the Yiddish theaters with three cousins, and volunteered as an assistant stage manager for an amateur thespian company that performed tragic comedies. Every Tuesday and Thursday night, he met with the Kimmelmen brothers, two amiable men who owned a grocery store next to the butcher shop. The *modus operandi* was always the same when meeting with the Kimmelmens. The place was Rubenstein's Grecian Tearoom, a small space with nine tables, a waiter dressed in a tunic, three blends of coffee, an assortment of sandwiches and pastries, but no tea. The time was eight until eleven. The location was the corner table under a display of enigmatic paintings by Rubenstein's wife, an untalented abstractionist who occasionally sold her impenetrable works to customers who appreciated confusion. There, under four original Rubensteins that had yet to sell and dense cigarette smoke, the three friends sipped coffee, munched on raisin bread, discussed politics politely, played checkers amiably, and attentively listened to Arturo Kimmelmen's original jokes. The jokes' scenarios were more or less identical. They always began with: "A man walked into a...." and ended with an allegedly humorless punchline. Most were banal. Few were funny. However, in the spirit of harmony and kindness, Leopold and Arturo's brother, Jacobi Kimmelmen, forced themselves to laugh. Neither suggested to Arturo that he vary the beginnings or inject actual humor into the endings. That would have hurt the amateur comedian's feelings. Occasionally, Jacobi Kimmelmen's wife joined the group. She was the source of Leopold's infrequent dates. Most of the women she arranged for him to meet were her relatives. A few were women she worked with at a sweatshop. Leopold always thanked her for arranging the dates and apologized after they didn't turn out as well as she had predicted. "Someday we'll find the right one for you," Jacobi Kimmelmen's wife was fond of saying when Plotkin periodically suggested that, perhaps, she might want to abandon her efforts to find him a wife.

On Saturday mornings, rather than praying in a synagogue with the Kimmelmen brothers, Leopold went alone to the National Zoo, where he visited Bruno, the listless orangutan that inhabited a cage with several energetic primates he and Ana Bloom had befriended in their youth. Bruno always seemed pleased to see him, shambling to the bars and extending his hand as he approached, which Leopold didn't grasp because a sign on the cage said, DON'T TOUCH THESE ANIMALS. Typically, Leopold fed Bruno grapes, while carefully avoiding contact, and gave him a brief synopsis of the week's events. He tried, without success, to teach Bruno to mimic his facial gestures, or to spend more time interacting with the other orangutans. When feeding Bruno, he usually thought about the Zoo conversation with Ana Bloom many years earlier, where he revealed his aspiration to become a professional intellectual. He often thought about her even when not feeding grapes to Bruno. Sometimes while lying in bed. Other times while waiting on customers, or laughing at Arturo's humorless jokes, or reading books, or eating dinner with the elders, or dating women who didn't pique his interest.

So it went, year after year. Three decades after his conscription into the family business, Leopold's father and uncles retired due to imaginary health problems. His mother joined them in retirement to attend to their illusory medical needs. "Our destiny is now entirely in your hands," Jacob told his son. "If the shop goes under, that will be the end of all of us. Keep in mind what a tragedy that would be. Everything depends on you. If you fail, we all fail."

The burden of failing weighed heavily on Leopold. In an effort to stimulate business, he extended the shop's hours and, with his father's permission, placed a sign in the display window announcing that the store was UNDER COMPLETELY NEW AND FRIENDLIER MANAGEMENT. He hoped the sign would encourage former customers who had been repelled by the previous management's rude behavior to return to the fold. Toward that end, he made radical changes to common practices. Rather than greeting customers with a frown, he approached everyone with a pleasant "Hello." Instead of ignoring the patrons' health-related complaints, he commiserated with them. He never placed his thumb on the scales, thanked each customer when handing them their purchases, and said that he looked forward to seeing them again in the near future.

Under his stewardship, the store's customer base expanded slightly and sales improved marginally. However, when adjusted for inflation, the shop's annual gross income declined to its lowest point in history. Desperate to avoid commercial extinction, he sought advice on how to generate additional income from Primo Astigmatopolous—his chicken plucker, close confidant, and best friend.

Astigmatopolous, an erudite, early middle-aged man with a high forehead, was born in a small, backwater region that was too insignificant to warrant a name. After receiving a joint degree in animal husbandry and foreign dialects from his Homeland's only university, he aspired to author a trilogy exposing the plight of the unwashed masses. Because most of the unwashed in his nameless country were illiterate, he decided to illegally emigrate to the Republic where his writing might find a wider audience. He disguised himself in a fake beard, dressed like a member of the Fettig *literati*, and risked life and limb crossing two mountain ranges to reach his destination. For sentimental reasons, Astigmatopolous brought several bags of mud from his Motherland, a place allegedly known for its unusually rich mud. Upon arrival in Fettig, he answered an advertisement for an entry-level chicken plucker's position at the butcher shop. Jacob Plotkin was so impressed by his command of the local dialect and knowledge of animals that he hired him. The job was ideal for his trilogical aspirations; he could think deeply about possible content while plucking.

Primo Astigmatopolous was thinking deeply when Leopold approached him for advice about the shop's dire straits. As Astigmatopolous plucked, the butcher revealed that the business faced a financial crisis more daunting than the bovine epidemics, vegetarian fads, and economic depressions it had weathered over the years. "No Plotkin in five generations has had to contend with anything like this," Plotkin bemoaned. "If we go under, I'll be disgraced. My father will never forgive me. My uncles will become more delusional. My mother will incessantly cry. I desperately need a viable business plan."

"Don't worry," the chicken plucker said calmly. "We'll find a way."

With the burden of devising a strategy weighing on him, the chicken plucker declared a moratorium on all trilogy-related ruminations so he could devise a business plan. Dedicated thinking, however, produced nothing usable. It was not until he had an epiphany while bicycling to work one morning that the vague outline of a plan finally emerged.

The epiphany stemmed from three incontrovertible facts: the sidewalk outside the shop was heavily traveled by carnivores; the overwhelming number of meat eaters passed the display window without looking inside; and no butcher in Fettig cut with Leopold Plotkin's flair.

Indeed, Plotkin's disassembling skills were unparalleled in the capital city. Through years of trial and error, he had perfected a flamboyant style of meat-cutting that was efficient as well as mesmerizing—an extraordinary amalgam of impeccable precision and graceful head, arm, and lower body movements. Even his competitors grudgingly admired his body of work.

"What do you recommend?" Plotkin asked after the chicken plucker revealed the incontrovertible facts that underpinned the epiphany.

"Simply stated," Astigmatopolous replied, "if we drag the dismembering table from the back of the shop to the front, place it near the display window so passers-by can watch you work, they will be drawn into the shop like moths to light, like bees to pollen, like ____."

"Like gawkers to a trained monkey," Plotkin interrupted with disappointment.

"I wouldn't put it quite that way," the chicken plucker gently disagreed.

"Unfortunately, your hypothesis ignores my nature and forgets that I am a private man with an aversion to being gawked at," Plotkin asserted.

"Desperate times call for desperate measures," the chicken plucker countered.

"The best laid plans of desperate men sometimes go astray," Plotkin retorted.

"Desperation is the mother of reinvention," the chicken plucker parried, adding that the loss of the shop would devastate Plotkin's father.

As the debate wore on, Astigmatopolous skillfully deflected each of Plotkin's arguments. Gradually, he upended the butcher's resistance. The next morning, after receiving authorization from his father, Plotkin repositioned the table. While bolting it to the floor, he told the chicken plucker, who hardly needed to be reminded, that he was doing so "with profound reluctance."

8

Soon after implementation of the business plan, pedestrians noticed Leopold Plotkin's unique repertoire: the exacting cleaves, cuts, chops, and slices of a surgeon; the perfectly synchronized leg movements of a ballerina; and the violent head-shakes of an orchestra conductor. The convergence of such talents in a single person generated the highest praise one in his position could expect to receive: He didn't seem like a butcher.

Word of Plotkin's performances spread through Fettig and then to the provinces. People of all ethnicities, genders, and ages came to watch him perform. Onlookers treated the spectacles as theater, giving standing ovations and uttering rapturous "bravos." They threw roses onto the shop's floor. They asked Plotkin for his autograph and to pose for photographs with their families. In a few instances, female admirers suggested after-work liaisons. When glowing reviews of his performances appeared in newspapers, the adulation rose to a level ordinarily reserved for demagogues.

The outpouring of reverence didn't translate into increased sales, however. Even at the height of his celebrity, Plotkin teetered on the edge of economic collapse. As one day followed the next, he gazed at the faces of admirers who never purchased his goods and felt exploited. Unable to cope, he summoned the chicken plucker to his flat for a consultation. "Do you think we should abandon your plan?" he asked. "Perhaps it would be best to return the dismembering table to the back of the store," he mused.

Still confident in the eventual success of his plan, Primo Astigmatopolous counseled against removing the table from pedestrian view. Congenitally unable to reach a decision without his father's knowledge and approval, Plotkin asked the patriarch what he should do.

"There's only one thing to do!" the paterfamilias hollered. "Take a bold, principled stand for once in your life! Cover the window with something! I won't have you taken advantage of by mobs of ingrates! It will destroy my reputation! It will make my beloved father turn over in his grave and his father turn over in his grave and so on up the line! If Primo still has that mud he always brags about, use it! Make it impossible to see in! Teach them a lesson: Plotkins can't be taken advantage of!"

Lacking the strength to reject his father's edict, that night, while the rest of Fettig slept, he lathered the inside of the shatterproof display window with the nonporous, multi-colored mud Primo Astigmatopolous imported from the Motherland. Primo assisted by stirring the mud.

"This is excellent mud," Plotkin commented as he brushed the yellow, black, orange, and purple substance onto the glass with horsehair paintbrushes borrowed from his uncles.

"Yes, it is," the chicken plucker replied each time Plotkin repeated the compliment, recalling that the Interior Minister of his nameless country described indigenous mud as "the finest in the world and the only thing we have to be proud of."

After completion of the project, every inch of the glass was covered in mud, making it impossible to see into the shop. The next morning, when Fettigians poured into the Small Business District, they were appalled to discover that the most coveted display window in the sector was now opaque. This unsettling phenomenon caused small groups to mill about and commiserate. To the best of anyone's knowledge, the complete shrouding of a commercial window was unprecedented.

The next morning, newspaper editorials condemned the transformation as a "desecration," an "affront," a "radical deviation from mercantile norms," and "beyond the pale." After breakfast, hundreds of citizens took to the streets in protest. Columns of agitated men, women, and children marched through the District, chanting that store windows were to be seen through and that only a merchant who had something to hide would work in secrecy. The butcher reacted badly to the demonstrations. Among other things, he suffered a temporary hearing loss, fleeting lower body paralysis, and a severe drooling bout.

Soon, posters appeared on buildings, accusing Plotkin of engaging in immoral activities and hatching sinister plots behind obscured glass. Placards were printed, describing Plotkin as an ANARCHIST BENT ON DESTROYING CAPITALISM and a SOCIALIST IN MERCHANT'S CLOTHING. Effigies of the butcher were burned. Patriotic songs were sung. Flags of the Republic were unfurled. As the protests became more vitriolic, a coalition of clerics from all organized religions and a smattering of disorganized religions convened silent candlelight vigils, offering an alternative to the noisy demonstrations. Plotkin's father insisted that he stay the course. When silence failed to achieve the desired results, the ecumenical consortium became disenchanted and joined forces with the demonstrators.

Fearing that Leopold Plotkin's behavior might jeopardize their efforts to bring socialism to the Republic, the Workingmen's Square expelled him, although the butcher had never been a member of the socialistic organization. Subsequently, the Talmudic Debating Society issued a statement condemning his act as "antithetical to the Five Books of Moses" and barred him from participating in future debates. Rabbis denounced Plotkin from the pulpit, criticizing him for bringing negative attention to the Jewish community and, thereby, imperiling its tenuous position in the Republic's melting pot. An editorial in the *Jewish Daily Angst* criticized Plotkin. "We are tolerated in this great bastion of freedom only if we don't make waves. Leopold Plotkin has made numerous waves with his radical act. In the interest of self-preservation, the Angst urges our most prominent rabbis to break bread with the butcher and convince him to undo what he has done before the voices of intolerance imperil our place in this great nation."

In the wake of the editorial, a delegation of rabbis confronted Plotkin at the shop. Its three spokesmen took turns urging him to clean the window—if not for himself, for his fellow Jews. He rejected their pleas after consulting with his father. Jacob proclaimed, "Nobody, except a Plotkin, tells a Plotkin what to do." The patriarch warned Leopold that he would lose paternal respect if he capitulated to the rabbinical pleas. Pursuant to Jacob Plotkin's instructions, the conflict-averse butcher added a layer of mud to the inside of the window as the rabbis looked on with chagrin. Agitated pedestrians, noticing that the mud had become thicker, hectored Plotkin the next day as he entered the shop. Feigning unflappability while shaking uncontrollably, Plotkin said, "Please go away."

When it became apparent that demonstrations would not break Plotkin's resolve, a clandestine group of militants emerged. Well-trained and disciplined, they hurled rocks at the shatterproof glass. As the projectiles bounced harmlessly to the pavement, the group's leader exhorted his men not to give up. Hours later, with the window still intact, the fatigued militants abandoned their leader to join the nonviolent protests.

In the second week of demonstrations, the size and frequency of protests increased geometrically. Over time, they grew exponentially. By the fourth week, thousands took to the streets. Word of the expanding movement spread from Fettig to the provinces, attracting mobs of angry rustics to the capital city to join their urban brothers and sisters. The outlanders infused the movement with new enthusiasm, ramped-up the level of anger, and extended the demonstrations beyond the Small Business District.

Professional commentators, unable to imagine a dispute without the benefit of their insights, weighed in. Economists forecasted the window's potentially devastating economic impact. Philosophers described the mud-encrusted glass as an affront to man's essence. Ethicists criticized the window's amorality. Political scientists predicted that the window could destabilize government. Even the most ardent solipsists described Leopold Plotkin as overly self-absorbed.

Not all citizens were against the meat merchant, however. As vitriol swirled around him, a confederacy of Deep Thinkers—mostly scholars in ill-fitting clothes and disheveled hair—rallied to his defense. They penned essays for obscure periodicals (read only by devotees) that advanced elegant, often inconsistent, theories to explain or justify his conduct. Some of the writings posited that his window was a harmless metaphor for the decline of Fettig society. Others described it as an innocent but misguided cry for help. A few speculated that the mud on the window was simply the inadvertent result of a lapse in Plotkin's sanitation standards.

As usual, the Deep Thinkers had no impact beyond a small circle of like-minded men. Accordingly, they decided to forsake their libraries and other intellectual cocoons and inject themselves directly into the upheaval by mounting counter-demonstrations. Although the finer points of their esoteric slogans were largely lost on most onlookers, they succeeded in confusing a small minority that didn't know what to think. These perplexed, loosely linked individuals, who called themselves Ambivalents, supported Plotkin one day, opposed him the next day, and every third day remained neutral.

The Jewish Anti-Slander Confederacy, a group dedicated to combating bigotry against Jews, took no formal position with respect to what Plotkin had done. The spate of anti-Semitic placards that began to appear in demonstrations did, however, alarm the Confederacy. Through its chairman, the organization issued a statement criticizing those who employed hateful sentiments to oppose Plotkin's window-related activities and imploring bigots to confine their remarks to the bedroom and dining areas of their residences. Offended by the Confederacy's statement, prominent anti-Semites accused the organization of being thin-skinned and intolerant. A spokesman for a group of Jew haters proclaimed, "We are not anti-Jewish! We are, instead, people of good faith who are not blind to the fact that Leopold Plotkin is an instrument of the international Jewish conspiracy of wealthy bankers and financiers to control the world's money!"

When months of demonstrations, vigils, bombast, dire predictions, demands for the butcher's arrest, bitter recriminations, and more expulsions from organizations Plotkin didn't belong to failed to trigger the mud's removal, clean-window proponents filed a raft of petitions with Prosecutor General Umberto Malatesta, urging him to charge the butcher with Crimes against the Republic. The petitions were met by a handful of letters from the butcher's supporters, urging Malatesta to leave Plotkin and the window alone. Ambivalents submitted two sets of petitions, one imploring Malatesta to prosecute, the other suggesting that he do nothing.

Comparing the large volume of material from Plotkin's opponents to the limited number of submissions from the butcher's supporters, Malatesta concluded that prosecuting Plotkin was in his professional interest. Since the Prosecutor General was generally unfamiliar with the laws he was supposed to enforce, he asked his Chief Minion to locate the law that Plotkin violated and to prepare an arrest warrant. The Chief Minion's exhaustive search revealed that no law prohibited what the butcher had done. To ease the disappointment, he told Malatesta that Plotkin's arrest was somewhat premature and that the logical way to proceed was to ask the Inner Chamber, the Republic's legislative body, to enact anti-window-covering legislation. Agreeing with the advice, Malatesta instructed the subordinate to draft a memo to Inner Chamber Leader Cicero Bookbinder, demanding that Bookbinder "correct this egregious oversight immediately."

Alter Ego Mendel Sprem

9

The memorandum Umberto Malatesta sent to Cicero Book-binder detailed Leopold Plotkin's heinous acts, the dire consequences a failure to prosecute would have on the Republic, and the shocking fact that no law made what the butcher did a crime. "This tragic oversight must be remedied to avoid descent into anarchy," the Prosecutor General asserted in the missive.

Malatesta's courier hand-delivered the memo to the Inner Chamber Leader's chambers. A clerk carried the message past Bookbinder's office and handed it to Mendel Sprem, Bookbinder's Alter Ego.

"More to read, sir," the clerk said matter-of-factly.

"Splendid," Sprem replied enthusiastically. "Did you happen to notice what the Leader was doing as you passed his office?"

"The usual," said the clerk. "He's engaged in a chess match with himself."

"Tap on his door and tell him it's time to go home," Sprem instructed. "He has a speech to give tomorrow and must be well-rested."

"Very good, sir," the servile clerk replied. "But what if he hasn't completed his match? You know he gets frustrated if he's interrupted before he wins."

"*I* become *more* frustrated when he ruins one of my speeches," Sprem retorted. "Better that he's frustrated than I'm provoked."

Mendel Sprem had been managing Cicero Bookbinder's legislative life for more than two decades. He engineered the Leader's election to the Inner Chamber after Bookbinder's opponent, an unbeatable incumbent, died unexpectedly hours before the polls opened. Once in office, he guided the little known politician's ascent to the pinnacle of power.

Unlike most Alter Egos, who merely assisted their Inner Chambermen, Sprem performed virtually all of Bookbinder's functions. Unless Bookbinder had to deliver a speech, debate a bill, or perform some other activity that required his presence, Sprem acted in lieu of him. The consummate substitute reviewed all documents sent to Bookbinder, prepared all correspondence signed by Bookbinder, drafted all laws proposed by Bookbinder, composed all speeches delivered by Bookbinder, formulated all policies promoted by Bookbinder, prescribed all votes cast by Bookbinder, and charted all tactics Bookbinder required to guide his party's Chambermen. As time permitted, Sprem informed Bookbinder of relevant events occurring outside Chamber walls to enable the incurious politician to appear conversant with developments under his jurisdiction.

Mendel Sprem's colonization of Cicero Bookbinder was by mutual agreement. Both recognized the Leader's limitations. Both understood that Bookbinder was a man of modest intellect who had no interest in or grasp of governmental operations. And both realized that Bookbinder's political survival depended on Sprem. They were also acutely aware of Sprem's unique qualifications: he was a highly cerebral man, steeped in the intricacies of politics, a voracious reader, an accomplished writer, and a man with boundless energy who was willing to work behind the scenes to achieve a well-defined political agenda.

Mendel Sprem was Cicero Bookbinder in all but name. Known in Chamber circles as "Bookbinder's Brain," Sprem was the de facto representative of Province 29 and Leader of the party that was perpetually in the majority. He appointed Chambermen to committee chairmanships. He was the gatekeeper and determined which bills would see the light of day. He was actually the second most powerful politician in the Republic—a mere rung below Emile

Threadbare, the High Minister. Though Sprem remained largely unknown outside the precincts of the Chambers Building, his reputation within the edifice was storied.

The Alter Ego reviewed Umberto Malatesta's request for an anti-window-covering statute. He decided to oppose it, not on doctrinal grounds, but for personal reasons. Years earlier, Malatesta unsuccessfully prosecuted three of Sprem's uncles, two aunts, a nephew, four nieces, and a stepsister for a criminal enterprise involving a family business that nearly destroyed the family structure. Still carrying a grudge, Sprem sent a reply, under Bookbinder's name, in which he thanked the Prosecutor General for his interesting suggestion, promised to give the matter careful consideration, and said that a more substantive response might be forthcoming in a few years. This prompted a venomous reply in which Malatesta accused Bookbinder of dragging his feet. Although Sprem relished Malatesta's displeasure, he recognized that a small dose of mollification might be politically prudent. Three weeks later, he dispatched a communiqué, under Bookbinder's signature, stating that the Leader was contemplating the selection of a committee to carefully explore the matter. He promised to apprise the Prosecutor General of further developments should there be any. The response incensed Malatesta. By return letter, the Prosecutor General called the convening of an exploratory committee an unconscionable act of legislative delay, accused Bookbinder of being a moral coward, and demanded that Bookbinder exhibit the leadership for which he was so unjustifiably revered. Sprem penned a reply that the Leader would not be bullied into pandering to the masses.

When several days passed without a response from Malatesta, Mendel Sprem assumed that Malatesta had abandoned his quest. The silence pleased Sprem. The pleasure was short-lived, however. As he was drafting a speech, a delegation of Cabinet Underministers appeared in his office to convey High Minister Emile Threadbare's demand for the immediate submission of a bill that criminalized the covering of mercantile windows with foreign substances. Sprem thanked the Underministers for their interest in the matter before telling them that the suggested legislation was inconsistent with the Leader's deeply held principles. Offended, because they knew that Bookbinder lacked deeply held principles, the delegation repaired to Gray House to confer with the High Minister.

High Minister Emile Threadbare with security official Olaf Dybyk

10

When told of Mendel Sprem's refusal to allow Cicero Book-binder to sponsor anti-window covering legislation, High Minister Emile Threadbare huddled with Olaf Dybyk, his Director of Internalized Security, to formulate a plan to secure Sprem's cooperation. After hatching a plan, they made an unscheduled appearance in Bookbinder's chambers demanding to see the Alter Ego. A clerk ushered them into a library where Sprem was eating his customary vegetarian lunch.

"The High Minister and Director of Internalized Security are here to see you, sir," the vassal announced stiffly.

"Mr. High Minister," Sprem said without enthusiasm as he brushed carrot droppings from his lap and stood. "It's a pleasure to see you," he lied.

"The pleasure is mine," Threadbare exclaimed disingenuously before seizing Sprem's hand tightly to demonstrate political virility.

"How is the Minister's wife?" Sprem asked after surviving the handshake. He and Cicero Bookbinder had spent most of a recent state dinner leering at Threadbare's statuesque spouse. Bookbinder secretly harbored an obsessive attraction to women of height.

"She's extremely well," said Threadbare. "I assume the Alter Ego's mistress is well as well?"

"Relatively well," Sprem replied, understating his consort's actual wellness to avoid overshadowing the First Female's health, a courtesy routinely shown to those higher on the political chain.

"And the Minister's children?" Sprem asked.

"Thriving," said Threadbare. "The Alter Ego's bastards?"

"Getting by," Sprem understated.

This prattle was followed by a series of questions about the welfare of other relatives. During the tedious exchange, Olaf Dybyk's eyes darted about the room wildly, searching for security breaches. Finally, the High Minister broached the reason for the visit.

"The Mud Crisis alarms me," Threadbare declared.

"With all due respect, Mr. High Minister, I think you are overreacting," Sprem replied. "The so-called crisis is a passing phenomenon of no importance."

"As usual, you are misguided," Threadbare proclaimed. "If something isn't done soon, I shudder to think what will become of the Republic."

Troubled by the direction the conversation was taking, Sprem tried to redirect it by offering the High Minister a carrot. Threadbare, however, wouldn't be deterred.

"The Crisis is a plague," Threadbare declared. "It has turned children against parents, fathers against sons, students against teachers, and so on and so forth."

"Soon our streets will be unsafe," Dybyk predicted.

"Crime will flourish," Threadbare postulated.

"As will incest," Dybyk opined.

"Morality will plummet," Threadbare mused. "Schools will close. Anti-Plotkin demonstrations will turn into anti-government protests. Our economy will collapse."

"My field operatives think that the muddying of the window is part of an international conspiracy of Jewish bankers; a plot by Jewish Bolsheviks to gain a foothold in the Republic, or possibly neither," Dybyk proclaimed. "Being a Jew yourself, I'm sure you're aware that ____."

Unwilling to listen to more anti-Semitic speculation, Sprem interrupted. "I'm certain, gentlemen, that the window is simply an isolated incident by a misguided merchant."

"How can I put this diplomatically, my good friend?" Thread-bare asked without expecting an answer. "Let's call your view 'wishful thinking,' a by-product of a hopelessly naïve and over-rated mind!"

"With all the meager respect I can muster, my dear friend," said Sprem, "Your view of my view is idiotic."

"Am I to deduce, sir, that you and, by necessary implication, Mr. Bookbinder, are refusing to sponsor anti-window covering legislation?" the High Minister asked.

"The simple answer to your question is 'Yes,'" Sprem replied.

The High Minister raised his bushy brows and looked knowingly at the Director of Internalized Security. "Mr. Dybyk informs me of some unspeakable indiscretions involving the Leader," Threadbare said gravely.

The reference to "unspeakable indiscretions" alarmed Sprem. Though aware that Cicero Bookbinder had engaged in many indiscretions during his years of civic service, he knew of only one that rose to the level of "unspeakability": a compulsion to ogle at or cavort with women who towered above him. Citizens demanded that their representatives be strong, proud and, above all, able to look down on women. It was universally presumed that any office holder who had liaisons with women of height wished to be dominated and, therefore, was unfit to govern. Despite Sprem's counsel to avoid even the appearance of mingling with taller women, the Leader's insatiable urges overwhelmed his political judgment, forcing him to engage in encounters with females as much as a foot taller. The Alter Ego's stomach churned as he studied Olaf Dybyk's smirking face. He wondered if the always suspicious head of security had discovered Bookbinder's one unforgiveable sin.

"Unspeakable indiscretions? I have no idea what you are talking about," Sprem stated with superficial calm.

"Show him," Threadbare commanded.

Dybyk reached into his suit jacket, removed a raft of photographs, and handed Sprem evidence of Bookbinder's unpardonable activities. There were pictures of the Leader at cafés, sipping coffee with towering females; hailing cabs with even taller woman at his side; embracing long-legged amazons in alleyways; nibbling the ears of ladies of height who were bending to accommodate him; ogling at Threadbare's statuesque wife from various perspectives at the state dinner; and other images that confirmed the Leader's pathology.

"Would I be correct to surmise from your wounded expression that the Leader has had a change of heart and now sees the need for clear-window legislation?" Emile Threadbare asked as Dybyk collected the incriminating evidence.

Sprem immediately recognized the dangers posed by the photographs.

"After reconsidering your arguments," he bleated, "I think they are persuasive. However, I propose something less drastic than legislation at this time."

"You are in no position to make proposals," Threadbare said dismissively.

"But I am," Sprem lied. "I have some deeply disturbing photographs which, if published, will put *you* in an extremely bad light."

"Can you be more specific?" Threadbare asked apprehensively, wondering which of his myriad indiscretions his enemies had recorded.

"Not now," Sprem said tersely.

"How can I be certain that such photographs exist?" Threadbare asked.

"The question offends me, sir," Sprem lied. "It's not my habit to lie." Although the Alter Ego *was* in the habit of lying, he presumed that Threadbare, like most politicians, had a perversion he didn't want exposed.

The High Minister knew that Sprem was an accomplished liar. Nevertheless, he was unsure that Sprem was lying on this occasion. Since he wasn't prepared to find out, he capitulated.

"Earlier," Threadbare said, "you mentioned a less drastic approach. Tell me more."

Sprem pursed his lips, his way of signaling he was about to say something important. "I'm confident," he said, "that a speech by the Leader at the offensive site *threatening* to introduce clear window legislation will be sufficient to bring the butcher to his senses. If this fails, though highly unlikely, the Leader will sponsor the legislation."

Ambivalent over Sprem's proposal, the High Minister's eyebrows arched in different directions—an involuntary movement that revealed his uncertainty about the proposal. Seconds later, the eyebrows returned to normal alignment, indicating that he found the proposal acceptable.

"I'm satisfied with the resolution of our slight differences," Threadbare lied.

"We're all adults here," said Sprem, "sensible, civilized men guided only by the desire to serve the people."

The Alter Ego and High Minister shook hands distrustfully to seal the pact. After the handshake, Threadbare and Dybyk left. Sprem resumed eating, relieved that he had avoided a political scandal that would jeopardize Bookbinder's career and his own.

Curator A. I. Gopnik

11

The poster was ubiquitous. It appeared overnight on the walls of coffeehouses, the counters of train stations, and other places where Fettigians congregated. Designed by the High Minister's Office to advertise Cicero Bookbinder's speech and ridicule Leopold Plotkin, it featured an unflattering caricature of the butcher smearing mud on his display window. Naked, except for a yarmulke and a skimpy apron, Plotkin's caricature was grinning like a madman. His pen and ink head, abnormally large in reality, dwarfed the remainder of his illustrated body. His sketched eyes bulged maniacally. His exaggerated hooknose flared demonically. Bookbinder's more benign caricature hovered in the background, delivering a speech. Below the drawings was an announcement that Bookbinder would be orating near the display window on a specified date and time. All "patriots and aspiring patriots" were encouraged to attend.

Several hundred copies of the poster had been pasted onto the high wall surrounding the Warehouse for the Purportedly Insane, a decrepit sanatorium located a block from the butcher shop. Most were still attached when chicken plucker Primo Astigmatopolous emerged from his hovel to embark on his daily bicycle trek to work. It was an arduous hour-long journey that required twelve miles of peddling along pockmarked streets, over steep hills, across rickety bridges, and through a serpentine tunnel. Conditions were inhospitable that morning. There was a steady drizzle and fog. The chicken plucker wore a white smock as protection from the elements.

Even before mounting his bicycle, Astigmatopolous felt exhausted. He had been awake most of the night, transcribing notes from interviews conducted in Fettig brothels, confessions overheard in churches catering to the poor, and bits of conversation gleaned in the capital city's seediest pubs. The notes were for his long-planned trilogy about people living on the margins of society. As originally envisioned, the process was to unfold in two stages: a year of collecting raw material; then the writing. Thirteen years after establishing this timeframe, the chicken plucker was still mired in the material-collection phase. Operating under the belief that he had yet to amass enough information to justify three books, he often re-interviewed the same people and returned to the same sites to eavesdrop. Since he was never without a notebook, his flat was littered with storage boxes containing the fruits of his labor.

After boarding his bicycle, the would-be author peddled in darkness. Navigating the uneven streets, challenging hills, and unstable bridges, he managed to exit the serpentine tunnel unscathed and turned onto Drabble Street, the last leg of the trek. It was eerily quiet, except for the rattle of his antiquated bicycle. Several blocks ahead, a pencil-thin man in tattered institutional coveralls stood at the Warehouse's outer-wall, ripping the posters from their brick moorings. As the emaciated man struggled to dislodge the last of the advertisements, he made cryptic references to matches and flames.

A moderately psychotic trustee on the Warehouse's garbage detail, Anatole Illianov Gopnik had plummeted from the heights of the Republic's artistic world to the depths of an insane asylum after setting fire to works displayed in the Museum of Despondent Paintings, where he had been the Head Curator. In the months preceding his plummet, Gopnik slowly devolved from a refined, rational person to a disheveled shell of himself, with a depression manifested by mania.

The unspooling resulted from a decade of work-related stress. While curating, Gopnik had specialized in the procurement of foreboding landscapes. In that capacity, he participated in hundreds of tedious art auctions, thousands of mind-numbing authentications, and countless dull seminars in which the meanings of works were discussed at length. He traveled extensively, searching the world for portentous pieces, an activity that required sleeping in strange beds and staring for hours at bleak canvasses. Immersion in the copious gloom led to bouts of hostility toward paintings he no longer considered sufficiently bleak to warrant hanging. One afternoon, he resolved to burn the undeserving works. Hiding in the facility after closing time, he removed a trove of the most egregious paintings from the walls, ripped the canvasses from their frames, carted the liberated items to the basement, arranged them into a neat combustible pyre, and lit a match. As the canvases burned, he muttered, "What choice did I have?" Fortunately for the Museum, the flames didn't spread to the upper floors. Satisfied with the outcome, the curator fell into a restful sleep.

The next morning, after Gopnik was discovered in the basement speaking gibberish near the mound of destroyed artwork, the Museum's Board of Directors had him committed to the Warehouse for the Purportedly Insane to ascertain whether he was a criminal who deserved to be prosecuted or merely crazy. A Warehouse diagnostician's examination yielded a tentative conclusion that Gopnik was either an obsessive-compulsive maniac with paranoid delusions, or a skilled arsonist masquerading as such. Operating under those assumptions, the diagnostician consigned Gopnik to a padded cell and told him to languish there until further notice. After several months of languishing, Gopnik convinced Warehouse personnel that his compulsion to burn artwork had diminished to the point where it was no more than a passing thought. Under a step-down plan, he was transferred to an unpadded cell without flammable items; then to a locked ward with a few flammable items; and, ultimately, to an unlocked ward containing numerous combustibles.

Eventually, Gopnik persuaded the powers that be that his arson-related demons had receded enough to justify his appointment to a trustee position on the inmate garbage detail, where he would be responsible for carrying burnable material from the institution to the public sidewalk for deposit in trash bins. He agreed to inform staff if uncontrollable urges to burn resumed.

Gopnik had encountered the poster advertising Cicero Bookbinder's speech while dragging bags filled with institutional waste through the Warehouse's main gate. Even when normal, he considered caricatures low art, insufficiently bleak, and unworthy of display. "These disgust me," he shrieked as his eyes darted across the mass-produced renderings. Ignoring his promise to inform his caretakers if the urge to burn returned, the former curator dropped the garbage bags, ripped the posters from the bricks, and arranged them in a neat pile near a row of collection bins.

It was while Gopnik was preparing the posters for immolation that the chicken plucker approached on his bicycle. Hearing rattles, the trustee turned to find their source. As he squinted into the fog-laden darkness, he saw a faint silhouette of what appeared to be either a man on a bicycle or a ghost on an emaciated horse. Suspecting that it was not an apparition, he ran into the street, thrust his arms outward, and shouted, "HALT!"

Preoccupied with his trilogy, the chicken plucker was oblivious to his surroundings. Startled by the shout, he refocused his eyes, looked ahead, saw Gopnik's body a few feet away, and swerved radically leftward to avoid a collision. The swerve redirected the bicycle to the high sidewalk curb parallel to the Warehouse wall. Moments later, the vehicle struck a curb, hurtling Primo Astigmatopolous across the sidewalk into the wall. His body came to rest, face-up, on the cement. Blood dripped from his scalp.

Gopnik sauntered casually over to the prone bicyclist. Peering at the accident victim he asked nonchalantly, "Are you alright down there?"

"Not too bad," the chicken plucker replied calmly.

"It was kind of you to swerve," said Gopnik.

"Think nothing of it," said the chicken plucker. "I'm sure you would have done the same."

"Probably not," Gopnik replied. "My name is Gopnik, a temporary guest of this facility. And you are?"

"Primo Astigmatopolous."

"Do you need a few seconds to acquire a second wind?" Gopnik asked. "Your breathing is labored."

"That isn't unusual," said the chicken plucker. "I'm a heavy breather."

"I tend to be a shallow breather, like most in my family," said Gopnik. "However, I was breathing hard just before flagging you down. The posters were stubborn. Too much glue."

"Do you mind if I take notes?" the chicken plucker asked, realizing that he had yet to interview a Warehouse resident.

"Notes of what?" Gopnik answered quizzically.

"Our interview," said the chicken plucker.

"May I ask why you want to interview me at this particular time?"

"I'm writing a trilogy."

"To be frank, I doubt that my life is interesting enough to fill three books."

"You'd only be a chapter."

"That's more realistic, but maybe not sufficient. I have a lot to tell."

"I'm sure you do."

"While I would be delighted to grant you an interview, this isn't a good time. The hour is growing late. The powers that be will start looking for me if I don't return soon. We have to focus on why I flagged you down. I need matches to burn posters. If you are capable of lifting your head slightly and turning your neck to the right, you'll see the pile I've assembled."

The chicken plucker managed, with some pain, to glimpse at the pile.

"Where do you intend to burn the posters?" he asked.

"On the sidewalk, about ten feet from your head, give or take three feet either way."

"This is a *public* sidewalk."

"I assumed so."

"Burning on a public sidewalk is a first degree *Fire Code* violation."

"That isn't surprising."

"I can't give you matches."

"You *can't*, or you *won't*?"

"Both, I suppose, although either is possible."

"I'm deeply disappointed in your response to my cry for help. I've offered to give you an exclusive interview, yet you refuse my request for matches. What kind of an ingrate are you?"

"I'm an unlawful immigrant."

"What does that have to do with refusing matches to a man who desperately needs them?"

"Burning on a public sidewalk is a deportable offense. If I give you matches, I could be sent back, which isn't a good option."

"You worry needlessly, my paranoid friend," said Gopnik. "Nobody will know where I got them. If your eyes weren't covered by blood, you'd be able to read the print on my coveralls attesting to the fact that I'm a trustee. I can be trusted not to reveal sources."

"Except for Mr. Plotkin, I trust no one," said the chicken plucker, almost to himself.

"Did you say *Plotkin*?" Gopnik asked with interest.

"I believe so," the chicken plucker replied.

"And the first name?"

"Leopold."

"Is he a somewhat idiotic looking man with heavy eye pouches and hair that resembles a den of snakes?"

"You might say that."

"Does he have a butcher shop on this street?"

"Yes."

"Extraordinary. A coincidence that defies statistical probability."

"What coincidence do you have in mind?"

"The image of the only person you trust defiles the posters I want to burn."

"*Mr. Plotkin's* image?"

"Of course *his*! Would you care to see an example before I look for a more cooperative person to flag down?"

"I would be deeply appreciative, if it isn't too much trouble."

Gopnik retrieved a poster and held it above the chicken plucker's body. As Plotkin's apostle cleared the blood from his eyes and studied the unflattering caricature, his normally heavy breathing rose to an alarming level.

"Are you still alright down there?" inquired Gopnik. "Your inhalations seem more labored than before."

"This poster does a disservice to Mr. Plotkin," the chicken plucker shrieked.

"It opens him to public ridicule!" Gopnik observed. "The person who produced this poster is insensitive and inartistic!" he declared for purposes of convincing the chicken plucker to part with one or two matches. "The abomination deserves nothing less than a good burning!"

The chicken plucker reached into a pocket, grabbed a box of matches, and said, "Take these and burn at will!"

"A most generous contribution to a vital cause," said Gopnik, "I'm forever in your debt. You are a prince among men and a kind-hearted gentleman willing to support a cause of vital importance. If I had more time, I would help lift you from the pavement. However, I don't. Remember, as you lay there recuperating, I am discrete to a fault and you have nothing to fear from me. My lips are sealed. They would have to torture me before I would reveal it was you who provided the matches. No, they would have to threaten my life before I would tell them where you can be apprehended. I will testify on your behalf should immigration officials attempt to deport you."

Gopnik turned and scurried to the poster pile, lit several matches, and strategically placed them on various parts of the pyre. The chicken plucker urged him on with contradictory cries of: "Burn them all," and "Save one for me."

As the flames rose and ashes danced on the sidewalk, Astigmatopolous hoped that he wouldn't be burnt in the process. Gopnik slipped the few remaining matches into a pocket, handed his accomplice a salvaged poster, and returned to the Warehouse with a sense of fulfillment. Minutes later, the chicken plucker lifted himself from the pavement. He then smoothed his rumpled clothing, used a handkerchief to dab at the cut on his forehead, righted his bicycle, and resumed his journey.

Inner Chamber Leader Cicero Bookbinder

12

icero Bookbinder and Mendel Sprem waded into the dense crowd gathered outside the butcher shop for the Leader's speech. Politicians and other prominent demagogues stood on the makeshift stage, waiting for Bookbinder's late arrival. Impatient to reach his destination, Bookbinder screamed, "Let me through!" Sprem pushed. Bodies parted. Bookbinder waddled.

As he ascended a stairway leading to the stage, the Leader reached into his coat pocket to retrieve the manuscript Sprem had written.

"It's not there!" Bookbinder whispered with alarm.

"What's not where?" Sprem whispered back.

"The speech isn't in my pocket."

"What did you do with it?"

"I don't know."

"This is a catastrophe waiting to happen."

"What can I do?"

"Just say a few words, then sit down."

As Sprem helped the portly Leader up the last rung of the stairway, he cautioned: "Remember your limitations."

Standing at the edge of the stage, looking at the sea of people below, Bookbinder struggled to recall passages from Sprem's lost text. His porous mind, however, couldn't remember more than the general thrust of the speech. None of the clever phraseology came into focus. Sensing that staring at the crowd for a few minutes would not constitute a speech, he opened his acclaimed mouth, formed a grave expression on his rotund face, cleared his golden throat, grasped the lapels of his topcoat, and bellowed in a stentorian voice, "Good afternoon!"

The audience erupted in applause. The applause soon spread to the tenements on both sides of the street, where tenants leaned from open windows to have better views of the revered politician. The only exceptions to the appreciative ovation were Jacob and Emma Plotkin and the twin uncles. The elders stood rigidly at their window in oppositional silence, wondering why the crowd was excited. "Anyone could have said that," the patriarch commented.

As the applause rose to a fever pitch, Leopold Plotkin emerged from the shop with the chicken plucker at his side. With the eyes of the assembled trained on the Leader, nobody took notice of them.

"My fellow Republicans," Bookbinder improvised in a mournful tone after the applause subsided, "word of the butcher's salacious activities has recently reached my sensitive ears. These repugnant and odious misdeeds have made the Inner Chamber queasy, if not actually vomitus." He patted his stomach, and then violently grabbed his throat in a choking gesture to pinpoint the exact locations of the Chamber's distress. The crowd applauded to acknowledge Bookbinder's clever body language.

Dizzy from the strangulation ploy, Bookbinder waited for his head to clear. When satisfied that he wouldn't faint, he continued. "I'm here to announce my position on this very troubling matter and to explain why the sinister butcher is an enemy of the City of Fettig, the Fettig River, and everything else bearing that revered name, et cetera, et cetera, and so forth! More important, he is an enemy of the Republic, without which Fettig would not exist and none of us would be here on this auspicious occasion."

Heads bobbed. Cheers erupted. Hats flung.

"Allow me to be frank, if not completely forthcoming," the orator resumed while many in the crowd searched for missing hats. "If truth be told, as it occasionally is, without store windows to look through, we are no better than beasts of burden left to our own devices or the devices of others…to labor in obscurity for posterity… after all is said and done…and cooler heads prevail!"

More applause. Mendel Sprem grimaced. The improvisation was worse than he had imagined. He began to consider strategies for extricating Bookbinder from the stage.

"Allow me to share a personal syllogism with you," Bookbinder elaborated. "All commercial establishments in this Republic have see-through display windows. Ergo, the place in question—the object of my heartfelt contempt—must either be a non-commercial establishment or…or…something else that has yet to be identified."

A sea of heads swayed to feign understanding of, and agreement with, the Leader's logic. The Alter Ego's head didn't move. Rather, he hunched his shoulders and looked away in despair. Plotkin and the chicken plucker, who thought the syllogism was illogical, rolled their eyes.

"I'm not here to cast a pall over the store that is the subject of my contempt, because a shop divided cannot stand and it is foolish to put the horse before the cart," the Leader shouted authoritatively. "No edifice is stronger than its weakest link, and a house of cards will collapse if one nudges the bottom card ever so slightly. Furthermore, it is important to note, though it is of no significance, that the perpetrator of this treacherous act is a radical of the Judaic sect. Therefore, it is incumbent on me to reach out to our clannish, boorish, weak-kneed Hebrew friends and ask them to join with their less peculiar Christian brothers in a campaign to bring a close to this matter. I remind all Jews, wherever they are or may be that this great Republic, while not embracing them, has allowed them to come to this land of the free in droves! Therefore, in gratitude for the welcome they have received, the followers of this mysterious faith, must encourage the owner of the offensive store to change his ways!"

Pockets of bigots in the audience began to chant, "Jews! Jews!"

Jews in the crowd, alarmed by the chanting, didn't join in. Even Mendel Sprem, a non-observant Jew who thought of himself more as a secular Republican citizen than a Jew, suddenly felt vulnerable.

"We should ask what we can do for this Republic, if not for ourselves," Bookbinder proclaimed when the chants subsided, "This is because the measure of a civilized people is how poorly those on top treat the degenerates beneath them, which brings me to the store's owner. Today it is Plotkin; tomorrow it may be Cohen or

Goldberg! A free society cannot remain free if merchants, particularly those of a conspiratorial sect, are allowed to work behind a dark window. While it is one thing for a government to work in secret, it is another for a merchant to do the same! Remember, as someone of significance once said: 'Ignorance is bliss but is bliss ignorance?'"

Bookbinder tore the right lapel of his suit in an effort to illustrate the point. Worked up to a feverish pitch, some in the crowd emulated the Leader by shredding articles of their own clothing. Leopold Plotkin and the chicken plucker shuddered, wondering what would happen next. Not wanting his wife to see men without shirts, Jacob Plotkin ordered her to back away from the window. The twins, not entirely understanding what was occurring but wanting to avoid any damage to their clothing, carefully removed their trousers.

Bookbinder urged the audience to cease and desist. "Shredding in public sends the wrong message," he shouted. "In a society that prides itself on tactful civil obedience, clothes must be above reproach!"

The Leader removed his gold-rimmed spectacles, which had been perched near the end of his bulbous nose, and started to polish the lenses with a handkerchief—something he did when he didn't know what to say next. The crowd, riveted on the handkerchief, waited in rapt anticipation to see what the esteemed orator would do with it after the polishing ended. Finally, words began to flow again as the handkerchief returned to its host's pocket.

"As I journeyed to this blighted street of stores, I carefully examined the windows to see whether the infection had spread. I saw a tailor shop. I saw a dry goods store. I may have seen a restaurant, a bank, and dozens of other retail establishments, although I can't be certain, because I have seen so much in my life that words alone cannot describe what I saw. What is more important is that I am certain, whatever I saw, I didn't see a single window with something smeared on it...*not one*...I tell you, *not one*...with the lone exception of the store in question, which is owned and operated by a troublemaker of the lowest order."

Inspired by the phraseology and believing that the reference to "not one" was a pithy catchphrase Bookbinder injected to stir them up, many in the crowd began chanting, "Not one! Not one!" Annoyed by the spontaneous chanting, the Leader threw up his arms to put an end to it and threatened to have the chanters arrested if they continued to interfere with his train of thought. Too upset to think of what to say next, he inserted snuff into a nostril and sneezed violently, causing many in the audience to gasp.

"This *wretched* merchant is an enigma," he said after regaining his composure. "That being so, if not now, when else? If not here, where? Given these juxtaposed realities, we must take a stand somewhere, for the beginning of a long journey starts in small steps and proceeds with much larger steps until the will to continue is sapped."

Mendel Sprem, despite being a situational atheist, silently prayed for the speech to end before the entire gathering realized that the Leader was unable to form an intelligible thought.

Bookbinder arched his eyebrows before resuming. "If this seditious window remains as is," he bellowed, "who can say that another window I might have seen en route to this speech won't have something on it tomorrow, or the day after? This two-headed monster must be nipped in the bud and pulled out by the roots before the stems get too thick to remove. Furthermore, if a leaf falls in a forest and nobody hears it, would anyone see it? I raise these profundities for your consideration to illustrate my indignation over the substance on that window, which if I am not mistaken, may be mud!"

Stirred by Bookbinder's indignation, the assembled masses applauded wildly until the Leader silenced them by threatening to summon the Constabulary to quell the unwelcome disturbance.

"Now to the official position," Bookbinder declaimed, pointing toward the overcast sky, while Sprem prayed for rain. Since he couldn't recall the official position, the Leader said nothing during the ensuing two minutes, while his fatigued index finger pointed upward and he endeavored to incubate a policy. Assuming that the legislative sage was prophetically pointing to the darkening sky, crowd members fixed a collective gaze on the gathering storm clouds. A silent consensus emerged that the Leader's metaphoric allusion to weather conditions was yet another oratorical maneuver, like the previous self-choking exhibition.

"Desperate measures call for desperate times," Bookbinder proclaimed, returning his gaze to the rapt assembly while furrowing his brow to evince desperation. "Therefore, I am issuing the following ultimatum to Plotkin and his crowd. First, and foremost, whatever is or is not on the window must be removed with all deliberate speed!" Applause erupted. "Second, all future activity occurring behind glass must be performed in full view, et cetera, et cetera and so forth!" More applause erupted.

Sprem was desperate to end the spectacle before the Leader's idiocy was fatally demonstrated and made a cutting gesture to his throat, indicating that Bookbinder should stop speaking. Ignoring Sprem, the Leader continued. "If whatever is or is not on the desecrated window is not forthwith removed, unspecified legislative action will be taken and criminal charges shall, will, may, or could be brought against the merchant at some time in the imminent or distant future."

Bookbinder's rich voice grew stronger. "As a civilized society, we cannot tolerate foreign things on mercantile windows!" he thundered. "Let noses press against clear glass! Let eyes gaze unimpeded! Let mouths gape like newly fallen snow on a springtime meadow, or whatever!"

The crowd, now in frenzy, thrust fists in the air and applauded wildly as Bookbinder descended from the stage with the assistance of his depleted Alter Ego, waved goodbye, and waddled down Drabble Street, trailed by Sprem and an entourage of fellow dignitaries who congratulated the Leader for delivering another thought-provoking address.

From behind their tenement windows, Jacob Plotkin and his semi-nude brothers paid no attention to the departing Leader. Instead, they attempted to determine which of the identical twins' discarded trousers belonged to which twin. When that task was successfully completed, they returned to the tenement's kitchen to argue about things unrelated to Bookbinder's speech.

Visibly shaken by the oration's portentous tone, the butcher and chicken plucker returned to the shop, mumbling "shit" or words to that effect. Realizing that if he capitulated, his father would call him a coward, Plotkin (shaking uncontrollably) told the chicken plucker that he could not remove the mud, despite wanting to. That evening, pursuant to the patriarch's instructions, he demonstrated ostensible resolve by adding several layers of mud to the glass. The next day, word of Plotkin's resistance reached Umberto Malatesta's desk. The Prosecutor General immediately informed High Minister Emile Threadbare's surrogates of the butcher's behavior. Soon thereafter, Threadbare reminded Mendel Sprem of Cicero Bookbinder's commitment to sponsor clean window legislation if the speech didn't bring Plotkin to his senses. To his profound regret, Sprem vividly recalled the promise and, unwilling to break it, readied himself to begin the process of criminalizing the meat merchant's mud-related activity.

Inner Chamber anarchist Milos Gorky

13

Seated on the side of the Inner Chamber reserved for Horizontal Party members, Cicero Bookbinder looked across the room and saw Giacomo Portabella, the Head of the Vertical Party, reading a newspaper. Apart from legislative debates, the archrivals never spoke. Their silence was a concession to philosophically pure constituencies that considered socializing with the enemy a mortal sin. Bookbinder lifted his corpulence, waddled past colleagues, and arrived at the Podium breathing heavily.

Turning to greet the Parliamentarian, he saw that the elderly man was asleep. Not wanting to disturb a functionary who had served the august body with distinction for more than a half century, the Leader didn't wake him. Instead, he removed a gavel from the slumbering official's gnarled hand, waved it, and called the session to order, demanding that the people's representatives direct their undivided attention to him. All legislative heads, except one, turned toward Bookbinder. The non-conforming head belonged to Milos Gorky, an anarchist with an oily goatee, who sat backward at a desk halfway between the Horizontal and Vertical parties.

Gorky was the body's lone member of the Dissident Party whose guiding belief was that laws were not only unnecessary to maintain social order but actually impeded a return to anarchy, man's natural state. Representing a district populated by disillusioned citizens opposed to lawmaking, he utilized peaceful means to obstruct legislation from advancing. The Leader was accustomed to viewing Gorky's back whenever he spoke and paid no attention to the bald spot on the crown of the anarchist's head.

"My fellow Chambermen," Bookbinder began, "it is time for this shining example of self-determination to do what it is elected to do, namely, legislate. The first item for consideration is Bill Number 101."

The Leader turned and saw that the Parliamentarian was still asleep. Knowing from experience that all ninety members of his party would support the Bill whatever its content, just as the sixty members of the opposition would vote against the proposal, Bookbinder did not disturb the official whose primary duty was to read bills aloud before a debate ensued. Instead, he dispensed with the formality of a reading and proceeded directly to the next step of the legislative process: addressing the merits of the proposed law.

Although nobody, including Bookbinder, knew what Bill Number 101 proposed, the debate proved vigorous. As the proponent, the Leader was the first to speak in its favor. He opened his highly flexible lips and read from Mendel Sprem's introductory statement: "The moment has arrived to do what must be done. Stated otherwise, I stand in support of this bill because a failure to enact now would be a disservice to the Republic, a dereliction of our legislative duties, and an inexcusable failure to seize the moment. As you must have noticed, the proposed statute is well crafted and comprehensively addresses the ills it is aimed to correct. In conclusion, it is for these reasons and others too imponderable to mention that you are urged to pass this landmark legislation!"

The Leader's endorsement brought forth raucous shouts of "Here! Here!" from members of his party to signal their unified support of the proposed law.

Opposition party operatives responded with a chorus of "Never! Never!"

Adhering to his usual *modus operandi*, Milos Gorky leaped to his feet to express disagreement with everyone but himself. "The moment to do something has yet to arrive, cannot arrive, and, will not arrive as long as I have the floor!" he proclaimed.

Awakened from slumber by Gorky's penetrating voice, the Parliamentarian declared the anarchist out of order and directed him to stop the unauthorized speechifying.

"Expel him!" Bookbinder's constituents shouted.

"Let him speak!" opposition members cried.

"This is none of your affair!" bleated a Bookbinder confederate.

"It is *always* our affair!" a Portabella aide croaked.

Amidst a rising crescendo of angry attacks and counter-attacks along party lines, fanned by Milos Gorky's demand to be heard, the Inner Chamber descended into chaos until the Parliamentarian threatened to have Gorky forcibly expelled if he refused to stand down. Gorky took his seat to avoid being manhandled and, after a round of perfunctory boos, hisses, and groans from Verticalist backbenchers, order was restored. The Parliamentarian called for resumption of the debate.

An array of representatives from Bookbinder's party rose to express unconditional and unequivocal support for Bill 101. Among the accolades, they described it as wise, comprehensive, effective and for the good of the Republic.

The opposition weighed-in, as more than a dozen Verticals blathered against the proposed law.

"This bill is beyond the pale," Portabella proclaimed belligerently.

"I can't, in good conscience, vote for this unprecedented piece of legislation," declared another, who demanded insertion of a series of unspecified amendments before voting began. Others in the opposition rose to criticize the Bill for being too specific, too vague, or both too specific and too vague.

Milos Gorky took the floor again. With a blue vein pulsating on his forehead, he declared in an ear-piercing tone, "the proposed law is disgraceful, an affront to the citizens of the Republic, unconstitutional on its face, and a graphic example of how out of touch Horizontalists are with the populace! I predict a catastrophic calamity if the proposal ever becomes law."

Contentious rounds of rebuttal, rejoinder, retort, and recapitulation in addition to elucidation and equivocation ensued. Several hours passed before the Parliamentarian announced, over Gorky's objection, that it was time to vote. The Bill was approved along party lines: 90 in favor, 61 against.

After enactment, the Parliamentarian read the text of the statute into the record to cure any technical defects stemming from his failure to do so before the vote. In a barely audible tone that exhibited the ravages of age, the beloved official muttered:

> *Whoever or whomever desecrates the window of a commercial business establishment by placing or perpetuating mud or any other foreign thing on, in, over, or behind said window shall be guilty of a Heinous Crime against the Republic unless said mud or other foreign thing constitutes a bona fide Work of Art. Upon conviction, the person or persons responsible for the desecration shall be subject to a lengthy term of imprisonment and an officer of the law shall forthwith remove the hereinbefore referenced mud or foreign thing from said window and expeditiously dispose of it.*

Horizontals applauded when learning what they voted for. Verticals didn't react. Milos Gorky muttered unintelligibly to himself, deflated by the passage of another law.

Prosecutor General Umberto Malatesta

14

On the evening of June 25, the day after the statute became law, Leopold Plotkin brushed more mud on the window to comply with his father's directive. The next evening, he repeated the exercise in accordance with Jacob Plotkin's wishes. Enraged by the butcher's defiance, Umberto Malatesta immediately convened a Secret Blind Jury to obtain an Indictment.

Under the *Criminal Cannons*, a citizen could be prosecuted if a Secret Blind Jury comprised of thirty citizens concluded, on the basis of "some evidence," that the citizen may have acted illegally. The *Cannons* envisioned a one-sided, *ex parte* presentation by the Prosecutor General's Office, in which neither the target of the proceeding nor the target's lawyer was permitted to attend or present evidence. To maintain secrecy, Jurors were blindfolded and told not to discuss anything about the proceeding with others.

In conjunction with standard practice, a Bailiff led thirty blindfolded adults to a secret room in the Courthouse and arranged them on benches. The Prosecutor General appeared with his Chief Minion. Looking at the sightless figures with disdain, Malatesta said sonorously: "For those few of you who do not recognize this compelling voice, the speaker is Umberto Malatesta, the Republic's *esteemed* Prosecutor General. Mr. Malatesta is here to inform you that something is rotten in Fettig!"

Pointing his index finger toward the ceiling, Malatesta shouted, "It is now a heinous crime for a merchant to cover a display window with *mud* or any other *foreign thing* unless it is a Work of Art! This vital law, enacted three days ago, also makes it unlawful for a merchant who covered a window *prior* to enactment to *perpetuate* a covering by failing to *immediately* remove it, or more precisely, *en flagrante delicto!*"

The blind jurors were impressed by Malatesta's use of Latinate.

"Through insertion of the word 'foreign,'" the prosecutor continued, "the legislation has in mind an object *in addition to* or *other than* glass, not necessarily an object from a foreign country, although such objects are certainly covered by said law."

Jurors listened attentively to Malatesta's rather interesting explanation of the term "foreign," except for an elderly man who raised his hand.

"Yes?" Malatesta exclaimed impatiently, dismayed by the interruption.

"May we have a recess?" the Juror asked. "This has gone on for quite a while, and I'm fatigued."

"Not now," the Prosecutor General sighed, relieved that it was fatigue rather than a substantive inquiry that prompted the interruption. "Umberto Malatesta's presentation is almost concluded. After issuing an indictment, you may recess for the remainder of your natural life for all I care."

Comforted by the revelation that there would soon be a recess, the Juror thanked Malatesta for his compassion.

"Where were we before this malcontent disturbed me?" Malatesta asked.

"You were telling us about foreigners," said a hollow-cheeked man seated near the exhausted elderly man.

"It's painfully obvious that you are either stupid or weren't listening," Malatesta corrected. "The Prosecutor General was actually discussing a recently enacted law making it illegal to place or maintain a *foreign thing* on a display window."

"Get rid of the idiot!" a rotund man shouted from the next to the last row.

"I'll get rid of *you* if you continue to disrupt this proceeding!" Malatesta boomed at the portly asserter.

After taking a moment to collect himself, Malatesta resumed. "The day after enactment of the law in question and a day after that day, Leopold Plotkin, a kosher butcher whose name will *forever live infamously*, abridged this *vital* law with malice aforethought, callous indifference, and contemptuous defiance, by lathering mud on the inside of his shop's display window...while you and your fellow law abiding citizens blissfully slept. Suffice it to say, the butcher lathered mud, from top to bottom, side to side, and in various and sundry other directions, on both occasions. These egregious acts have been attested to by several nameless informants."

The Jurors gasped in horror. Several cried out, "The bastard!"

Malatesta continued after the hostility subsided, "In addition, the belligerent meatmonger also maintained a pre-existing mud-covering on said window after passage of the aforementioned law by failing to remove it!"

Secret Jurors responded to the revelation with additional color-ful epithets.

Buoyed by the positive feedback, Malatesta directed his Chief Minion to place photographs of the window on easels in order to demonstrate what the butcher had done. Using a wooden pointer, he said, "If you weren't effectively blind, you would see three pho-tographs of the window in question: one depicting it minutes be-fore enactment of the aforementioned law; the others depicting its condition thereafter. In light of these pictures, here can be no doubt that the volume of mud increased to a frightening degree after pas-sage of the new law!"

Malatesta paused to allow this graphic proof to sink-in. "When one considers the quantitative disparities before and after, one is left with but one conclusion: the butcher twice crossed the line that separates the lawful from the unlawful, the good from the bad, the benevolent from the malevolent, and so on and so forth, *ad hoc.*"

"No question about it," remarked a Juror, enamored with the timbre of Umberto Malatesta's voice.

"What kind of person covers a window with mud more than once?" another shrieked.

"A sadist with no respect for authority!" a Bailiff chimed-in.

"A scoundrel with no reverence for the law!" the Court Stenog-rapher opined.

"Is there any need for Umberto Malatesta to say more?" Malatesta asked, buoyed by the supportive comments.

"What more can be said?" a man in clerical garb shouted hysterically. "He's a sinner! Pictures don't lie! Anybody can see what he did while those of us God-fearing people slept! He's an obvious atheist! In the face of this reign of sinfulness, I implore all of my temporarily blind brothers of faith to find this beast guilty as charged and to pray that he will be condemned to live his remaining years among the rabble that inhabit our prisons! As God is my witness, there is no need for a trial! Justice delayed is justice denied! The people have spoken! I say hang him and let him burn in Hell with fellow sinners! May God have mercy on his soul!"

"My sentiments exactly," said Malatesta despite suspecting the speaker was insane. "Before a perfunctory vote, however, does anyone have a question?" he asked, required to do so by the *Criminal Cannons*.

A short man with droopy eyelids raised his hand meekly.

"What is it?" Malatesta asked impatiently.

"Before we vote," the Juror muttered, "shouldn't we hear some testimony from someone who saw the scoundrel putting mud on the window?"

"Remove this troublemaker!" Malatesta ordered. "I won't tolerate sarcasm in this proceeding!"

A man in the ninth row raised his hand to ask if Jurors should discuss the issue before voting. Declaring the question "unnatural," Malatesta had the Juror removed.

Seeing no other raised hands following the ejections, Malatesta proclaimed, "There being no other questions, the time to vote has arrived. All in favor of declaring that Leopold Plotkin may have committed Heinous Crimes, raise your hands."

All of the Jurors who had not been disgorged from the room raised their hands.

"Let the record show," Malatesta announced, "that Leopold Plotkin has been indicted by acclimation."

Commandant Jean-Pierre Proust with Aide-de-Camp

15

On the day of the butcher's indictment, the Prosecutor General's Office published the following notice in all newspapers of record:

Under the guidance of Prosecutor General Umberto Malatesta, a Secret Blind Jury has issued an Indictment against Leopold Plotkin, the man whose abominable crimes precipitated the Mud Crisis. To celebrate this crucial first step in the legal process, members of the public are cordially invited to attend his arrest at 12 o'clock this Thursday afternoon at ABRAHAM PLOTKIN AND OTHERS KOSHER MEAT PRODUCTS, situated on the last block of Drabble Street, near the Warehouse for the Purportedly Insane. Due to the large number of people expected to attend, early arrival is recommended.

At noon on Thursday, a battalion of constables from the National Constabulary, commanded by Commandant Jean-Pierre Proust, descended on the butcher shop. The battalion members, dressed in ceremonial blue uniforms adorned with gold epaulets, formed two perfectly aligned columns. Following Proust's lead, they marched smartly toward the establishment's front door to the accompaniment of the Constabulary's Fife and Drum Corps. Throngs of onlookers, standing behind several rows of dignitaries, applauded the militaristic precision.

Executing a plan conceived by Proust's Aide-de-Camp, the constables gained entry to the shop by demolishing its unlocked door. Without the door to impede them, they stepped single file into the establishment before diverging into five semi-columns, a configuration designed to foreclose any avenue of escape. Plotkin and the chicken plucker were chatting in the back of the shop as the semi-columns advanced. The butcher had just returned from a slaughterhouse after disemboweling a cow. His hands and clothing were covered with blood. Primo Astigmatopolous was de-feathering a chicken. His hands and clothing were shrouded in feathers.

Alarmed when he heard the door cave in, Plotkin became light-headed. Equally alarmed, Astigmatopolous dropped the chicken he was plucking onto the floor. As the constables approached, both raised their hands toward the tin ceiling to signal submission. They remained as still as statues, except for Plotkin's body spasms.

Commandant Proust issued an order: "Unfurl the document!" As rehearsed, his Aide-de-Camp unfolded a copy of the poster that had announced Cicero Bookbinder's oration. Pointing to the butcher's caricature, Proust asked his vassal: "Which of these two imbeciles most resembles Plotkin?"

"As best as I can tell," the Aide-de-Camp replied after comparing each of the potential arrestees to the caricature, "it is the one shaking on my right, although I can't rule out the still one on my left or possibly both or neither."

Satisfied with the identification, Proust directed a constable to shackle the "asshole on the right."

As the constable moved toward Plotkin, it occurred to the chicken plucker that a first-hand description of the arrest was sufficiently important to include in the trilogy he planned to write. Seizing the opportunity, he reached into his apron pocket to retrieve a notebook. When Proust saw this sudden movement, he shouted, "The one on the left has a weapon!" With that, Proust dove to the floor and contorted into a fetal ball. Battalion members instantly reacted to the felon who caused Proust's reversion to infancy. They trained pistols at Astigmatopolous' head, surrounded him, reached into the suspicious pocket, and removed the notebook.

It only took a moment before the recumbent Proust realized that he had plunged to the floor to avoid a notebook. He reclaimed his feet with a tinge of embarrassment, brushed sawdust and feathers from his uniform, and announced that he was resuming command of the operation.

Turning to Plotkin, Proust reissued the order to shackle the butcher, adding that a few punches on the ribs would deter him from refusing to cooperate. The chicken plucker watched in horror as battalion members pelted, hog-tied, hoisted, carried his employer and dear friend through the void that was once the shop's front door, and tossed him into the back of a police wagon like a sack of spoiled meat. Stirred by the Constabulary's rough treatment of the villain, crowd members urged members of the battalion to kick, stomp or punch the meat merchant. Proust resisted a strong temptation to accommodate the mob's base instincts when he appealed for restraint. He reassured the mob that Plotkin would be systematically abused when admitted to Purgatory House of Detention.

As the wagon sped away from the butcher shop at breakneck speed, Plotkin was thrown against its walls and ricocheted in various painful directions. "Is this how it ends?" the butcher wondered.

Warden Hans Gogol

16

Purgatory House of Detention was constructed in an era when prison facades were designed with aesthetics in mind. Still considered an architectural wonder, its exterior was an amalgam of soaring walls, leaning towers, high minarets, low parapets, flying buttresses, dipping cornices, fluted columns, graceful windows, and menacing gargoyles. Behind the lovely façade was a cluster of profoundly overcrowded, vermin-infested cellblocks that housed the worst of the worst, the best of the worst, and the relatively bad.

The institution reeked of fear. Weak inmates feared strong inmates. Strong inmates feared guards. Guards feared low-level administrators who, in turn, feared the Warden. The Warden feared the Board of Overseers, a body that didn't oversee but occasionally threatened to visit the facility.

When admitted to Purgatory, Plotkin was harassed by a Reception Room corporal, slapped by a Reception Room sergeant, and humiliated by a lieutenant who elected to strip-search him in the

presence of a female nurse. During the extensive ocular inspection of his naked body, the butcher was required to squat, spread
his buttocks, cough, lift his testicles, cough again, open his mouth,
wiggle his tongue, and display his ears. Because the inspection revealed nothing of interest in or near his orifices, Plotkin's blood-
drenched clothing was returned to the embarrassed butcher. Once
dressed, he was handed off to a pockmarked guard who shackled
his limbs, ushered him into the bowels of the prison, and threatened to beat him to a pulp if he caused trouble.

Purgatory's bowels were dark, dank, and foul smelling as well
as noisy and chaotic. As Plotkin shuffled across a rotunda that
led to a six-tier cellblock, he heard a cacophony of noises echoing
off the ancient walls. Among the discordant sounds were inmates
shouting at each other, guards shouting at inmates, administrators
shouting at guards, and cell doors clanging. Thrust into an environment whose level of conflict seemed worse than anything he
had experienced while living with his parents and deranged uncles, the butcher became paralyzed by fear. As a result, the pace of
his shuffling declined precipitously.

When the pockmarked guard noticed Plotkin's glacial pace, he
accused Plotkin of attempting to start a riot and called for assistance. A pack of cohorts rushed to the scene. After the guards
pelted him with nightsticks, they carried him up five flights of
stairs to the top tier. Once upright, he was ordered to walk. As the
butcher obediently shambled down the catwalk, leering prisoners
extended arms through cell bars in welcoming gestures. Several
expressed an interest in stealing his food or beating him when the
opportunity arose. Plotkin heard another promise to get to know
him better. Unnerved, he wondered if his refusal to capitulate to
Cicero Bookbinder's demands had been a mistake.

Plotkin was dragged to a cell at the far end of the tier. Attached
to the cell's gate was a sign bearing the inscription: COMMUNAL
SANCTUARY FOR WEAKLINGS. Designed to protect the frail and
the puny from assault by their stronger brethren, the practice of
collecting weaklings in a common site, though logical in theory,
achieved only marginal success in practice. Experience showed
that, when bored, the least weak of the weaklings preyed on the
lower end of the spectrum.

When making arrangements for Plotkin's pretrial incarceration,
Prosecutor General Umberto Malatesta, basking in the glow of the
indictment, insisted on the butcher's placement in the Sanctuary to
ensure his survival until the trial ended. "After that, you can feed

the bastard to the wolves, for all I care," Malatesta told Warden Hans Gogol.

The Sanctuary was designed to uncomfortably accommodate six standard-sized adult weaklings. On the day of Plotkin's admission, it housed nineteen weaklings of various dimensions. Plotkin studied the overcrowded repository while the guards were removing his shackles. He saw the occupants lying head to head on the floor, like packaged sardines. Doubting that there was room for one more, he politely asked whether there was somewhere else to store him.

The pockmarked guard, a man with a deep-seeded distrust of inmates, construed the question as an attempt by Plotkin to destabilize the institution. "You've been a thorn in my side since your arrival," the officer proclaimed, slapping each side of the butcher's head before clubbing both knees. When tired of abusing Plotkin, he opened the Sanctuary door and pushed the butcher inside.

Plotkin crawled toward the back of the cell, careful not to bump any of his cellmates too hard. As he crawled, the weaklings noticed his bloodstained hands and clothing still moist from the morning's cow-slaughter. Inferring from the volume and location of the blood stains that Plotkin had taken one or more lives in the hours preceding his arrest, they migrated to the unit's four corners, ceding Plotkin most of the floor. Plotkin thanked them for their generosity.

Plotkin was depleted by the morning's events and took no interest in socializing. With the intention of taking a recuperative nap, he closed his eyes. The weaklings cowered together in small groups, worried that the butcher might target them for reprisals if they disturbed his sleep. In hushed tones, they debated whether he selected the victims randomly or for good cause. Before they were able to reach a consensus, the pockmarked guard entered the cell and jerked Plotkin to his feet. Again threatening to beat him if he caused any trouble, the officer dragged him out of the Sanctuary onto a long corridor with numerous false turns, confusing intersections, and hidden dead-ends. The labyrinth led to a door with a sign that read: WARDEN'S CHAMBERS. STAY OUT UNLESS INVITED IN.

The pockmarked guard knocked gently on the door, meekly identified himself, and asked permission to enter.

"Do you have the prick?" a deep voice boomed from inside the chambers, prompting Plotkin to visualize the speaker as a person of colossal size.

"Yes, sir," the pockmarked guard replied in a subdued tone.

"The prick is here."

"Bring the son of a bitch in," the baritone directed.

Once inside the room, Plotkin immediately recognized his misconception regarding the warden's size. Gogol was a short, skinny, balding man with a flinty mustache and an air of arrogance. He sat at a large desk whose dimensions were noticeably out of proportion to his body. His Lilliputian fingers toyed with the mustache as he fixed on Plotkin with a malevolent stare. To placate the official who appeared to have a Napoleonic complex, Plotkin pretended to be slightly more frightened than he actually was.

"I've received hundreds of complaints from reliable sources that you have destabilized the Sanctuary and disturbed the tranquility of my institution," Gogol shouted. "While I hoped that, in time, you would learn to fit in, I realize now that I was naïve. I underestimated. It won't happen again."

"What do your sources say I did?" Plotkin asked politely, thinking he had been a model prisoner.

"That's privileged information," Gogol answered, studying the bloodstains on the butcher's shirt and hands. "If anything, my sources have minimized the trouble you have caused."

"How reliable are your reliable sources?" Plotkin inquired, believing that even the most reliable of sources occasionally made mistakes.

The inquiry offended Gogol. He leapt from his chair and aligned his balding pate with the butcher's lower chest. He raised his head to glare at Plotkin. "Put this asshole in the basement next to the lunatic!" Gogol boomed. "I won't have him questioning the reliability of my sources!"

"Do you want me to put the asshole next to the lunatic in the same cell or next to the lunatic in a different cell?" the pockmarked guard asked, confused by what he considered a latent ambiguity in Gogol's directive.

"Next to the lunatic in the *next* cell, idiot!" the Warden shouted, irritated that the dim-witted guard insinuated that the directive was not crystal clear.

Embarrassed by being humiliated in the presence of an inmate, the pockmarked guard angrily dragged Leopold Plotkin from the Warden's office to a poorly lit stairway. After the butcher negotiated the steep entrance to the basement, with only a few minor falls, he was pushed into the moldy, semi-dark basement with a stench he wasn't quite able to identify. He was then hustled down a narrow corridor and thrown into a cave-like structure with a low ceiling, naked light bulb, stained floor mattress, and chamber pot. Plotkin bent, waddled into the windowless repository and, within seconds, fell asleep.

The lunatic in the adjacent cell, the only other occupant of the basement, was a defrocked lawmonger recently convicted of embezzling from his law firm. Sane when committing the crime, he had gone mad during the two-year wait for trial. Animated by a delusion that his conviction was a conspiracy to drive him out of the legal profession, he routinely stayed awake all night, staging mock trials that closely resembled his own trial, endlessly proclaiming his innocence to an imaginary jury, spouting legal maxims to a non-existent judge, railing against his defense attorney, defaming former law partners, castigating his billing clerk, condemning his estranged wife, and ridiculing former mistresses and various other people, real or imagined, he believed had taken part in the conspiracy. It was afternoon when Plotkin entered the adjoining cage. The lunatic was asleep and snoring innocently.

During Plotkin's first evening in Purgatory's basement, he discovered that the lunatic's nocturnal behavior precluded any sleep at night. The next morning, he appealed to his neighbor to confine the irrational behavior to daylight hours. The lunatic, who was mildly paranoid even when sane, rebuffed Plotkin with the accusation of conspiring with enemies to silence him. Since it was obvious there was no way to reason with the madman, the butcher had no choice but to alter his lifelong sleeping pattern and make due with fitful daytime naps.

Against the backdrop of the lunatic's nightly trial reenactments and protestations of innocence, Plotkin occupied his time battling armies of cockroaches that invaded his cage every night. The swatting noise agitated the lunatic. "Quiet! Court is in session," he demanded. "You're disrupting my concentration. If I'm convicted, there will be hell to pay!"

Not wanting to antagonize the only other human occupying the basement, Plotkin abandoned the insect wars. With little else to do, he began ranting as well, often about the same things the lunatic railed against, but more coherently. The lunatic began to sense from the parallel ranting that Plotkin was a kindred spirit, not a conspirator. As a sign of good will, he introduced himself and offered to talk if the butcher ever felt the need. Soon, the subterranean neighbors were immersed each night in long, rambling discussions about things Plotkin had no interest in but valued as a means of passing time.

Despondent and fearing he would soon die a forgotten man in Purgatory's basement, Plotkin began to long for his previous life: the stench of the butcher shop; the anxieties caused by living in a cramped apartment with his overbearing father and deranged uncles; the incessant verbal skirmishing with extended family members; and the lack of meaningful social outlets. Over time, Plotkin grew increasingly morose, and plagued by nagging self-doubt. Day after day, when the lunatic was not shouting, he wondered whether he should have ignored the patriarch and cleaned the window. He thought about the *Divine Comedy*, one of his favorite books as a child, and speculated about which Circle of Dante's Inferno he had descended to. He even prayed for the first time since the bar mitzvah fiasco, promising, as he confessed his sins, that he would attend Sabbath services if he survived.

17

The morning had already been unkind to Plotkin. After managing to lapse into a superficial sleep despite the fetid air and marauding insects, he was awakened when the pockmarked guard threw an envelope into his cell. The butcher opened the envelope and read the first letter he had received since his admission to Purgatory. The missive, written by the chicken plucker, said:

I was deeply disturbed by the way the constables mishandled you. Even in the backward republic of my birth, a man of your stature is treated with dignity when taken into custody and is not abused until imprisoned.

Minutes after you were thrown into the wagon, I informed your father, mother and uncles of your arrest. Your mother already knew; your father and uncles did not. The uncles could not understand why you were arrested and denied any knowledge of the Mud Crisis, which both of us know is untrue. I'm afraid the shock of not having you around to belittle has badly affected their memory. Your father is also experiencing memory problems. He insists that the idea to cover the window with mud was yours and says that you have disgraced the family with your "irrational behavior." He also vows to blame you if the business is forced into bankruptcy in your absence. He says that he'll write if and when he feels like it.

The elders have mixed feelings about your plight. As noted, your father blames you. Your uncles blame your father. Your mother blames herself. She says she should have paid more attention to you while you were growing up.

I have persuaded the elders to come out of retirement to fill the void created by your departure. So far, with a few minor exceptions, all has gone well since their return to the shop. Yesterday, one of your uncles almost severed his thumb (the right one) while chopping ribs. The doctor hopes it will not die and says it may be usable in two or three years, if there is a miraculous recovery.

Your other uncle threatens to cut off his hair to protest your arrest. I held a mirror up to his mostly bald head to demonstrate why this would be an inadequate means of protest. He now says he will start a partial hunger strike (foregoing dairy products) until you return.

Your mother has assumed the responsibilities of taking customer orders, calculating all purchases, and making change. She cries most of the time over your situation. This upsets everybody, including our few patrons. Despite your father's demands to calm down, she insists on crying and promises to continue until your release.

Protesters still come every day and are louder than ever. The noise has slowed progress on the trilogy. Business is much the same as ever. Customers complain about being threatened and jostled by protesters. Bankruptcy looms.

I visit Bruno every Saturday at the Zoo. He seems depressed. He won't eat the grapes. He sits and sulks. I think he misses you.

The Kimmelmen brothers also miss you, particularly Arturo who says he always appreciated your laughter at his jokes. He promises to send you a letter with a few jokes to cheer you up. Jacobi sometimes accompanies me to the Zoo but complains that Bruno is too depressing to spend much time with. He suggests that lettuce might be better to feed Bruno rather than grapes.

On a happier note, your father and uncles are as combative as ever. They fight with each other and the few relatives who continue to visit. They defend you when relatives accuse you of staining the family name, but then accuse you of the same as soon as the relatives are expelled. One of your third cousins plans to change his name to distance himself from you. Four other family members are considering returning to the Old Country, where the Plotkin name is not held in such low regard.

I hope to visit Purgatory soon to interview you about your experiences. I believe the vicissitudes of your incarceration deserve a chapter in the trilogy. My readers will be keenly interested in the subject.

In closing, I wish you the best while you rot in prison.

Sincerely and truly yours,

Primo

Moments after Plotkin finished reading the letter, the pock-marked guard returned and shouted: "Stand up, moron! Your lawyer is upstairs!"

"You must have me confused with somebody else," the butcher replied. "I don't have a lawyer."

"Are you disrespecting me?" the easily offended guard roared.

"Not in the least," Plotkin responded. "I was merely correcting a possible mistake."

"I'm not mistaken, asshole," the guard shouted.

Accusing Plotkin of insolence, the pockmarked guard unlocked the cell, pulled the butcher up from the floor, shackled his legs, and dragged him to a stairway leading to the Legal Consultation Room. At the foot of the stairway, the guard was met by a phalanx. Warden Gogol was at the head. The martinet ordered the pockmarked guard to lower Plotkin's head so his short arms could reach the butcher's skull. Once the head was properly positioned, Gogol struck the butcher's head from various angles. When Gogol grew tired, the rest of the phalanx carried the butcher upstairs to the Legal Consultation Room.

A mesh screen dissected the room, splitting it into two unequal parts; the larger for lawyers, the smaller for inmates. Because the prisoner's side had no furniture, Plotkin asked for a chair. The request was denied on grounds that he was too disruptive to be trusted with a weapon. His handlers vacated the room and locked the door.

The butcher stood under a naked light bulb, wondering who the lawmonger was and what he wanted. Taught by his father since childhood never to trust lawyers, Plotkin waited with trepidation.

Public Defender Felix I. Bleifus

18

A decade before Plotkin was dragged to the Legal Consultation Room to meet with attorney Felix I. Bleifus, the Republic's High Court of Final Supplications held that indigent citizens charged with serious criminal wrongdoing had a right to "apparent representation" and would "no longer be expected to be convicted entirely on their own." Writing for the majority, the High Court's Lead Justice elaborated:

> *It is evident from the syntax of Item Six of the Constitution that the illusory right to apparent representation contemplates that poverty-stricken rabble be accompanied by an attorney at every stage of a prosecution that may lead to incarceration. This right — a testament to the Republic's acute sense of fairness for even the lowest among us — requires that lawyers assigned to impecunious pond scum be duly licensed, of reasonably sound mind, and have the capacity to sit or stand in close proximity to the accused during all critical events. In the interest of judicial restraint, this*

Court refrains from delineating anything else that such lawyers must do prior to the rendering of a guilty verdict.

After issuance of the opinion, indigent criminals were not left to fend for themselves. If they chose, they could be ostensibly assisted, without charge, by attorneys employed by The Society for the Apparent Representation of Indigent Criminal-Types—a poorly funded, understaffed, ineffectual agency, established by the Republic's Inner Chamber to provide superficial services to tens of thousands now in need of lawyers. With its meager budget, the agency was able to lease substandard offices, purchase minimal supplies, and pay paltry salaries to procure the employment of idealistic or bottom-tier attorneys.

Felix I. Bleifus was among the lawyers originally hired by the Society. In ten years of public service, he had met and, occasionally, exceeded the agency's modest expectations. Lethargic, with limited intelligence and poor study habits, Bleifus was attending a substandard legal seminary when the Court discovered the right to apparent representation. Lacking the ambition, pride, and minimal competence to effectively practice law, he had feared that he would be unemployable until reading an announcement pinned to a seminary bulletin board. The announcement read:

EMPLOYMENT OPPORTUNITIES FOR OUR LEAST DISTINGUISHED STUDENTS HAVE MATERIALIZED DUE TO THE HIGH COURT'S RECENT DETECTION OF A CONSTITUTIONAL RIGHT TO FREE, APPARENT LEGAL REPRESENTATION FOR POOR CITIZENS CHARGED WITH SERIOUS CRIMES. THE INNER CHAMBER HAS CREATED AN ENTITY KNOWN AS THE SOCIETY FOR THE APPARENT REPRESENTATION OF INDIGENT CRIMINAL-TYPES TO DELIVER THE NEGLIGIBLE SERVICES TO WHICH INDIGENT DREGS ARE NOW ENTITLED.

BECAUSE SATISFACTION OF THE NEW RIGHT REQUIRES LITTLE SKILL OR WORK ON THE PART OF LAWYERS, THE SOCIETY IS IN NEED OF RECENT GRADUATES FROM THIS AND OTHER LOW-LEVEL LAWMONGERING SCHOOLS WHO RANK IN THE BOTTOM FIFTH OF THEIR CLASS AND HAVE DEMONSTRATED THAT THEY LACK THE AMBITION OR SKILLS

THAT WOULD MAKE SUCH EMPLOYMENT UNSAT-
ISFYING TO MORE ACCOMPLISHED GRADUATES. IF
YOU BELIEVE YOU QUALIFY AS A CAREER CIVIL SER-
VANT IN THIS AGENCY, YOU ARE ENCOURAGED TO
APPLY. STUDENTS WHO ANTICIPATE GRADUATING
IN THE UPPER FOUR-FIFTHS; WHO HAVE A MODI-
CUM OF LAW-RELATED AMBITION, PRIDE, OR SKILLS,
SHOULD LOOK ELSEWHERE.

Certain that he was well qualified to work at the Society, Bleifus
submitted an application. The application illuminated his poor academic achievements and listed several professors who could attest
to his lack of ambition and other qualities the Society coveted. In a
paragraph riddled with grammatical errors and which made little
sense, he begged for an opportunity to demonstrate his mediocrity
in an area of the law that had never interested him.

Impressed by his lusterless background, Society administrators
invited him for an interview. He clearly exhibited the ineptitude
the agency was looking for during the brief encounter. Bleifus'
phlegmatic behavior particularly impressed the interviewers, as it
rendered him virtually unemployable elsewhere and increased the
likelihood that he would remain at the agency for decades to come.
The Society hired him as a Temporary Probationary Lawmonger
Second Class.

After securing a license to practice, the novitiate embarked on
a career that, despite squalid working conditions, a paltry salary,
and the lack of intellectual challenges, proved immensely satisfying. For his first five years, Bleifus showed an aptitude for artfully
feigning representation in a variety of contexts: preliminary hear-
ings, trials, post-conviction appeals, and the like. In time, the Society promoted him to a Permanent Probationary Lawmonger Second Class position, subject to an annual renewal, if he continued
to exhibit the necessary lack of ambition and skills needed to cope
with the superficiality of his work.

The Society rotated staff lawmongers to a different function every few weeks in an effort to preserve their limited attention spans.
Bleifus was assigned to the Intake Unit the day Plotkin was summoned to the Legal Consultation Room. As an intake lawyer, his
primary functions were to ascertain whether the potential clients
were sufficiently poor to qualify for the agency's apparent services,
convince them that going to trial was a poor option, and lay the
groundwork for guilty pleas. He was not expected to veer into the

exotica of discussing the facts of a case unless a client insisted. If a factual discussion proved unavoidable, Bleifus was told to caution clients against elaboration, something the agency considered a waste of its limited resources. Consistent with the agency's *modus operandi*, he had not reviewed Plotkin's file before meeting with him.

19

Felix I. Bleifus tottered into the Legal Consultation Room, clutching a briefcase with one hand, a handkerchief with the other. Ashen and stoop-shouldered, he personified chronic illness.

The lawyer eased into a chair without acknowledging Plotkin. It was not his custom to look at potential clients during initial intake sessions. When meeting prospective clients for the first time, he ordinarily fixed his eyes on the Society's intake sheet or his watch.

"I am Bleifus, a permanent probationary attorney with the Society for the Apparent Representation of Indigent Criminal-Types," he said as he removed a set of papers from his briefcase. "And you are Nussbaum?"

"No, I'm Plotkin," the butcher corrected.

"Where's Nussbaum?" Bleifus asked before emitting a fusillade of raucous coughs.

"I have no idea," said Plotkin." Alarmed by his visitor's coughing, he backed away from the screen that separated him from the lawyer as a precautionary measure.

"You shouldn't be here," Bleifus exclaimed. "Plotkin is sixteenth on the list. Nussbaum is first."

"I can leave," Plotkin offered deferentially.

"No, I might as well get rid of you now; Nussbaum can wait," said Bleifus.

The lawyer placed a single piece of paper on a table.

"Repeat your name to ensure that it isn't placed in Nussbaum's file by mistake. If that happens, you'll never hear from the agency again. You'll be left out in the cold."

"I'm Leopold Plotkin," the butcher repeated.

The notorious name meant nothing to Bleifus. The lawyer was a man of limited curiosity who rarely read newspapers or discussed current affairs. Although vaguely aware of the Mud Crisis, Bleifus knew nothing about its origin or the person who ignited it.

"Age?"

"Forty-three."

"Wife's name?"

"I don't have a wife."

"Children, legitimate or otherwise?"

"None."

"I assume you're familiar with the Society?"

"Not at all."

"That's *unfortunate*," Bleifus droned with regret. "Due to your ignorance, I'm obliged to explain what the Society is...does...does not do...will not do...cannot do...and has never done—unless you're willing to listen to a *condensed* version of our services that glosses over most of the information I'm otherwise required to provide. I hope you're willing to hear the short version. I have more than two dozen criminals to see today."

"The condensed version is fine," said Plotkin, who didn't want to spend any more time with the sickly-looking lawyer than necessary.

"Thanks for being so flexible and disinterested," Bleifus said, still not looking at Plotkin. He removed the condensed version from his briefcase and began to recite. "'Reduced to its essence, the Society represents criminals who are too poor to purchase the actual services of private lawmongers and provides them with the apparent services now required by the Constitution.'"

"Did you say *apparent* services?" Plotkin asked.

"I may have," Bleifus replied.

"That bothers me a little, if you did," said Plotkin. "Linguistically speaking, the word connotes something superficial, ephemeral, ostensible, specious, or pretended."

Glancing at his watch, Bleifus saw that a minute of the eight minutes allotted to intake sessions had already slipped by. Always concerned about time, he returned to the condensed version without bothering to address Plotkin's concern.

"'Why has a Society representative come to see me? You are probably asking yourself,' the lawyer read. "In a nutshell, there are two reasons. The first is to determine if you are poor enough to qualify for the Society's array of apparent services. The second is to propose a strategy that will bring about a speedy and just resolution of your legal nightmare and remove the dark clouds of uncertainty hovering over you and possibly over a loved one, if you have any.'"

"I have several," Plotkin interjected, not wishing to be seen as someone without loved ones.

"As we get to know each other intimately during our brief time together today," Bleifus said without enthusiasm as he reviewed the remaining sections of the truncated sketch, "the Society hopes we will form a strong enough bond so you will accept my advice without questioning its wisdom. Do you understand?"

"I believe so," Plotkin replied.

"Now we turn to the eligibility standard for our broad range of services," said Bleifus. "To be eligible, one must be indigent. Do you consider yourself to be at or near the poverty level and, if so, why?"

"I suppose so," Plotkin replied. "My business barely makes a profit."

"How meager are your typical earnings?"

"Extremely meager."

"Do you have any dependents?"

"Yes."

"How many and who?"

"Four. My elderly father, decrepit mother, and two unhinged uncles."

"Considering the number of mouths you have to feed, the ages of the mouths, and other factors that need not be discussed, you qualify under our sliding scale for the entire range of apparent services, which in the Society's estimation need not, should not, and, hopefully, will not have to be delivered in this instance."

After surviving another coughing fit, Bleifus resumed reading from the shortened script. "'Now that we've forged an intimate and trustful relationship, this is a good time to touch upon the Society's overarching policy. What is the policy? Simply stated, it is to encourage clients the Society apparently represents to plead guilty and throw themselves on the mercy of the Court rather than risk a trial, an event replete with catastrophic possibilities for you and your loved ones, not to mention Society lawmongers. A superficial in-depth study shows that, in most instances, clients who insist on a trial and waste the Court's time receive harsher punishments when it comes time to sentencing.'"

Bleifus consulted his watch again. After determining that several more precious minutes had elapsed, he resumed reading at a slightly faster pace. "'This remarkable cause and effect phenomenon—a slight reduction in sentence in exchange for foregoing trial—is most likely due, if it exists, to judicial gratitude for having been spared the burden of presiding over yet another trial. That said, I can assure you with sincere disingenuousness that the Society cares deeply about its apparent clients and will be at or near your side every step of the way to conviction, even if you foolishly choose to hold-out for a trial. We are committed to a high level of apparent representation whether you have sufficient intelligence to plead guilty or stubbornly require our over-taxed lawyers to sit beside you for however long it takes to convict you. Should you reject a mercy-throwing, an attorney assigned to apparently represent you will introduce himself minutes before trial and remain in your general vicinity, a foot or two away, until you are led from the courtroom in chains, a broken man, to serve your sentence.'"

Still staring at the intake manual, Bleifus asked Plotkin if he had any questions, hoping that he didn't.

"I have a three-part question," Plotkin said.

"Oh," said Bleifus with bitter disappointment.

"What do Society lawyers do to prepare for trial when an inmate decides not to throw himself on the court's mercy; how long, before trial, does preparation begin; and how much time is usually spent preparing for trial?" Plotkin asked.

Surprised by the uniqueness of the inquiry, Bleifus needed a moment to compose a reply. "As far as I know, most of us don't prepare. However, if you're hooked-up with an idealist, you might get one who prepares a little."

When Plotkin said that he had no other questions, Bleifus was delighted.

"Before I call for a guard to take you back to your cell, I'd like to confirm that you will participate in a mercy-throwing," Bleifus said.

"Actually," Plotkin replied, "I haven't decided. It's something I have to discuss with my father. Can I tell you later?"

Shocked by his potential client's obstinacy, Bleifus looked at the butcher for the first time. Squinting through the mesh screen that separated him from Plotkin, he struggled to make sense of the morose man standing on the other side of the divide. When squinting, he saw the bloodstains on Plotkin's clothing.

The lawyer suspected that the stains were the residues of a violent crime and asked with uncharacteristic curiosity, "What's that on your shirt?"

"Splattered blood," Plotkin replied nonchalantly.

"That's a lot of splatter," Bleifus noted with disgust. Violent criminals were his least favorite clients.

"Unfortunately," Plotkin lamented, "the shirt is ruined. I was standing too close to the jugular when I severed it."

"You cut the throat?" Bleifus shrieked, his stomach churning.

"Correct."

"Did anybody see you do it?"

"This time?"

"There were *other* times?"

"Of course. It's what I do for a living. Unlike most of my competitors, I do my own slaughtering. I don't like to delegate. When I do it myself, I know it's done right."

"You say that...*proudly.*"

"It's nothing to be ashamed of, though it isn't exactly fulfilling."

"How many times have you done...this?"

"Sever jugulars or the other stuff?"

"What *other stuff*?"

"Disemboweling, removing brains, livers, testicles, hearts, and so on."

Stunned by the disclosures, Bleifus fell silent before gagging. When able to speak, he asked, "Did anybody witness you...cutting the jugular *this* time?"

"Probably. Is that important?"

"Isn't its importance *obvious*?"

"I didn't think so."

"Who might have seen you?" Bleifus demanded.

"Not to seem ignorant, I think this line of questioning is probably beside the point," Plotkin said cordially. "If I were you, I'd ask something like why I covered it with mud rather than boards or a curtain."

"You covered it with mud?"

"You seem surprised."

"I'm not surprised! I'm *appalled*! Have you no respect for the dead?"

"What has that to do with my case?"

"Don't you recognize the *heinousness* of your acts?"

"*Heinousness* is a little extreme, don't you think? You must be a vegetarian."

"*Heinousness* doesn't begin to describe your depravity! Don't pretend to be naïve!" Bleifus screamed.

The lawyer tugged at his beard anxiously. "Under the circumstances," he mumbled, "I don't see how I or anybody associated with the Society can possibly represent you!"

Unimpressed with the Society's services, Plotkin didn't object.

Bleifus collected his belongings and pounded on the door, demanding to be let out. When a guard arrived, the apoplectic lawyer told the guard not to fetch Nussbaum or any other potential clients for interviews; he was leaving for the day. As Bleifus fled to his office, Plotkin was led to the basement. The butcher now understood why his father had such a low opinion of lawyers.

The Lunatic, Pincus Barrenblat

20

After the dustup with Felix I. Bleifus, Plotkin worried about being tried without the assistance of counsel, something he had not previously thought about. Knowing virtually nothing about the workings of criminal trials, he felt legalistically adrift. In a moment of desperation, he sought advice from the lunatic while the defrocked attorney muttered legal maxims from his cell door. The lunatic was flattered by Plotkin's request but rejected the overture, stating that he wasn't accepting new clients for the foreseeable future. The next morning, as Plotkin lay sleeping, the erstwhile lawyer hollered, "Get up! The time to prepare has arrived!"

Elated by his neighbor's change of heart, the butcher approached the bars of his cell to be closer to the lunatic's acquired wisdom.

"I originally intended in this lecture series to address the ten critical stages of a trial," the madman whispered. "Unfortunately, due to intervening circumstances beyond my control, namely, the presence of eavesdroppers listening to my every utterance, I can't risk having all ten parts fall into enemy hands. It is one thing for my enemies to acquire a portion of my knowledge; it is another for them to appropriate everything. I will, therefore, limit my remarks to *five* critical stages, leaving the remainder to your imagination and for my enemies to speculate about."

Although Plotkin was disappointed that half of the critical stages would be omitted, he held out hope that possibly after commencement of the lecture series, the lunatic would be less delusional and reveal the full complement of stages. To plant that seed in the lunatic's mind, he whispered, "Perhaps, as the lectures proceed, you'll be willing to share additional critical stages with me."

"More than five is out of the question!" the lunatic shrieked. "If you continue to imply that you will only be satisfied with a ten-part presentation, I will cancel the lecture series and leave you to your own devices. I rest my case and respectfully ask the court to strike the witness' incendiary suggestion that more than five critical stages be revealed, and, more importantly, admonish the witness not to offer any more rude provocations."

Unaware that the lunatic expected him to function as the judge as well as the recipient of his wisdom, the butcher didn't rule on the motion to strike.

"Will the Court *please* rule?" the lunatic repeated with obvious frustration. "I am distracted from the central, seminal, all-important point I was about to make and must put the matter to rest before I can continue."

"The last statement is stricken and the witness will offer no more rude provocations," Plotkin said judiciously, hoping the lunatic, as a result of the ruling, would remain focused long enough to begin the lecture.

"Thank you, Your Honor," the lunatic said.

"Is there anything else before we proceed?" Plotkin asked, still in a judicial mode.

"Of course there is more," said the lunatic. "There is always more."

"What is it?"

"The record must reflect that there will be no charge for my services. Without such a reflection, there could be an appearance of impropriety on my part which, given my history of alleged improprieties, I must scrupulously avoid. As I believe I might have told the Court on more than a few occasions, I have been unjustly convicted of repeatedly receiving fees from clients in exchange for services not rendered, and can't afford another conviction on the same grounds. In addition to reflecting that I will receive no remuneration for my services, the record must state that the inflated billings were entirely my clerk's fault. He was a poor scheduler; too many cases to handle; too much to do. I couldn't be in two places at the same time or, in some instances, three places at the same time. If anybody deserved to be convicted it was him."

"The record will reflect everything that you said," Plotkin proclaimed. "Is there anything else before you begin the lecture?"

"Yes," the lunatic replied. "One housekeeping matter. I want those in attendance to feel free to ask questions anytime a question comes to mind. Ask even if I am in mid-sentence or deep in thought. Unlike other lecturers who are hostile to being interrupted by questions, I welcome interruptions. Interruptions show that I am getting through. So interrupt me at your pleasure. I believe that___."

"Which of the five critical stages of a trial are you lecturing on tonight?" Plotkin interrupted.

"How *dare* you interrupt me mid-sentence! Here I am, giving up my limited free time without remuneration to assist you in acquiring the insights that might enable you to one day walk from this place a free man, and you have the audacity to interrupt my train of thought! I hand you nuggets dredged from the slime of three decades of exhausting work, without seeking or requesting remuneration, and you shamefully speak while I am speaking! Your constant interruptions sap my energy! I can't continue under such trying circumstances!"

"I won't interrupt anymore," Plotkin promised.

"Will you stipulate to that on the record?"

"I will."

"Well?"

"I stipulate."

"Sit and listen," the lunatic declared. "The only way to master the five critical stages of a trial is to listen to what I say and to take copious notes. If this lecture series is to have any beneficial effect, you will have to take copious notes. Do you know how to take copious notes?"

"I occasionally took copious notes before I was expelled from the Talmudic Debating Society," Plotkin replied. "Earlier in life, I took copious notes at the National Library of Pedantic Writings," he added to reassure the lecturer of his fitness to attend the lecture.

"Excellent," said the lunatic. "You can't rely on your memory. Those who rely on memories are doomed to repeat their mistakes.

Were you aware of that?"

"Not until now," said Plotkin.

"You must be careful not to allow your notes to fall into the wrong hands," the lunatic warned. "Any hands other than yours are the wrong hands. Make sure to take the notes to the trial. Unless you do, they won't do you any good. And if they don't do you any good, what have I been doing here, every night, day after day, week after week, advising you without remuneration?"

"The only hands that touch the notes will be mine," Plotkin assured the lunatic.

"That gives me some comfort, although I'm not sure how much comfort it gives me since I haven't ruled out the possibility that you are conspiring with governmental officials and my former secretary lover to further do me in on additional, baseless charges."

"I assure you I am not conspiring with anyone to do you in. I wish you no harm."

"I'm exhausted," the lunatic announced. "We'll have to continue the lecture series tomorrow night, at the same time and location. If for some reason you aren't able to attend, give me advance notice in writing. I will clear my schedule for you tomorrow night but, if you give me advance notice that you are unable to attend, I can put the cleared time to good use working on my appeal from the horrendous miscarriage of justice inflicted on me."

"I'll be here tomorrow night at the same time," Plotkin assured the lecturer.

"And bring the notes you have taken tonight," the lunatic recommended.

"I don't have any notes."

"What have you been doing all this time?"

"Listening."

"That won't do. If you are derelict in your note-taking tomorrow night, that will put an end to the lectures. I refuse to waste my time attempting to help somebody who refuses to help himself."

"I understand," said Plotkin with feigned understanding.

"I hope you do," the lunatic proclaimed angrily. "Now let me sleep. I have to regain my strength."

The next evening, the lunatic announced that he was ready to lecture. Satisfied that Plotkin had pen and paper in hand to record the insightful observations he was about to convey, he proceeded. "The first topic I will address tonight," he said professorially, "is the Closing Argument or Tirade. As the names suggest, this comes near the end of the trial, just before the judge orders the jurors to deliberate—an unrealistic order, given the intellectual shortcomings of most of the idiots who are impaneled."

The lunatic paused to ask Plotkin to read back his notes. The butcher gave a verbatim reading of the two sentences uttered by the lunatic. "Excellent. It is self-evident that you are an avid note taker," the lunatic said enthusiastically.

"I learned to take avid notes when studying at a librarian's feet."

"It's unhealthy to study at anybody's feet—particularly a librarian's. Feet are filthy carriers of bacteria, germs, toxins, poisons, secretions, and numerous other nasty things."

"I don't disagree."

"Whether or not you disagree is beside the point. It ignores the irrefutable fact that without avid notes, you'll be lost at trial."

"I can't afford to be lost at trial."

"Even if you aren't lost, you are almost certain to lose. Most defendants do. I did.

"That is something I hope to avoid at all costs."

The lunatic coughed nervously. "Was your reference to avoiding costs a subtle allusion to conspiratorial accusations that I have solicited fees for my lecture services?"

"No.   It was merely a figure of speech," Plotkin assured the lecturer.

"Please avoid all figures of speech that can be construed to relate to a fee for my services or I will be forced to put an abrupt end to the lecture series. For purposes of avoiding any possibility that your reference to costs will lead to another prosecution and further disgrace on my part, I move to strike the phrase 'at all costs' from the record and ask that the jury be instructed to disregard it."

"The phrase 'at all costs' is stricken from the record and the jury is instructed to disregard it," the phantom judge declared. "Please feel free to proceed."

"Where were we before the unseemly reference to *costs*?"

"You said you were going to discuss the Closing Argument."

"I did?"

"Yes. That is what my notes say."

"Well, if that is what your notes say, it must be true, unless you are an inaccurate note taker."

"I usually take accurate notes."

"Then it must be true. Now that we have resolved this troubling issue," the lunatic said appreciatively, "unless you have a question, I will proceed directly to the topic of the Closing Argument, the most critical stage of a trial other than possibly the Opening Argument, cross-examination, jury selection, and several other stages that need not be mentioned, since I will only be able to discuss the five critical stages of a trial rather than ten. The less said about the deleted stages the better, given my justifiable concerns over the persistent level of surveillance I have been subjected to without justifiable cause. Don't you agree?"

"Without a doubt," Plotkin conceded for mollification purposes, although still disappointed that the lunatic's lectures would cover only five of the ten critical stages of a trial. Fearful that the deletion of half the critical stages would impair his chances of gaining an unlikely acquittal, he asked, "Can you at least tell me something about the five deleted critical stages so I will recognize them as they occur?"

"Absolutely not," the lunatic replied. "In fact, I find your request both insulting and belligerent, and ask the Court to hold the witness in contempt. This is at least the third or sixth time this witness has acted contemptuously. If these proceedings are not to get out of hand, he must be punished."

"The witness is held in contempt of court," the judge declared obediently.

"And?" the lunatic intoned.

"And *what*?" Plotkin replied.

"Isn't the Court going to instruct the bailiff to remove the witness and place him in a cell until the witness purges himself of the contempt?"

"Very well," said Plotkin in his judicial capacity. "The Bailiff is instructed to remove the witness and place him in a cell until the witness purges himself."

Without waiting for the imaginary bailiff to remove the recalcitrant witness, the lunatic continued. "Now that this matter has been resolved, my lecture series is over."

"Over?" inquired the shocked judge, jury and witness.

"Yes. Completely and irretrievably."

"What about the five critical stages you were going to lecture on?"

"The less said about the critical stages, the better, given the furtive eyes and ears that litter these hallowed chambers. Moreover, my energy is dissipated. I am too exhausted to continue. Please fend for yourself and let me sleep. I am through talking. I suggest that you sleep too. You'll need your strength for the trial."

As the faint light of dawn filtered through the only window in the basement, Plotkin wasn't able to sleep. Fretting over the loss of potentially useful information that might enable him to navigate the froth of self-representation, the butcher tossed and turned on the floor of his cage, imagining the worst.

Ana Bloom

21

Plotkin stood in the Visitation Room for Disruptive Prisoners waiting for his unidentified visitor to arrive. Told only that the visitor was a woman, he assumed it was either his mother or an aunt. The door on the other side of the mesh barrier opened. A handsome woman emerged wearing a blue, high-collared dress. The door closed behind her. As she gracefully approached, he had no idea who she was.

"Leopold?" the woman asked skeptically.

"Yes," he replied.

"Do you recognize me?" she asked.

"No," he said, squinting through the mesh.

"Would you like a hint?" she asked.

"That might be helpful," he said.

"Do you remember Hinta Gelb?" she asked.

"Very clearly," he said.

"Do you recall a girl who studied with you at her feet?"

"Do you mean Ana?"

"You remember her name!"

"Nothing remarkable in that. She was my only friend."

"*I'm* Ana!"

Astounded to be seated across from the person he had incessantly thought about over the years, Plotkin couldn't help feeling ambivalent about the revelation. On one hand, he was excited to see her. On the other, he was embarrassed to be seen by her in a prison visiting room as an accused criminal who looked bad and smelled worse. Not knowing how to react, he merely said, "Oh."

Bloom was shocked by how much he had aged since his disappearance from the library. After seeing his sallow skin and the purplish pouches beneath his eyes, she felt foolish asking, "How are you?"

"Not too bad," he said. "Except for languishing in a filthy basement infested with insect colonies, residing next to an insane, defrocked lawyer who babbles all night, and a few other hardships, things could be worse."

"You're living in a basement?" she said with horror.

"Actually, I think it's a sub-basement," he replied.

"Why would they put you in a sub-basement?" she asked.

"They think I'm disruptive," he answered.

"That's ridiculous," she said.

"They have all of the power," he explained.

"Power corrupts," she sighed philosophically.

"It always has," he sighed back.

"I would have visited sooner," Bloom said. "Unfortunately, when you were arrested, I was on a six-month library tour of semi-illiterate countries and didn't find out about it until a few days ago. I read an article about you in *the Monthly Contrarian*. You're quite the hero, taking on the powerful government. You've come a long way from the shy boy I knew."

"Not a hero," he said somberly. "A fool."

"Still the self-effacing person I knew," she said, looking at his somber face.

"You must still love books," he said in order to change the subject.

"I *do*. And you?"

"Only in theory now. They ban all books in here. The only things I'm allowed to read are letters, after the Mailroom Censor examines them for escape plots and corrects any grammatical errors."

"They're barbarians."

"I agree."

"What do you do all day?"

"Mostly languish, squash insects, and listen to my neighbor rant. Sometimes, they allow me to walk in circles outside my cage for a few minutes."

Knowing nothing about Plotkin's post-pubescent life apart from his arrest and imprisonment, and feeling too depressed to hear more about his travails in Purgatory's basement, Bloom asked what he had done in the three decades since his disappearance. Plotkin didn't want to burden her with too many unpleasant details, so he gave her only a brief overview of the downward trajectory his life took after his father banned him from the library. Included in the narrative were the bar mitzvah debacle, his conscription into the butcher shop, the extinguishment of his dream of becoming a professional intellectual, the difficulties of sharing a small flat with his argumentative father and unhinged uncles, and the frustrations of being the sole proprietor of a financially struggling business that was always on the verge of bankruptcy. Deducing from the moisture in Bloom's eyes that even the watered-down version was making her sad, Plotkin changed the subject.

"How has *your* life been since I disappeared?" he asked.

Fearing that an accurate synopsis of her generally positive biography would compound Plotkin's suffering, Bloom carefully edited the narrative. She spoke of experiencing self-doubt after finishing only fifth in her secondary school graduating class; barely earning dual doctorates in literature and biology; and succeeding Hinta Gelb as the Head Librarian of the National Library, by default, because nobody else applied for the position. She also disclosed that her once-wealthy father had declared bankruptcy due to poor investment decisions, and that her mother experienced "spells" during which she talked to herself. Omitting all references to her wide circle of friends and former lovers, she misrepresented that most of her free time was spent reading biographies to her father of financially ruined capitalists and attempting to engage her mother in conversation. Bloom also revealed that she had never married and pointed out that she had twice lived unsuccessfully with misogynistic men whose conservative political views eventually caused her to end the relationships.

After exhausting the edited version of her life, Ana Bloom steered the conversation to other topics. She and Plotkin discussed the current state of Republic politics, the philosophical underpinnings of death in its various forms, the subliminal messages contained in Flavio Plumage's classic poem *The Inferno Below,* and the nuances of reductive dialectical materialism in the Bleak Ages. The conversation was easy and comfortable, flowing without impediment. Each felt a longing to return to those innocent times when they debated theorems, deconstructed syllogisms, and debunked inferences drawn by adult members of the intelligentsia. Both thought of the days of their youth when they read in the catacombs of the National library with the comforting sounds of Hinta Gelb re-shelving books in the background. He told her that, until his incarceration, he regularly visited with Bruno the orangutan at the National Zoo and that Bruno was still lethargic. As she parted her lips to reveal how much she had missed their friendship, a guard banged on a door to announce that the visit would end in two minutes. She quickly asked Plotkin whether he had a lawyer. He revealed that he didn't and that he was too poor to purchase the services of one on the open market. As she was ushered out the door, she told him that she would attempt to locate an attorney who was willing to take his case pro bono.

"Make sure there aren't any hidden costs," Plotkin managed to exclaim before a guard extracted him from the room. "I can't afford to pay."

Attorney Bernard Talisman

22

O n the trolley ride from Purgatory, Ana Bloom read an advertisement in the *Monthly Contrarian* announcing the formation
of the Women's Association for the Prevention of Cruelty to
the Truly Despised. The ad described the Association as a legal ad-
vocacy group dedicated to aggressive protection of the rights of the
categorically loathed. The organization's first public meeting was
scheduled for the following week at All Sinners Nondenomination-
al Church. Persons seeking its services were invited to attend.

Bloom was the first person to speak at the meeting. Myra Rabinowitz-Pritzker, the organization's President, sat at the center of a
table, directly across from her. Rabinowitz-Pritzker's seven lieuten-
ants sat at her flanks. Bernard Talisman, the group's volunteer Legal
Consultant and partner in the elite law firm of *Talisman, Steinbloom,
Rogoff, Babel, and Barebottom,* sat off to the side, at a separate table.
He was Rabinowitz-Pritzker's half-brother. Vaguely handsome, he
wore an imported pinstriped suit, a heavily starched white shirt,
and a red necktie. His moustache was neatly trimmed. Round,

gold-plated reading glasses rested at the end of a patrician nose as he edited a memorandum of law for one of his firm's clients.

Following a brief intra-committee conversation, Rabinowitz-Pritzker announced that she and her confederates were ready to hear from Bloom.

Ana Bloom rose gracefully, nodded cordially, and said with appropriate obsequiousness, "It is an honor to appear as a surrogate before a body that so generously devotes its time to helping despised people."

"Likewise, it is an honor to hear from a surrogate appearing on behalf of a despised person," Rabinowitz-Pritzker said.

The Chairwoman's confederates nodded sternly as Bernard Talisman continued working on the memorandum.

"I am here on behalf of one of the Republic's most despised men," Bloom continued. "This truly gentle person is rotting in Purgatory, unrepresented and unappreciated. He is without counsel or hope; destined to be convicted and sentenced to one of our Republic's horrendous prisons merely because he smeared mud on his shop window. As I will explain, he___."

"Say no more," Rabinowitz-Pritzker interrupted. "We are very familiar with Mr. Plotkin's troubles."

"His predicament is well known to us," added a Committee member on Rabinowitz-Pritzker's left.

"This is very heartening," said Ana Bloom, surmising they had already decided to assist Plotkin.

"There is no doubt that Mr. Plotkin is widely despised and that his prosecution is animated, in large part, by the loathing of broad segments of the non-despised community," Rabinowitz-Pritzker explained.

"No doubt, whatsoever," several Committee members echoed.

"I am gratified that you recognize this injustice," said Bloom.

"Only the willfully blind would fail to see the loathing at the root of this discrimination," said Rabinowitz-Pritzker.

"One has to be heartless not to see it," a member at the end of the table chimed in.

"Unfortunately," Rabinowitz-Pritzker continued, "though Mr. Plotkin may well be the most despised person in the Republic, the Association cannot assist him. Our Founding Charter won't permit it. We advocate only for those who are despised because they belong to a despised *group*—not for reasons *unique to themselves*. Mr. Plotkin is what we call a *randomly despised* person—hated for something he has done or not done, said or not said and so forth, rather than for belonging to a certain group. Although the fact that he's Jewish isn't entirely irrelevant, it's clear that Mr. Plotkin is essentially despised because of the window, not his religion. Therefore, our hands are tied."

Her colleagues nodded as Rabinowitz-Pritzker turned to her half-brother, and asked, "Do you agree, Bernard, that our hands are tied?"

Because Bernard Talisman had heard nothing that preceded the question, he asked his half-sister to recapitulate. While Rabinowitz-Pritzker recapitulated, the lawyer looked at Ana Bloom for the first time. A man of unusual rectitude, he wasn't in the habit of leering at women. In this instance, however, he couldn't resist. Erotic excitement—more intense than anything Talisman had experienced at trials or appellate arguments—surged through his loins as he studied the handsome woman who waited to see whether he agreed with his half-sister.

Until that moment, Talisman had been consumed by the law, assiduously avoiding amorous entanglements, fearing that relations with women would dilute his creative energy and thwart his advancement. His days and nights had been devoted to searching for precedents, analyzing, ruminating, brainstorming, crafting memorable bon mots, and turning eloquent phrases. He had directed his amorous energies toward romancing judges, juries, and clients. Lawmongering had made Talisman wealthy and famous beyond anything he imagined when he opened a small office above an umbrella store decades earlier. Through the years, he had built a large and powerful partnership that now occupied an entire building in Fettig's Government and Justice District. Despite professional success, Talisman faintly sensed something was missing from his life, though he couldn't say what.

After his half-sister's recapitulation, Talisman issued a concurring opinion while continuing to stare at Bloom. "Regrettably, my half-sister is right," he said with profound regret, "The Association's hands are tied."

Disappointed, Ana Bloom blushed and apologized for her ignorance of the Association's mission and for wasting its time. She smiled politely and slowly retreated from the room. Talisman ached to stop her, offer condolences, and ask whether he could see her again, perhaps later that day. His rigid sense of decorum, however, wouldn't allow this. As Bloom drifted from view, he willed himself back to the memorandum.

In the ensuing days, the lawmonger couldn't purge Bloom

from his thoughts. When drafting briefs, reviewing contracts, casting about for legal precedents, offering documents into evidence, cross-examining hostile witnesses, conferring with judges at sidebar, and exhorting juries, she never left his thoughts. When remonstrating, obfuscating, and performing other lawyerly functions, he recalled her forlorn look when leaving the room.

Within a week, Bloom had become an obsession. The obsession adversely affected his work. Talisman's writing deteriorated, becoming hackneyed, disjointed, and mediocre. His forensic arguments lost the penetrating focus that once distinguished him from less talented rivals. Desperate, he asked his half-sister to write Bloom at the address Bloom entered in the Association's Meeting Registry and invite her for tea at their mansion. Despite having misgivings about the ethical implications of her brother cavorting with a former supplicant for the organization's services, Rabinowitz-Pritzker agreed to do it.

The invitation raised Ana Bloom's spirits. She speculated that it signaled a change in the Association's position. When she arrived at the mansion, Rabinowitz-Pritzker warmly greeted her. They drank several cups of tea while engaging in repartee about things neither had an interest in and politely laughed at each other's quips. As the conversation neared its natural death, Bernard Talisman entered the room, feigning surprise at finding Bloom with his half-sister. "Pardon me," he said disingenuously to his half-sister. "I didn't realize you were hosting a tea."

Rabinowitz-Pritzker introduced him to Bloom. Talisman played with his moustache pensively and said that Bloom looked vaguely familiar. The reluctant host of the tea shook her head, mildly put off by her half-brother's dishonesty.

"I was a surrogate last week at a meeting of the Women's Association for the Prevention of Cruelty to the Truly Despised," Bloom reminded Talisman.

"Is that so?" Talisman said coyly, while his half-sister rolled her eyes.

"Would you like to join us, Bernard?" Rabinowitz-Pritzker asked, as rehearsed.

"That would be nice," he said with broad understatement. "My afternoon appointment is cancelled and I have nothing pressing. Do you mind if I join you, Miss Bloom?"

"Not at all," Bloom said, looking forward to discussing Plotkin's case.

After more tea and idle chatter, Rabinowitz-Pritzker excused herself, claiming that she had a headache. Her tactical departure allowed Talisman to become better acquainted with the object of his obsession.

Repairing to the study, they discovered a mutual interest in the emerging field of Neo-Darwinism. After a lengthy discussion on this subject, they agreed to meet the next day at a coffeehouse to delve into Neo-Creationism, a theory that had emerged to counter the underpinnings of Neo-Darwinism. The next day, they sat in a corner of a smoke-filled denizen for caffeine addicts discussing Neo-Creationism, before turning to foreign literature. During these exchanges, Bloom refrained from any mention of Plotkin's need for legal representation, as did Talisman.

Captivated by Ana Bloom's mind, personality, and appearance, Bernard Talisman arranged to dine with her and his half-sister the following evening at one of Fettig's most pretentious restaurants. There, the inchoate couple immersed themselves in each other, essentially ignoring Rabinowitz-Pritzker. Over the course of several days, as Talisman grew more comfortable with Bloom and Bloom with him, their mutual attraction deepened to the same degree that Rabinowitz-Pritzker felt ignored. One evening, while the half-siblings were alone, Rabinowitz-Pritzker announced that she would no longer chaperone his rendezvous with Bloom.

The object of Talisman's affection decided to raise Plotkin's need for legal representation during her ninth rendezvous with Talisman, a performance of the Fettig Symphony. As kettledrums combusted, she confessed that she did not feel "comfortable" enjoying time together with him while the butcher rotted in Purgatory without counsel. Clutching his hand, she pressed her moist lips against Talisman's ear. When she captured his full attention, she asked whether he would represent Plotkin, gratis, either through the Association or his law firm. On stage, a string section played as she pleaded the butcher's case. Overcome by the emotion of the moment, Talisman consented to represent Plotkin without charge. Though aware that representing the notorious meat merchant would scandalize his partners and not sit well with the Captains of Industry, banking cartels and others on the firm's client list, Talisman's desire to please Ana Bloom overwhelmed his judgment. Thrilled by Talisman's offer to represent the butcher, she embraced his hand and smiled tenderly.

The next morning, three months after Plotkin's imprisonment, a Talisman middleman posted bail for the butcher. Word of the reviled inmate's imminent release reached Purgatory Warden Hans

Gogol. When the paperwork was completed, the disappointed administrator came to Plotkin's cell to give him a farewell slap. As the guards removed Plotkin from the basement, the lunatic in the adjoining cell hysterically demanded to be released along with him, claiming that he and the butcher had been co-conspirators and, therefore, should be simultaneously released. Ignoring the lunatic's irrational pleas, Gogol's guards dragged Plotkin upstairs to the exit gate and threw him to the ground. Looking up, Plotkin saw the outstretched arms of Ana Bloom and his chicken plucker, Primo Astigmatopolous, welcoming him back to society. The welcoming party helped Plotkin to his feet as they showered him with hugs and kisses. Moved by their conviviality, he returned their affection in kind.

While Plotkin and his friends waited to board a trolley to the Small Business District, Bloom revealed that a highly successful lawyer she knew had agreed to defend him, free of charge. Plotkin quizzed her about the existence of hidden charges. She assured him there were none. The butcher was relieved.

During the trolley ride, Bloom was careful not to mention her dalliance with Talisman and the growing romance that inspired the lawmonger to defend Plotkin. According to her fictionalized explanation, Talisman was motivated by a long-standing interest in the case and a desire to prevent a miscarriage of justice.

After Plotkin, Bloom, and Astigmatopolous disembarked in the Small Business District, Bloom left for the National Library of Pedantic Writings. The chicken plucker accompanied Plotkin to the butcher shop. Standing outside the establishment, Plotkin beheld the display window for the first time since his arrest. He noted, while studying the glass from various angles, that the mud had lost none of its luster. "There is no finer mud than the mud of my country," the chicken plucker proudly reiterated, drawing an appreciative nod from Plotkin.

"Without your mud, none of this would have been possible," the butcher remarked, not without irony.

23

Plotkin's reunification with his family was emotional. When he entered the flat, his father accused him of staining the family name, his mother complained that his arrest nearly killed his father, and his uncles insisted that he was responsible for the finger injury. The elders asserted that he looked and smelled bad and didn't seem pleased to see them.

"Have you cracked up?" Jacob Plotkin asked.

"What happened to you?" Emma Plotkin asked. "As a child, you were so well-groomed."

"I don't like the look of his eyes," the twins exclaimed.

"You destroyed our lives by putting mud on the window," the patriarch said mournfully.

"But it was your idea, Papa," Plotkin reminded his father.

"Your mind is playing tricks on you," the patriarch responded angrily. "As a man of moderation, I wouldn't have told you to do something that radical."

Unable to disagree with his father, Plotkin responded cryptically. "Perhaps mistakes were made," he said.

Jacob Plotkin was offended by his son's use of the passive tense. He launched an interrogation that eventually extracted an admission from the butcher that he "overreacted" by muddying the window. "Looking back on things now, it would have been better had I left the window alone," Plotkin conceded.

The matriarch began to sob. Plotkin hugged her and begged for forgiveness. "I'll try to forgive, but I can't forget," she replied, freeing herself from his clutches.

"The best we can do is *try*," said his Uncle Misha. "With such deep wounds, we're pessimistic about forgetting. Your stupidity nearly killed me and your parents. Whatever you did, it was wrong. You should have known better."

Moving to the next item on their repatriation agenda, the elders demanded an accounting of Plotkin's time in Purgatory. Over the course of an hour-long inquisition, they elicited the nature of his suffering in excruciating detail, permitting him to pause only for food and water. They listened attentively, when not interrupting, and were particularly incensed by an incident when the prison physician refused to treat his imaginary asthma ailment. Jacob Plotkin concluded that the doctor was a "quack" who deserved to lose his license. "My son could have died and left us with nothing to live on," the *paterfamilias* moaned.

As the day wore on, throngs of uninvited extended family members appeared, demanding to be included in the homecoming festivities. They relished the opportunity to blame Leopold for soiling the family name and told him how bad he looked. The relatives listened attentively as Jacob Plotkin repeated his earlier criticisms of his son for their benefit. Later, they formed an "Amen" chorus, echoing each of the patriarch's accusations verbatim. Eventually unnerved by the mirror-image criticisms of his only child, Jacob told them to cease and desist. Unwilling to do either, they ignored the injunction. Soon, he evicted them en masse.

Several hours later, darkness fell. The members of the close-knit family, exhausted from the proceedings, agreed to suspend hostilities until morning. With a temporary cease-fire in place, they shook hands and retired to their bedrooms to reflect on the day's events.

24

Not wanting to interfere with Plotkin's reunification with his family, Ana Bloom waited a week before inviting him to dinner. The evening of the dinner, Plotkin groomed himself. He bathed, shaved gray stubble from his cheeks, chin, and neck, clipped the stray hairs from his nostrils, and trimmed his moustache. Once groomed, he removed a photograph that he kept hidden under his mattress. It was a black and white image of him standing next to Ana Bloom outside the National Library of Pedantic Writings. In the photograph, he was thin and stiff. She was gangly but poised. He was frowning. She was smiling. He held *Crime and Punishment*, his favorite novel, in one hand, and *The Death of Ivan Ilych* in the other. She clutched a kite. Comparing the boy in the picture to the middle-age man in the mirror, Plotkin was disappointed by how his face had wrinkled and sagged. He had never considered himself very much to look at. However, the comparison made him realize how extensively his modest looks had declined over the years. In contrast, he appreciated how Ana had improved over time. All aspects of her had come together harmoniously. In his eyes, she was comparable to a perfectly aged cheese.

Plotkin got dressed in his only suit. He purchased a rose at a flower shop and boarded a trolley to Ana Bloom's neighborhood. When he arrived at the narrow row house she had shared with her parents since Leonard Bloom's financial collapse, Plotkin handed her the flower. She thanked him for his thoughtfulness and led him to the dining room table to join her parents. Leonard Bloom shook Plotkin's hand weakly. Ida Bloom vaguely smiled.

During the meal, the bankrupt former owner of Bloom's Department Store gave a floor-by-floor description of the defunct emporium, followed by a detailed yearly accounting of philanthropic donations he made when times were good. At the end of the accounting, he said with tears welling in his sad eyes, "Perhaps I gave too much." After regaining his composure, he summarized the good times, the years when the store was at its zenith; when he and his wife enjoyed holidays in exotic places, belonged to an exclusive Jewish social club, and attended symphonies, operas, and ballets. Through her husband's reminiscences, Ida was in the throes of one of her spells, talking to herself. She occasionally nodded, as if to say her husband's summary of better times was essentially accurate.

As Leonard Bloom continued his mournful narrative, Plotkin was intrigued by how successful elements of the First Wave of Migrants (the wave that preceded the elders' Wave) lived. Until then, the butcher had only heard about the phenomenon second-hand, through his father's jealous complaints. Plotkin found the meal a delightful diversion from the dinnertime combat he routinely experienced at his own family gatherings, despite Leonard Bloom's depressive nature and Ida Bloom's spell.

As the butcher prepared to leave, Ana kissed his forehead tenderly. Buoyed by the kiss, Plotkin speculated that she might be mildly attracted to him, despite his shortcomings. As the weeks passed, the resurrected friendship blossomed as they jointly attended enigmatic lectures, obtuse plays, opaque poetry recitals, and dark a cappella songfests on evenings Bernard Talisman was otherwise occupied. They also frequented coffeehouses that catered to pseudo intellectuals and political dissidents who had emigrated to the Republic in search of new opportunities for disagreement. Occasionally, they returned to parks and other places they had frequented during Hinta Gelb's socialization experiment.

When Plotkin was with Ana Bloom, he relished the opportunities to gaze at her pale face, inhale her meadow-fresh aroma, hear her desultory voice, listen to her infectious laughter, and admire her inquisitive mind. Sometimes, he imagined kissing her lips rather than her cheek or forehead, as was the norm. A practical man who accepted his limitations, he realized that co-mingling with her lips would never be more than an imagined pleasure. Sometimes this made him sad. Usually, it didn't. A friendship with a beautiful, intelligent woman who enjoyed his company and took him from his cocoon now and again was sufficient, he convinced himself.

One evening, they attended a play at a Yiddish Theater, in which renowned actor, Yehuda Moskowitz, played a wandering Jew expelled from a dozen countries before finding a permanent residence. During intermission, Bloom suggested, with tact, that removing the mud from the window might be in his best interest. Plotkin thanked her for the suggestion before rejecting it. "Unfortunately," he said with regret, "my father now admits that the mud was *his* idea, not mine, and has threated to disown me if I disturb the window." Ana knew that Plotkin had a desperate need to feel respected, if not loved, by his father, and recognized the futility of pushing the issue any further. They returned to their seats and enjoyed the remainder of Yehuda Moskowitz' brilliant performance.

Psychiatrist Seymour Peltz

25

L eopold Plotkin's post-Purgatory nights were plagued by recurring nightmares of being buried alive after digging his own grave and selling tickets to the funeral. Hearing this, Ana Bloom persuaded him to consult with Dr. Seymour Peltz, the Permanent Acting Director of Admissions and/or Discharges at the Warehouse for the Purportedly Insane. Peltz, who subsidized his Warehouse salary with a private psychiatric practice, specialized in treating the symptoms of sleep-related anxieties and other neuroses. Not wanting to be seen in a psychiatrist's office, Plotkin made arrangements, through Bloom, for Peltz to make a house call.

More comfortable with inanimate objects than people, Peltz sat in the Plotkins' kitchen, staring at a teapot. He hadn't spoken since entering the tenement flat. To ease the tension, Bloom offered the psychiatrist a cup of tea. Peltz accepted with an unenthusiastic nod. After tea was poured, he shifted his gaze to the teacup.

"What is the color of your urine?" the doctor finally asked, appearing to direct the question to the teacup rather than the patient.

"My urine?" Plotkin answered, surprised that his urine was of any clinical significance.

"Yes, your *urine*," Peltz confirmed emphatically.

"I have no idea," said Plotkin.

"No idea?" Peltz said with alarm.

"Is that a *problem*," the butcher asked.

"It's more than a *problem*," Peltz responded. It's *extraordinary*. I am dismayed that a man your age doesn't know the color of his urine. It is one thing to be unaware of the color of the urine of others; quite another to be oblivious to one's own liquid excretions."

"What does this mean, doctor?" Bloom asked with concern.

"Difficult to say," Peltz replied gravely, meticulously folding his cloth napkin into six equal parts and four subparts. "It could be a bad sign. On the other hand, it could mean nothing. Only time will tell."

The diagnostician removed a notebook from his medical bag and recorded his thoughts: "Patient claims no knowledge of his urine's coloration. May indicate disorientation as to time/place/ smell, or that he urinates with eyes closed. Both possibilities are troubling."

Peltz looked at the ceiling, focused on a light bulb, and asked, "How would you describe your health?"

"Poor to atrocious," Plotkin answered.

"Why do you say that?" Peltz inquired.

"I'm racked with disease," Plotkin stated.

"What diseases currently rack you?" the diagnostician demanded of the light bulb.

"Late-stage pleurisy, transient headaches, pseudo-consumption, recurring foot tremors, irregular heartbeats, insipient leprosy, vascular degeneration, parasites___."

"What kind of parasites?" Peltz interrupted.

"Yet to be determined."

"Anything else?"

"Low grade pain in my colon, high grade pain in my spleen, descending pain in ___."

"That's enough," Peltz said. He wrote: "Patient suffers from undifferentiated solipsism, resulting in a morass of hypochondriacal illnesses."

Peltz removed a measuring tape and stethoscope from his bag and approached Plotkin.

"What are you doing?" Plotkin asked with concern as Peltz prepared to measure his head.

"I'm about to determine the circumference of your skull, locate and count the undulations, palpate the lower portion of the cranium to determine its density, and listen inside for irregularities," Peltz revealed while unrolling the tape measure.

"I don't like being touched by strangers," Plotkin said, as images of the traumatic shaking incident with the part-time rabbi during his bar mitzvah crossed his mind.

"Nobody likes to be touched by strangers," Peltz proclaimed. "Nor do most people like to touch strangers. However, without direct tactile access to your head, I can't conduct this examination properly."

"Let the doctor measure your head, Leopold," Bloom calmly instructed. "I'm sure he knows what he's doing."

Peltz proceeded. First, he determined the diameter of the butcher's large skull. Then, he located and counted the number of folds on its surface, palpated the lower sphere, and listened with the stethoscope for any aberrant noise. When Bloom saw Peltz wince, she asked if he had found something. Peltz said that other than his realization that Plotkin probably had difficulty locating hats large enough for his head, nothing of clinical importance was discovered.

"How long have you had a death wish?" the psychiatrist asked the measuring tape.

"I didn't say anything about a death wish," Plotkin replied.

"Do you deny having a death wish?"

"I've never given it much thought."

"So you neither confirm nor deny?"

"I suppose so."

"I recommend that you give some thought to it after I leave."

Peltz lifted the teacup and stared at it from multiple angles. "Look at this cup," he directed. "Does it resemble a breast?"

"Should it?"

"That's for you to determine."

"Is this a trick question?"

"Does the question embarrass you?" Peltz asked the handle.

"A little."

"That's very revealing."

"What does it reveal?"

"That you may have an aversion to sex."

Plotkin didn't react, other than a slight coloring of his cheeks.

"Let me approach this from a slightly different angle," Peltz said while fondling the teacup. "What *do* you think about when engaged in intercourse with a person of the opposite gender?"

"I haven't done that," Plotkin replied, blushing.

"Assuming that sometime in the future you engage in that disgusting act, how do you imagine this would make you feel?"

"I would prefer a change of subject; there's a woman in the room."

"Very well. Turning to a closely related but entirely different topic, I must ask, for the sake of completeness, whether you have ever fantasized about engaging in sex with a mannequin," he inquired.

"Not as far as I can remember. Does anyone?"

Fearing that Plotkin may have detected that he harbored mannequin-related fantasies, Peltz' normally colorless face turned crimson. He abandoned the inquiry and fixed his attention on the kitchen sink.

"Some colleagues at the Warehouse speculate that you covered the shop window with mud to humiliate your mother. Others theorize that your choice of mud suggests an immature fixation on excrement that has no relationship to your oppressive mother. What should I tell them?"

"Tell them I had my reasons."

"Do you care to share the perverse reasons with me?"

"I prefer not to."

"In light of your refusal to cooperate, I'll put this extremely important question to Miss Bloom. How would you describe Mr. Plotkin's mood?" Peltz asked while staring at the tablecloth.

"He seems to be on edge," she replied.

"What do you mean by that?"

"His nerves are frayed,"

"Given the anxiety-laden circumstances surrounding him — the fact that he is universally despised and hung in effigy daily — frayed nerves are to be expected," Peltz explained as his gaze moved to Ana Bloom's shoes. "It would be abnormal if they weren't. However, the extent of fraying is what is critical here. Would you characterize the level of the nerve fraying as severe, moderate, or negligible?"

"Severe, I suppose," she estimated.

"Now is not the time to *suppose*, Miss Bloom. I need your *unvarnished* observations. Without them, my conclusions may be skewed. And in my profession, skewing a conclusion is unacceptable."

"I would say moderate to severe, then."

"In addition to being on edge and having moderately severe frayed nerves, have you observed other symptoms of lunacy on his part?" he inquired of her demurely-crossed ankles.

"Yes, he sometimes feels shame and guilt about things he didn't do."

"Didn't do when?"

"Didn't do ever."

"That's interesting. It is also disconcerting," Peltz remarked as he wrote "floridly hallucinatory" in his notebook.

Peltz grabbed his medicine bag. "Now to the scribblings," he said, removing a collection of primitive drawings done by Warehouse inmates. He used the material to troll for mental aberrations. Peltz showed the butcher a scribbling of wildly intersecting red, black, and blue lines. "What do you see?" he asked.

"Lines," Plotkin replied succinctly.

"Of course you see lines!" the psychiatrist fulminated. "What do the lines suggest?"

Plotkin turned the drawing in several directions and squinted, but the lines suggested nothing to him. Fearing Peltz might find him abnormal if he had nothing to report, Plotkin lied. "I see the angel of death," he said.

"What is the angel of death doing?"

"Lurking in a hospital hallway."

"Do you see anything else?"

"Yes."

"What do you see?"

"Dead patients on the floor. Dead fish lying beside the dead patients. A dead doctor attended by a dying nurse. Soon to be dead visitors having massive strokes. Mounting death all around."

"Are any of the people naked?" Peltz asked while furiously taking notes.

"Possibly."

"Are the naked ones engaged in sexual congress?"

"What?"

"Are they *fornicating*?"

"I doubt it. They're either dead or dying."

Peltz scratched his head before he made the following entry: "Patient has dark side, exacerbated by morbid preoccupation with deviant sex. Possible split personality with overlay of persecution complex and underlay of grandiosity."

Peltz showed Plotkin a second drawing filled with dozens of black rectangles and cone-shaped objects resting on each rectangle.

"What does this suggest?" the psychiatrist asked.

"Garbage cans filled with debris," the butcher lied creatively now that he understood the sort of response Peltz seemed to appreciate.

"What kind of debris?"

"Rotting fruit with roundworms and mounds of carrier pigeon droppings."

Peltz sipped his tea and swished it around his mouth several times before swallowing. "This is bad," he said with a pained expression.

"The *tea* is bad?" Ana Bloom asked.

"No, my *tentative diagnosis* is bad," Peltz said.

"What is it?" she probed anxiously, glancing at Plotkin to see how he was holding up after Peltz' revelation.

Unable to recall the particulars of his preliminary findings, Peltz referred to his notes. The notes were illegible and of no use. The diagnostician closed his eyes to refresh his memory, ruminated, cleared his throat, ruminated some more, and finally opened his eyes so he could focus on the stove. In a hushed tone, he said, "I fear the patient is *possibly* afflicted with a form of insanity or *possibly not*. Although things now look bleak for him, there is some small measure of hope that he will regain his sanity, if he is, indeed, insane."

"What are you saying?" the confused butcher asked.

"I'm saying you *could* or could *not* be insane and am recommending that you place yourself under my auspices and the auspices of my colleagues for the next thirty days or so, give or take several months."

"What do you think, Leopold?" Ana Bloom inquired, trying to gauge Plotkin's reaction.

"Perhaps he's mistaken," Plotkin answered.

Outraged that a man who saw rotting fruit with roundworms in the scribbling doubted his tentative diagnosis, Peltz leaped to his feet, stared at himself in the wall mirror, and addressed his reflection. "You sicken me!" he said, intending the misfocused remark for Plotkin. "I despise you!" he added.

With that, the Permanent Acting Chief of Admissions And/Or Discharges threw his evaluation tools into his bag, ran to the door, jerked it open, lurched into the hallway, descended five flights of stairs to Drabble Street, and ran home.

After Peltz' frenzied departure, Plotkin and Bloom sighed in unspoken agreement that the evaluation had not gone well.

26

The morning was raw. Snow fell on Leopold Plotkin and the chicken plucker as they began their trek to the law offices of Talisman, Steinbloom, Rogoff, Barebottom & Babel. Dressed in tattered overcoats and hats, their well-worn shoes left deep impressions in the snow. Clouds wafted from their nostrils. Envy occupied Plotkin's mind.

"Why do these stores thrive while we struggle?" the butcher asked morosely while passing shops with long customer queues.

"Who knows?" Primo Astigmatopolous replied. "Some things are unfathomable,"

"The trial is on the horizon," said Plotkin. "Will it be included in the trilogy?"

"It will be the centerpiece of the third book," Astigmatopolous revealed.

"The *sine qua non*?" the butcher asked.

"The *raison d'être*," the chicken plucker assured him.

"I'll read it while I'm rotting in prison."

"It will be dedicated to you."

"I'm flattered."

"And I'm appreciative. Without you, there wouldn't be a third book."

Continuing on their journey, the butcher and his companion approached the Northeast Quadrant of Fettig, a landmass that encompassed the Low-Culture District, the Flat District, as well as the Government and Justice District. Entering the Low-Culture District, they canvassed the decaying remains of abandoned burlesque palaces, freak-shows, dance halls, and other tawdry establishments that once flourished in the twelve-block area. Plotkin hadn't set foot in the seedy precinct since his early childhood when, every Sunday morning, he, his father, deranged uncles, and other male relatives bathed naked together in the bathhouses of Liverpool Street. On those weekly outings, he had watched as the adults sweat profusely, bemoaned business setbacks, argued politics, decried life's inherent unfairness, and attacked each other in Yiddish. The young Plotkin had always been careful to keep his distance from the warring factions, worried that the combatants would come to blows or that his father would suffer a heart attack during the confrontations.

The vestiges of the bathhouses stirred long-buried memories of how much he hated those Sundays. "I came here as a small boy, every week to commune with naked relatives," he told his confidant, as tears filled his eyes.

Misconstruing the tears as a nostalgic by-product of happy childhood memories, Astigmatopolous patted Plotkin on the shoulder. "When I think of my country of origin and see the slums I joyfully played in as a boy, I also feel sad." Too despondent to disabuse the chicken plucker of his misunderstanding, Plotkin said nothing.

As snow continued to fall, the moist-eyed butcher and his misguided confidant reached the outer edge of the Flat District, where dilapidated row houses harbored the City's finest brothels. Innovative marketers, the courtesans attracted clientele by posing provocatively at street-level windows, fully clothed to add to the allure. Despite opposition from moralists, feminists, and anti-hedonists, they and their handlers were tacitly permitted to practice their profession as long as they remained in the circumscribed area.

Already that morning, clients of varying sizes, shapes, and ages had entered the bordellos. Plotkin had always been curious about houses of ill repute, and studied them and their occupants as he trudged on. The women at the windows wore dresses hiked-up several inches to reveal bare ankles, a gesture regarded as highly sensual in the sexually repressed Republic. Their lank hair, garishly dyed and parted just left of center, hung below the shoulders, unlike the pulled-up, natural-colored hair of women in polite society. Their faces were heavily rouged. Their lips were densely painted. Their half-closed eyelids, darkened with coal dust, pulsated with allure. Sleeveless dresses revealed multi-colored tattoos of copulating couples in positions rarely attempted in real life; depictions calculated to arouse even the limpest male members and stimulate commerce.

Plotkin's normally inert libido stirred when he viewed the window-women. Experiencing an erection, he checked his overcoat to make certain it obscured the bulging protuberance. Unfortunately, it didn't. Though oblivious to the bulge, the chicken plucker noticed that Plotkin's complexion had turned abnormally ruddy; even the gray pouches beneath his eyes were vibrantly red. He thought Plotkin might faint. It was at that moment that a cry came from a brothel doorway.

"Primo!" a comely prostitute called out.

When Astigmatopolous ignored her, she waved frantically and, in a surprisingly clear soprano, issued another "Primo!"

"Do you know her?" the bewildered butcher asked. He had always assumed the chicken plucker, an avowed celibate, was asexual and, therefore, had never frequented the brothels.

"Who are you referring to?" Astigmatopolous inquired innocently, feigning ignorance of the source of the greeting. He was too embarrassed to admit that he cavorted with the prostitute, if only for literary purposes.

"I'm referring to *her*," Plotkin said, pointing to the doorway.

Fearing that Plotkin would not believe that his relationship with the woman was strictly book-related—limited to frequent nightly interviews for the trilogy—the chicken plucker lied. "I have no idea who she is," he muttered.

"Where have you been lately?" the woman called again, suspecting that Astigmatopolous had not heard her previous greetings.

The chicken plucker grabbed Plotkin's elbow. "Please, let's go. She's confused."

"Are you sure you don't know her?"

"As God is my witness."

"It seems that he doesn't know you," Plotkin shouted to the woman. "I would appreciate it if you leave him alone. You're making him uncomfortable."

"He's just shy!" the woman insisted. "He knows me intimately!"

Persuaded by the vehemence of the chicken plucker's denial, Plotkin moved on. Astigmatopolous anguished as he kept pace with the butcher, regretting any pain he might have caused the woman he had so frequently interviewed.

Fighting the wind, they trudged past more brothels where prostitutes came to the door and also called out the chicken plucker's name. Although the repeated cries of "Primo!" raised questions in Plotkin's mind regarding his friend's veracity, he was willing to give his employee and best friend the benefit of the doubt.

The trekkers moved ahead, past rows of tawdry bars, dilapidated boarding houses, downtrodden hotels, decrepit pawnshops, and seedy strip joints. Eventually, they came to a brick boundary wall that marked the end of the blighted District and the beginning of the sumptuous Government and Justice District—home to all Republic governing bodies, courthouses, national museums, and law firms. Plotkin hadn't been in the Government and Justice District since he and Ana Bloom visited it during the socialization experiment. He recalled being unnerved while observing a contentious debate in the General Assembly's Inner Chamber. Entering the district for the second time in his life, he hoped that his visit with Bernard Talisman would be less anxiety inducing.

The Concierge

27

Plotkin and Astigmatopolous shambled along the Avenue of Importance, past the Inner Chamber Building, the Department of Internalized Security, and the National Museum of Only Successful Wars. They crossed the Park of the Governed, a sprawling urban green that emptied onto the Boulevard of the Judiciary, home to four cathedral-like buildings: the Low Court of Criminal Transgressions, the Low Court of Civil Transactions, the Medium Court of Appellate Pursuits, and the High Court of Final Supplications. Except for their heights, the structures looked identical. The High Court dwarfed the others.

In contrast to the flocks of tourists who were gawking at the architectural wonders, Plotkin and his companion paid no attention to the buildings before turning onto The Street of the Troubles, host to hundreds of lawhouses that accommodated the insatiable demands of the Republic's litigious populace. Although it was early in the morning, the street was already inundated with attorneys, shrieking sidewalk barkers enticing people to visit certain firms, and consumers making their way to appointments.

Plotkin's mouth was open wide as he surveyed the towering gray granite structure occupied by *Talisman, Steinbloom, Rogoff, Barebottom & Babel*, a baroque office building that dominated everything around it. The impressed travelers pushed open the building's double doors and entered a lobby whose floors, walls, and ceiling were faced with imported white marble. The decorous chandeliers and other lavish accoutrements made the atrium a monument to profligate spending and testament to the enormity of the firm's success.

As melting snow dripped from their overcoats, a refined nasal voice called out to them from a counter at the far end of the lobby, "Didn't you see the sign?" The query came from the lawhouse's Concierge, a pink-skinned man dressed in an immaculate mouse-gray suit.

"What sign?" Plotkin asked.

"The sign that says: NO TRESPASSING," the Concierge exclaimed.

"We're not trespassers," Plotkin said timidly.

"Then, *why* are you here?"

"My business associate and I have come to see Mr. Talisman."

The Concierge suspiciously motioned for them to approach. When the bedraggled pair stood before him, he inquired in a slightly more civil tone, "For what purpose?"

"To consult."

"Do you have an appointment?"

"I believe so."

"What is your last name?"

"Plotkin."

"Yes, I see it here," said the Concierge after glancing at the Appointment Registry. "A 9:30 tentative appointment."

"Why tentative?"

"To give us flexibility; to enable us to push you to the back of the queue if important clients without appointments have to be seen first."

"Have I been pushed back yet?"

"Certainly. Two slots so far; probably more to come as the day wears on."

"What do my business associate and I do in the meantime?"

"Wait, of course."

The Concierge rang a polished brass bell. Immediately, meticulously etched double doors opened and the Waiting Room Attendant, dressed in a tuxedo, emerged. "Please escort these…these *tentatives* to the couch on the fringe of the room," the Concierge instructed.

The Attendant walked stiffly ahead into a large wood-paneled area filled with well-dressed men and women seated on puffed chairs. The clients sat rigidly—sipping tea, reading, smoking, and exchanging pleasantries as the Attendant escorted Plotkin and Astigmatopolous to the fringe where a pair of hard, non-puffed chairs awaited them. Eyeing the butcher and his companion, patrons reacted with controlled disdain. Some mumbled scornfully. Others contorted eyebrows or quietly sighed.

After the butcher and chicken plucker were seated, the Attendant lowered his head to Plotkin's ear and asked, "May I bring either of you a newspaper?"

"If there's no charge, we'd appreciate *The Monthly Contrarian*," Plotkin replied meekly.

"I'm afraid we don't have radical periodicals," the Attendant said. "However, I can recommend a less controversial newspaper from our selection."

"Thanks, but less controversial newspapers have ruined my reputation," Plotkin replied.

"I'm sorry to hear that," the Attendant said as he slinked away.

Although a few patrons returned to their previous activities, most stared at the new arrivals, wondering why such marginal characters had been admitted to one of the most exclusive waiting venues in the Republic. Women clutched their handbags. Men sat poised, ready to flee if the ostensible vagrants made any sudden moves in their direction.

Unaware of the practice of whispering in high-pedigree waiting rooms, Plotkin enumerated the medical dangers of visiting brothels to the chicken plucker, specifying the diseases fostered by paid-for copulation. Because the enumeration was sufficiently loud to be overheard, clients were appalled by the crude details. They tried a number of ways to subtly signal their displeasure. Some coughed. Others murmured. A few sighed. When those efforts failed, a leather-faced man seated in the middle of the cavernous room sprang to his feet and rapidly exited. Moments later, the Concierge entered and briskly walked past red-faced patrons to the couch on which the butcher and chicken plucker sat.

"There has been a complaint about you," the officious overseer said gravely.

"Can you be more specific?" Plotkin replied.

"I am told that you and your *business associate* are discussing brothels, sexual diseases, and other disgusting matters."

"Is that prohibited?"

"Don't be coy," the Concierge exclaimed. "If you wish to continue waiting, you must comport yourselves according to the rules of polite society. Any further complaints will require more extreme measures."

Satisfied that he had restored order, the room's overseer left the room. Soon, Plotkin resumed his outline of the dangers inherent in frequenting brothels, thinking his voice was sufficiently low so as not to be heard by others.

"This is outrageous!" the leather-faced man bellowed as he again leaped from his chair. He strode from the room, sucking angrily on his cigar.

Seconds later, the Concierge re-appeared and stepped carefully over the prostrate bodies of a few patrons who had fainted during Plotkin's narrative. He leaned within inches of the butcher's face. "I see you are at it again!" he whispered. "Your vulgarity has made everybody in this room *queasy*," he declared, punctuating his words with a stream of spittle that passed through gaps in his teeth. "We have a conundrum," the Concierge proclaimed.

"A conundrum?" asked Plotkin, reaching for his handkerchief to remove the spray of saliva from his brow.

"Exactly," said the Concierge. "On one hand, you are a patron who is expected to be treated courteously while waiting. On the other, you are a rude and obnoxious irritant who has forfeited any right to courtesy. Then too, you have a tentative appointment to meet with a Named Partner. However, you are unfit to wait here due to vulgar behavior. Since we can't have you here, what shall we do?"

The other patrons listened attentively to the Concierge's framing of the conundrum, aware that its resolution would affect the remainder of their waits. The Concierge paused while he considered the options. During the pause, several patrons recommended an expulsion.

"As I see it," the Concierge resumed, "there are two choices. One would be cancelation of the appointment and eviction from the premises. The other, exile to our basement until Mr. Talisman can see you. Which will it be?"

Traumatized by his stay in Purgatory's basement, Plotkin felt squeamish about banishment to the firm's subterranean. "I don't do well in basements," the butcher said with existential dread.

"Then, you leave me no alternative but to evict," the Concierge exclaimed as he stood to his full height and straightened his waistcoat.

"May we have a moment to confer?" the chicken plucker asked, realizing that without Bernard Talisman, Plotkin's conviction and return to prison were inevitable.

"A moment, no more," the Concierge replied.

The chicken plucker pleaded with Plotkin to agree to go to the basement, whispering that the stay would be less onerous than a trial without counsel. "I'll help you get through this," he offered as an inducement.

After mulling it over, the butcher accepted the advice. "I'll go," he said with palpable reluctance.

With that, Plotkin and his companion followed the Concierge toward a portal to a steep stairwell. When the door was locked behind them, grateful patrons politely applauded.

Prime Thinker Guda Prikash

28

The firm's basement was uninviting. It was poorly lighted, cold, and smelled like rotting cabbage. Water dripped from the ceiling. Exotic insects crawled on the walls.

"This reminds me of Purgatory," Plotkin lamented as he surveyed the premises.

"I'll expose it in the trilogy," Primo Astigmatopolous vowed.

"I'd leave if I didn't need Talisman."

"Desperate times call for desperation and the lesser of two evils."

As they conversed, Plotkin and the chicken plucker were unaware that Guda Prikash, the lawhouse's reclusive Prime Thinker, was editing a brief in his cloister on the other side of the basement. A member of an ancient lawmongering order of ascetics known as Prime Thinkers, Prikash had practiced below ground for many years. In that people-free environment, he was able to focus on the firm's most demanding cases without distraction and avoid many of the negative aspects of practicing law that would have been intolerable for him.

Endowed with a brilliant mind and an obsession with the law from early childhood, Prikash had always aspired to be an attorney. However, extreme social anxieties made it difficult for him to appear in public. Recognizing that his phobias rendered him unfit for a traditional legal practice, he attended the Republic's only legal monastery for aspiring Prime Thinkers, where he studied under Master Blix, the order's preeminent educator.

The onerous process had required six years of isolated work to hone the skills required of a Prime Thinker. With Master Blix at his side, but never too close to make him uncomfortable, he learned to formulate legal theories that commonplace lawyers could not envision; to frame legal arguments that would not occur to mainstream practitioners; and to write clearly, cogently, and logically, in contrast with the often muddled, verbose, adjective-stuffed, grammatically-fractured expositions of members of the traditional bar. Just as important, he learned to accept with equanimity that he would work in obscurity, without the public recognition typical lawyers craved. The fact that he would never have to attend settlement conferences, participate in trials, meet with judges, or perform other functions that required public appearances, more than trumped any regrets he might otherwise have had over the lack of attribution.

In the tradition of his order, Guda Prikash took a vow of humility and agreed not to cut his hair, trim his beard, marry, or wear suits. After bidding an emotional farewell to Master Blix, he became the Talisman firm's Prime Thinker. Living and working in the solitude of his basement lair, Prikash nimbly scrutinized work prepared by others; corrected errors created by others; rid the products of the banality or incoherence overlooked by others; developed novel legal theories beyond the expertise of others; and performed other tasks that exceeded the capacities of his colleagues, irrespective of the time of day or day of the week.

Prikash was an ideal fit for the law firm and vice versa. He had no family, friends, or social aspirations. He was content to eat, sleep, and occasionally bathe in seclusion—pleased to enlighten lawmongers who were not his intellectual equals and enable them to better represent clients he would never have to see. The cloister had all that he required: a hot plate, a narrow work and eating table, a chair, an iron bed, two tea kettles, a wash basin, shelves for a few dishes, forks, and food staples, an armoire for his limited items of clothing, and a water closet. There were no paintings, photographs, professional certificates, licenses, or wallpaper to interfere with his concentration. A low-wattage light bulb dangling from an electric cord above the work and eating table provided sufficient illumination for reading the books and documents that typically cluttered it. Through a side door, he had access to a library that contained all published opinions of the Republic's appellate courts. He required nothing else and loved what he did.

On the opposite side of the library, the butcher and the chicken plucker waited through the afternoon for the tentative appointment with Talisman. By early evening, they were still waiting.

29

Oblivious to the fact that Leopold Plotkin was in love with her, Ana Bloom told him the day before he was to meet with Bernard Talisman that she was romantically involved with the lawyer. The butcher was speechless, crushed by the disclosure.

When finally released from the lawhouse's basement to Talisman's office, the butcher used the few moments of awkward silence to stealthily study the lawyer from across a lavish mahogany desk. Talisman's flawlessly coiffed hair, sculpted moustache, and dignified bearing attested to why Bloom had formed a romantic alliance with the attorney.

"Shall we begin, gentlemen?" Talisman inquired.

"Before beginning," the chicken plucker interjected somberly, "I have something important to say."

"You are Mr.____?" Talisman inquired.

"Primo Astigmatopolous, Mr. Plotkin's intimate friend and business associate," the chicken plucker revealed with pride.

"What is it that you wish to say, Mr. Astigmatopolous?" Talisman asked.

"Approximately two Sunday's ago," said the chicken plucker, "I confessed my normal bundle of sins to my priest, Monsignor Lorenzo Sagittarius of The Church of Lost Causes. He is an elderly but influential priest who, as it happens, is a distant cousin of Umberto Malatesta—the prosecutor who wants to destroy Mr. Plotkin's life and, by extension, the lives of Mr. Plotkin's mother, father, and deranged uncles, all who must depend on him for daily sustenance and will be devastated when Mr. Plotkin is tried, found guilty, and imprisoned, which is a foregone conclusion in the Plotkin household and elsewhere, as far as I can tell."

"I'm quite familiar with Mr. Malatesta and of Mr. Plotkin's financial importance within the family circle," Talisman said.

"Before asking the Holy Confessor to grant absolution for my offenses," Astigmatopolous continued, "I informed him that I had an additional sin to relate that day; one that weighed so heavily on my conscience that I found it difficult to eat, sleep, drink, bathe, or be in Mr. Plotkin's company without feeling severe pangs of guilt. His Holiness asked, from his side of the confessional, what I had done to arouse pangs so strong that I had difficulty carrying on my normal daily activities. To set the stage for my explanation, I informed the Good Father that I work in the butcher shop whose display window led to the so-called Mud Crisis, a fact that I had not previously revealed, since where I work had never been particularly relevant to my confessions. After the revelation, Father Sagittarius, a normally sedate man of the cloth, expressed intense hatred toward Mr. Plotkin. Among other things, the Holy Father called my dear friend 'the father of the Mud Crisis,' a 'plague on the Republic,' and other sentiments I didn't agree with, but chose not to dispute since I didn't want to antagonize the Good Priest and risk being excommunicated. After listening to His Eminence's ranting for several minutes, still holding my silence, I confessed that some of the fault for the alleged mud crimes was mine. I told the Holy Father that I furnished the mud to Mr. Plotkin and helped by keeping the mud well-stirred while he brushed it on the window. Sobbing as I confessed, I recounted how my employer was imprisoned in Purgatory in conditions unfit for an animal; how his parents and uncles suffered like abandoned pets while he rotted in prison; how he and they would suffer even more after he is convicted and re-imprisoned; and how, despite my role in this affair and apart from a few pangs of guilt, nothing bad has happened to *me.* I told His Eminence that while Mr. Plotkin will be imprisoned for many years after he is tried and convicted, I will be free as a bird while he rots, slowly but surely, until there is nothing left of him but a vague memory."

"May I inquire, sir, before you provide any more minutiae about your confession to Father Sagittarius, what your point is, so I might appreciate its relevance?" Talisman asked in a low voice, masking a growing impatience.

"Please don't interrupt him," Plotkin interceded politely. "He over-speaks when nervous. If you interrupt, it will only get worse. What I am trying to say, without trying to cause trouble, is that a little patience will go a long way."

"With the greatest of respect, sir," the chicken plucker said, "as Mr. Plotkin cogently explained, if you stop interrupting and allow me to complete my thoughts, you will eventually see the point. The end is in sight. Those in your trade don't seem to realize, unlike people in my profession, that patience is a virtue."

"Very well," the lawyer said with more than a tinge of impatience. "Please continue."

With a grateful nod, Astigmatopolous resumed his narrative. "After expressing contrition to Father Sagittarius for my role in the

crimes and the troubles I have caused Mr. Plotkin and, by extension, his father, mother, and uncles, I asked His Grace for forgiveness so I could resume eating, sleeping, drinking, bathing, and
sharing Mr. Plotkin's company without pangs of conscience. When
the Saintly Father granted me absolution for the mud-related sins,
he told me that ecclesiastical forgiveness, alone, would not be sufficient to enable me to resume life as I once knew it. He explained
that, due to certain psychological factors, which he had neither the
time nor expertise to discuss, I could expect the pangs to plague me
all the days of my sinful life unless I confess my crimes to his distant cousin, Umberto Malatesta, and beg the Prosecutor General to
permit me to testify against Mr. Plotkin. I thought that you might
comment on Father Sagittarius' advice."

Talisman ruminated for a moment, and asked, "Have you been
questioned by Malatesta, any of his minions, or a member of the
National Constabulary?"

"Not to my knowledge," the chicken plucker answered, having
less than full confidence in his ability to recall important events.

"It seems to me, with all due respect for Father Sagittarius' advice," said Talisman, "that his recommendation to confess to Malatesta is misguided. Betraying Mr. Plotkin will only add to your
guilt feelings and increase the likelihood of a conviction. In this
instance, less is more."

"Good point," said Astigmatopolous. "Anything I can do, or
not do, to avoid injuring Mr. Plotkin, I'll do, or won't do."

Touched by Astigmatopolous' loyalty, Plotkin tenderly placed
a hand on his acolyte's shoulder.

"Shall we move on, then?" asked Talisman.

"Why not," said Plotkin.

Over several frustrating hours, during which the butcher and
the chicken plucker frequently corrected or supplemented each
other's statements, the lawyer tried to unearth the facts surrounding the display window project: its genesis, the procurement of
the mud, the timing and sequence of the muddying episodes, the
methodology of applying the mud, the existence or non-existence
of any witnesses to these events, and the particulars of the arrest.
While slowly extracting the details, most of which he already knew
from reading newspaper accounts and speaking with Ana Bloom,
Talisman thought about possible legal defenses. One-by-one, he
eliminated the Six Standard Excuses: self-defense, defense of others, defense of property, duress, compulsion, and mental unhingement. When the lawmonger reached the end of his patience, he

announced that he had no further questions at this time, escorted Plotkin and Astigmatopolous to an elevator, and wished them well on their return journey.

Returning to the heavy snow and wind, the butcher and chicken plucker began an exhaustive postmortem of the day's events as they made their way from the Government and Justice District to Plotkin's tenement.

30

A few days after meeting with Leopold Plotkin, Bernard Talisman sent the following missive to Prime Thinker Guda Prikash:

> This concerns *The Republic against Plotkin*, a vexing prosecution pending in the Low Court of Criminal Transactions. Our firm represents defendant Leopold Plotkin, a butcher shop owner who allegedly violated a recently enacted statute that makes it a crime to cover a display window with mud unless the window, so covered, constitutes a Work of Art.
>
> By way of background, the client is a virtuoso of sorts, possessing cutting skills that exceed anything previously exhibited in the butchering industry. Legions came to the window to watch him cut, cleave, chop, et cetera. When Plotkin realized that most of his admirers didn't purchase his meat, he took the unprecedented step of covering the window with mud to foreclose peering. Citizens then took to the streets, demanding that he remove the mud. Editorials condemned the act and called for his prosecution. Inner Chamber Leader Cicero Bookbinder gave a speech at the site, demanding that Plotkin clean the window. When Plotkin ignored the demand and brushed additional mud on the glass, an anti-window covering statute was passed.
>
> Subsequent to the legislation, the butcher put more mud on the window. He was arrested, charged with three violations: one, for perpetuating the original mud, the others for adding mud on two separate occasions.
>
> Although Plotkin's behavior initially brought to mind an insanity defense, during an interview I realized that whatever insanity he has doesn't satisfy the rigorous standard for legal insanity because he understood the nature of his acts. I also ruled out the other traditional defenses.
>
> Last week, I visited the crime scene, hoping something there might be inspirational. Regrettably, what I found at the site was either unsettling or comical and failed to inspire me. A crowd was gathered in front of the shop burning effigies of Plotkin. Surrounded by angry men and women, I studied the window and found it aesthetically unappealing, not in the least artistic. Plot-

kin introduced me to A. I. Gopnik, an eccentric man with an inappropriate smile who claims to be a retired art curator. Mr. Gopnik is currently a patient at the Warehouse for the Purportedly Insane. The poor fellow went on at length about how the mud-encrusted window was one of the "most accomplished" paintings he had ever seen and that, if acquitted, Plotkin should devote himself, full-time, to art.

While Gopnik blathered, I concluded that he was either delusional or had been enlisted by Plotkin to lay the groundwork for a Work of Art defense. Though the client has only eight years of schooling, it is obvious that he has a clever mind. However, if he intended to plant the seed of the defense in my mind, he was too clever by half. Nobody who views the window with any degree of objectivity could conclude it is artistic.

Without troubling you with further details, suffice it to say the excursion to the butcher shop failed to inspire me. It is in this state of dismay and frustration that I reach out to you. I fear that should you fail to identify a defense I may have overlooked or rejected improvidently, the butcher will surely be convicted. It is my hope that you can devise a stratagem to avoid this outcome. Please give this matter your immediate attention. I look forward to receiving your insights in the near future.

31

D espite serious doubt that a muddy window could constitute a work of art, Guda Prikash didn't entirely dismiss the possibility. Hoping to dredge up useful precedent to support a Work of Art defense, his encyclopedic brain sorted through two centuries of High Court opinions embedded in it. Moments later, Prikash recalled the case of *Pogrebin against Pogrebin*, an obscure decision handed down in the Court's early years that defined works of art for litigation as opposed to aesthetic purposes. He cautiously opened the side door of his hermitage and squinted into the darkness to assure that no humans were in the vicinity. When certain he was alone, he made his way to the book stacks. Turning down the aisle where *Pogrebin*-era opinions were stored, he found the correct volume, returned to his cloister, and read the following:

> *This estate conflict raises a perplexing question not heretofore decided: namely, what constitutes a work of art? At the core of this dispute is a food-preparation table that the testator, Silvio Pogrebin, owned at his demise. In his will, the testator bequeathed all personal property except "works of art" to his daughter, Hortence Pogrebin, the Appellee. "Works of art" were left to the testator's son, Pavel Pogrebin, the Appellant. The issue we must determine is whether the table constitutes a work of art, as a matter of law, or is simply inartistic personal property.*
>
> *The evidence adduced at trial established that, until the testator's death, the table was situated in his mansion's pantry, having served many years as locus for preparation of family meals. When the testator expired, its top was marred with numerous cuts, holes, excavations, undulations, incisions, gashes, hollows, burn marks, singes, abrasions, and other markings.*
>
> *Appellant's expert testified that the markings were consistent with artistic expression inasmuch as they appear to depict ferocious military battles. An expert purchased by Appellee testified that the markings were no more than the random consequences of knives, choppers, forks, dishes, bowls, and pots wielded by culinary staff and cannot be said to depict anything synonymous with art.*
>
> *Lacking the wisdom of this Court, the trial judge and panel*

of intermediate appellate judges erred in finding for the Appellee. Among other things, they erroneously concluded that to qualify as a work of art for litigation purposes, an item must be nominally pleasant to behold; created by a professional or amateur artist who holds himself out as such; and the product of a medium conventionally associated with art such as paint, pastel chalk, marble, and the like. In light of these and other mistakes, We reverse and remand.

To guide the trial judge on remand and put this decades-long dispute to rest, We set forth the correct analytical framework. The logical starting point (which the lower courts inexplicably failed to consider) is Flummenbaum's Dictionary of Common Usages, the definitive authority on our language. Flummenbaum defines "work" as "a noun suggesting exertion directed to produce or accomplish something; something made or done; or the application of force acting upon a body." It denominates "art" (i.e. art of a graphic nature) as "a noun meaning the production through the rendering of images, shapes, patterns, or symbols, in a realistic or abstract format, in solid or liquid form, irrespective of commercial value or how aesthetically pleasing or displeasing the rendering may be, and without consideration of the medium used to create the object." From these definitions and exercise of common sense, this Court makes the following findings regarding the characteristics of litigational graphic art:

First, that which has been produced by exertion need not be appealing, marketable, or worthy of display. To the contrary, it can universally be regarded as appallingly ugly, yet still constitute a work of art.

Second, the person whose exertions produced the alleged "work of art" need not be an artist, hold himself out as such, or even be considered within the community-at-large as possessing artistic talent.

Third, the term "art" must be liberally construed to encompass a broad spectrum of forms, including, but not limited to, weavings, pottery, sculptures, drawings, etchings, woodcarvings, and, of course, paintings.

Fourth, the medium utilized may include such conventional artistic materials as paint, wood, clay, and marble or materials not traditionally associated with art, the enumeration of which We leave to the imagination of those who create art.

Fifth, and foremost, to qualify as a work of art, that which has been produced must depict something and the trial judge or Jury must determine whether, *in fact, there has been a <u>depiction</u>. The opinionated testimony of experts—though* not *required—will often be of consequence since laymen (whether Jurists or Jurors) frequently are incapable of detecting depictions on their own, particularly when art is abstract or minimalistic.*

Encouraged by the expansive standard established in *Pogrebin* for identifying works of art, Prikash dispatched the following memorandum to Talisman:

I may have a stratagem that affords a small glimmer of hope in the matter you recently brought to my attention regarding the mud-laden window. It derives from a High Court opinion issued in the case of Pogrebin against Pogrebin, which establishes the analytical framework for identifying works of art for legalistic purposes. A loose application of Pogrebin will allow you to argue that the glass in its current state is a Work of Art and, therefore, does not violate the anti-window covering statute. The volume containing Pogrebin is attached. I have taken the liberty of marking the relevant passages.

As you will gather from the High Court's analysis, it is of no moment that a purported artistic item is unpleasant to the eye, was not produced by a practicing artist, and consists of non-traditional constituents. Moreover, the Court has endorsed the use of experts to assist the trier of fact in ascertaining whether the item is a work of art. It seems to me that all of this operates to your client's advantage, given the opinion expressed by the aforementioned A. I. Gopnik.

While I understand why, at first blush, you might be reluctant to predicate Mr. Plotkin's defense on the opinion of this insane gentleman, I trust that on further reflection you will conclude, as I have, that the former curator's unhingement does not necessarily detract from his opinion. As I recall from my time living among people, it is widely known (and even expected) that members of the artistic community, including connoisseurs, are mentally aberrant to one degree or another, yet still enjoy considerable respect within the non-artistic world.

In closing, if you are unable to locate a sane expert to vouch for the window's artistic nature, I recommend that arrangements be made through the Warehouse for the Purportedly Insane to bring this disturbed individual to the butcher shop for reexamination of the display window as a precursor to his preparing a report attesting to its artistic bona fides. Though what he purports to have seen within the four corners of the window is likely the product of a psychosis, I believe this man represents the best hope of securing an acquittal.

ernard Talisman had arranged for A. I. Gopnik to be brought to the window to examine it. He waited anxiously on the sidewalk while Gopnik and the chicken plucker made their way through mobs of demonstrators. Accustomed to the bizarre behavior of his fellow inmates, the former curator was not intimidated by the mob. The lawyer was pleasantly surprised by how normal Gopnik looked compared to most of the demonstrators. Were it not for a strange grin on Gopnik's face, Talisman wouldn't have suspected that he was insane.

After reaching the window, Gopnik was re-introduced to Talisman and Leopold Plotkin. Grinning at the muddy glass, he asked, "Where's the painting you want me to examine?"

"You're looking at it," Talisman replied with concern, wondering how the connoisseur could have forgotten a window he had praised only a few days earlier.

"This muddy thing?" Gopnik said skeptically.

"I was under the impression that you called this a *magnificent painting* last week," said Talisman.

"You're badly mistaken, sir," said Gopnik. "I've never seen this thing before. Whether it's a painting, let alone magnificent, has not yet been determined. I recommend that you stop trying to unduly influence me. I must be above reproach and left to my own devices. In my fragile condition, I can be easily influenced. If too easily influenced, the integrity of any conclusions I arrive at will be highly questionable and my reputation as a respected curator will be irreparably damaged."

"I certainly had no intention of unduly influencing you," said Talisman defensively.

"Now that we've narrowly avoided a scandal," said Gopnik, "you and your cohorts need to back away. I require room to work. Without sufficient room, the examination will be incomplete and my reputation will be destroyed. A person in my field can never be too careful. I must be exacting, scrupulous, precise, exhaustive, and meticulous. Please back away! Give me room to work!"

Talisman, Plotkin and a gaggle of curious demonstrators backed away.

"Where's the alleged artist?" Gopnik asked when satisfied that he had sufficient room to work.

"There," said the chicken plucker, pointing to Plotkin who was holding a meat cleaver.

"This man looks like a *butcher*," Gopnik said.

"He's an artist when not selling meat," Talisman lied.

"He doesn't have an artist's bearing," Gopnik said skeptically.

"He came to art late in life," Talisman misrepresented.

"Magnifying glass, please," said Gopnik.

Talisman handed Gopnik the magnifying glass he had purchased at the curator's behest. Pressing the instrument against his inquisitive right eye, the connoisseur began a scrupulous assessment of the lower fifth of the window. As the examination of the lowest region progressed, Talisman saw that Gopnik's face was expressionless, raising concerns that the madman didn't visualize the painting he once extolled.

"What do you see?" asked Talisman, unable to contain his anxiety.

"I see that I need a ladder," Gopnik responded. Does anybody have one? Without a ladder, I can't complete my appraisal. Without a complete appraisal, this will be a waste of time."

Primo Astigmatopolous appropriated a stepladder from the butcher shop and placed it near the window. Lifting his pant legs to avoid an accidental fall, Gopnik climbed to the top rung and began to scrutinize the upper fifth of the window, progressing from right to left, then up and down, and, finally, corner to corner. After completing the upper fifth, he proceeded to the middle fifth. When finished, he returned to terra firma and made entries in a notebook. Closing the notebook, he announced stolidly, "I'm finished and ready to return to the Warehouse."

"Is it your opinion that this is a Work of Art, sir?" Talisman asked, hoping to get a sense of the expert's irrational thoughts.

"That *is* the question, isn't it?" Gopnik replied.

"Yes, it is," Talisman agreed.

"I'll have a written answer at some future time," Gopnik stated.

"When might that be?" Talisman inquired.

"It might be soon or it could be much later," Gopnik replied. "Please don't ask me to predict more precisely when it might be. I have an artistic temperament and in the fragile emotional state I am in, I can't tolerate stress. Some days, even simple tasks, like taking out the garbage, are more than my nerves can handle. It could be weeks, if not months, before I muster the emotional wherewithal to prepare a written report." Gopnick's eyelids fluttered. "On the other hand, it could be hours or days."

"Would it be too stressful, sir, before returning to the Warehouse, to tell us in a word or two whether you detected a Work of Art?" Talisman asked judiciously, not wanting to upset the man who represented the only hope for a defense verdict.

"It would," Gopnik replied nervously. "It isn't my practice to reveal findings orally. If you want an oral opinion, I recommend that you hire a hack. Otherwise, you need to leave me alone and allow my dear friend, whom I believe is either a chicken plucker or trilogist, to escort me back to the Warehouse."

"I understand," Talisman replied disingenuously, "as does my client, whose life depends on you." Talisman gestured to Plotkin standing dolefully at the shop's door.

With that, Gopnik hugged the chicken plucker to demonstrate enormous affection for his newfound friend. The chicken plucker reciprocated. Thereafter, Talisman shook both of Gopnik's hands. Plotkin did not want to offend the disgraced curator by withholding a farewell gesture, so he patted Gopnik's shoulders. After the polite social niceties ran their course, Astigmatopolous took Gopnik's elbow and announced that it was time to leave. They walked along the sidewalk toward the asylum. Demonstrators quietly observed them, wondering who the grinning man was and why he had examined the window with a magnifying glass.

33

Immediately after returning to the Warehouse, A. I. Gopnik drafted a preliminary report. In it, he described the window as "an extraordinary painting by an immensely talented artist; a creation that ushers in a new school of art." Inspired by Gopnik's findings, Bernard Talisman drafted an Exposition of Defenses, a submission required in all cases where an accused insisted on a trial rather than pleading guilty. In the Exposition, Talisman revealed that his client would be offering a defense predicated on two propositions: the statute under which Plotkin was being prosecuted "exempted works of art" and the display window was "a painting."

Prosecutor General Umberto Malatesta was appalled by what he considered outlandish contentions and filed a caustic reply. He characterized the defense as "brazenly asinine, audaciously disingenuous, wholly frivolous, entirely spurious, and categorically insane."

When the issue was joined and ripe for disposition, the matter was referred to the Low Court's Pretrial Motions Judge whose function was to decide potentially dispositive matters before a case was assigned to a Trial Judge. After reviewing *Pogrebin against Pogrebin* and hearing arguments from the competing sides, the Motions Judge held, in a one paragraph opinion:

> *Despite the patent absurdity of equating a muddy window with art, the High Court, in its infinite wisdom, has determined that whether or not a given item alleged to be artistic is so is a question of fact that must be decided at trial. Therefore, the defense's ridiculous assertion that the window is a Work of Art must be determined either by a Judge or by the butcher's peers, to wit, a jury.*

34

Wearing a dark gray bowler, charcoal gray greatcoat, off-gray serge suit, and other grayish sartorial trappings of the law-monger elite, Bernard Talisman walked resolutely toward the Low Court of Criminal Transgressions. Leopold Plotkin, limping several paces behind, wore a beret and brown gabardine suit with elbow patches, furnished by the firm to leave the impression that he was an artist as well as a butcher. Pessimistic about an acquittal, he had recently added a limp to his collection of imagined infirmities.

Plotkin's parents, uncles, Ana Bloom, the chicken plucker, and the Kimmelmen brothers were next in line. All but Bloom were draped in funeral-black clothing and shared the butcher's pessimism. A few members of the extended family followed, not far behind. They also wore black, not to mourn the anticipated verdict but to reflect the belief that the trial would cast aspersions on all Plotkins, even those with surnames other than Plotkin. Holding up the rear guard were several Jewish Deep Thinkers. As usual, they were dressed shabbily and lost in thought.

In the months preceding Jury Selection, Bernard Talisman and Prime Thinker Guda Prikash had worked assiduously to prepare the butcher's defense. They propounded interrogatories, filed motions, argued petitions, analyzed evidence, compiled exhibits, authored affidavits, drafted questions, conceived a trial strategy, and wrote, revised, and rehearsed an Opening Rant to the Jury. While Leopold Plotkin's advocates prepared, the butcher spent most of his time worrying about the impact of a conviction: his consignment to Fishgrund Penitentiary for the Already Convicted; the collapse of ABRAHAM PLOTKIN AND OTHERS KOSHER MEAT PRODUCTS; the dispersal of loved-ones to asylums for the elderly; and an array of additional painful consequences that led to sobbing bouts, fitful sleep, and a diminished appetite. Incessant worry about the bleak post-conviction future eventually took its toll on Plotkin's fictive health status, exacerbating existing hypochondria-inspired illnesses and giving rise to new ones. In addition to the limp, he imagined a partial paralysis of his upper arms.

"Look what the stress has done to his leg," his mother mumbled.

"That's nothing compared to the upper arms," his father murmured.

"What's wrong with his upper arms?" his uncles muttered.

"They don't move," Jacob Plotkin edified. "Those dogs in Purgatory made him a cripple."

The elder Plotkin's mournful recounting of his son's most recent disabilities prompted sighs from the butcher's uncles, tears from the butcher's mother, moans from the butcher, but no reaction from Talisman, Bloom, or the chicken plucker. The lone response from extended family members came from Hanna Blin, Leopold Plotkin's half-aunt, who described the limp and paralyzed arms as figments of her half-nephew's morbid imagination, a contention that set off a heated intrafamilial debate.

While the debate raged behind him, Plotkin's heart quickened when he saw what loomed ahead. Several hundred feet from where he limped was a scrum of demonstrators gathered on the Plaza of the Condemned, a public square adjacent to the Low Court, named in honor of trials that ended particularly badly for defendants. He observed people of varying sizes, genders, and ethnicities parading in the Plaza, waving anti-Plotkin placards, shouting anti-Plotkin obscenities, and raising their arms to display muddied hands—a gesture designed to remind onlookers of the butcher's criminal activities. He also saw placards containing anti-Semitic messages, such as WHAT DO YOU EXPECT FROM A KOSHER BUTCHER?

Staring at the demonstrators, the butcher's stomach churned as he inventoried the canvas of bulged eyes, twisted mouths, and flared nostrils. Despite daily exposure to acrimonious rallies near the butcher shop, Plotkin shuddered as he observed the vehemence of the activities occurring in the shadow of the Courthouse.

"They look ferocious!" whispered Meyer Mandelbrot, the aged family peacemaker. "Perhaps we should turn back!"

"We're marching into the jaws of the enemy," said the fourth cousin nobody had recognized at the bar mitzvah rehearsal, and still did not recognize.

"Who is this *interloper?*" Jacob Plotkin demanded, pointing to the distant cousin nobody knew.

"Now isn't the time to ask about *me*," said the still-unemployed college professor. "Now is the moment we must focus on our safety and turn back."

"Whoever he is," wailed Isaac Fassbinder's former mistress, "he makes sense."

"I never trusted her," said Jacob Plotkin, referring to the former mistress.

"If Papa were alive to see this, he'd turn over in his grave," said both uncles, as the mistress began to retreat.

"Wait! I'll join you!" said the relative no one recognized. Seconds later, the two walked arm in arm, bantering cheerfully, before disappearing from view.

"We're better off without them," Jacob Plotkin proclaimed. Turning his attention to the remaining relatives, he declared, "If there are any other cowards here, join the *deserters*. Only loyal family members are welcome."

Though other members of the extended family considered leaving, none did.

The noise of demonstrators and the acrimony of the familial exchanges left Plotkin light-headed. He told the chicken plucker that he feared a Major Medical Incident and dropped behind to walk with Ana Bloom. Bloom sensed a problem when she noticed that Plotkin no longer limped and that his paralyzed arms now moved. To comfort him, she grasped his elbow, and instructed him to breathe deeply.

"My son is having a Major Medical Incident!" Jacob Plotkin yelled. "He needs a doctor!"

"Your son is quite alright," said Bloom. "He's just a bit nervous. Under the circumstances, he's holding up quite well. There's no need for a doctor."

"He looks weak," said the patriarch.

"No, he looks fine, all things considered," Bloom corrected. Turning to Leopold, she said, "Try not to look so grim. Remember what Mr. Talisman told you; if you look grim, the Jury will think you're guilty. Try to project confidence."

"How can I project confidence in this outfit?" Plotkin asked, repositioning his beret with his newly mobile arm. "Maybe I shouldn't have severed ties with The Society for the Apparent Representation of Indigent Criminal-Types. Maybe Felix Bleifus wasn't as incompetent as he seemed. Some people make bad first impressions. He deserved another chance. I overreacted by letting him leave the visiting room without asking him to stay."

"Forget about Bleifus," Bloom whispered gently, seeking to avoid further agitation. "If you hadn't cut ties with him, you wouldn't have the best lawyer in the Republic on your side. Don't forget how hard Mr. Talisman has worked on your case. Nobody else would have done what he has."

"Pay no attention to the demonstrators," Bernard Talisman

commanded from his lead position, as the Plotkin's supporters drew closer to the Courthouse. Fearful but unwilling to retreat, the retinue cautiously made its way along the Plaza of the Condemned, where officers from the National Constabulary formed a porous shield around the butcher. A few constables felt conflicted by the role of protecting a person they despised, but shouted, "Let the son of a bitch through," and other words to that effect.

Flanked by his confederates, Plotkin followed Talisman to the Courthouse's main entrance as mob members attempted to snatch his beret. Once inside, the butcher resumed limping. He and his allies crossed the building's Rotunda to the soothing sounds of Milos Kafka's Opus 123 in C Minor played on a great pipe organ—a daily ritual during working hours. Reaching a bank of elevators, they boarded one and slowly ascended. Plotkin's mother rested her hand on her son's shoulder and said, "I'm sure you'll do fine. You always did well in school. Things will return to normal when this is over."

"Wishful thinking," Hanna Blin interjected. "He doesn't have a chance."

"Don't contradict my wife!" shouted Jacob Plotkin.

"Hanna's just being realistic," Mordecai Himmelfarb said.

"Keep out of this!" said Jacob Plotkin.

"This isn't the time to fight," said Meyer Mandelbrot.

"Mind your own business," the deranged uncles chimed in.

They disembarked from the lift in heated debate and navigated a hallway to hand- carved double doors bearing the inscription: COURTROOM 9.

"This is it," Bernard Talisman said soberly, opening the doors to the theatre where jury auditions in *The Republic against Plotkin* would soon begin.

"This *is* it," Plotkin thought despondently, as he bade farewell to his father, mother, twin uncles, the chicken plucker, Ana Bloom, and the other supporters who, like all citizens, were prohibited from entering the room until the proceeding was concluded and seven citizens were selected to determine the butcher's fate.

Justice Wolfgang Stifel

35

Justice Wolfgang Stifel, appointed to preside over *The Republic against Plotkin*, was revered by prosecutors for his unwavering pro-prosecution philosophy, reviled by defense attorneys for his copious lack of integrity, and despised by accused criminals for his injudicious temperament. The diminutive judge was easily perturbed, disdainful, cynical, unsociable, discourteous, rude, unprincipled, and a master at shaping trials in ways that facilitated convictions. His affinity for prosecutors was rooted in a troubled childhood on the streets of the Flat District, where crime flourished, sometimes with Stifel as its victim. Due to his small stature, he was assaulted on a recurring basis by young bullies and robbed by more mature thugs.

Animated by a compulsion to punish people like those who ruined his formative years, Stifel attended law school and, after completing his studies, secured a position in the Prosecutor General's Office. There he acquired a sterling reputation among his peers as a zealot who was willing to ignore legal niceties in the interest of securing guilty verdicts. After a decade of prosecutorial misconduct, the Republic's High Minister, who respected Stifel's single-minded pursuit of convictions at any cost, called him to the Bench. He thrived on the Bench in the years that followed, enjoying a reputation for imposing stiff sentences.

"My philosophy," he told his psychiatrist during their weekly sessions, "is that it's better for dozens of innocent scum to be unjustly convicted than for one asshole to be unfairly acquitted." In the tradition of the mind-healing arts, where silence was considered golden, the psychiatrist noted the comment in his patient's file and remained steadfastly silent.

When selected to preside over Plotkin's trial, Stifel was elated. His closest sycophants noticed a minor quickening of his gait, a slight straightening of his back, and a marginal lifting of the fog of forgetfulness that plagued him in recent years. They were pleased that a jurist with such immense biases had been chosen to superintend the proceedings.

Buoyed by congratulatory letters imploring him to follow his base instincts and do whatever was necessary to assure Plotkin's conviction, Stifel envisioned the trial as a way of establishing his legacy for generations to come. His only disappointment was that a jury, rather than he, would render the verdict; that his role would be limited to ruling in favor of the prosecution on evidentiary objections, shaping jury instructions in favor of the Republic, establishing a conviction-oriented atmosphere throughout the trial and, if all went well, sentencing Plotkin to the maximum term allowed by law.

36

"All rise!" a Bailiff brayed as Justice Stifel trundled into the Courtroom for commencement of Jury auditions. While the decrepit Jurist inched his way toward the base of the Great Bench, all rose: Leopold Plotkin and Bernard Talisman at the Accused's Table, Umberto Malatesta and his minions at the Prosecution's Table, Courtroom personnel on lower tiers of the Bench, and members of the Jury Ensemble in the Pews.

No longer capable of climbing the staircase that led to the Great Bench's summit, Stifel boarded a dumbwaiter to reach his destination. Moments later, he stepped onto the Judicial Perch, grasped its banister with both mottled hands, and cast his beady eyes on the assemblage below. The Justice was still insecure from indignities experienced during his formative years, but felt somewhat better about himself as he noted each lowered head, bent knee, and other manifestations of obeisance emanating from the gathered. He allowed himself a few extra moments of adulation before stepping back and disappearing into his chair.

"Sit and listen!" the Bailiff wailed. "God save this Court, the Republic, and anything else worth saving!"

"It is now time to commence Jury auditions in *The Republic against Plotkin*," Stifel's disembodied voice intoned imperiously from his seated position. "So that even the most judicially ignorant in the Ensemble may understand, it is now time to select seven legalistically untrained persons from this ill-equipped troupe to decide the fate of Leopold Plotkin, a butcher charged with Crimes against the Republic. The accused will now stand and display himself."

Squeamish about displaying himself in public, Plotkin slowly stood and turned toward the Pews to face the Ensemble. He was met with hostile glares and mouths contorted in anger. Standing inert next to Bernard Talisman, quivering hands hidden in the pockets of his borrowed suit trousers, the butcher stared expressionless at the prospective Jurors, hoping he wouldn't have to stand throughout the auditions.

Stifel expectorated into a spittoon strategically located at the base of his chair for ready access. Following a series of full-throated expectorations, he began his preliminary remarks.

"This unfortunate situation—the need to select a group of feck-less laymen such as yourselves to adjudicate the guilt or innocence of the alleged reprobate standing before you—exists because the accused has insisted on a trial by Jury," the Jurist decried. "As a result, instead of having a highly educated, experienced, and er-udite officer of the law distinguish truth from fiction, right from wrong, and pretext from subtext, a group of seven unqualified, uninformed people will be performing these functions. For rea-sons too obvious to require mentioning, the defendant has elected to leave the ultimate determination of guilt or innocence to seven *virginal* fact finders. This highly regrettable situation, one that our Founding Fathers authorized, is counterintuitive, counterproduc-tive, and inconsiderate. More to the point, it is ridiculous. Allowing criminal-types to insist that untrained novices, such as yourselves, render the ultimate decision, rather than leave that function where it rightly belongs—with a robed professional like myself—defies logic."

While members of the Ensemble wondered how the Found-ing Fathers could have made such an egregious mistake, Stifel said peevishly: "Under the *Jury Selection Protocol*, the winnowing of fifty legalistically ill-equipped fools in your ranks to seven ignoramuses for empanelment unfolds in two Stages. In Stage One, each side has an unlimited right to banish tainted Ensemblers for Gross Unfit-ness to Serve. This requires proof that a prospective Juror, before hearing any evidence, has formed an *inalterable opinion* that the ac-cused is guilty—an opinion so *firm* that nothing he may hear or see once trial begins could *conceivably* change it. If the Court agrees—in the exercise of its vast discretion—that an Ensembler's mind is *en-tirely* and *irrevocably* closed to the possibility of innocence, he will be purged. On the other hand, if the Court concludes that an En-sembler's mind is closed, but not *irrevocably so*, he will be deemed *merely unfit* and permitted to remain in the Jury pool for Stage Two."

The prospective Jurors, curious to discover who among them might be grossly unfit or merely unfit, scanned the Pews in search of telltale signs. Plotkin also eyed the assemblage, unsure of what to look for but willing to make some assumptions. He deduced from the rows of scowling faces glaring back at him that the entire Ensemble had an inalterable belief that he was guilty and conclud-ed that possibly the whole collection should be disqualified. Pros-ecutor General Umberto Malatesta also perused the angry visages and concluded that all was well.

"What is Stage Two? You should be asking now if you have

any sense," Stifel scoffed. "It is a tedious exercise where both sides expel auditioners for no expressed reason. Seven of the survivors will then be selected, three each by the respective sides and one by mutual agreement, to form the Jury that will *usurp* this Court's adjudicatory authority."

Following several additional complaints that his power to decide was being expropriated, the Judge boarded the dumbwaiter and left the Courtroom for his first recuperative in-chambers nap of the day; a hiatus that could last an hour or more.

37

After returning to the Courtroom, Justice Stifel launched Stage One of the purging process. He posed three questions to Ensemble members: Were they "familiar" with the facts associated with Plotkin's alleged crimes; if so, had they already formed a "firm belief" that Plotkin was guilty; and if they firmly believed Plotkin was guilty, could they "temporarily set aside the belief until hearing some evidence."

Because the citizens auditioning for Plotkin's Jury coveted the opportunity to participate in the butcher's conviction, all but one of them lied. Some misrepresented that they knew little or nothing about the underlying facts. Others said their beliefs in Plotkin's guilt were less than firm or firm but not irrevocable when, in reality, the beliefs were calcified and not subject to change. Several disingenuously said they could suspend their beliefs until hearing some of the evidence.

The only person who said that his mind was "irrevocably closed" about Plotkin's guilt was Yitzhak Lepidus, a once-revered Talmudic scholar who had retired from the profession after losing a series of debates to Plotkin. Humiliated by the defeats, he hated the butcher. Bernard Talisman asked for an opportunity to question the former Talmudic scholar at sidebar, a right guaranteed by the *Jury Selection Protocol*. Having no choice, Stifel reluctantly granted Talisman's request.

Talisman turned toward Lepidus, who was sandwiched between him and Umberto Malatesta, and asked, "How long have you known Mr. Plotkin?"

"Time is relative, as are many other things in this enigmatic world," Lepidus replied bitterly. "I have known him much longer than anyone should have to know a person like him. Let me leave it at that. I don't care to be any more specific."

"Thank you," said Talisman, unconcerned that the prospective Juror declined to be more specific.

"And thank *you*," Lepidus replied, "for not pressing me on the subject of how long I have known him. It is still painful for me to think about him. They say time heals all wounds. In this instance, time has had no effect on my wounds. My wounds, most of which are psychological, are still open, like festering sores. As long as the wounds continue to fester, I cannot possibly pinpoint exactly how long I have known the man. However long I have known him, I have despised him with every pore of my heavily-mottled skin."

Malatesta, a surprisingly squeamish person for a prosecutor, shuddered as he imagined open, festering sores on a wide swath of wrinkled skin. Talisman was unaffected by the image depicted by the retired scholar and resumed his interrogation.

"As a result of knowing my client for however long you have known him, sir, and due to the various open sores you attribute to him, would it be fair to say that you harbor enormous ill will toward the accused or, as a biblical scholar such as yourself might say, a considerable amount of *wrath* with respect to him?" Talisman proposed.

"Yes, it would be fair to say that," Lepidus answered. "However, it would be fairer to say that I *despise* him, in the biblical sense of the word. Though we are taught not to hate or to harbor jealousy against our fellow man, I found it impossible in this instance not to hate or harbor jealousy against your client. As a result, I withdrew from the Talmudic Debating Society and discontinued attending shul."

"Would it also be fair to say, sir, that as a result of the hatred you feel toward my client, you would vote to convict him regardless of the evidence elicited at trial?"

"Yes, it would be fair to say that. However, it would be fairer to say that I would vote to convict him even before the trial begins."

"In light of your deeply-rooted hatred of the accused and willingness to convict him without the benefit of a trial, sir, is it also fair to say that it is not *conceivably possible* that you can keep your mind even *slightly* open regarding the accused's guilt or innocence until the commencement of trial, let alone the introduction of evidence?"

"From an existential standpoint," Lepidus replied, "virtually anything is *conceivably possible*. However, from a practical perspective, there is no degree of possibility that I can manage to keep my mind open in this instance because of the overwhelming disgust I hold for the man you are representing."

Confident that the retired scholar's testimony established the prerequisites of Gross Unfitness to Serve, Talisman looked up to Stifel and said, "Your Honor, the defense respectfully moves to eliminate this individual from the Ensemble."

"And what facts do you believe would justify such an extreme measure?" the Jurist asked with feigned consternation.

"Your Honor," Talisman replied with great restraint, "as exhibited by this good man's *unequivocal admission* that he would vote to convict my client even before the trial begins, and acknowledgment that there is no practical possibility that he could vote to acquit Mr. Plotkin, it seems self-evident that this individual cannot *conceivably* keep an open mind regarding Mr. Plotkin's possible innocence and is, therefore, *grossly unfit to serve.*"

"It may seem self-evident to *you*," Stifel stated acerbically, "but it is certainly not to *me*. This man has admitted the existential possibility that he could change his mind. Therefore, the motion is denied and you will take your seat next to the accused."

Talisman was appalled by the Court's ruling but, careful not to react to it, he thanked Stifel for the adverse decision and calmly returned to the Accused's Table. Stifel announced that it was time for another intermission and that after his return, the final phase of the winnowing process—Expulsion For No Stated Reason—would begin.

The Jury

38

Lawyers who represented wealthy criminal-types often retained Disgorgers to assist in determining which Stage One survivors to strike. Steeped in the science of physiognomy, Disgorgers didn't rely on intuition. Instead, they focused on body type, posture, skin pigment, hair density, hand size, neck length, head shape, nasal configuration, and other such things to predict how a Jury candidate might vote.

Bernard Talisman secured the services of Gunter Spigelgass for this purpose. Aware that most Republicans despised Plotkin, Spigelgass sought to lower Talisman's expectations by telling the lawyer that the best he could do would be to eliminate the most hostile of the haters. "To hope for more is unrealistic," he said.

Gunter Spigelgass was seated at the Accused's table when Justice Stifel returned from the intermission and announced the commencement of Stage Two. Almost immediately, Talisman exercised his first strike, eliminating Yitzhak Lepidus from the Ensemble. After Talisman struck the former Talmudic scholar, Spigelgass left his chair and walked up the aisle of the Spectator Pews to study the profiles of the auditioners. His eyes darted back and forth, meticulously assessing countless nostrils, eyebrows, ear lobes, and other features of significance. At his behest, the entire Ensemble stood and rotated their bodies so he could observe them both frontwards and backwards.

Over the course of several hours, Talisman, in collaboration with Spigelgass, methodically designated Juror aspirants for elimination. When it was his turn, Malatesta chose at random, often without bothering to look at the Ensemble.

Among the Talisman-Spigelgass casualties were a studious-looking man with unusually long fingers (a trait Spigelgass identified as reflecting an extreme pro-prosecution proclivity); a man with exceptionally poor posture (which Spigelgass believed evinced an inability to resist peer pressure); an impeccably dressed man (a strong indication, according to Spigelgass, that he was hostile to mud); a few excessively thin individuals (indicative that they were probably vegetarians and likely to be repelled by a purveyor of meat); several men with no discernible chins (suggesting a weak will and lack of resolve to resist the pressure to convict); and a man with permanently raised eyebrows (indicative that he was too skeptical to accept the proposition that the window constituted a painting).

When the process of elimination ended, seven auditioners were selected for empanelment. Stifel grudgingly congratulated them for being designated to perform "the most important civic function in the Republic; the unique opportunity to sit in judgment of another human being and exact *retribution* on behalf of the state."

A Bailiff ushered the Jurors into their Stall and administered the Oath. Reduced to its essence, the Oath required them to follow the dictates of the judge, no matter how arbitrary or irrational they seem; to avoid a miscarriage of justice regardless of how enticing a miscarriage might seem; and to set aside any strong and settled biases they may have against the accused or criminals per se for as long as possible, hopefully until the receipt of most, if not all, of the evidence.

Closely studying the Jurors as they took the Oath, Leopold Plotkin found something unsettling about each. The fish-shaped mouth of Juror No. 4 disquieted him, as did the poorly constructed toupee of Juror No. 6, the triple chins of Juror No. 2, the anteater-like nose of Juror No. 3, the age of the octogenarian seated as Juror No. 5, the prominent nasal moles of Juror No. 7, and the furtive eyes in the oblong face of Juror No. 1. More troubling still was the presence of mud on the hands of several of the designated Deciders, a reality that caused him to infer that they had participated in the demonstrations outside the Courthouse.

39

"**B**efore the attorneys' Opening Rants," Justice Stifel announced gravely, "the Court will deliver its Sermon. Listen with your untrained ears. Absorb with your limited minds. Try to comprehend a small portion of what is said, despite your intellectual shortcomings. Otherwise, this will be a terrible waste of judicial resources, an intolerable expenditure of wasted effort on a collection of misfits who are not up to the task!"

The Jurors nodded courteously after each of Stifel's disparagements. Plotkin wondered why the Jurors seemed to appreciate the discourtesies. He attributed their reaction either to a lack of self-esteem or a failure to understand what Stifel was saying, neither of which he thought bode well for any chance of an acquittal.

"Unfortunately, it will be left to you, not the Court, to decide whether the accused committed Abominable Crimes against the Republic," Stifel muttered again with disappointment. "This is because Leopold Plotkin has opted for a trial by a jury of his feckless peers rather than a trial by judge trained in the law, a disturbing scenario that defies both logic and common sense."

Stifel heaved a sigh to exhibit frustration. The Jurors smiled appreciatively.

"Under the Republic's *Rule of Law* paradigm," he continued, "even obviously guilty rabble must be treated as *technically* innocent until *formally* convicted. For this reason, a trial must *precede* conviction, not the other way around. Were this a perfect world, a more direct and efficient route would be taken...to wit...conviction, then trial."

Several heads bobbed in the Jury Stall to reflect agreement with the proposition that the better approach would be to convict first, then proceed with the formality of a trial. The Jury's reaction troubled Plotkin, who believed that having a trial first was the better approach. He looked at Talisman to see whether the lawyer was also disturbed by Stifel's preference for a verdict-first approach and the Jury's agreement with it. As always, Talisman's face was inscrutable. In some way, the lawyer's unflappability offered the butcher a degree of comfort. Perhaps the lack of reaction signified that Stifel's preferred approach hadn't infected the Jury.

"In our system," Stifel growled, "an accused may be convicted only if the prosecution shows 'beyond a Nagging Doubt' that he committed the crime in question. Even for those few of you who aren't abysmally stupid, Nagging Doubt is a difficult concept to grasp. This is because what *nags* one person doesn't necessarily *nag* another; what is one person's *doubt* is another's belief; and what is *beyond* to one individual has *not yet reached* for another."

Stifel expounded further in a minimalist effort to address the concept. "To one degree or other," he lectured, "all of you are human and, therefore, experience doubt in your mundane lives. Some doubt is to be expected as you struggle to survive in the societal jungle, riddled with sophisticated lies, rampant dissembling, and gross exaggerations, all of which make you barely better than apes. Without occasional doubt, you would not be what you are—imperfect, flawed, sinful, and superficial. Doubt is not something to fear. Nor is it something to be overly concerned about...unless it paralyzes you and leaves you unable to decide."

The Justice moved his hamster-like tongue over his crooked front teeth in a polishing motion. While polishing, he gathered from the Jurors' blank stares that they were having difficulty grasping the Nagging Doubt calculus. With no reason to believe that further elucidation would make a difference, he skipped to the next item on his agenda.

"During this trial, witnesses will be called to testify. As in life, some may tell the unvarnished truth. Others may offer quarter or half-truths. Several may exaggerate, conveniently forget, or altogether lie. Because the law assumes that you have had first-hand experience with liars and persons with impaired or selective memories, it is left to each of you to determine whether you are being lied to, told something by a well-intentioned person with a flawed memory, heard from a truthful person with good recollection, or some combination thereof."

Stifel sipped water to irrigate his throat, a narrow passageway that parched easily. While he drank, politicians in the Dignitaries Section of the Spectator Pews squirmed uncomfortably, fearing that the references to lies and liars might cause some to look disdainfully in their direction.

Once Stifel's throat was irrigated, he resumed his instructions. "To avoid mindlessly soaking-in testimony like the inert sponges you naturally are, you should endeavor to use common sense, in the event you have any, and try to decide whether a witness is worthy of belief. Discard the unworthy and embrace the worthwhile, and so on and so forth."

Plotkin could see the Jurors struggling to comprehend Stifel's vague instructions. The only member who seemed to understand the instructions was the octogenarian. Moreover, unlike his peers, the old man refrained from nodding in agreement with every utterance and insult. Instead, he seemed bemused by Stifel's lack of judicial restraint or respect for the Deciders. This seemed to offer the butcher a glimmer of hope. Perhaps there was one Juror who was not an inert sponge; an independent thinker who would resist a rush to judgment.

Stifel's mind drifted. "Where was I?" he called down to the Courtroom Scrivener.

"You just completed the Inert Sponge Analogy," the Scrivener called up from the second tier of the Great Bench.

"Very well," Stifel sighed.

Aware that his energy was waning, he sniffed a box of smelling salts kept on his Perch for such occasions and barked a series of asides. "The Court reminds you of your overarching responsibilities as the Deciders to attempt to keep a *somewhat* open mind about the accused's guilt for as long as feasible and to avoid a premature determination. Though it is difficult to keep a mind somewhat open for any appreciable length of time—particularly in a criminal case involving alleged *heinous acts* that may threaten the Republic—you must strive to do so if the *appearance of justice*, the central fiction of our adjudicatory apparatus, is to have any meaning."

Bernard Talisman bristled at Stifel's reference to the *appearance* of justice. Like a few of his more liberal colleagues, he believed that *actual* justice should be required by the Constitution. He hoped that someday, a majority of the High Court of Final Supplications would adopt that enlightened position.

Stifel paused to expectorate into his spittoon. Once rid of the phlegm, he turned to the next item on the agenda. "If you have the capacity and predilection to read newspapers," he said, "you may not do so before rendering a verdict. This admonition is primarily based on the fact that there is no practical reason to read about a trial you are attending."

Because none of the Jury members was interested in reading about the trial, they weren't disappointed by the admonition.

"On a *minor* matter," Stifel continued, "you may not discuss these proceedings among yourselves prior to entering the Deliberation Room to render a verdict. Once inside, you will have ample opportunity to chat about this case—whether before or after reaching a decision. Some juries prefer to discuss the facts before issuing a verdict, others afterward or never. Should you bother to discuss, it needn't be in depth. Having observed your vacuous expressions, the Court assumes that any discussion you might choose to engage in will be brief and superficial."

At that juncture, having no appetite to say more, the Judge announced that the time had come for the competing sides to deliver their Opening Rants.

40

Four hours into his prolix Rant, Umberto Malatesta thanked the Jurors for their "obvious appreciation" of his performance and proudly sauntered back to his minions. He was pleased that he had parroted his subordinates' lines with only a few minor mistakes and convinced that he had mortally wounded Plotkin. Justice Stifel thanked Malatesta for his *concise* summary and cautioned Bernard Talisman against *verbosity*. "Follow the Prosecutor General's example," the Judge admonished. "The less said the better."

Talisman rose, undaunted by Stifel's hypocrisy. He genuflected politely toward the Great Bench, bowed courteously to the Prosecutor General, nodded amiably to the Jury, and nearly vomited.

Talisman had become nauseous toward the end of Malatesta's presentation. Now that he stood, he felt dizzy. Stoic by nature, he didn't ask for a recess. Instead, he positioned himself behind Leopold Plotkin, grasped the back of Plotkin's chair, and waded into the Rant.

"Gentlemen of the...Jury," he moaned between deep breaths. "The man I stand behind, both literally and figuratively....has been derided by my hyperbolic...adversary as a repulsive reprobate, a malignant growth, a pustule, a fiend, and...a degenerate. In truth, he is none of these things. Instead, he is an obedient...son to his elderly father; a generous child to his infirm mother; a selfless caretaker...to his emotionally impaired...uncles; and a butcher whose unparalleled meat-cutting skills were once...were once...revered."

The lawmonger paused to retch, causing uneasiness in the pit of Plotkin's stomach. The butcher assumed that the man on whose shoulders his future rested was either a poor public speaker or, more generally, incompetent. The butcher's father whispered to the deranged uncles that his son's lawyer was "tongue-tied" and Ana Bloom worried that the love of her life might be experiencing aphasia as a result of a transient stroke. At the Prosecution's Table, there was palpable relief that the adversary was proving to be mediocre. They had not expected such an easy match.

The nauseous lawyer inhaled slowly and declared, "Like most of us, my client bleeds when cut; cries when sad; and sleeps when... tired."

Recognizing the difficulty of seducing Jurors from the distance of the Accused's Table, the lawyer abandoned the security of Plotkin's chair and shuffled unsteadily toward the Jury Stall. Fearing that he might purge before arriving, he reached under his robe for a handkerchief. After securing it, he placed it over his mouth and crossed the Courtroom Well in short, rubbery steps.

Reaction to his unorthodox gait varied. Jurors were intimidated. Justice Stifel was bemused. Malatesta was elated. Courtroom personnel were puzzled. The chicken plucker was nonplussed. The Plotkin elders were confused. Myra Rabinowitz-Pritzker was concerned. Cicero Bookbinder and the High Minister were pleased. Other onlookers were disquieted or delighted—depending on their allegiance.

Talisman managed to reach the Stall without incident. Grasping its railing, he steadied himself. "For most of his adult life," Talisman said, "Mr. Plotkin labored in obscurity…in an unprofitable butcher shop situated on the fringe of the Small Business District. As he entered middle-age, he perfected unique…butchering skills never previously seen in the Republic. It was then that his problems began. Pedestrians soon noticed his novel cuts and cleaves… and stopped to look through the display window as he worked. His surgically precise hand movements, fluid pirouettes, and overall flamboyance…astonished them. They believed his performances rivaled the City's finest opera…and ballet productions. They registered their approval with…applause, rose-throwing, and other acts of adulation."

Talisman's head throbbed. His chest tightened. Resisting the temptation to end the Rant prematurely, he gasped for air. Lacking sufficient air, he squealed, "Word of Mr. Plotkin's…virtuosic exhibitions…spread, drawing hordes of men, women, and children to the window. Citizens from the four corners of the Republic…made pilgrimages to the shop…to pay homage."

Members of the audience and several Jurors, appalled by the unpleasant rasp of Talisman's voice, covered their ears. As Talisman's breathing became more labored, his voice acquired an even more unpleasant, nasal quality. Simultaneously, his ribs began to ache. Massive pools of perspiration emerged on his neck, chest, and lower back. Growing progressively weaker, he leaned against the Jury Stall's railing. As he continued to deteriorate before their eyes, Jurors wondered why a man so frightened to speak in public had agreed to participate in such a prominent trial.

Talisman plodded on. He managed to string a few fitful words together to portray Plotkin as victim rather than villain. Before long, he began to speak ungrammatically. In the middle of a particularly mangled sentence, he fell silent and collapsed.

Pandemonium erupted. Shocked by the collapse of her paramour, Ana Bloom left the Spectator Pews, rushed to Talisman's side, and cradled him in her arms. Overcoming a brief pang of jealously, Plotkin rushed to Talisman's other side and listened for a heartbeat. Outraged by the display of the defendant attending to his fallen adversary, Umberto Malatesta leaped to his feet to demand a mistrial. In the oral motion, he accused Talisman of feigning illness and the butcher of pretending to render compassionate emergency services to curry sympathy with the Jurors.

Unwilling to subject himself to another round of tedious Jury auditions, Justice Stifel denied the motion. He was thoroughly insulted by the pandemonium, and immediately ordered Bailiffs to clear the venue of *rubble*. With a degree of order restored, a physician on trial for medical malpractice in another courtroom was summoned. The incompetent physician gave Talisman a cursory examination and opined that the prostrate attorney was probably sick. Placing smelling salts under Talisman's nostrils, the doctor succeeded in awakening him. Bloom continued to cradle the fallen lawmonger with one arm and massaged his neck with the other. While still on his back, Talisman regained consciousness, looked heavenward, and in a labored voice asked Stifel for a brief postponement. Stifel, who required counsel to stand when addressing him, denied the motion because Talisman hadn't complied with his rules. Ascertaining from a courtroom clock that it was too late in the day to begin the evidentiary phase of the trial, the Justice announced that testimony would begin the next morning, with or without Talisman's presence.

41

In the hours following Bernard Talisman's admission to Our Lady of the Albatross Hospital, staff gauged his body temperature, analyzed his blood, evaluated his urine, examined his stool, studied his ears, and cultured his throat. He was poked, palpated, probed, needled, reflexed, turned, rotated, sat-up, sat-down, told to remain still, and urged to move. Physicians discussed exploring his spleen, heart, kidneys, intestines, and lungs.

Due to Talisman's wealth and professional status, he was housed in a private room rather than on a ward. Three of his partners—Steinbloom, Rogoff, and Babel—hovered over his bed as Talisman thrashed about and mumbled incoherently. Noting that the mumbles made oblique references to Guda Prikash, the partners enlisted a nurse to interpret what he was saying. According to the nurse's translation, Talisman was claiming that Guda Prikash was the only one in the firm who knew the case well enough to carry on, and must be enlisted to take his place. The partners tried to reason with him, pointing to the Prime Thinker's phobic fear of public places and lack of trial experience as disqualifying factors. When Talisman continued shrieking Prikash's name, Steinbloom, Rogoff, and Babel reluctantly agreed to undertake the quixotic mission of enlisting Prikash in order to calm their partner's nerves. Before the partners left to contact Prikash, the nurse provided them with the name of Bartok Golub, a psychiatrist who specialized in treating most major social phobias.

At the time Steinbloom knocked on the door of Prikash's basement hermitage, the Prime Thinker was drafting a memorandum of understanding that only he entirely understood. The room was in its normal state of disrepair. Discarded drafts were strewn on the floor. Law books and used clothing littered his unmade bed. Dishes were piled haphazardly in the sink. Thick layers of cigarette smoke hung in the air.

Babel had tapped gently on the door to avoid alarming Prikash. He told Prikash that he, Rogoff, and Steinbloom had come to confer about an urgent matter. Unnerved by the intrusion, Prikash asked what the urgent matter concerned. Babel said it was too sensitive to discuss through a door and asked to be admitted. Not wanting to argue the point, Prikash let them in.

The Prime Thinker felt uneasy that three men had invaded his refuge. He lit two cigarettes in an effort to calm his nerves. While Prikash puffed, Babel described Talisman's untimely illness, Justice Stifel's refusal to postpone the trial, and their fallen partner's belief that Prikash was the only member of the firm capable of trying the case.

Anticipating what Babel was about to ask him, Prikash preemptively rejected the request and reminded the intruders of his aversion to public places. Undeterred, Babel opined that Prikash's prodigious mind could overcome the phobia through the sheer force of intellect. Prikash countered that his intellect had its own limitations. Steinbloom took over when he sensed that Babel was failing in the attempt to persuade Prikash to replace Talisman. In a thinly disguised appeal to Prikash's conscience, Steinbloom argued that withholding the Prime Thinker's services would deprive Leopold Plotkin of a fair trial and inevitably lead to a conviction. Prikash reminded Steinbloom that he had never tried a case and that serving as Plotkin's counsel would even more inevitably result in a guilty verdict. Convinced that further efforts to entice Prikash to try the case through rational discussion would be futile, the partners retreated to the firm's conference room, where Rogoff telephoned Dr. Golub and arranged for the psychiatrist to come to the law office that evening.

When the partners met the mind healer in person, they were struck by his slovenly appearance. Golub's unkempt hair, unruly beard, and wrinkled suit were eerily reminiscent of Prikash, as was the odor of stale cigarette smoke embedded in his overcoat. They realized that Golub was their only viable option to secure the Prime Thinker's trial services, and overlooked his grooming shortcomings as they greeted him effusively. Clutching his elbows, they led the psychiatrist to the conference room, where they summarized the nature of Prikash's phobias and explained why it was critical to cure him without delay. When Golub felt satisfied that he knew enough about the situation to treat the patient, he said guardedly, "It is likely, but far from a certainty, that the underlying pathology will subside to one degree or another following hypnosis, either for the short, medium, or long-term. After treatment, he may be capable of functioning in a trial setting either proficiently or marginally, depending on the variables, which are numerous but not altogether all-encompassing."

Without understanding any part of Bartok Golub's prognosis, the partners escorted him to Prikash's sanctuary. Once admitted,

Steinbloom introduced him as a prominent, medically ordained psycho-hypnotherapist who specialized in treating irrational fears of public places and other phobic disorders. Prikash stated that he was at peace with his phobias and had no wish to be cured. Steinbloom further explained that Golub had been roused from his sleep to treat him. The selflessness of the psycho-hypnotherapist's dedication persuaded the Prime Thinker to listen to what he recommended.

As Golub expounded on his professional bona fides and regaled Prikash with case histories of successful therapeutic outcomes, Prikash was impressed by the psychiatrist's disheveled appearance and felt at ease with the stranger who reminded him of himself. Despite the amazement of experiencing this rare connection with another human being, he reiterated that he was comfortable with his phobias and wished to maintain the status quo. Golub was accustomed to such resistance. He pivoted easily to identify many things the Prime Thinker had missed out on due to his reclusive existence: strolls through parks, the scents of flowers, the company of women, the luminescence of summer skies, the sounds of musical instruments, plays, communal baths, and other activities. The recitation of sights unseen and opportunities missed eventually convinced Prikash to take another approach. He agreed to participate in an experiment he assumed would fail, telling Golub, "If this doesn't work, I wish to be left alone."

With Guda Prikash's capitulation, Bartok Golub reached into his medicine bag and removed a miniature gold-plated pen. Directing the hermit to lie face up on the unmade bed, he positioned the Prime Thinker's skull at a right angle to the headboard, and placed the tip of the pen inches from the end of Prikash's considerable nose. Through a series of imperceptible wrist movements, the psycho-hypnotherapist caused the pen to move slightly. Golub next instructed Prikash to concentrate on the tip of the pen and to count backward from three hundred, in increments of six, until losing consciousness. In a matter of moments, Prikash's crossed eyes closed tightly and he descended into a deep slumber.

While Prikash slept, Golub prepared him for the role of Plotkin's substitute counsel through a series of post-hypnotic suggestions. Pressing his lips against Prikash's left ear lobe, he told the patient to think of himself not as a Prime Thinker but as a skilled litigator who thrived in the courtroom; as an incisive cross-examiner who was capable of improvising at the spur of the moment; and as an exceptional orator who addressed juries without relying on notes.

Golub suggested that Prikash had participated in hundreds of trials and enjoyed enormous successes, particularly in cases decided by juries involving artistic issues. After the psychiatrist completed summarizing Prikash's fictionalized history as a prolific trialmonger, Babel described the interior of the Courtroom; pinpointed Justice Stifel's judicial philosophy; read aloud sections of the *Uniform Rules of Procedure* that were likely to be of relevance during the trial; detailed proper grammatical constructs for posing questions to witnesses; and emphasized that Prikash was an extrovert who preferred the society of people, particularly juries, to solitude.

When the partners were satisfied Prikash was prepared to assume stewardship of Plotkin's defense, Golub told the Prime Thinker that he would be awakened by a soft handclap and that after awakening, he would remember nothing that occurred that evening. "Avoid places where raucous, sustained applause is likely to occur or you will revert to your reclusive ways," Golub cautioned the sleeping phobic.

Looking down at Prikash, the psycho-hypnotherapist quietly gave a single clap of his hands. As the Prime Thinker's eyelids fluttered, Golub and the three lawyers left the hovel. Moments later, Prikash heard knocking on the hovel's door. He got out of bed and invited the partners inside with a natural warmth and enthusiasm.

Designated to speak, Steinbloom said grimly, "During his opening oration today in the Plotkin trial, Mr. Talisman collapsed. He is hospitalized and unable to continue. The presiding judge refuses to postpone the proceedings. Instead, he insists that substitute counsel be ready to proceed tomorrow morning. As a result, there's an urgent need to___."

"I would be honored to step in," Prikash interrupted enthusiastically.

"You would?" Rogoff asked with a tinge of skepticism. Until then, he had doubted the efficacy of hypnosis on a brilliant, strong-willed subject.

"Certainly," Prikash confirmed ebulliently. "If I may be frank, I was disappointed that Mr. Talisman didn't ask me to second-chair him. Although I am sorry, of course, to hear that he's ill, I'm elated to have the opportunity to try the case. As you know, gentlemen, it's in the courtroom where I experience my greatest challenges and pleasure."

"And where you have had enormous success," Steinbloom effused.

The partners took solace in Prikash's new litigational outlook, but not his current physical appearance. With that in mind, they arranged for him to be groomed. In short order, they had his hair cut, beard trimmed, and nails manicured. After a series of baths, the partners fitted him in a robe, a trial wig, and dress shoes. Later that night, Prikash was relocated to the guest wing of the Talisman estate and placed under the supervision of Talisman's half-sister, Myra Rabinowitz-Pritzker. They cautioned her to be sure he wasn't exposed to any loud applause for the duration of the trial and was well fed.

Guda Prikash Repurposed

42

Wearing the donated robe, wig, and other clothing provided by the firm, Guda Prikash strode into the Courtroom for the first day of testimony. He walked down the central aisle, calm, resolute, and delighted to find the Spectator Pews filled to capacity. Heads turned. Curious eyes darted in his direction. Lips moved. Prikash attributed the spectators' reactions to their awareness that a seasoned trial attorney had entered the fray. Acknowledging the ostensible admirers, he doffed his wig.

Dr. Bartok Golub sat in the Pews, studying the Prime Thinker. Retained by the firm to monitor Prikash and attend to him if he relapsed, Golub was satisfied with Prikash's behavior so far. The recluse's gait was proud. His demeanor seemed to be within normal range. Carrying a borrowed briefcase with the élan of a lawyer who had lugged legal documents his entire professional life, Prikash manifested the air of confidence instilled in him the night before. All seemed clinically appropriate to the psychiatrist.

As Prikash entered the Courtroom, the Well was bustling with activity. The Scrivener stood at the first level of the Great Bench reviewing entries in the *Journal of Proceedings* from the day before. Ushers darted around the room, filling water glasses. Bailiffs worked at dusting Justice Stifel's chair. Umberto Malatesta was conferring at the Prosecution's Table with his minions. The Courtroom Crier was practicing the commands he delivered at the opening of each trial day.

Amidst this activity, Prikash strode toward the Accused's Table, eyeing the Prosecution's Table, the Great Bench, the Flag of the Republic, the Witness Closet, and the Jury Stall—all of which seemed familiar due to Babel's vivid descriptions during the psycho-hypnosis session. Delighted to be where he imagined he had been many times before, Prikash was radiant as he joined the seated butcher. He had been introduced to Plotkin earlier that morning. During the brief encounter, he managed to allay most of the butcher's concerns, assuring him that he was well-prepared, enjoyed excellent health, expected to complete the trial unscathed by illness, and was accustomed to trying cases on short notice.

As Prikash was about to sit, the Crier ordered everyone to stand. The door connecting Justice Stifel's Chambers to the Courtroom burst open. Surrounded by a coterie of Bailiffs, Stifel stepped into the Well, boarded the dumbwaiter, exited on the Judicial Perch, and glared down from on high while Prikash, Malatesta, and the Prosecutor General's minions genuflected. When satisfied with the intensity of the genuflections, the Jurist sat and receded from view. Soon thereafter, a Bailiff herded Jurors into their Stall.

The Justice then said with great solemnity, "Members of the Jury, have you reached a verdict?"

Since no testimony had been elicited or evidence adduced yet, the Courtroom erupted in confusion. Leopold Plotkin complained to Prikash that he hadn't received a fair trial. Guda Prikash rose to demand a mistrial. Umberto Malatesta remained seated and gasped. Bailiffs called for order. Spectators stirred. Jacob Plotkin moaned. Plotkin's mother sobbed. Extended family members shuddered. Representatives of the Women's Association called for Stifel's impeachment. The head of a contingent of prison guards readied his men to shackle Plotkin the moment the guilty verdict was announced. Cicero Bookbinder marveled at the genius of the Jury system. Jurors frantically huddled in the Stall to formulate a response to the Judge's inquiry as to whether they had reached a verdict.

The Scrivener had reviewed the *Journal of Proceedings* only moments earlier, and thought that Stifel's question was somewhat premature. Based on that assumption, he mounted the stairway to the Judicial Perch and, breathing heavily, asked, "May I make a slight observation, Your Honor?"

"Now is not the time to observe!" Stifel scolded sourly. "The Jury is about to render its verdict. Return to your station!"

Willing to endure Stifel's ire in order to protect him from a serious memory-related *faux pas*, the Scrivener whispered, "It appears that Your Eminence is requesting a verdict before testimony has begun. I believe the Court will agree this is a bit out of the ordinary, even in a case whose outcome is too obvious to require testimony. Perhaps the Court might wish to reconsider and withdraw the question."

"I fear, sir, that your memory has abandoned you," Stifel snapped. "There has been an abundance of testimony—more than necessary, in fact, as I vividly recall."

"Your Honor," the Scrivener whispered earnestly, "I am quite certain there has been no testimony."

"Get the *Official Journal* and bring the damn book here *ex delicto!*" Stifel demanded.

"I have the *Journal* with me, Your Transcendence," said the Scrivener, showing Stifel the bound volume swaying in his quivering hands.

"Read back the first question put to the last witness and the last witness' complete answer to the initial inquiry," Stifel ordered.

"I am afraid there was no *last witness*, Your Sustenance," the Scrivener said.

"Very well," Stifel stated incredulously. "Then read back the last question put to the *first witness* and the entirety of the first witness' response to it."

"I am afraid there was no last question put to the first witness, Your Prominence, because the first witness has yet to appear," the Scrivener replied.

"Are you sure?" Stifel probed.

"Quite sure," the Scrivener gently affirmed.

"Very well," Stifel proclaimed gruffly. "Slink back to your station and write nothing about this incident in the damn *Journal!* Delete the question and replace it with a reference to my welcoming the Jury to today's proceedings and a cautioning against reaching a premature determination."

As inconspicuously as a faint nocturnal shadow, the Scrivener crept down the Bench's stairway while Stifel demanded silence and announced authoritatively, "To satisfy certain technical matters and, thereby, assure all T's are dotted and I's are crossed, announcement of a verdict will be postponed until further notice."

Depleted by the morning's events, the Jurist declared an adjournment and returned to chambers for a recuperative nap. In his absence, the Jury was led from the Stall to its Sitting Room; Malatesta was entertained by fawning minions; Prikash attempted to persuade Plotkin that Stifel was not as mentally brittle as he appeared; Jacob Plotkin and the twins went to the water closet; Ana Bloom worried about Talisman's health; Inner Chamber Leader Cicero Bookbinder and High Minster Emile Threadbare engaged in awkward banter; Director of Internalized Security, Olaf Dybyk, scanned the Courtroom looking for possible security breaches; former Head Librarian Hinta Gelb read; and other spectators chatted.

43

The prosecution's first witness was Primo Astigmatopolous. The chicken plucker was in the Witness Closet due to an indiscretion committed by Monsignor Lorenzo Sagittarius of The Church of Lost Causes. The Holy Father, believing that his familial relationship with Umberto Malatesta trumped the confidentiality of clerical confessionals, had disclosed to his cousin everything Astigmatopolous told him about Leopold Plotkin's display window activities. After interviewing the disillusioned trilogist, Malatesta named him as an unindicted co-conspirator, immunized him from prosecution, and informed him he would be subpoenaed to testify against his employer and best friend.

The day following the interrogation, the chicken plucker attempted to evade subpoena by fleeing the Republic for his Motherland. He was willing to return to his native village, a place where he had no literary future, to avoid betraying the butcher. Before sunrise, he set out on a bicycle for his nameless country, carrying some of his worldly possessions. A notable exception was his store of trilogy-related materials. Too voluminous to carry in a suitcase, he hid the containers under the floor in his shanty. He hoped to retrieve the valuable information sometime after Plotkin's conviction, when his evasion of process would be merely a vague memory in the Prosecutor General's porous mind.

Several hours into his flight, the chicken plucker was spotted peddling erratically as he headed north toward the Republic's border. A constable was immediately summoned to apprehend him. After being taken into custody, the authorities turned Astigmatopolous over to Umberto Malatesta, who arranged to place him under house arrest until his appearance at the butcher's trial.

Standing rigidly in the Witness Closet, the reluctant unindicted conspirator nervously waited for the examination to begin. He looked at Plotkin's somber face. Although the butcher had repeatedly thanked him for his selfless act and said that he shouldn't feel guilty for helping the prosecution to convict him, Astigmatopolous felt remorseful for what he was about to do.

"Are you Primo Astigmatopolous, the accused's chicken plucker and closest friend?" Malatesta asked.

"I am," Astigmatopolous answered sheepishly.

"Are you here pursuant to a subpoena?"

"To the best of my knowledge, I am."

"Prior to being served with a subpoena to appear in this proceeding, did you attempt to evade service by taking flight to your homeland, a backward foreign country that isn't sufficiently important to have a name?"

"Actually, I wasn't taking flight. I was returning to my village to comfort my ailing father who I haven't seen for many years. He was lonely and urged me to return home for a brief visit."

"While taking flight to avoid service of a subpoena, were you disguised in a fake beard, driving erratically by bicycle toward the Republic's border?"

"I wore the fake beard merely as protection from the wind. My face is sensitive to the elements. I believe I was driving within the posted speed limit, give or take a few minor exceptions while I was thinking about my ailing father."

"While erratically fleeing the Republic in disguise, did you find yourself on a bridge, with a constable pursuing you by motor vehicle?"

"I believe so. My memory isn't completely intact. It's not very dependable. I suffered a head injury in childhood. My father accidentally dropped me. So did my mother."

"Did you hear the constable order you to stop peddling?"

"I heard sounds but couldn't understand what he was saying. He slurred his words."

"As the constable drew near, did you jump fully-clothed into a river?"

"I think it was a *leap* rather than a jump."

"After the constable dragged you to the riverbank and you regained consciousness, did he ask your name?"

"I don't recall. I was having difficulty breathing. The beard had lodged in my throat. My mind was confused. There wasn't enough air going to my brain."

"Did you tell the constable that you were Otto Glick, a third-violinist with the National String Symphony?"

"In the condition I was in, I might have said anything."

"A day before jumping into the river, were you interviewed by Prosecutor General Umberto Malatesta about your confession to Monsignor Lorenzo Sagittarius of The Church of Lost Causes?"

"I might have been."

"After repeating the church confession to Mr. Malatesta, did you subsequently provide Mr. Malatesta with a letter from a charlatan named Stanley Lillian Rothblatt, M.D., Ph.D., M.A., C.P.A., and Q.R., in which the quack claimed you were terminally ill and asked that you be excused from testifying because the stress of betraying Mr. Plotkin, your intimate friend, was likely to kill you as the trial date approached?"

"I have only a vague memory of that. Again, being repeatedly dropped on my head while a child, my mind isn't what it once was."

"Can we assume from your appearance today that you have yet to die?" Malatesta asked sarcastically, prompting laughter in the Pews. Plotkin didn't laugh. He was concerned by the loss of color in his friend's face and feared that Astigmatopolous, like Bernard Talisman, might collapse in open court.

"Yes, we can assume that I haven't died yet," the chicken plucker acknowledged gravely. "However, who knows how much longer I have?" He tapped a trembling finger in the area of his heart to suggest the once robust organ wasn't functioning well.

Loping with the practiced agility of a panther closing in on its prey, Malatesta drew near the base of the Great Bench, periscoped his massive neck toward the heights of the Judicial Perch, and roared: "In light of irrefutable proof that the degenerate cowering in the Witness Closet attempted to evade the subpoena and the disgraceful way he has conducted himself in this Courtroom, the prosecution asks that Primo Astigmatopolous be declared a hostile witness and allowed to be treated in the manner befitting that lowly status for the remainder of this interrogation!"

Rising from the Bench in order to see the witness, Justice Stifel declared: "It is obvious from this man's extreme efforts to avoid testifying—including but not limited to his jeopardizing the life of a constable in the performance of official duties and wearing a fake beard—that he is hostile to the core and deserves to be treated as such for the entirety of his examination."

44

Umberto Malatesta returned to the newly declared hostile witness and stared at the chicken plucker with an exaggerated scowl. "Isn't it true," he demanded, "that you were raised in a small, nameless, impoverished, stupendously inconsequential foreign country several hundred miles to the north which you contend is *known* for its mud?"

"I was and it is," the chicken plucker said proudly, drawing derisive giggles from the Pews and smirks from the Jury Stall.

"Isn't it also true, that when you illegally sneaked into the Republic, you surreptitiously smuggled several bags of foreign mud with you?"

"That's possible, although with my poor memory, who knows?"

"After entering the Republic with at least nine bags of undeclared mud in your possession, did you apply for and obtain employment as a chicken plucker in a seedy establishment known as ABRAHAM PLOTKIN AND OTHERS KOSHER MEAT PRODUCTS?"

"I did."

"Over time, did you become the accused's friend, confidant, and self-proclaimed apostle?"

"I also became his business associate and close advisor."

"Last February, did you deliver the undeclared bags of mud to the accused?'"

"I believe so, though it might have been March. Time has a way of blurring in my mind."

"Regardless of the month, sir, describe for the *good* members of the Jury how you delivered the bags to the accused."

"I handed them to him."

"What did the accused say when you handed him the bags?"

"Thanks."

"And what did you say after he thanked you?"

"You're welcome."

"In addition to 'You're welcome,' did you tell him the mud came from your nameless homeland, a republic that is allegedly known for its mud?"

"I don't recall," the chicken plucker lied, fearing that an affirmation would strengthen the prosecution's case.

"Allow Umberto Malatesta to refresh your selective memory," the prosecutor expelled ominously, before plucking a notebook from a pile of exhibits.

In a menacing baritone reserved for special intimidation purposes, Malatesta asked, "Over the past decade, have you been taking notes for a trilogy you have yet to begin on the purported plight of the dregs of our society?"

"Actually, it's only been seven and a half years," the chicken plucker mumbled while eying the notebook with trepidation.

"In response to a *subpoena duces tecum* issued after you leaped from the bridge, did you deliver this notebook to the Prosecutor General's Office along with hundreds of other volumes of material prepared for the so-called trilogy?" Malatesta probed.

"What choice did I have?" the chicken plucker asked rhetorically. "You told me I'd be thrown into Purgatory if I didn't."

Jurors, spectators, and Plotkin shuddered at the mention of the notorious prison.

"Let the record show," the Prosecutor General said, "that Umberto Malatesta is handing the hostile witness Volume 109 of the notebooks that were produced in response to the subpoena. Let the record also show that Mr. Malatesta has directed the uncooperative testifier to turn to page 57, which contains the entries for February 11 of last year, and to read the first paragraph out loud."

Embarrassed by having to share his most intimate thoughts with strangers, Primo Astigmatopolous began reading in an anxious monotone:

> As usual, the day began with a single poached egg and half-slice of bread with a third of a spoonful of peach jam, followed by a six ounce glass of tonic water to settle my stomach. After cleaning my teeth and plucking hairs from my nostrils, I bicycled to the whorehouse to interview Magdalena for the seventh time. She seemed delighted to see me. Throughout the interview, my lower member pulsated with amorous agitation as I stole glances at her sensuous lips, tongue, teeth, nose, earlobes, and ankles. Over-stimulated, I wasn't able to concentrate on her description of life in the brothel and cut the interview short. During the ride to the shop, my thoughts remained with Magdalena, though they shifted to her beautifully shaped hands, soothing voice, engaging personality, and intimate knowledge of the underclass. I imagined someday caressing her fingers or neck while she described life as a prostitute.

The chicken plucker paused. "Is that enough?" he asked with agony etched on his face.

Malatesta glared. "Continue!" he demanded shrilly.

Primo Astigmatopolous resumed reading, his voice quaking with each word.

> *The workday proceeded as normal. As I plucked, I daydreamed about the lovely Magdalena, considered topics for the trilogy, and listened to Mr. Plotkin being harangued by contentious customers. At five o'clock, Mr. Plotkin placed the Closed for Business sign on the front door and reminded me to meet him that evening for the Display Window Project. After he left for his hovel, I returned to the brothel for some follow-up questions. Magdalena appeared pleased to see me. Between clients, she spoke about her difficult childhood in the slums of Fettig. Just being near her was stimulating. Unable to concentrate on what she was saying, I told her I had a headache and returned to the shop. When Mr. Plotkin reappeared, he asked me to hand him some of the mud I brought from the Motherland. I reminded him that my former country is known for its mud. Thereafter, we ___.*

"Enough!" the Prosecutor General interrupted, thrusting his intimidating arm toward the Witness Closet to signal the chicken plucker to stop.

"Do these obscene entries remind you, sir, that you told the accused last February that the mud you provided came from your Motherland, a nameless *foreign* entity that was allegedly known for its mud?"

Derisive giggles surged through the Courtroom over the witness' pride for the quality of his nondescript country's mud. When Jacob Plotkin berated a nearby spectator for mocking his former chicken plucker, a Bailiff called for order and threatened to expel the patriarch from the venue if he didn't cease and desist.

"More or less, I suppose the entries do suggest this, if you read between the lines and take my words out of context," the chicken plucker acknowledged with regret.

"Tell the Jury what occurred after you gave the bags of mud to the accused and bragged about its quality," the prosecutor ordered.

Too humiliated to look at Plotkin or anyone else, Astigmatopolous cast his eyes downward and began to describe the events of that night—careful to hew to the narrative documented in his notebook to avoid having to read aloud any additional Magdalena-related entries in a public forum.

"After Mr. Plotkin commented on the mud's richness," the chicken plucker recounted nervously, "he said that the Window Project would proceed in two stages: first, he would swab an undercoat on the glass; then, lather an overcoat over the undercoat. My job was to inspect the quality of his work after both coats were applied."

"Did he, in fact, lather both coats?"

"Yes."

"What implements did he use?"

"A stepladder, horsehair brushes, and a palette."

"When you began the Project, was the glass in pristine condition."

"Other than a few pigeon droppings, some smudges, and dust, it was mostly clean."

"In the period preceding the fouling of the glass last February, isn't it true that people of all strata, genders, sizes, and shapes were drawn to the window like bees to honey, to peer into the malodorous establishment and watch the accused cut, cleave, slice, and chop meat?"

"I suppose so."

"Isn't it also a fact that peering citizens registered approval of the accused's meat cutting with applause, cheers, and the tossing of bouquets of roses and other precious flowers?"

"As best as I am able to recall."

"These outpourings of approval, however, didn't translate into increased demand for the accused's meat products, did they?"

"Not according to Mr. Plotkin's accounts receivable."

"This lack of demand, in turn, led to resentment, agitation, and antagonism on the accused's part—did it not?"

"You might say that."

"And the extraordinary resentment, agitation, and antagonism the accused harbored in his dark heart led him to the so-called Display Window Project, a *seditious* plan to prevent pedestrians from seeing into the butcher shop—isn't that so?"

"I wouldn't call it *seditious*."

"Did Umberto Malatesta *ask* what you would call it?"

"I suppose not."

"In the end—after both coats were applied the evening of February 11 under cover of darkness—every inch of the window was covered in mud, is that not a fact?"

"As best as I could tell, with my poor eyesight."

"What instructions did the accused give you that night regarding the *sinister* Project?"

"He told me to make sure the mud was thick enough to prevent peering."

"The peering of pedestrians of all genders, ethnicities, and religious persuasions?"

"Yes."

"The peering of the wealthy, the poor, and the huddled masses who came to this Republic seeking freedom from tyranny, disease, and persecution?

"Yes."

"The cripples, the imbeciles, and the insane—unfortunate people who have no entertainment outlets other than recreational peering?"

"I assume so."

Murmurs of disgust inundated all sectors of the Courtroom.

"Tell the Jury why, on February 11th of last year, the accused—with wanton disregard for the welfare of pedestrians—wanted to prevent the citizens of this Republic from peering into his shop."

"Because most of those who peered didn't...didn't___."

"Didn't what?"

"Didn't buy his meat."

"Reduced to its ugly essence, sir, you are saying that the butcher's heinous decision to cover the window with a foreign substance was animated by *economic*, not *artistic* reasons."

"I suppose so."

Repetitive gasps coursed through the forum.

"Earlier in your hostile testimony, you admitted the accused used a horsehair brush and a palette to apply the topcoat, did you not?" Malatesta asked.

"He actually used two horsehair brushes and a palette, or possibly___," the chicken plucker said before the impatient prosecutor cut him off.

"However many brushes or palettes were *wielded*, you idiot, after February 11, did the accused apply mud to the window a *second* time under cover of darkness?" Malatesta asked.

"Yes," the chicken plucker answered.

"When was that?"

"I believe it was the evening of March 3rd."

"Tell the Jury what prompted the rodent to apply additional mud on the window that night."

"It was Mr. Bookbinder's speech."

"Are you referring to the memorable oration in which the universally admired Leader of our great Republic's Inner Chamber implored the accused, *with remarkable restraint* and *civility*, to remove the mud from his window or face the consequences?"

"Actually, Mr. Bookbinder wasn't very restrained. He called Mr. Plotkin treacherous, a degenerate, a monster, and an enemy of Fettig."

"Did the accused hear the memorable oration?"

"It was impossible not to; the stage was almost inside the shop."

"Describe the accused's reaction to the speech."

"He didn't approve of it."

"In fact, your thin-skinned employer reacted to a few *innocuous* remarks by a luminary of the Republic by muddying the window even more later that day, isn't that so?"

"As I said, Mr. Bookbinder called him a___."

"That's enough!" Malatesta violently shrieked, causing several Jurors to recoil in fear.

Malatesta squinted at the witness. "On or about June 25th of last year, did you learn about the passage of a statute making it a crime to cover the window of a mercantile establishment with a foreign substance or maintain a previously covered window unless the window, in covered condition, is a *Work of Art*?"

"Only in passing."

"On or about that day, did you discuss the newly enacted law with the accused?"

"Briefly."

"Did he call the new law a *'travesty'* that he could not respect?"

"I believe he used those words."

"On the evening of June 25th of last year—a day that shall forever live *infamously* in the annals of the Republic—did the accused smear more mud on the window?"

"To the best of my vague recollection, he did."

"Did you assist?"

"No, he wanted to do it himself."

"How much of the window did the new layer of mud cover?"

"All of it."

"Was the same procedure repeated the following night, the evening of June 26th?

"I believe so."

"At any time prior to or after the four mudifications you have confirmed, did the accused tell you that he believed he was creating a *'Work of Art'* or, more specifically, a *painting,* in connection with the *ignominious Project*?"

"I don't remember," the chicken plucker lied inaudibly. "I was thinking of other things."

"What are you mumbling, sir?" Malatesta demanded. "Speak up. You can't crumble now, you moral coward. Speak up like a man, not the corrupt degenerate you are and, I suspect, always have been!"

"I don't remember," the chicken plucker repeated somewhat louder.

"If we were to read through your *disgusting* journal, would the phrase 'work of art' or the word 'painting' appear in connection with these heinous events?"

"I don't think so."

"Do you concede, sir, that your *immoral* notebooks don't contain a single word reflecting that your co-conspirator ever told you he was creating a Work of Art or, more specifically, a painting?"

"Probably," the chicken plucker acknowledged with self-loathing regret.

"As you cower in the Witness Closet, sir, tell this Jury whether the accused has *ever* stated that the window is a *painting* or any other *specimen of artwork*," Malatesta demanded.

"Not that I recall," the chicken plucker admitted melancholically.

Turning his back on the witness and strutting toward his fawning minions, the Prosecutor General announced, "Umberto Malatesta has no more questions."

The Court Scrivener requested a water closet recess. With reluctance, Justice Stifel announced a brief break in the proceedings.

45

During the water closet break, a woman walked to the railing that separated the Well from the Pews. "Mr. Prikash," she called out.

Guda Prikash turned and saw the ravishing woman.

"Yes?" he replied.

"I'm Magdalena. I'm concerned about Primo. He's a very sensitive person. Please be gentle with him."

"I will," Prikash said, as he admired the supplicant for her alluring beauty as well as her concern for the chicken plucker's well-being.

With the Scrivener's return to the Courtroom, Justice Stifel announced the resumption of the chicken plucker's examination.

Distancing himself from Astigmatopolous to avoid increasing the chicken plucker's anxiety, Guda Prikash said, "You testified on direct examination that Mr. Bookbinder's disparaging speech described___."

"Objection, Your Honor!" Umberto Malatesta wailed, before Prikash could complete the question. "The assertion that the Leader's speech was *disparaging* has no basis in fact and is an affront to one of our most beloved citizens. In the interest of fundamental fairness, it must be stricken!"

Aroused by Umberto Malatesta's impassioned plea, Justice Stifel struggled to his feet, wagged a menacing finger at Guda Prikash, and declared: "Without a grain of evidence, sir, you have maligned a politician whose sensitivity to those he humiliates is almost legendary! Your grotesque mischaracterization of the Leader's speech is an affront to the exalted civil servant whose presence in this Room speaks volumes about his character, priorities, and dedication to the scrupulous enforcement of our laws! The Court will not tolerate character assassination! The objection is sustained and the Jury is instructed to disregard the entirety of the partial question!"

Grateful for Stifel's compliment, Cicero Bookbinder rose in the Pews, smiled broadly, waved to the Judge, and thanked him for the compliment. Moved by the Leader's eloquence, the audience broke into thunderous applause.

The loud clapping stunned Guda Prikash, causing his eyes to

flutter. The hypnotic state induced by Bartok Golub soon evaporated and Prikash reverted to his former phobic self. Utterly confused, the lifelong hermit couldn't grasp why he was standing in a courtroom surrounded by an exuberant mob.

Studying Prikash's anguished face, Golub realized that the Prime Thinker was on the brink of an emotional collapse. Desperate to aid his patient, he pushed past applauding spectators, drawing indignant looks as he did. When he reached the perimeter of the Well, the mind healer cried out, "Plotkin, bring your lawyer to me at once!" The butcher approached Prikash to take hold of his hand. Worried that Plotkin intended him harm, Prikash recoiled and yelled hysterically, "Don't touch me!"

The mounting chaos infuriated Stifel. He pounded his gavel and demanded silence. Cowed by the Judge's command, Prikash went silent and meekly permitted Plotkin to lead him to Golub.

"I'm here to help," Golub told Prikash reassuringly.

"Do I know you?" Prikash asked with trepidation.

"Yes," Golub replied in a calming professional cadence.

"How?" Prikash asked.

"We can't talk now," Golub declared. "You must ask the Judge for a recess and then we'll talk."

"What Judge?" Prikash inquired.

"That Judge!" Golub replied, pointing up to the Perch where only the upper fringe of Stifel's wig could be seen.

"I don't see a Judge," said Prikash, who saw only the top of the wig.

"It doesn't matter," Golub said frantically. "Ask for a recess."

"Why?"

"There's no time to explain."

"Why not?"

"Please! Ask for a recess!"

"Your Honor, may I have a recess?" Prikash muttered obediently.

"For what reason?" Stifel demanded.

"Why am I requesting a recess?" Prikash asked Golub.

"For a water closet break," Golub replied.

"To relieve myself," Prikash exclaimed.

"This is highly irregular," Stifel responded.

"Tell him that you have a highly irregular bladder," Golub advised.

"I have a highly irregular bladder," Prikash echoed.

"Very well," Stifel said reluctantly. "Empty your bladder

quickly. Time is of the essence."

Golub led the Prime Thinker from the Courtroom to a small water closet at the end of the hallway. After they entered, Golub locked the door, sat Prikash on the toilet and removed a pen from his suit jacket. Focusing on the pen, Prikash's eyes grew heavier. His descent into a full hypnotic state was interrupted, however, by loud knocking.

"It's occupied!" Golub shouted.

"Unlock the door!" Jacob Plotkin insisted.

"Go away!" Golub hollered.

"Where am I?" the partially hypnotized patient asked. "What are you doing?"

"Hypnotizing you," Golub replied, as the demands to unlock the door grew more insistent.

"Why?" Prikash asked groggily.

"For the greater good," Golub explained.

More knocking and demands to open the door reverberated through the tiny room.

Knowing he couldn't hypnotize Prikash as long as the commotion distracted the Prime Thinker, Golub unlocked the door.

"What are you doing to him?" Jacob Plotkin asked accusatorily, when he saw the semi-conscious lawmonger sprawled on the toilet.

"This isn't your concern," Golub replied, moving Prikash from the toilet to the lavatory's sink.

"Are you robbing him?" Misha Plotkin inquired as he entered the water closet with his older brother and twin.

"This man is representing my son!" Jacob said with concern.

"I am?" Prikash mumbled.

"He is?" Moishe Plotkin asked, having no recollection of Prikash.

"Who are these people?" Prikash asked.

"How should I know?" the anxious psychiatrist replied.

"We'll report you to the authorities!" Misha threatened.

"What gall! Robbing a lawmonger while court is in session," said Jacob.

"Are you finished?" Golub squealed.

"Don't rush us!" said Jacob, who was sharing the toilet bowl with his brothers.

"We don't like being rushed," the uncles declared in unison.

"I would appreciate if you finish your business and leave," said Golub.

"Don't talk!" Jacob insisted. "We need to concentrate."

"That Michelangela must be a beauty," Misha speculated while concentrating.

"Her name is Modigliani," Jacob corrected.

"The chicken plucker has no chance with her," Moishe opined.

"He's out of his depth," said Jacob.

"The chicken plucker is no writer," said Misha. "Papa was a good writer."

"He was a genius with words," said Jacob.

"He was an intellectual," Moishe added.

"Are you gentlemen finished?" Golub asked, as Prikash stared vacantly.

"I told you, we can't be rushed!" Jacob asserted.

"We can't concentrate if you keep interrupting us," said Misha.

"This man has a lot of nerve," said Jacob. "He assaults my son's attorney in the water closet of a courthouse when court is in session and interrupts when we try to relieve ourselves."

"Are you finished?" Golub asked hysterically.

"This process requires time!" Jacob protested.

As they leisurely relieved themselves, the brothers continued to discuss the attributes of their deceased father, which unsettled Golub and weakened Prikash's resolve to sacrifice himself for the greater good. Glaring at Golub after they completed their mission, the brothers buttoned their trousers. When exiting the water closet, they threatened again to report him to the authorities.

With quiet restored, Golub again sat Prikash on the toilet and successfully completed the psycho-hypnotic procedure—this time telling Prikash he would remain hypnotized until he heard three whistles, something Golub believed was unlikely to occur in a courtroom. Golub then led the re-hypnotized lawyer from the water closet to rejoin the Courtroom hostilities.

Magdalena

46

As Guda Prikash approached the Courtroom with Bartok Golub at his elbow, the Prime Thinker focused on the chicken plucker's admission that he didn't recall Plotkin referring to "art" or a "painting" during the Window Project. Realizing that if not diluted, that testimony would badly weaken the Work of Art defense, he sorted through his prodigious mind for an effective line of questioning.

"Do you recall the prosecution asking whether Mr. Plotkin mentioned *art* or a *painting* when brushing the window on February 11th?" Prikash asked when he resumed the cross-examination.

"Vaguely," Primo Astigmatopolous replied.

"Do you recall testifying that you were thinking of *other things* as he brushed?" Prikash asked.

"Yes," the chicken plucker answered squeamishly.

"When you observed Mr. Plotkin window-brushing on subsequent occasions, were you also thinking of *other things*?"

"Yes," he acknowledged more squeamishly.

"Would it be fair to say, sir, that those *other things* concerned the woman referred to in your notebook as 'the lovely Magdalena'?" Prikash asked.

"It would be fair to say, but embarrassing," Primo Astigmato- polous confessed.

"Isn't it a fact that you thought about Magdalena incessantly and redundantly while Mr. Plotkin brushed?" Prikash probed.

"It is," the chicken plucker mumbled.

"As Mr. Plotkin applied mud, did those thoughts stimulate your libido, sir?"

"Do I have to answer?"

"If there is to be a complete record, you must."

"Yes, my libido was stimulated."

"Isn't it a fact, Mr. Astigmatopolous, that you were focused on Magdalena's fertile mind, convivial personality, knowledge of the underclass, alluring eyes, pouting lips, sensuous neck, abundant breasts, well-shaped ankles, and curvaceous buttocks, and soon were overcome by such intense feral lust that you were incapable of thinking of anything else, including what Mr. Plotkin may or may not have said when brushing mud onto the window?"

"Objection!" cried Umberto Malatesta, scanning the faces of several Jurors who appeared to be sexually aroused by the ques- tion. "The defense's explicit reference to feral lust is calculated to stimulate the latent prurient interests of Jury members and, there- by, deflect attention from the issues! The reference is demeaning to this Court and of relevance only to perverts!"

Malatesta flailed his arms. "The prosecution implores His Hon- or to strike all sexual references from the question; instruct Jurors to forget all indecent portions thereof; and have the Scrivener read a sanitized version of the inquiry for the witness' response."

Justice Stifel, whose mind had been wandering when Guda Pri- kash asked the question, nevertheless, sustained the objection and ordered a cleansed reformulation. After deleting what he assumed were the offensive elements, the Scrivener read the following: "Isn't it a fact, Mr. Astigmatopolous, that you were focused on… and were so… that you were incapable of thinking of anything else, including but not limited to what Mr. Plotkin may or may not have said when brushing mud onto the window?"

"Yes," the chicken plucker replied to the amended question.

"Did the fog in which you were mired adversely affect your brain functions so that if Mr. Plotkin did utter the words 'art' or 'painting,' you wouldn't have had the capacity to understand what he said?" Prikash asked.

"Objection!" Malatesta roared. "Conjecture related to the impact fog might have had on this pervert's brain lies exclusively within the province of an *expert physician,* not a *chicken plucker!*"

"Sustained!" Stifel wheezed.

Undaunted, Prikash asked: "Whatever the cause, did you fully comprehend what Mr. Plotkin said as he brushed the window the nights in question?"

"No, most of what he said sounded like gibberish to my otherwise occupied mind."

Sensing that he needed more than words to convince Jurors of the chicken plucker's inability to comprehend what Plotkin had said on the nights in question, Prikash asked, "Is Magdalena in the Courtroom?"

"When I last looked, she was," the chicken plucker answered sheepishly.

"Please point her out," Prikash said.

Astigmatopolous pointed to the back of the Pews.

"Please stand," Prikash said, courteously extending an arm in Magdalena's direction.

The prostitute slowly rose. Magdalena had scrubbed all vestiges of lipstick, skin powders, and rouge, as she always did in off hours. Her hair was neatly arranged. In all respects, she was attractive in an understated way.

Jurors stared. The Scrivener put aside his pen to gape. Cicero Bookbinder cast a lupine glance her way. Jacob Plotkin and the deranged uncles turned to assess her. Even the part-time rabbi (who had presided at Plotkin's bar mitzvah without once looking up) interrupted his reading to admire her. Plotkin, who also turned to look, was astounded by the revamped version of the woman who had called to the chicken plucker from the brothel's doorway the day they trekked to Bernard Talisman's office.

"Objection!" Malatesta protested, after he noticed several Jurors with mouths agape. "This is thoroughly improper, inadmissible as a matter of law, and an egregious abuse of the trial processes!"

"Indeed!" Stifel gasped as he stood to ascertain what the entire Courtroom was staring at. "The woman standing in the Pews shall immediately sit-down! Jury members are instructed to forget they saw her and refrain from drawing any inferences!"

Despite the Judge's instructions, Jurors couldn't forget what they saw or dismiss the possibility that Magdalena's allure was so compelling that the chicken plucker didn't hear Plotkin mention 'art' or a 'painting' on the nights in question.

"Resume the interrogation!" Stifel insisted angrily.

"My learned opponent asked whether you *ever* heard Mr. Plot-kin state that the display window is a painting or other form of artwork," Prikash posited. "Let *me* ask you *this*: Has Mr. Plotkin ever stated in your presence that the window is *not* a painting or *not* some other species of art?"

"No," the chicken plucker replied.

"*How often* has he not told you that?"

"Very often."

"*Where* has he not told you that?"

"Inside the butcher shop. On the sidewalk in front of the butch-er shop. On the stairs to the Plotkin flat. Inside the flat. Almost everywhere we have been together."

"In the months since the mud-brushing, have you ever observed Mr. Plotkin admire the window?"

"Yes, on and off; more on than off."

"When did he admire the window as though it were a Work of Art?"

"Objection!" Malatesta thundered. "The question calls for rank speculation and is calculated to upend the prosecution's good faith efforts to secure a conviction."

"Sustained!" Stifel squealed. "The Court admonishes defense counsel that it will not tolerate rank speculation or undue interfer-ence with the prosecution's good faith efforts to convict. In accor-dance with the *Uniform Rules*, the Jury may not speculate on how the witness might have answered the question, had he been permit-ted to."

Several Jurors nodded to assure the unseen Jurist they would not speculate. Leopold Plotkin muttered something about judi-cial bias. Jacob Plotkin and his brothers argued among themselves whether the Judge had exceeded his authority by precluding the Jurors from speculating. Ana Bloom was disheartened. Malatesta and his minions were delighted.

"At any time subsequent to the mud-brushing," Prikash asked, "did you hear Mr. Plotkin comment on the window?"

"Yes. He often commented on it prior to his arrest."

"What did he say?"

"Every work day he referred to it as 'the great achievement' of his life; something that had made his father proud of him for the first time."

"Objection and move to strike!" Malatesta growled somewhat

belatedly. "This is rank hearsay and yet another illustration of defense counsel's willingness to deviate from *The Rules of Evidence and Procedure* as if they don't apply to him!"

"Absolutely," Stifel replied with smug condescension. "The testimony is hereby stricken. The Jury is instructed to forget this intrinsically unreliable information. Defense counsel is admonished to stick to the *Rules* or suffer the consequence. He is trying the Court's limited patience and making a mockery of this proceeding."

After the adverse ruling, Guda Prikash announced he had no more questions for the chicken plucker. Umberto Malatesta followed suit. Relieved that there were no more questions, Primo Astigmatopolous left the Courthouse for the relative calm of a violent thunderstorm.

Satisfied that enough incriminating evidence had been adduced for one day, Justice Stifel adjourned the proceedings and repaired to his Chambers to disrobe. Umberto Malatesta left for the Prosecutor General's Office, where his Chief Minion was polishing a draft of questions for the next witness' direct interrogation. Guda Prikash returned to the law firm to put the final touches on queries for the next witness' cross-interrogation. Leopold Plotkin retired to his tenement to critique the day's events with family and supporters. Ana Bloom visited Our Lady of the Albatross Hospital to deliver tender kisses and news of the trial to Bernard Talisman. Myra Rabinowitz-Pritzker went to the mansion she shared with her half-brother to await Prikash's late arrival for dinner.

47

D espite A. I. Gopnik's documented history of insanity—something that might be expected to destroy the former curator's credibility as a witness—Umberto Malatesta realized that juries acted unpredictably at times and could embrace Gopnik's expert opinion that the display window was a Work of Art, thus, paving the way for the butcher's acquittal. Unwilling to risk the humiliation of an acquittal, Malatesta had met with his most trusted minions several months before the start of trial to explore creative ways to assure that would not occur.

At the outset of the brainstorming session, the Prosecutor General spoke passionately about the "vital interests" at stake in *The Republic against Plotkin*—namely, his reputation. He told his underlings that merely purchasing an expert to counter Gopnik's opinions wouldn't, in itself, eliminate his concerns. Furrowing his brow to accentuate the extent of his concerns, Malatesta invited the minions to expand their horizons beyond the unsavory practices normally employed in the Office and venture into the realm of the unethical. Inspired by the broad latitude given by Malatesta and appreciative of his confidence in their deviousness, the small collection of advisors proposed a litany of unscrupulous tactics. Malatesta's Chief Minion rejected all of the proposals, however, calling them either "unsound" or "impractical." Malatesta agreed.

As the frustrated Prosecutor General was about to end the exercise, a bug-eyed subordinate offered an idea. The bug-eyed speaker told Malatesta about a hysterical letter he had received months earlier from a pathological liar named Pincus Barrenblat, an unscrupulous lawyer he had prosecuted for overbilling clients and embezzling from his firm. The minion recalled Barrenblat's claim that Leopold Plotkin inhabited a nearby cell in Purgatory's basement and was plotting to kill him. Despite Barrenblat's cries for protection, the bug-eyed minion confessed that he tore the letter up and did nothing to protect the supplicant because "Barrenblat was not only a liar; he was insane."

"So why are you telling me this?" Malatesta asked impatiently.

The minion explained that Barrenblat might be willing to relate a false jailhouse confession in which Plotkin allegedly admitted that the display window wasn't a Work of Art. Impressed by the proposal, Malatesta took credit for the idea and instructed his Chief Minion to visit Barrenblat in Purgatory to suborn the habitual liar's perjury.

The following afternoon, Malatesta's emissary met with Barrenblat in Warden Hans Gogol's office. Initially, the Chief Minion was put off by Barrenblat's slovenliness, irritated by the disgraced lawyer's repeated protestations of innocence, and appalled by his assertions that the conviction had been a miscarriage of justice. The Chief Minion's commitment to the mission, however, overcame these aversions and he listened with ostensible interest to everything the inmate had to say. After Barrenblat finished blathering, the Chief Minion reminded him of Plotkin's plot to kill him and suggested that testifying against Plotkin would be sweet revenge for the lunatic. Initially, Barrenblat refused to testify, saying it would be hypocritical for him to complain about *his* miscarriage of justice while participating in *another's* miscarriage. Desperate to convince the liar to cooperate, the minion offered the lunatic inducements to testify against the butcher: relocation to a larger cell, bi-monthly outdoor exercise, and appointment to a trustee position in Purgatory's basement, all of which the Warden had approved in advance. Satisfied by the offer, Barrenblat agreed to commit perjury.

Soon after the Purgatory meeting, the Chief Minion prepared a script for the lunatic to memorize. Among other things, it portrayed Plotkin as repeatedly shouting from his cell: "The window is not a Work of Art! Only a madman would call it art! My lawyer has hired a madman to tell the imbeciles on the Jury that the window is art! The imbeciles will believe the madman and acquit me!"

During rehearsals, the Chief Minion cautioned the defrocked lawyer to avoid any references to his purported miscarriage of justice and to focus exclusively on the butcher's confession. With tranquilizers prescribed by Purgatory's part-time doctor, the outbursts and erratic behavior of the perjurer-in-waiting diminished to the point where he seemed normal when delivering his lines. On the eve of the lunatic's scheduled testimony, the impressed minion reported to Malatesta that Barrenblat now had sufficient control of his faculties to appear credible.

48

Pincus Barrenblat seemed saner than Plotkin had anticipated. Freshly shaved and dressed in a suit—casting alert eyes directly at the Jury Stall and speaking in a measured cadence—Barrenblat was nothing like the lunatic the butcher had known while cohabitating with him in Purgatory's basement. Without once referring to the alleged miscarriage of justice that had resulted in his conviction and disbarment, Barrenblat calmly testified that he was currently incarcerated in Purgatory House of Detention, had practiced in the areas of estates and trusts prior to his incarceration, was a profoundly changed man since discovering religion in the prison's basement, and was recently made an inmate trustee due to his now sterling reputation for trustworthiness.

Relieved that the witness had not deviated from script up to that point, Umberto Malatesta began to lay the testimonial groundwork for the introduction of Plotkin's false jailhouse confession. The Prosecutor General turned toward the Accused's Table and pointed to Plotkin with an angry finger. "Did there come a time," he thundered, "when you and that *reptile* were housed together in Purgatory's basement?"

"Unfortunately, there did," the lunatic replied, managing to look troubled, as rehearsed.

"When was that?" Malatesta asked.

"I can't recall," said Barrenblat, unable to remember that portion of the perjured testimony. "Whenever it was, I have no doubt that the time came—a terrible time, almost too painful to recall; a time that nobody should have to experience."

"How close were your cells to each other?" asked Malatesta in an attempt to redirect the witness to his scripted responses.

"Only inches apart," said Barrenblat. "Much too close for comfort."

"How long did the two of you reside in adjoining cells?"

"Too long. It wasn't a happy time. He was a nuisance, always swatting insects or babbling. The swatting nearly drove me crazy. The babbling became intolerable. I couldn't sleep. I was exhausted. I was at the brink of collapse, gasping for air. Later, the swatting, interspersed with babbling, made me sleep too much. Oversleeping sapped my energy. When awake, I would lie there, praying he would stop."

"When you lived in the vicinity of this extraordinarily *selfish* man, did you have occasion to hear his voice when he was not babbling?"

"Regrettably, I did. I can still hear it when I'm not paying attention."

"Why do you say *regrettably?*"

"When he wasn't babbling, he shouted, ranted, raved, and occasionally railed—depending on his mood. All of this was much louder than the babbling. He was obviously insane. He nearly drove *me* insane, repeating the same thing over and over, in that bone-chilling loud voice."

Plotkin was troubled as he looked at his former jailhouse neighbor in the Witness Closet. Not only was Barrenblat now speaking calmly and in fully understandable sentences, the lunatic was effectively portraying *him* as the one who was insane. Something had caused a dramatic change. Plotkin thought to alert Guda Prikash to the suspicious turn-around. However, he saw the lawyer taking copious notes and decided not to disturb him.

Umberto Malatesta had reached the moment where he was to elicit from Pincus Barrenblat the butcher's alleged jailhouse confession. Dramatically raising both hands above his head and circling them counterclockwise in order to increase the anticipation, the prosecutor asked in an exaggerated *basso profundo:* "What was the accused incessantly shouting, ranting, raving, and/or railing about; what did he repeat over and over until you were on the verge of losing your mind?"

Barrenblat glanced at Plotkin and saw the look of a man who obviously felt betrayed. The downcast expression reminded the lunatic of his own reaction when the firm's bookkeeper testified against him at his trial. A tinge of guilt from his underdeveloped conscience caused him to hesitate and, then, to ask Malatesta to rephrase the question.

"What did the accused repeatedly say until you almost went off the rails?"

Jurors leaned forward, spectators craned their necks, Guda Prikash tilted sideways, and Leopold Plotkin slumped in anticipation of the climactic answer. Barrenblat stood rigidly, catatonic but for eyes that darted back and forth between Plotkin and Malatesta.

"The witness will answer the question!" Stifel demanded from the Judicial Perch.

"That voice. Where is it coming from?" the lunatic asked frantically, looking around but unable to see the seated Stifel.

"From here," the pocket-sized Jurist said after standing to reveal himself.

"Thank God! I thought I was hearing voices again," Barrenblat sighed.

"What did the accused repeatedly say?" Malatesta asked again.

"Until the miscarriage of justice," Barrenblat exclaimed as his eyes widened, "I trusted the law. The trust was misplaced. The miscarriage destroyed my life. It also destroyed the lives of my parents, my wife, two or three mistresses, several siblings, and countless others who claimed to love me. Soon, it will destroy the lives of my brothers' and sisters' unborn children. Later it will destroy the lives of the children of my brothers' and sisters' children. After that, it will___."

"Thank you for those heart-rending comments," Malatesta said, struggling to maintain his composure. "However, please answer the question, if you don't mind."

"Why should I mind?" said the lunatic.

"Well?" said Malatesta, expecting a substantive answer to the pending question.

"What was the question? With all your badgering, I forgot it."

"I asked what you heard the accused repeatedly shout from his cell."

"I don't know," the witness replied.

"You *don't know*?" Malatesta gasped, triggering a profusion of other, even louder gasps at the Prosecution's Table.

"Yes, I don't know," the lunatic repeated.

"How is that possible, *sir*?"

"Whatever he said was unintelligible, even to a man of my intelligence."

"Isn't it a fact, sir, that you heard the accused shout day after day, until you nearly lost your mind: *it's not art*, a confession by a guilt-ridden deviant that the window was neither a painting nor any other kind of artwork?"

"Objection!" Guda Prikash hollered up to the Judicial Perch.

"What is the justification for this *unorthodox* objection?" Justice Stifel groused dismissively.

"The question is impermissibly leading," Prikash explained, shocked that even a judge as biased as Stifel would request an explanation.

"Objection denied," Stifel ruled. "In light of the witness' obvious hostility to the prosecution as manifested by his feigned inability to recall a statement that almost drove him crazy, it is more than permissible for the prosecution to lead him by the nose until he provides a substantive response to a perfectly proper question. Defense counsel is admonished to step down and let the testimony continue without specious interruption."

As Prikash resignedly returned to his seat, Malatesta crooned appreciatively, "Thank you, Your Omniscience,"

"You are most welcome," Stifel purred.

"What did the accused say?" the prosecutor asked Barrenblat again.

"May I have a moment to think about that?" the lunatic asked.

"Take your time," Malatesta said, sensing that the lunatic had been chastened.

After a lengthy pause, during which Jurors and spectators stared intently at Barrenblat, the lunatic finally said, "Alright, I've thought about it."

"And?" said Malatesta.

"I recall what the accused said," the lunatic declared.

"Tell the Jury what you recall," Malatesta directed.

"He said, 'It's not a fart.'"

"It's not a *fart*?"

"Yes, it's not a *fart*," the lunatic repeated as the Jurors exchanged bemused glances. A general tittering could be heard in the Pews.

"Don't lie to the Jury!"

"Don't call me a liar!"

"Permission to refer to this witness as a liar, Your Honor," Malatesta pleaded.

"Permission granted," said Stifel.

"I submit, sir, that you are a liar and have changed your story to suit yourself," Malatesta shouted.

"My story has never changed and lying is not part of my nature," said Barrenblat.

"I further submit, sir, that what you heard the accused shout day after day, week after week, and season after season was *not* 'it's not a fart,' but rather, 'it's not art'."

"And I submit to you, sir, that, as a legal practitioner trained in the art of precise listening, I heard what I heard. He definitely said, 'It's not a fart'. I am a man of great rectitude, from a profession known for its integrity. It's not my practice to lie. If someone has told you otherwise, they are lying. Lying is rampant. It's everywhere—in the trees, the sky, the air we breathe, the____."

"That's enough!" Malatesta groaned as he observed the witness emotionally unravel. Realizing that any further questioning would be futile, he looked up to the Judicial Perch and said, "The prosecution has no more questions to put to this ignoramus." Disappointed and embarrassed, Malatesta skulked back to his table to join his deflated minions.

Guda Prikash, delighted with the lunatic's testimony, informed Justice Stifel that he had no questions for Barrenblat. With that, Stifel ordered constables to remove the lunatic from the Witness closet. As the lunatic was led across the Well, he shouted that another miscarriage of justice had just been committed against him. In the midst of his tantrum, he winked at Plotkin. Grateful for Barrenblat's benign testimony, the butcher's face muscles contorted into a rarely fashioned, partial smile.

Art Expert Hippolyte Thwaite

49

The jousting of art experts began with Hippolyte Thwaite's entry into the Witness Closet. In response to Umberto Malatesta's questions, Thwaite detailed his copious accomplishments with self-aggrandizing adjectives: graduation from a *renowned* college; a mentorship under the *eminent* curator, Bruno Wittgenstein, at the *esteemed* Museum of Iconoclastic Culture; directorship of the Museum after Wittgenstein suffered a nervous breakdown; membership in innumerable *exclusive* professional societies; authorship of *seminal* essays in *venerable* journals; recipient of the title "Professori of Arts" from the National Center for Honorifics; and *memorable* expert appearances in courtrooms across the globe. Thwaite concluded the description of himself as the "preeminent assessor of art in the world and an icon whose analyses are universally respected and embraced."

After eliciting Thwaite's pedigree for the better part of an hour, Malatesta asked the Court to recognize him as an expert on all things artistic. When Guda Prikash declined to challenge Thwaite's unassailable qualifications, Justice Stifel granted the connoisseur license to expound on anything he believed was pertinent.

Speaking deferentially to a witness accustomed to obeisance, Malatesta asked: "During this examination, would you prefer to be addressed as 'Professori' or simply 'sir'?"

"As 'Professori,' of course," Thwaite spat. "Anything less would be an insult."

"Understood," Malatesta lapped obediently.

"Were you retained by the Prosecutor General's Office to assess the display window at ABRAHAM PLOTKIN AND OTHERS KOSHER MEAT PRODUCTS?" Malatesta asked.

"Of course I was *retained*," Thwaite replied. "Why else would I be here? It isn't my practice to make unilateral assessments. To assess without retention would be unseemly and, more important, unprofitable."

"When retained, were you given instructions?"

"Certainly, I was given instructions. It would be senseless to make an assessment without knowing what I am expected to do. Only an amateur would proceed without instructions."

"Please tell the Jury what the instructions were."

"I was asked to utilize my vast storehouse of knowledge and the most modern techniques of my profession—virtually all of which I invented—to determine whether the window in question is a Work of Art or a haphazard aggregation of mud."

"Did you subsequently visit the butcher shop, Professori?"

"If I didn't visit it I would have no reason to be here, would I?"

"What did you do after arriving at the shop?"

"Unfortunately, I did much more than anticipated or desired. Upon arrival, I encountered an unruly mob. The vermin were carrying placards whose crude content I won't repeat. They were also chanting vulgarities more disgusting than the placards. Jostled by the ruffians and threatened with bodily harm by an elderly woman who appeared to be leading the mob, I miraculously avoided injury by convincing the riffraff that I was not allied with the accused. Despite the clarification, I remained in harm's way but completed my task for the agreed-upon fee."

"Please tell the Jury what occurred after your brush with violence."

"I took up a position perpendicular to the window, equidistant between the left and right perimeters of the glass. From that vantage point, I was able to study the glass straight-on, while my assistant stood guard to make sure I wasn't attacked from behind."

"What did you see as you commenced the study?"

"I saw mud."

"Nothing more?"

"Nothing *more* and nothing *less*."

"After assessing the window straight-on, what did you do?"

"I looked up, down, vertically, horizontally, longitudinally, acutely, obtusely, obliquely, abaxially, rhomboidally, and anaclinally—the Eleven Cardinal Geometric Positions from which competent connoisseurs scrutinize alleged works of art. I invented the procedure twenty-three years ago and it has been in vogue ever since."

Fascinated that Thwaite had risked his life to assay the window from a multitude of angles, Jurors scribbled *"cardinal," "geometric,"* and *"competent"* in their notebooks to remind them of the significant points. Spectators marveled at his thoroughness under fire. Plotkin, who encountered angry mobs daily when entering and exiting the shop, was unimpressed.

"From the Eleven Cardinal Positions, Professori, what did you observe?"

"Again, I continued to see mud."

"After ascertaining that the window contained only mud, what did you do?"

"My assistant took photographs of the window, while *I* stood guard."

"How many pictures did he take?"

"Eleven."

"Why eleven, Professori?"

"Because there are eleven geometric positions. Anything less is insufficient; anything more is superfluous."

"Have you brought the photographs with you, Professori?"

"I have."

"Are those the photographs you are holding in your authoritative hands?"

"They are."

"Please tell the Jury what they depict."

"In a word, mud."

"Only mud?"

"Mud and nothing else."

With authenticity established, Malatesta moved the photographs into evidence and sought Justice Stifel's permission to allow the Jury to inspect them. The Judge granted the request without asking Guda Prikash whether he objected. After the Jurors studied the items, the Prosecutor General asked: "What did you do after your assistant took the pictures, Professori?

"I asked myself whether the mud-laden window could plausibly be a Work of Art or, more particularly, a painting."

"Did you reach a conclusion in that regard?"

"If I didn't, I wouldn't be here."

"Please tell the Jury what you concluded."

"I will momentarily," Thwaite said, clearing his throat, adjusting his tie, fingering his moustache, and checking his pocket watch, all of which was meant to raise Juror anticipation for his answer. Summoning as much pomposity as he could muster, he stated haughtily: "I concluded that the mass of mud was neither a painting nor any other art form."

Thwaite's opinion sent a surge of excitement through the Courtroom.

Plotkin, who had anticipated the opinion, was neither excited nor surprised. Having read Thwaite's expert report, he accepted the damaging evidence with the aplomb of a defendant expecting to be convicted.

"Does your opinion rise to the level of a *reasonable* degree of professional certainty?" Malatesta asked.

"It rises much higher than that," Thwaite replied, staring at the ceiling. "It soars to the height of *absolute* certainty! It is *indisputable fact,* not mere opinion; an uncontradictable reality; an irrefutable certitude; an unmistakable truth!"

"Objection!" Guda Prikash cried.

"On what basis?" Justice Stifel inquired irritably.

"Under the *Uniform Rules of Evidence,* Your Eminence," Prikash argued, "an expert opinion may not exceed a *reasonable degree of professional certainty* and may not rise to the fanciful heights the witness claims to have reached. By exceeding prescribed boundaries, he is, in effect, trying to usurp the role of the Jury as the finder of facts."

"The Court has given defense counsel's objection considerable thought," Stifel replied as soon as Prikash finished, "and finds it specious, trivial, and worthless."

After Prikash cordially thanked the Jurist for rejecting the motion, Umberto Malatesta placed one hand on the Witness Closet railing, thrust the other toward the ceiling, and said, "Professori, please tell the Jury why you have concluded that the window is not a Work of Art or, more particularly, not a painting."

"Because I know art when I see it," Thwaite said with disdain.

"Can you elaborate, Professori?" Malatesta asked, surprised by the brevity of the response, which omitted virtually everything Thwaite had agreed to say.

"If you insist," the witness said.

"That would be appreciated," said Malatesta.

"My painstaking examination of the window revealed it is ugly in the extreme; unappealing; and of no significance apart from preventing one to see into the shop. Furthermore, the workmanship shows no skill by the clod who lathered the mud onto the window. To the contrary, there are unmistakable indicia of random, haphazard swipes by a manual laborer. It is a prototypical example of artlessness, clumsiness, and crudeness. Because paintings fall within the rubric of Art, the lack of even rudimentary skill in this instance, of necessity, precludes the possibility that the window is a painting. It is an abomination, a monstrosity that only a madman could find artful."

The Jurors, most of whom were manual laborers and had insanity running in their families, found Thwaite's comments offensive. Unaware that his expert was alienating the Jury, Malatesta plowed ahead with the line of questioning.

"When you referred to a '*madman*,' Professori, did you have anyone in particular in mind?"

"I certainly did," Thwaite said, rolling his eyes disdainfully.

"To whom were you referring?"

"To A. I. Gopnik, the so-called connoisseur who will be testifying for the defense."

"What led you to conclude that Gopnik is a madman, Professori?"

"Objection to this witness testifying about Mr. Gopnik's mental state," Guda Prikash interposed. "Mr. Thwaite has been proffered as an *art* expert, not as a specialist in the workings of *minds*. This inquiry is beyond his purview."

"The Court takes judicial notice of the fact that, as humans, we are all exposed to insane people on a daily basis," Stifel announced. "Therefore, one does not have to be a specialist to diagnose diseased minds. We all know a diseased mind when we see one. In light of this reality, defense counsel is admonished to be more prudent with his objections. The Court is losing patience with the constant interruptions."

To avoid offending the thin-skinned Jurist, Prikash thanked the Court for its ruling.

"Where was Umberto Malatesta when his opponent needlessly interrupted him?" the Prosecutor General asked the Scrivener.

"What led you," read the Scrivener "to conclude that Gopnik is a madman, Professori?"

"Please enlighten the Jury," Malatesta asked Thwaite.

"Two things in particular, the latter more persuasive than the former," said Thwaite.

"Would you begin with the former, Professori, and then proceed to the latter, if you will?"

"After your Office retained me, I confirmed that Gopnik had been a resident of the Warehouse for the Purportedly Insane for some time. Later, I had the displeasure of reading his so-called expert report. The report confirms that he *belongs* in the Warehouse; that he is of unsound mind; that he is suffering from severe delusions, if not outright hallucinations."

Waving Gopnik's written report with disdain, Malatesta asked: "What is it about this that convinces you he is delusional, if not hallucinatory?"

"It is obvious he sees things that are not there."

"What do you mean 'not there'?"

"He refers to things that exist only in his imagination—to things that would be seen only by a man who has completely lost touch with reality."

"Taking it one step further, Professori, do you have an opinion as to whether the report itself is crazy?"

"I do."

"What is your opinion?"

"The report is undoubtedly crazy."

"Is that your considered opinion?"

"It is more than 'considered.' In all my years of reviewing expert reports, I have never seen a report as insane as this one. There was a time, before his descent into madness, that I *almost* admired Gopnik. Sadly, there is no ignoring the fact that now both he and his report are profoundly unhinged!"

Extracting all he had hoped to from his expert, Malatesta thanked Thwaite and strode confidently back to his minions who, silently mouthed, "Well done, sir," to which he mouthed-back, "Of course."

"Does the defense have any questions for this witness?" Stifel inquired.

"It does," Guda Prikash replied.

"Get on with it, then!" the Jurist demanded.

50

When preparing for trial, Bernard Talisman had rummaged through Hippolyte Thwaite's published essays for impeachment material. He discovered *What Is Or Is Not Art,* a monograph Thwaite co-authored decades earlier with Fyodor Shebolsky, a radical scholar who subsequently left academia to become a Trappist monk. Astounded to find passages in the writing that mirrored the High Court's analysis in *Pogrebin against Pogrebin,* he was poised to use it as the centerpiece of Thwaite's cross-interrogation, until collapsing during the Opening Rant. Guda Prikash held *What Is Or Is Not Art* behind his back when putting his first question to the witness.

"Does the name Fyodor Shebolsky mean anything to you?" Prikash asked in a subdued tone.

"Fyodor Shebolsky?" Thwaite replied with concern; his eyelids blinked nervously.

"Yes, Fyodor Shebolsky," Prikash repeated.

"I believe he's a monk of some sort."

"Wasn't he an art historian who taught at the College of Classical Didacticism when you were a student there?"

"With so many professors milling around the place, how can I possibly be expected to know if he was there or not?"

"Didn't you and Shebolsky co-author a monograph titled, *What Is Or Is Not Art* soon after your graduation from the College?"

"Having co-authored countless monographs with innumerable parasites, it's impossible for me to recall the names of every cipher who rode my coattails."

"Let the record show that I am handing Mr. Thwaite a copy of *What Is Or Is Not Art.* Please review it, sir, and tell me whether this refreshes your recollection with regard to you and Shebolsky co-authoring this scholarly writing."

Thwaite laboriously slogged through the monograph, trying to think of a way to avoid Prikash's unanticipated trap.

"Now that I have had the opportunity to scan this," he said after sufficient time elapsed to formulate a plausible response, "I remember clearly it was not a scholarly writing at all, but a parody Shebolsky and I put together to mock the growing number of so-called critics who saw art in virtually everything they looked at.

Shebolsky had a wonderful sense of humor, and a great sense of the absurd, not as wonderful as mine, but rich, nevertheless. Yes, a keen, biting wit. He was always lampooning one thing or another until he took a vow of silence and disappeared into a Trappist monastery. A terrible waste of comedic talent, indeed."

"Can you show me where on the cover page or anywhere else it states that *What Is Or Is Not Art* was a parody?"

"There was no need to state the obvious. Anyone who bothered to read could see that it was a parody. As a matter of fact, I recall Shebolsky laughing hysterically when I asked him whether we should note in the monograph that it was a parody. Later, during a dinner party with Shebolsky and various admirers, we read it aloud and drew hysterical laughter from the adoring audience. I'm certain if Shebolsky were here rather than in a cloister, he would tell you this was a satirical piece, nothing to be taken seriously."

"Let us review, sir, what you and Shebolsky wrote in regard to the question posed by the monograph's title, namely what is or isn't art. Please turn to the second page and read the third and fourth paragraphs out loud."

"Is he allowed to badger me like this?" Thwaite whined, desperately looking at Umberto Malatesta for extrication.

"*Who* is being badgered?" Justice Stifel demanded when Thwaite's query roused him from a stupor.

"I am!" Thwaite replied.

"And you are?"

"Hippolyte Thwaite, the prosecution's most important witness."

"There will be no badgering of this witness," Stifel announced menacingly. "He is to be treated with the respect I assume he is due."

Prikash resumed the interrogation. "Please read the previously identified paragraphs to the Jury, sir."

"You may read," said Malatesta, convinced that he had no plausible basis to object, even under Stifel's lenient pro-prosecution standards.

"If I must," Thwaite groused as he located the paragraphs and recited in a dull monotone:

> *The question of what is and is not art has been with us since our primitive ancestors lived in the virgin forests of the Republic and were drawing images of beasts on the walls of caves. While it is within the ambit of professional art connoisseurs to opine on the*

quality of art, it is presumptuous for even the most sophisticated maven to exclusively determine what is and is not art since art can come in virtually limitless forms, shapes, and sizes, and, in the last analysis, is a matter for the eye of the beholder, however uneducated, untrained, or undiscerning his eye may be. Thus, the answer to the inquiry of what is or is not art—as discussed in greater detail below—does not fall solely within the domain of professional connoisseurs; rather every individual, no matter how naïve or uninformed, may determine this for himself.

Thwaite stopped reading and tried to return the monograph to Guda Prikash, who refused to take it. Instead, Prikash directed him to read the next paragraph aloud. The expert lowered his head and went on mournfully:

In addition to brushing oily resins on canvas—the conventional means by which our artistic forbearers rendered portraits, pastorals, and other primitive paintings—our ancestors utilized various less conventional but equally acceptable methods to create art, such as applying mud on cave walls and, later, stained glass. This is persuasive evidence that genuine paintings and other authentic works of art have historically come in forms as varied as man's imagination allows. In fact, mud as an artistic medium actually precedes oily resins, and glass has been used for artistic exposition at least as long as canvas, if not longer. To dismiss such media as "non-artistic" is at odds with our rich creative history and deserving of reproach.

For the second time in the trial, a smile crinkled across Plotkin's face. The manuscript was a fortunate find. He looked to the Jury to see if any of them recognized the import of the passage as support for the defense that the mud on his display window was, indeed, a Work of Art. Only two Jurors jotted notes; the rest seemed lost in the rhetoric. One of the note-takers was the octogenarian. Plotkin knew he had to restrain himself from reading too much into the Jurors' behavior, but there had been precious few moments of optimism until now and he wanted to enjoy the sense of vague confidence that all was not yet lost.

"Thank you," Prikash said, as color drained from the witness' face.

"May I add something, Your Honor?" Thwaite squealed.

"No question is pending!" Prikash reminded the Judge. "Therefore, I respectfully suggest that it would be inappropriate for the witness to add anything. He will have the opportunity to add later, if the prosecution wants to re-question him."

"This is a search for the truth, sir!" Stifel reacted scornfully. "The witness may add!"

Clearing his throat, Thwaite declared with obvious displeasure, "What I was just forced to read did *not* represent my views *when written,* does *not* represent my views *now,* and will *never* represent my views as long as there is a breath in my flawless body. I reiterate that the monograph was a parody. Shebolsky and I were satirizing."

The expert then turned to address the Jurors directly. Looking at them with darting eyes, he said, "If you don't believe this explanation, I offer four alternative explanations, any one of which you have my permission to accept as the truth. First, Shebolsky's name is listed above mine on the cover page. This confirms that *he,* not *I,* was the *principal* author. Second, the monograph was published more than thirty years ago, long before I became the consummate, universally esteemed, unrivaled, peerless connoisseur I am now. I was young and my thoughts on art were still evolving, and not fully formed. Ergo, this ancient document hardly represents my current thinking. Third, what I was forced to read was taken out of context. Therefore, it means nothing. Fourth, anyone with a grain of sense, which some of you may have, would know from the exaggerated tone of the document that Shebolsky and I were merely trying to provoke debate, stimulate thought, arouse curiosity, and stir intellectual discourse. I would *never* suggest that the determination of what is or is not art should be left to the uneducated masses, and I doubt that Shebolsky thought so then or would think so now, if he ponders non-religious questions between prayers."

Thwaite arched his left brow for emphasis. "Even if one assumes *arguendo* that I once seriously contended that mud was an acceptable artistic medium, there is not a single documented instance of a *reputable* art connoisseur recognizing mud on *glass* as art," he added.

"The Court thanks you for the erudite clarification," Stifel gushed.

Though disturbed by the Court's gratuitous comment, Prikash maintained his composure. "Now let us turn to A. I. Gopnik, the witness you demeaned as a 'madman'," he said calmly. "Do you acknowledge, sir, that this so-called madman was a luminary in art appreciation before he was committed to the Warehouse?"

"I suppose so, to those who didn't know better," Thwaite replied snidely. "However, he is now a shell of his former self, a deranged has-been who wouldn't recognize a Work of Art if it fell on him."

The testimony prompted Leopold Plotkin to recall his twin uncles. He was offended by Thwaite's choice of words.

"Have you seen Mr. Gopnik since his commitment, sir?"

"Fortunately, I haven't."

"So you have no first-hand knowledge of his current mental state?"

"True enough. However, his report—which I read with an equal measure of laughter and astonishment—confirms that he is still crazy, to say the least."

"Do you have a degree in psychiatry, sir?"

"I do not. However, as an art expert, it is incumbent upon me to understand the human condition and, since an early age, I have had the ability to distinguish diseased from healthy minds."

"Isn't it true, sir, that Bruno Wittgenstein, your former superior at the Salon of Iconoclastic Art, was widely regarded as clinically insane before he severed his ear, attempted to sever the ears of several subordinates, was forced to retire and dispatched to an insane asylum?"

"Perhaps so. However, I was not among those who questioned his sanity before the ear incident. In my opinion, he was confused and misunderstood, not insane. To this day, I continue to view Mr. Wittgenstein as relatively stable and would have no apprehension visiting him in the insane asylum, provided he is unarmed and adequate security is nearby."

"Isn't it a fact, sir, that there is a rich history of insanity within the artistic community: Andre Austerlitz's untimely cutting of his nose when his paintings were criticized as mediocre; Francis of Matawan's removal of an eye when his works were rejected by the Museum of Natural Arts; and Ricardo de la Verdi's claim that he was a bird, after a bird destroyed his most prized painting with droppings, among the most noteworthy examples?"

"I am not sure I would call the history 'rich'."

"Isn't it a fact that many art connoisseurs have continued working through bouts of insanity and commitments to asylums?"

"To a *limited* degree, perhaps. However, you are vastly overstating the prevalence of lunacy within the profession."

"The Court agrees," Justice Stifel interjected, "and takes judicial notice that *most* artistic connoisseurs aren't crazy. Now that this is resolved, has the defense asked its *last* question?"

"I have a few more, Your Honor."

Looking directly into Hippolyte Thwaite's hooded eyes, Prikash said, "Isn't it true that most painters use horsehair brushes and palates when creating art?"

"That seems to be the case," Thwaite replied rather coldly.

"Isn't it also true that the mud on the butcher shop's window is multi-colored and resembles paint in that regard."

"One *might* say that."

"Do *you* say that, sir?"

"I suppose so."

"Nothing further, Your Honor," said Prikash, reclaiming the monograph and moving it into evidence.

Plotkin was impressed by Guda Prikash's partial dismantling of the pompous witnesses' testimony. It seemed obvious to the butcher that his defender had honed his skills as a trial attorney over many years of in-court experience. When the Prime Thinker returned to the Accused Table, the butcher nodded appreciatively. The gesture reminded Prikash why he loved trying cases.

Social Scientist Kierkegaard Thumbnail

51

T he statute Plotkin allegedly violated didn't require proof of negative repercussions. The Prosecutor General's Chief Minion realized, however, the inflammatory value of illuminating the real or imagined consequences of muddying the window. Thus, he persuaded Malatesta to address the issue at trial. Toward that end, the prosecution purchased the services of social scientist Kierkegaard Thumbnail to create a List of Horribles—a catalog of all bad things that might conceivably result if the mud were not removed, no matter how unlikely or remote the possibilities might be.

After being accepted as an expert in the field of social science, Thumbnail stared morbidly at the Jury, as was his typical demeanor. He recited his inventory of possible catastrophic results from the current opacity of the display window: increases in airborne diseases, stress disorders, alcoholism, hospital admissions, mortality rates, aggressive behavior, major depressions, suicide attempts, agnosticism, inflation, unemployment, workplace accidents, unwanted pregnancies, arsons, and fraudulent insurance claims. In a parallel vein, he predicted marked decreases in reading comprehension, church attendance, agricultural yields, birthrates, and marriages.

The mood in the Courtroom grew progressively darker as Thumbnail continued adding to the mountain of disasters he claimed to envision if Plotkin were to be acquitted and the window remained muddied. Plotkin was depressed by the bleak exposition. By the time the direct examination ended, most members of his family were also depressed.

During a vigorous cross-examination, Guda Prikash extracted admissions from Thumbnail that the link between the muddy window and the predicted consequences was tenuous, that it was predicated on a skewed statistical analysis, and that his predictions were based on extrapolations that few, if any, in his profession would make. Thumbnail also conceded that he had a generally bleak outlook, stemming from a difficult childhood with overly strict parents, and that he could not rule out the possibility that those factors may have influenced his predictions.

Feeding his expert impermissible leading questions on re-direct, despite Prikash's objections, Malatesta enabled the social scientist to explain that a tenuous cause and effect relationship between the Mud Crisis and bad outcomes did not negate the existence of a link; that no study was perfect; and that any failure by others in his profession to agree with his extrapolations was due to professional jealousy or a lack of imagination.

When Thumbnail left the Witness Closet, a parade of non-experts described the Mud Crisis' impact on their lives. A college professor testified that he lost his will to teach after seeing the window. A nun lamented that her faith was depleted after discovering the window mired in mud. A long-married couple related that they spontaneously developed irreconcilable differences after passing the window. A mapmaker testified that the window caused him to lose all sense of direction. Each of the tragic scenarios produced tears in the Jury Stall and sobbing in the Spectator Pews.

Despite Guda Prikash's probing cross-examination, the lay witnesses refused to concede that changes in their lives they attributed to the mud could have resulted from something else. After the last traumatized figure stepped from the Witness Closet, Malatesta announced that he had concluded the prosecution's "airtight case." This, in turn, triggered Guda Prikash's *pro forma* motion to dismiss all charges, followed by Justice Stifel's equally *pro forma* denial of the motion.

"The defense will commence its presentation tomorrow morning," Stifel announced officiously, prompting snickers in the Pews from onlookers who felt certain there was no case of any consequence to present.

52

"What is your name, sir?" Guda Prikash asked the man standing serenely in the Witness Closet.

"Anatole Illianov Gopnik," the witness replied with humility, exhibiting none of Hippolyte Thwaite's smugness.

"And what is your profession?"

"I am an art connoisseur and a former museum curator who specialized in the procurement of bleak paintings."

"What piqued your interest in that motif, sir?"

"Actually, nothing. A museum position was available and I was unemployed at the time. As they say, beggars can't be choosers."

"Please summarize your educational background and professional experiences."

"My journey began at the Collegia of Artistic Expression, where I studied the Grand Masters, the Fabulists, and other schools of painting that have come into and out of fashion over the years. After learning to appreciate each school, I copied notable works and made some original paintings, usually of nudes since my interests lay almost exclusively in the naked body. Although I was reasonably proficient in replicating the works of others, it became obvious that I lacked originality. Graduating near the bottom of my class, I gravitated to a nomadic colony of failed artists on the Republic's eastern slopes led by Octavio Benito Medici, a painter of meager talent who, in more than three decades, had never sold a painting to a non-relative. It was through this wonderfully mediocre and supportive man that I learned how to appreciate art, regardless of its quality or sales potential."

"Mr. Medici taught me not to rely on the tastes of the consumer-class to determine whether a piece is worthy of respect or hanging. Like him, during the years I resided in the colony, I never sold a painting to anyone outside my family, although I exhibited a few works at the Salon des Mediocrities, an outlet dedicated to displaying the works of failed or failing artists."

When the Jurors recalled Thwaite's pomposity, they found Gopnik's humility reassuring and easier to digest. They immediately warmed to him. Several saw in Gopnik a man very much like themselves, resigned to a life with few successes. It was evident from their attentive body language that they preferred this man of humility to the egocentric Thwaite.

"Did you eventually leave the art colony?" Prikash asked.

"Yes, I did."

"What prompted you to leave?"

"One morning, Mr. Medici summoned me to his hovel. Speaking like the mentor he had become, he implored me to venture out, to fail as an artist in society at large and, after a respectable period of failure, to teach at an obscure art school where I could share my knowledge of failure with students who were destined to fail in their artistic endeavors. He said that teaching a generation of mediocre artists how to fail with dignity would be a noble calling."

"Responding to my beloved mentor's recommendation, I left the colony. Soon, I managed to obtain employment at an obscure institution of higher learning for two years, where I taught hundreds of untalented students how to fail with their dignity intact."

Gopnik lowered his head, as if embarrassed. "I left the school when a suspicious fire of unknown origin destroyed its exhibition hall and I wasn't able to account for my whereabouts when the conflagration began," he admitted. "The administration suspected that I set the fire and declined to furnish me with a letter of recommendation. Without a letter, my life as an academician ended and my next opportunity to fail had to be in another context."

"After leaving academia, what did you do?" Prikash asked.

"I managed to secure a position as Head Curator of the Museum of Despondent Paintings. While there, I also edited a bi-monthly journal in which I critiqued paintings under the pseudonym Isaac Koplinsky, an associate from the art colony. Koplinsky used to complain about laboring in obscurity. I wanted to bring this tragic man some degree of the notoriety he craved. Unfortunately, when a fire I started damaged the Museum, I was committed to the Warehouse for the Purportedly Insane. As a result, I lost my job and my efforts on Koplinsky's behalf came to an end."

Jurors admired Gopnik's attempt to bring Koplinsky a morsel of recognition. None could imagine Thwaite being so benevolent. Leopold Plotkin was both struck by Gopnik's attempt to help the unfortunate Koplinsky, and proud to have the disgraced former curator on his side.

"In addition to editing the bi-monthly journal, have you authored any learned treatises?" Prikash asked.

"I have," Gopnik answered.

"Please tell the Court about them."

"While teaching, I presented numerous monographs at local

and regional conferences of failed artists, the most memorable one was *On Being an Artistic Non-entity: Challenges and Rewards.* The entire list of monographs is contained in the *curriculum vitae* I prepared at the behest of attorney Talisman, who I understand collapsed on the first day of trial while addressing the nice people in the Jury Stall. My heart goes out to him, his family, and the Jurors who must have been traumatized by the event."

Jurors were moved by Gopnik's empathy and nodded admiringly at him. Prompted by their kind gestures, Gopnik faintly waved his hand. Though outraged by the Jury's behavior, Umberto Malatesta decided against interposing an objection so as not to offend the Deciders. Instead, he muttered obscenities under his breath.

"Before your commitment to the Warehouse for the Purportedly Insane, were you a member of any professional societies?" Prikash asked.

"I was," Gopnik answered.

"Please identify them."

"Prior to being committed to the Warehouse, I belonged to the local chapter of the Society of Minor Artistic Pedagogues, the regional chapter of the Society of Unknown Artistic Exhibitors, the National Society of Failed Artists, and the International Society of Occasional Expert Witnesses. There may be others. However, residing in an insane asylum has dulled my memory a bit."

"Over your career as a failed artist, an educator of aspiring failed artists, a member of organizations dedicated to failing artists, a journal editor, a monograph author, and a museum curator, have you ever been certified to opine as an art expert?

"I have."

"Have you prepared a list of the cases where you have been certified?"

"I have. The two cases are listed in alphabetical order in my Curriculum Vitae."

"I show you a document titled *Curriculum Vitae of Anatole Illianov Gopnik.* Is this a true and correct copy of the Vitae?"

"It is."

After offering Gopnik's bonafides into evidence, Prikash passed the witness to Malatesta for cross-examination. Convinced Gopnik was sufficiently expert under the relaxed criteria governing expert witness qualification and fearing that Justice Stifel would commit reversible error if he declined to recognize Gopnik's expertise, Malatesta elected not to oppose certification. Instead, he informed the

Court he would not challenge the "insane, disgraced, arsonist's meager qualifications to opine" and would permit the Jury to hear Gopnik's "irrational testimony." He concluded by saying, "Let them determine for themselves how unworthy of belief this prostitute's opinions are, with respect to whether the muddy window is a Work of Art."

Prepared to reject Gopnik as an expert and disappointed by Malatesta's failure to challenge him, Stifel stated with regret: "Without an objection to this admittedly mediocre man's qualifications, this Court recognizes him as an expert to opine on whether the window is a Work of Art or merely a large pane of mud-ridden glass that violates the anti-covering statute."

53

After establishing the date, time, and method of A. I. Gopnik's examination of the display window, Guda Prikash asked him to describe what he saw.

"I saw a brilliantly crafted, multi-colored mural divided into two separate yet unified parts," Gopnik testified. "The left side is an exquisitely rendered landscape consisting of an untilled wheat field, a solitary figure of indeterminate gender standing near a tiller, a denuded forest, a mountain range, a cluster of quaint shops, houses, churches, graveyards, and other objects painted in thin, airy brushstrokes that evoke tranquility. The right side is an equally impressive cityscape comprised of rows of grimy factories, drab tenements, stores, thugs, prostitutes, traveling salesmen, mounds of dead fish, garbage cans, and other objects rendered in thickly applied dark swirls created either with a palette knife or extraordinarily skilled fingers. The heaviness of the application evokes the frenetic amoral sexual activity typical of the Promiscuous Movement in vogue last century. Were the great Juan Pablo Ionesco not dead, I would have thought this aspect of the masterpiece was his creation. I believe the heaviness is an homage to this great amoralist, probably by one of his disciples."

Gopnik took a moment to review his notes, so he could be certain not to overlook any of his observations. While Gopnik reviewed, Leopold Plotkin scanned the Jurors to see their reactions to what Gopnik had already described. Most of their faces reflected disbelief. A few were blank. He desperately hoped that one or more of the blank stares had not yet concluded that Gopnik was delusional.

"The contrasting halves of the painting," Gopnik resumed, "are seamlessly joined by interconnecting scratch marks and subtle stippling. This is a remarkable achievement, attainable by few painters other than Juan Pablo and those who mimicked him after his assassination by a jealous competitor."

"After examining the window, did you subsequently return to the site?" Prikash asked.

"I did," Gopnik answered.

"For what purpose?"

"To create a replica of the window."

"Why did you do that?"

"Mr. Talisman asked me to."

"Did you create the replica?"

"I did."

"Is it an exact replica?"

"It is."

"Is the replica in the Courtroom?"

"It is."

Prikash looked up to the Judicial Perch. "Your Honor, the defense respectfully requests permission for Mr. Gopnik to leave the Witness Closet in order to use the replica to illustrate his observations with respect to the painting."

"The *alleged* painting," Justice Stifel corrected.

"Of course, the *alleged* painting," Prikash conceded.

"Does the prosecution object to this request?" asked Stifel.

"Not at all," Umberto Malatesta replied confidently. "Allowing the Jury to view a copy of the inartistic monstrosity is an excellent idea."

"There being no objection, the witness may leave the Closet for the purpose so specified. The Court cautions the insane witness' Warehouse handlers to keep a close eye on him to assure that Jury members are not placed in harm's way."

Gopnik walked from the Closet to the replica. Prikash handed him a pointer. The Jurors repositioned themselves in their seats to have an unobstructed view of the exhibit.

"Please show the Jurors where on the alleged painting the two unified haves are located," Prikash instructed.

"The landscape is here," Gopnik noted with the aid of the pointer, "the cityscape is there."

"For the Jury's edification, sir, please point out the features you previously identified on the landscape side and explain their artistic significance. After doing that, please do the same for the cityscape side," said Prikash. "Should there be other features you wish to refer to, which you did not previously directly identify, kindly do that as well."

Squinting through a magnifying glass, Gopnik pointed to the wheat field and said, "This is the wheat field. This symphony of white, yellow, orange, and a speckle of off-brown brushstrokes is rendered impeccably. At its center is a figure standing stiffly behind a tiller. A ray of light filtered through dew-induced fog falls directly at this person's feet, drawing one's eyes inexorably to him or her, whichever is the case. The scale of this person relative to the leafless trees and structures off to his or her left is flawless, as is the perspective, composition, and harmony of the scene. The tiller's clothing, a white hooded robe, would be appropriate for either gender, making the representation universal in appeal. The congruence of melancholic verticals and horizontals, the dead forest, and the absence of human activity in the village proper, suggests the agrarian way of life is nearing a denouement and invites the eye rightward, toward the emerging cityscape."

Gopnik tapped the pointer at various items on the urban side whose swirls, he said, were reminiscent of the best works of the great Juan Pablo. "In contrast with the laconic tone of the agrarian landscape," he declared, "the urban sector is vibrant, infused with vitality and élan. The smokestacks, sewers, open garbage bins, gangs of marauding hoodlums, drunkards, and dead fish littering the streets are rendered so powerfully, one can almost smell the noxious odors. A street scene, painted with extraordinary subtlety in gray tones, suggests the decadence of the prostitution district—depicting women seated seductively at windows, enticing men who are skulking along the sidewalk, wrestling with whether to venture inside for hedonistic pleasure or to go to work. To evoke the tension and ambivalence of the male figures, they have been drawn without noses, mouths or eyebrows."

The spectators squinted at the replica in vain attempts to see what Gopnik's artistic eye purportedly discerned while Gopnik tapped the pointer. "As one's eye moves from these faceless figures," he said, "it is drawn to a bluff where we find a collection of churches of unspecified denominations. All the churches are painted in dark colors, suggesting competition for the souls of the faceless men and, perhaps, their seducers. Unexpectedly, a frameless still life of an apple, three oranges, and two cantaloupes rests on the largest church's steps. A stooped man is destroying the still life's canvas with a knife, while a crowd applauds. This is the most moving part of the painting, illuminating the violence and lack of respect for paintings that permeate our emerging urbanized society."

Jurors seemed dubious. Unable to detect any of what Gopnik claimed to see, several rolled their eyes or furrowed brows in skeptical arches. Spectators giggled at the testimony. Even Plotkin's most ardent supporters had to struggle to suppress laughter. The butcher saw these reactions as bad omens.

Stepping back from the replica to gain a broader perspective, Gopnik said, "This mural incorporates certain unmistakable aspects of the Ashkenazi-Rejectionist School. However, it is not derivative. Instead, it is the next logical step on the Ashkenazi-Rejectionist continuum, a *masterpiece* ushering in a new and technically better school of art, one that encompasses subtle minimalist and symbiotic features the Ashkenazi-Rejectionists never dared to incorporate. The breathtaking range of techniques and stylistic improvisations of this work reveal its creator as a genius."

As Jurors turned to the recipient of Gopnik's fulsome praise, Leopold Plotkin was unable to suppress a prideful beam. He appreciated the compliments of a man who respected the quality of his unintentional efforts. In the Pews, Plotkin's mother was overcome with pride as well. She whispered to Ana Bloom, "He always was a good drawer."

"The boy is no *drawer!*" Jacob Plotkin angrily corrected. "He's a *creative genius!*"

Guda Prikash turned to the expert witness and asked the central question in the trial: "Have you formed an opinion, to a reasonable degree of professional certitude, as to whether the display window is a Work of Art or simply an undifferentiated conglomeration of mud?"

"I have," Gopnik replied gravely.

"Please tell the Jurors what your opinion is," Prikash instructed.

"The window is a Work of Art or, more precisely, a painting of breathtaking quality. To be even more precise, it is a painting of majestic quality; a remarkable aesthetic achievement that one would expect to find in the finest museum, not on a butcher's storefront."

Prikash tilted his head slightly to suggest he had one more line of inquiry for the unhinged connoisseur. "Do you acknowledge that most people who look at the window will see only mud, not the painting you have described?"

"Of course," Gopnik conceded.

"Will you explain why that is?"

"I would be pleased to," Gopnik said convivially as he turned toward the Jury Stall. "The painting is so subtle, only a few select people, those blessed with a heightened degree of aesthetic sensibility, will see it. That is its *genius*. One must have what I call *The Gift* in order to appreciate it."

"Do you have *The Gift*, sir?"

"I do."

"Is *The Gift* something only persons trained in the arts are endowed with?"

"Not necessarily. Although it is more likely a person trained in the arts will have it, others can as well."

"What percentage of people would you expect to have it?"

"Only a small percentage; perhaps three to five percent, give or take a percent or two either way."

With that, Prikash passed the witness to Umberto Malatesta for a cross-interrogation. Sensing that Malatesta could benefit from time to prepare, Justice Stifel announced an early lunch recess—one that would last an hour longer than normal.

54

Umberto Malatesta's Chief Minion was troubled that the Jurors seemed to like A. I. Gopnik. He realized that Leopold Plotkin's conviction would be subverted if even a single Juror accepted Gopnik's testimony, as a result of an affinity with the insane expert witness. Over lunch, the minion recommended that Malatesta assault Gopnik's character to eliminate that possibility. "Assassinate the character and the opinion will fall," he whispered conspiratorially to his superior.

After eating, the Prosecutor General approached Gopnik, holding a set of baseless, accusatory questions prepared by the underling.

"You admitted during your direct testimony that you appropriated Isaac Koplinsky's name in conjunction with your bi-monthly journal," Malatesta reminded Gopnik. "Isn't it also a fact that you used an array of other pseudonyms during your failed career: Andre Shostakovich, Misha Goldberg, Eliezer Cohen, Dmitri Kropotkin, Misha Halpern, and Mordechai Melig, to name a few?"

"Koplinsky was the only one that I appropriated," Gopnik replied respectfully.

"Do you also deny using the pseudonym Isaac Perlmutter in the course of your meaningless career?

"Yes."

"And Benjamin Kornbluth?"

"That also."

"In addition to appropriating the names of others, isn't it a fact that while your mentor, Octavio Benito Medici, treated you like the son he never had, you betrayed him by engaging in sex with his wife under his bed while he was sleeping?"

"Objection! Prikash exclaimed.

"What is the reason for this untimely interruption?" Justice Stifel demanded.

"The question has no *conceivable* relevance," Prikash replied. "Whether Mr. Gopnik engaged in connubial activities with Octavio Benito Medici's wife under a bed has no bearing on his expert opinion."

"The objection is quashed!" Stifel huffed. "The witness' alleged sexual exploitation of his dying mentor's distraught wife, while he was being treated like a son the barren couple was unable to conceive, is directly related to whether he has a propensity to lie."

"Well, sir?" Malatesta asked Gopnik, spreading his arms like wings. "What have you to say?"

"Would you be kind enough to repeat the question?" said Gopnik.

"If you insist," Malatesta said disdainfully. "Isn't it a fact, sir, that while the aged, crippled, and naïve Octavio Benito Medici treated you like the son his wife never gave him, you betrayed this pathetic, terminally ill man by flagrantly and repeatedly fornicating with the licentious woman beneath the dying man's bed while he writhed in pain and pleaded with you to stop?"

"Until now, I didn't know Octavio Benito Medici had a wife," Gopnik replied. "In fact, before you posed the question, I wasn't aware he was crippled, on his deathbed, or in pain."

Malatesta was undeterred. "Assuming *arguendo* that Octavio Benito Medici had a wife and that this immoral woman had offered to engage in connubial pursuits with you under his deathbed, would you have permitted his children to watch?" he asked.

"Objection!" Prikash cried.

"What is the basis for *this* interruption?" Stifel asked impatiently.

"The question assumes facts not in evidence, lacks foundation, is hypothetical, and is irrelevant. Its only purpose is to blacken the witness' character."

"The Court will permit the impermissible question and instruct Mr. Perlmutter, or whoever he claims to be at this time, to speculate as to whether he would have taken advantage of his mentor's wife, had he a wife, while the hopelessly naïve Octavio Benito Medici, a man of great rectitude and infertility, was sleeping and his five illegitimate children were eating under the bed."

"I had too much respect for Mr. Medici to do such a thing while his children were eating. Furthermore, I wouldn't have taken advantage of Octavio Benito Medici's wife unless he insisted. At that time, I had no interests of a sexual nature."

Justice Stifel, who had many interests of a sexual nature, instructed the Jury to disregard the witness' answer on the ground that it was likely to confuse them. He recommended to Malatesta that it might be best to move on from the Medici Affair to another scandal perpetrated by the witness.

"How often have you committed adultery during your troubled marriage?" Malatesta asked next.

"Unfortunately, I have never married," Gopnik replied sadly, arousing the envy of several unhappily married Jurors.

"So, no woman would have you?" Malatesta suggested.

"Actually, despite several proposals from suitors, I chose to fail alone rather than burden another person with my failures," Gopnik said selflessly.

"Turning from your *selfish* decision not to marry and bring children into this world to a matter that is equally repulsive," said Malatesta, "how many paintings did you forge during your *dismal* career as a failed artist?"

"None," Gopnik replied.

"Were you a charter member of a subversive secret society known as Artists for the Expansion of Art, whose guiding principle is that anything—however inartistic—is art as long as one proclaims it so?"

"I was not a member. In fact, I've never heard of the group."

"Since the society is secretive, you can't be expected to openly acknowledge that you were among its founders, can you, sir?"

"I suppose that's true," Gopnik conceded.

"Now let us turn to what you have egotistically referred to as *The Gift*," Malatesta spat. "Isn't it true that this so-called *Gift* to see what others don't see is actually an *illusion within a delusion;* that the painting you claim to see on the window is merely a byproduct of a grossly diseased mind that resulted in your involuntary commitment to the Warehouse for the Purportedly Insane?"

"It is *not* an illusion within a delusion," Gopnik replied. "Although I am the first to admit that I have a touch of insanity, I *saw* a Work of Art on the window. It's an exquisite creation rarely seen in this or any other lifetime. I saw a masterpiece."

"Motion to strike, Your Honor!" Malatesta shouted, unhappy with the answer. "The witness' response was unresponsive to the question and redundant."

"The Jury shall disregard the entirety of what the witness said," Stifel ruled, without permitting Guda Prikash to weigh-in. "The witness shall respond responsively in the future and avoid repetition."

Confident that the witness would not be able to recall what he claimed to have seen on the display window replica when questioned by Prikash, Malatesta said with a flourish: "Do you concede, sir, that if you *don't* see something now that you claimed to see when testifying on direct, it necessarily follows that your so-called *Gift* is nothing more than the excrement of a diseased mind?"

"That would be a logical inference, I suppose," Gopnik agreed.

"Point to where the solitary figure with an erection is standing," Malatesta insisted with a scowl.

"The solitary figure doesn't have an erection," Gopnik corrected. "I said that he or she is standing erect in a wheat field. Because the person's back is turned, it's impossible to tell whether there *is* an erection, assuming the figure is of the male gender."

"Point to the deluded forest," Malatesta insisted.

"Actually, it's a *denuded* forest, not a *deluded* one," Gopnik replied as he pointed to the exact location he had cited in his direct testimony.

"Where are the faceless nuns and rabbis you mentioned?" Malatesta asked, hoping to trick the witness, who had not mentioned either during direct interrogation.

"I never said there were nuns or rabbis," Gopnik replied without hesitation. "I referred to faceless men cavorting in a prostitution sector of the cityscape. There they are." He pointed to the faceless men's precise location.

"Point to the cantaloupes, the oranges, and the goddam cluster of churches!" Malatesta shouted, drawing disapproving frowns from a few Jury members.

Again, without hesitation, Gopnik pointed to each object as Malatesta glowered at him.

"Show Umberto Malatesta everything else you purport to see."

"Here are the grimy factories…drab tenements…cheap stores…dead fish…thugs, prostitutes…pimps…traveling salesmen____."

"That's enough!" Malatesta cried, sensing that the exercise was enhancing rather than eroding Gopnik's credibility. After regaining most of his composure, the Prosecutor General resumed the interrogation, pursuing a line of questioning that ignored the legal maxim: *A TRIAL LAWYER SHOULD NOT ASK A QUESTION IF HE DOESN'T ALREADY KNOW THE ANSWER.* The line of questioning also deviated from the Chief Minion's script, another potential pitfall.

"You testified on direct, sir," Malatesta said sardonically, "that only rare individuals endowed with the so-called *Gift* are able to see a painting on the window. Other than yourself, can you identify a *single* person on this planet who has claimed to see anything but mud on that God-forsaken piece of glass?"

"Yes," Gopnik replied matter-of-factly.

"What was that?" Malatesta groaned, clearly shocked by the answer.

"I said 'yes,'" Gopnik repeated. "I can identify such a person."

The nonplussed prosecutor blindly forged ahead. "*How* do you know that someone else has claimed to see a painting on the window?"

"I heard his compliment."

"A compliment about the *window*?"

"Yes."

"Tell me *exactly*, word-for-word, what you heard."

"He said, 'That's a nice painting'."

"Where were you when you imagined hearing this?"

"On the sidewalk, next to the window."

"How far away was he from you?"

"A few inches."

"Describe him."

"He had a small head, a prominent nose, a short white goatee, a small growth on___"

"That's sufficient, sir! How long have you been seeing and hearing from imaginary people?"

"I've never experienced visual or auditory hallucinations, as far as I know."

"I take it that you heard the alleged compliment by the alleged man with a big nose on the day you examined the window as the accused's so-called expert?"

"No, it was three days after that."

"Why were you on the sidewalk, inches from the window, three days after the examination and not in the Warehouse where you belonged?"

"I was on a field trip to the National Zoo with other patients."

"So, the other person who professed to see a painting is a fellow insane patient?"

"Well, actually, he was a psychiatrist."

Giggles emerged in the Pews. Unnerved but unwilling to abandon his quest, Malatesta asked, "What is the name of this purported psychiatrist?"

"Dr. Milton Zilberstein."

"Zilberstein?"

"Yes, Zilberstein."

"In the weeks after Zilberstein allegedly called the window a '*nice painting*,' how often did you observe him in the Warehouse for the Purportedly Insane talking to himself, mumbling incoherently, drooling, or exhibiting nervous tics?"

"Never. As soon as we arrived at the Zoo, he collapsed and

died."

"So, this alleged psychiatrist is *unavailable* to refute your *hearsay* contention that he saw a painting?"

"I suppose that's true."

"Are you sure Zilberstein is dead? More to the point, isn't his very existence, another product of your florid delusions?"

"I'm quite certain he is dead."

"Why?"

"The Zoo's veterinarian said so."

"What exactly did the veterinarian say to suggest that Zilberstein had died?"

"He said, 'This man isn't breathing.'"

"Other than the veterinarian's offhand remark that Zilberstein wasn't breathing, is there any other evidence of his death?"

"Yes, his obituary was tacked to a Warehouse bulletin board."

Sensing once again he had only enhanced Gopnik's credibility by asking a blind question, Malatesta decided to retreat. In a quavering voice, he announced that he had nothing more to ask of the "hopelessly insane witness."

Jurors wondered whether they had overestimated the prosecutor's talent. Spectators were appalled by his mishandling of the Zilberstein affair. Plotkin was surprised by his nemesis' ineptitude. Justice Stifel was chagrinned.

Badly damaged, Malatesta limped back to the Prosecution's Table where he was met by his minions' blank stares.

"Does the defense wish to belabor the points raised by the prosecution's cross-examination, or is it willing to leave it at that and move on?" Stifel moaned from his Perch.

"The defense has nothing more for Mr. Gopnik," Prikash replied, content with the ground gained from Malatesta's mishandling of the interrogation.

"That being the case," Stifel groaned, "the witness may return to the Warehouse and reunite with fellow madmen. The defense shall call its next witness."

"The defense has no more witnesses," Prikash stated.

"Does the prosecution have any rebuttal witnesses?" Stifel inquired solicitously.

"It does not," Malatesta answered flatly, still disconsolate over his clumsy cross.

"Very well," said the disappointed Judge. "As neither side has anything more, the evidentiary record is shut and the parties' Closing Diatribes will commence in the morning."

55

Umberto Malatesta's self-regard enabled him to efficiently forget his recent Courtroom stumbles. By the next morning, he considered the cross-examination of A. I. Gopnik an unqualified success. With his confidence restored, the prosecutor rose to begin the Diatribe. Strutting toward the Jury Stall, he stopped, pointed sharply at Plotkin, and thundered, "The proof is overwhelming that this *degenerate* has engaged in one of the most *horrific* crime sprees in modern history; a spree that has shaken the Republic to its core and will do irreparable damage unless abated by a guilty verdict and a thorough cleansing of the *immoral* display window!"

Malatesta then initiated a scathing narrative of half-truths, flagrant lies, and occasional references to the actual trial record. He embellished the dire predictions of social scientist Kierkegaard Thumbnail. He twisted Pincus Barrenblat's testimony to portray a jailhouse confession rather than a denial by the butcher that he had farted. He reminded the Jury of the chicken plucker's testimony that Plotkin never referred to the window as a Work of Art and falsely claimed that Primo Astigmatopolous overheard the butcher deny that it was a painting.

Tapping disparagingly on Gopnik's replica of the window as Plotkin sunk further into his chair, the Prosecutor General shouted: "The preeminent art connoisseur, Professori Hippolyte Thwaite, swore under oath that this monstrosity is neither a painting nor any other species of art known to Mankind. During his unforgettable testimony, the Professori stated, without equivocation, that the workmanship reflects no skill on the part of the clod who layered the mud; that the mud-infested window is a prototypical example of amateurishness by a stranger to the art world that only a madman would find artful."

Malatesta paused to observe the Jurors' appreciation of his Chief Minion's phraseology. "The reference to a *madman*," he resumed disdainfully, "brings to mind Anatole Illianov Gopnik—the disgraced curator, admitted arsonist, and betrayer of Octavio Benito Medici. The prosecution submits that Gopnik's *delusional* opinions offend both common sense and aesthetics, and lend support to the widely held belief that crazy people should be seen and not heard. If you recall nothing else after being locked into the Deliberation Room, remember that Gopnik is a longtime resident of the Warehouse for the Purportedly Insane; adopted a variety of pseudonyms during his failed career to hide his true identity; belonged to a secret society; betrayed his mentor by repeatedly engaging in inappropriate sex with the dying man's wife; and arrogantly claims to have the ability to see what others cannot!"

As Jurors listened attentively to the Prosecutor General's misrepresentations, Malatesta tapped the mud-covered glass and defied them to see what the profoundly unhinged man purported to see. He added that if they saw anything but mud, they would be as insane as Gopnik.

Plotkin stole a glance at Guda Prikash to ascertain whether Malatesta's mangling of the record disturbed his lawyer. He saw a calm expression on Prikash's face. Although he didn't understand why, Prikash's unruffled exterior mildly comforted the butcher. Perhaps he has confidence in the Jury's ability to see through the Prosecutor General's distortions, the butcher thought.

Malatesta moved closer to the Jury Stall. "It is now time to address Milton Zilberstein, the mysterious *phantom* the *madman* claims made a passing, utterly ambiguous statement while walking to the Zoo with a group of other crazy people!" he declared.

Anticipating that Malatesta was about to blacken Zilberstein's character, Jurors leaned forward in their chairs; spectators leaned forward on the benches; Courtroom personnel leaned forward at their stations; and Justice Stifel leaned sideways to position his good ear in the prosecutor's direction. Seated upright, Prikash readied his pen for note taking. Neither leaning forward nor sideways, Plotkin braced himself for the worst.

"As you will recall," said Malatesta as he gazed amorously at Jurymembers, "the accused's so-called art expert sought to bolster his preposterous opinion with a stray, out-of-court comment attributed to Zilberstein, an alleged psychiatrist from the Warehouse for the Purportedly Insane who, more likely, was an inmate of the institution. According to Gopnik's virtually incomprehensible account, one that defies common experience, Zilberstein either said that the window was a 'nice painting' or that it was a 'nice day for a walk to the Zoo.' Whatever Zilberstein did or did not say, assuming for the sake of argument that he isn't a figment of Gopnik's vivid imagination, there are deeply *troubling* aspects to this inherently unreliable testimony."

"First, the alleged statement is rank *hearsay*. Whatever was said, it was muttered on a street, not in a court of law and, therefore, not given under oath or subject to cross-examination, the sacrosanct hallmarks of reliability. Second, apart from Gopnik's self-serving testimony regarding the purported statement, we have no confirmation that Zilberstein even *existed*. Where is Zilberstein's alleged obituary? Where is Zilberstein buried? More important, where is his medical license? Third, assuming *arguendo* that Zilberstein once walked this earth and was a psychiatrist of some sort, there is no testimony that he was sane when he made the passing comment about the weather."

"As you are no doubt aware, men who devote their lives to tending to the insane are at least as mentally ill as their patients, often crazier. Moreover, even if Zilberstein were *sane* when he said it was unlikely to rain, we are left with troubling questions that have never been answered to anyone's satisfaction. What caused his death? Was Gopnik complicit in his apparent murder? When Zilberstein denied seeing a painting, did Gopnik become enraged and follow him to the Zoo, poisoning him with tainted peanuts? You should ponder these and other troubling questions about Gopnik's mysterious ways when you are taken to the Deliberation Room to render a guilty verdict. If you are unable to resolve them, Umberto Malatesta highly recommends that you reject the insane witness' testimony in its entirety."

Inferring from the concerned expressions of Jurors that his comments about Zilberstein's possible murder had piqued their interest, Malatesta's confidence soared and he decided to supplement his Chief Minion's prepared remarks with some thoughts of his own.

"The more one thinks about it," he declared, "the more one realizes that Zilberberg is either another of Gopnik's delusions or a calculated invention by a congenital liar. Is it likely a man so young would have died, especially the same day he allegedly said 'the window is filthy'? Assuming, for argument's sake, that Zilberwitz made an oblique reference to a painting, *what painting* was this profoundly emotionally disturbed man referring to? Was it a portrait he saw on a Warehouse wall? Was it a still life he had admired in the National Art Gallery? Who knows? How can anybody know? These are mystifying questions only one person can answer, and he is not here."

Delighted with the Jurors' perplexed expressions, the Prosecutor General returned to the prepared remarks. The puzzled looks of jurors were mirrored throughout the Courtroom. Plotkin silently hoped Malatesta would prolong the rambling to thoroughly confuse everyone prior to his attorney's illumination of the truth. But the prosecutor seemed to be on firmer footing when he said, "As Umberto Malatesta thanks you for your abiding attention to the compelling case he has presented against the *monster* smirking at the Accused's Table, he urges you to convict not because the accused has placed our great Republic in harm's way; not because your fellow citizens overwhelmingly deplore his antisocial acts; not because you will be hated by friends, family members, and acquaintances if you acquit him; and not because you will be unable to look yourselves in the mirror if you fail to find him guilty. Instead, Mr. Malatesta implores you to convict based on the evidence he has just summarized. In the final analysis, unless you are more dull-witted than Umberto Malatesta imagines, you will come to the only conclusion that makes sense: the butcher is *guilty*."

Looking at the glazed eyes of each Juror, the silver-tongued prosecutor intoned: "When you recede to the Deliberation Room to convict, remember Umberto Malatesta's final words: The painting Gopnik professes to see is *an illusion within a delusion.*"

Enamored with the pithiness of his parting words and pleased to see a few Jurors scribbling in notebooks, Malatesta smiled broadly, thanked the Deciders in advance for returning a guilty verdict, and strode victoriously across the Well to rejoin his comrades.

Plotkin's doleful eyes followed Malatesta's confident return to the Prosecution's Table. His hopes sank so low they were barely discernible. He found it less likely now that even a single Jury member would embrace the Work of Art defense and, thereby, produce a hung Jury.

56

"**H**aving the rare *Gift* to see what most others cannot," Guda Prikash declared at the outset of his Closing Diatribe, "Anatole Gopnik described the masterful window painting crafted by Leopold Plotkin. He showed you precisely where the elements of the painting are situated: the wheat field, the solitary tiller, the cantaloupes, the denuded forest, the mountain range, the rows of grimy factories, the mounds of dead fish, the tenement buildings, the portentous clouds, the prostitutes, the pimps, the churches, and the grave yard. He did this, both on direct testimony and on cross-examination, with a precision that belies the existence of an *illusion within a delusion*, the derogatory phrase my opponent coined to ridicule this learned, highly respected curator."

Prikash raised his index finger for purposes of emphasis. "There is no dispute over the fact that Mr. Gopnik is insane. His insanity is a matter of record. However, there has been no proof that he is *delusional*; that he *imagines* things that are not there. I submit that the Prosecutor General, in an act of desperation, has resorted to personal ridicule and pejoratives, just as men did when visionaries theorized that man evolved from apes."

Leopold Plotkin immediately thought of Bruno, the orangutan, and wondered whether his primate friend would miss him, or only the grapes, when he was re-consigned to prison. At the same time, it occurred to him that Bruno often seemed to share his dejected mood. Was that an indication of how close they were on the evolutionary scale? When he had more time, perhaps while disintegrating in prison, he vowed to think more about the matter.

"Let us not forget the vast presence of insanity within the artistic community," Guda Prikash said. "Andre Levinson's incessant threats to become a Christian evangelist when his paintings were criticized as mediocre; Morris Goldstein's contention that he was a bird, after a sparrow destroyed his most prized painting with droppings; and, of course, Wittgenstein's partial amputation of his nose while Director of the Museum of Iconoclastic Art."

Prikash gestured to the prosecution's expert, Hippolyte Thwaite, seated in the Pews between Inner Chamber Leader Cicero Bookbinder and High Minister Emile Threadbare. "The only testimony that Mr. Gopnik suffers from delusions, as opposed to generalized insanity, came from Professori Thwaite, who may be steeped in the arts but has no qualifications to diagnose mental aberrations."

Satisfied that he had adequately addressed the illusion within a delusion theory, the Prime Thinker turned to *What Is Or Is Not Art,* the monograph Thwaite co-authored with Fyodor Shebolsky. Displaying the writing to the Deciders, he reminded them of the monograph's confirmation that mud on glass paintings actually predated oil-based canvas works. "For Professori Thwaite to call mud on glass 'non-artistic' is diametrically at odds with the Republic's creative history," Prikash proclaimed. "Moreover, it contradicts what he and Shebolsky wrote in their monograph. Here again is what Thwaite and his co-author said:

> *In addition to brushing oily resins on canvas—the conventional means by which our artistic forbearers rendered portraits, pastorals, and other primitive paintings—our antecedents utilized other less conventional but equally acceptable methods to create art, such as applying mud on cave walls and, later, stained glass. This is persuasive evidence that genuine paintings and other authentic works of art have historically come in forms as varied as man's imagination allows. In fact, mud as an artistic medium actually precedes oily resins, and glass has been used for artistic exposition at least as long as canvas, if not longer. To dismiss such media as 'non-artistic' is at odds with our rich creative history and deserving of reproach.*

Prikash paused to allow Jurors to digest the words. He then said, "For Professori Thwaite to characterize the window as non-artistic also ignores this passage from the writing:

> *The question of what is art has been with us since our primitive ancestors lived in the virgin forests of the Republic and were drawing images of beasts on the walls of caves. While it is within the ambit of professional art connoisseurs to opine on the __quality__ of art, it is presumptuous for even the most sophisticated maven to determine __what is not art__ since art can come in virtually limitless forms, shapes, and sizes.*

"I submit that Leopold Plotkin's mud on glass painting is an homage to his artistic forbearers which, after subtle modifications to the Ashkenazi methods, ushered in a new School of Art that will inspire future generations of painters, critics, and historians."

With no other exculpatory nuggets to extract from the mono-graph, Prikash shifted to a topic that he suspected weighed on the minds of Jurors—Plotkin's alleged confession in Purgatory's base-ment, which Umberto Malatesta misrepresented as fact. After re-counting the lunatic's testimony regarding the butcher's repeated cries from his cage, the Prime Thinker narrowed his eyes and said, "When one applies logic and normal rules of grammatical con-struction to the phrase 'It's Not a Fart,' it is obvious that this was an innocent explanation that whatever Mr. Barrenblat thought he heard that day had not actually originated from my client's rectum. My learned opponent's intimation that a denial of flatulence was a confession that the window is not art has the stench of prosecuto-rial overreaching."

Unable to mask their appreciation of Prikash's clever turn of a phrase, Jurors giggled before Justice Stifel ordered them to sup-press their "inappropriate" reactions. The Prime Thinker's clever wordplay unsettled Malatesta, who found it unseemly for anyone but him to play with words. Plotkin vaguely smiled, impressed by the impact of the witticism on Jurors, as did Ana Bloom, Myra Rabi-nowitz-Pritzker and others in Plotkin's small circle of supporters.

Prikash transitioned to his next argument. "Just as the Prose-cutor General has attempted to mislead you about the import of Mr. Plotkin's flatulence-related statement," the Prime Thinker as-serted, "he has tried to confuse you about the significance of what Dr. Zilberstein said on the sidewalk. According to Mr. Malatesta, the remark, 'That's a nice painting,' raises mystifying questions. I suggest that the only thing *mystifying* are the questions my learned opponent *claims* are raised."

Prikash gestured toward Malatesta. "The Prosecutor General is keen on explaining away Milton Zilberstein's illuminating apprais-al of the window because it confirms both the existence of *The Gift* Mr. Gopnik identified and the Work of Art the connoisseur vividly described. Don't allow the so-called *mystifying* questions to distract you. Don't accept the Prosecutor General's invitation to enter the *fantasyland* he has populated with a Warehouse psychiatrist he sug-gests may actually have been a patient; could have been murdered; possibly never existed; might have said 'It's a nice day' during a to walk to the Zoo rather than 'It's a nice painting' and____."

"Enough examples!" Justice Stifel interceded. "Move on!"

Prikash moved on. In the course of doing so, he stressed the significance of the High Court's opinion in *Pogrebin against Pogre-bin* (a case Stifel had refused to mention); the exaggerations and irrelevance of social scientist Kierkegaard Thumbnail's dire predictions; and the unimportance of the chicken plucker's failure to recall whether Plotkin mentioned art or a painting when he brushed mud on the window. In mid-declamation, Stifel suddenly declared that only two minutes remained in the argument—a newly devised time constraint not imposed on Malatesta, whose Diatribe went on much longer.

With insufficient time to address all that he had planned to address, Guda Prikash abandoned some finer points and proceeded directly to the conclusion. In an effort to bond more intimately with Jurors through false flattery, he thanked them for their "selfless civic contributions to the world's greatest deliberative process." "I have observed your copious note taking and obvious attention to detail," he lied, "and infer from this that you are intelligent, fair-minded men with common sense and the ability to appreciate the subtleties of this case, including the painting in question. I sincerely believe you have sufficient self-control not to fall for the prosecution's bombast, misrepresentations, and skewing of facts."

"Enough of the *ad hominems*!" Stifel shouted.

Scanning the Jurors' inscrutable faces, Prikash softly intoned, "As the ultimate arbitrators, you hold Mr. Plotkin's fate in your hands. Depending on how you exercise your awesome power, he will either continue to live among us as a free man or be consigned to prison to live out his life in filth, degeneracy, and boredom, far from loved ones, unable to operate his beloved butcher shop like the five generations of Plotkins before him, a frustrated genius, unable to create art for future generations to appreciate. Before you deliberate, bear in mind your Oath to endeavor to avoid a miscarriage of justice. While you deliberate, I will keep a vigil with him and his sick and elderly parents to await a verdict that reaffirms the finest traditions of our judicial system."

As Prikash walked from the Jury Stall to the Accused's Table, Justice Stifel announced that due to defense counsel's "prolixity" the Court would deliver its Directions after a recess. At the Table, Plotkin complimented Prikash for his "excellent speech" and thanked him for all he had done in a "futile effort" to prevent the inevitable destruction of his life and the lives of his parents and uncles.

"I am honored by your gratitude," Prikash said. "In my years of trying cases, clients have rarely expressed appreciation for my work."

57

J ustice Stifel delivered his Closing Directions from the edge of the Judicial Perch. His reedy voice, weakened by the rigors of the trial, wafted downward to the Jury Stall, then to the Tables where the combatants sat, and, finally, to the Pews where hundreds had gathered, shoulder-to-shoulder, hoping his guidance would lead to a speedy conviction.

"You have heard the evidence and arguments of counsel," the Jurist proclaimed dourly. "Tragically, it will now be left to you, not the Court, to decide whether the accused committed Crimes against the Republic. Before being sent to the Deliberation Room to wield your undeserved power, try...despite your severe limitations...to comprehend a few of these instructions."

Stifel frowned as he looked disdainfully at the Jurors.

"You would not be faulted if you view the accused as odious and reprehensible," the judge snarled while Plotkin and members of his immediate family winced. "Such perceptions are understandable in light of the evidence. However, in rendering the appearance of justice, you are expected to ignore a compulsion to convict merely because the accused may be despicable and has caused a Crisis that may negatively affect your lives. Instead, you must decide whether there is or is not a Nagging Doubt in your vacuous minds regarding the accused's guilt."

Despite Stifel's admonition, several jurors were unable to ignore the perception that Plotkin was odious, reprehensible and despicable. They glared at the butcher. The glares unnerved the defendant. He averted his eyes and abandoned his last sliver of hope. Images of Purgatory cascaded through his mind. A future without a future took hold in his mind. "Why did I listen to my father?" he asked himself. "I was a fool."

"This trial is the most momentous event of your sterile lives," Stifel exclaimed, prompting a rash of nervous fidgeting within the Jury Stall. "It has been closely monitored by your fellow citizens— from sea to sea, shore to shore, and mountaintops to valleys. Politicians, local as well as national, have opined on the consequences of what you will decide here. Try not to allow these powerful forces to influence you."

As the Justice listed other things that should not affect the Jury's verdict, Plotkin's heart pounded. Behind him, spectators smiled, and the butcher's supporters muttered angrily to themselves, particularly the patriarch who now blamed himself for ruining his son's life. Malatesta looked on appreciatively at the effect that the Stifel's statements seemed to have on the Deciders. Every so often, Stifel scornfully looked down at the waxen figures in the Stall, still jealous that they were the finders of fact.

"*The Rules* require that the Court caution you against holding the accused's refusal to testify against him," Stifel declared with obvious displeasure. "In accordance with this *unrealistic* dictate, you are expected to overlook the fact that by exercising his privilege to remain mute, he denied you an opportunity to hear his rendition of the events and escaped a probing cross-examination by the Prosecutor General."

"On another point, if you were paying attention, you might have heard some of the Court's interactions with the lawyers. You are instructed not to allow any perceived antipathy on the Court's part toward defense counsel, or affinity for the prosecution, unduly influence you. In the event you infer that the Court harbors animosity toward the accused, for example, and was signaling its preference for a conviction, treat this inference, more or less, with a grain of salt."

Stifel scowled at Prikash, then smiled at Malatesta. Plotkin winced. Prikash patiently retained a practiced calm as the Justice resumed his directions.

"The statute the accused allegedly violated is straightforward and sufficiently clear for even those of you with particularly low intellects to understand," Stifel said. "On its face, it prohibits the covering of a commercial window with any *foreign thing* unless the *thing* is a Work of Art. To ascertain whether the accused's mud-mired window is artistic in any sense of the word, you must use your eyes and common sense, to the extent either or both are in working order. In the event this does not resolve the issue, ask yourself whether the opinion of a *madman,* to wit, Anatole Gopnik, is as believable as the prosecution's *esteemed* art critic, Professori Hippolyte Thwaite."

Stifel knitted his eyebrows and gazed malignantly at the Jurors as they mulled over those insights. "Since your ignorance of the law is breathtaking," he proclaimed, "the Court finds it necessary to explain that a proper verdict requires unanimity, meaning that all seven of you will have to reach the same conclusion. In pursuit of that objective, you will be locked into a small, windowless room, barely larger than a janitor's closet, for as long as necessary, unless the Court determines, in its wisdom, that you are hopelessly stalemated and discharges you. In the unlikely event you are unable to render a verdict, the Court and your fellow citizens will be greatly displeased. To avoid the shame and stigma that are sure to follow from a stalemate, you must rise above your limitations and reach a decision!"

As the Jury was led to the Deliberation Room, everyone in the Courtroom expected a quick guilty verdict. With that shared conviction, nobody bothered to leave. Stifel remained on the Great Bench. Personnel remained at their stations. Spectators remained in the Pews. Newspaper reporters stayed in their cubicle. Opposing counsels continued to occupy their respective Tables. Plotkin's heart raced as he slouched at Guda Prikash's side.

58

The Jury's first act was to select a Chairman. Because nobody else expressed an interest in the position, a Juror with an ant-eater's nose was chosen by acclimation. Once installed, he thanked his colleagues for recognizing his leadership qualities, promised to devote his full energies to the position, and declared it was time to vote. A Juror with a poorly constructed toupee congratulated him for his bold decision and tireless efforts to bring the deliberations to a close. "Without you, I doubt we would have reached this point."

"Shouldn't we discuss the evidence before voting?" the octogenarian asked timidly.

Astounded by the old man's audacity, the anteater accused him of being an apologist for the butcher. "I'll have you expelled if you continue obstructing us," he threatened.

The first among equals ripped a sheet of paper from his notebook, tore it into seven uneven pieces, kept the largest remnant for himself, and instructed his colleagues to be sure to write "guilty" on the ballots before returning them.

Moments later, he counted six "guilty" votes and one "undecided." Appalled, the anteater demanded that the lone dissenter reveal himself.

"It was me," the octogenarian admitted, raising a gnarled hand.

"Are you a *moron*?" the anteater asked apoplectically.

"I don't think so," the octogenarian replied.

"Well, I do," the anteater asserted sharply. Gesturing across the table to the Juror with the poorly constructed toupee, he said, "The bastard's guilt is as obvious as the squirrel on that guy's head."

"You make fun of my hairpiece when *you* have the snout of an animal that feeds on insects!" the toupee rejoined.

"I was making a point; not mocking your silly hairpiece!" said the slope-nosed Chairman.

"Well, make your point with *his* ridiculous mouth!" seethed the toupee, pointing to a Juror with a fishlike mouth.

"Keep my mouth out of this!" fish-mouth shot back. "The prick's guilt is as obvious as *his* three chins!" he declared, pointing at two mounds of flesh that supplemented a multi-chinned Juror's original chin.

As the analogies expanded to craggy skin and other physical flaws amenable to mockery, the exchanges grew louder. Soon, a Bailiff arrived to tell the Deciders that they had disturbed the Judge's sleep. The anteater apologized for his colleagues' misbehavior.

After the Bailiff left, the anteater glared at the octogenarian. "Explain your vote!" he barked.

"Well," the octogenarian shrugged innocently, "like I said, I think we should talk a little before convicting the asshole."

Exasperated that the aged Juror expected a discussion before finding Plotkin guilty, the anteater tried to bully him into changing his position. When threats failed, the anteater summoned the Bailiff to report that the Jury was stalemated and needed the Justice's advice on how to resolve it. The Bailiff suggested a letter summarizing the problem. Minutes later, the anteater handed the Bailiff a hastily scrawled missive. The Bailiff carried it to Stifel on the Great Bench, where the Jurist silently read the following:

> *Deer Justis Steeple. The jurie has a big problum and begs for You're help. Six of us have voted the bucher GILTY. One old man who is sinile won't convict him unlest we discust the facts befour officille voting him gilty. Me and the five other Jurors I am overseening think what the old man is doing is hiley irreguler and we want to no weather he has a write to do that. If he don't, will you pleaze throw him off of the jurie so he can't introfere with are work. If he does have the write, what shud we do? None of us, accept maybe him, wants to see the bucher get off scot free. We hope to hear from you soon so we don't have to sit all day doing nothing but looking at each other and getting into argumints. Yours trueli, the Chairman.*

Although the *Uniform Rules of Procedure* required that all Jury inquiries be addressed in the presence of the parties, Stifel decided to dispense with the formality. He prepared a response and instructed the Bailiff to deliver it *ex parte* to the Deliberation Room. The Bailiff, in turn, handed the response to the Chairman who, because he was a poor reader, passed it to the toupee to read to the group. The epistle stated:

> *This is in response to your poorly spelled, grammatically atrocious letter. At the outset, be advised that the Court's name is Stifel, not Steeple. The Bailiff will provide you*

with a dictionary, which you are to use if you find it nec-
essary to write again. The Court hopes that your inability
to write properly does not reflect on your capacity to rea-
son or oversee your fellow Jurors.

As for your question, the Court sympathizes with your
frustration. Unfortunately, a demand to discuss some
facts before voting to convict, though irritating, is not a
basis for an expulsion. While juries are not required to
discuss facts before voting to convict and often do not,
they may do so if any Juror insists. The Court suggests
that you try to resolve the impasse by appeasing the re-
calcitrant member with a brief discussion of a few facts
before rendering a guilty verdict.

The anteater heeded Justice Stifel's suggestion by announcing there would a superficial chat before taking another vote. Pleased by the change in position, the octogenarian extended his hand as a peace offering. Not wishing to appear weak, the anteater withheld his hand and warned the old man not to gloat.

Under the anteater's direction, a facts-based discussion ensued. Among other topics, the Jurors speculated on the spelling of Gopnik's alleged pseudonyms; whether Hippolyte Thwaite's self-importance exceeded Umberto Malatesta's; if Bernard Talisman's malady was life-threatening or chronic; what the fallen trialmonger might have said had he continued his Opening Rant; and whether the chicken plucker was a practicing celibate or simply too timid to engage with Magdalena in matters of the flesh.

As the discussion progressed, the anteater noted something he considered decisive: the fact that the only persons who claimed to see a painting amidst the mud were Gopnik and Zilberstein, the butcher's fellow Jews. The room became oppressively stuffy as some of the anteater's allies discussed the propensity of Jews to stick together and other conspiracy theories. This led to disagreements. Soon, the discussion devolved into personal affronts and threats of bodily harm. Disturbed by the outbursts, Stifel dispatched the Bailiff to tell Jury members that deliberations were adjourned until the next morning, when they were expected to return in less combative moods.

59

The second day of deliberations began with the anteater's declaration that discussion was closed and it was time to vote. All but the octogenarian agreed. He suggested that the Jurors examine the replica of the display window before voting.

"Will nothing satisfy you?" the Chairman snarled.

"Looking at the replica will," the octogenarian replied calmly.

"Write the Judge and get him thrown off the Jury," fish-mouth whined, prompting nods from others.

Utilizing the editorial services of the toupee, the anteater drafted another letter to Stifel, reporting a stalemate due to "the ridiculous old man who wants us to look at the replica before voting." He begged Stifel to expel the octogenarian. In his written reply, Stifel stated that, though the replica was of dubious significance, he would not risk reversible error by banishing the obstinate holdout. "To avoid a stalemate," Stifel wrote, "look at the goddam replica!" Bitterly disappointed, the Chairman asked the Bailiff to bring the exhibit and a magnifying glass to the Deliberation Room.

The octogenarian reviewed his notes of Gopnik's testimony and prepared a list of the items that Gopnik claimed to see on the window. Then, looking through a magnifying glass, he quietly studied the exhibit. After the study, he broke his silence. "I see churches," he stated matter-of-factly.

"Where?" the anteater demanded.

"There," the octogenarian replied, placing his thumb where Gopnik had claimed to see a cluster of churches.

The anteater seized the magnifying glass. Squinting through it, he reported with disdain, "I only see mud!"

"Only mud," three-chins agreed after hovering over the site.

"Definitely, nothing but mud," exclaimed the Juror with nasal moles.

"Without a doubt, mud and not a thing else," the toupee declared.

"Satisfied?" the anteater asked.

"There's more to look at," said the octogenarian.

"Hand the goddamn magnifying glass back to him so he can finish," the anteater ordered.

The octogenarian resumed his study.

"I see the graveyard," he reported.

"You're as crazy as Gopnik," said the anteater, eliciting concurrences from comrades.

"It's well cared for," the octogenarian added.

"Give me that damn thing," three-chins brayed, yanking the magnifying glass from the octogenarian. He examined the site and declared, "It isn't a graveyard."

As others searched in vain for a graveyard, they accused the octogenarian of being Gopnik's dupe, easily led, stupid, insane, or a secret supporter of the butcher intent on exonerating him despite overwhelming proof of guilt. Undeterred, the octogenarian continued examining the replica. He paused after each sighting to enable fellow Jurors to register withering criticism of his discovery of the wheat field, the solitary human in the field, the forest, mountain range, village, houses, factories, tenements, businesses, mounds of dead fish, ladies of the night, faceless men, grime, and a portentous section of sky.

"I think I have *The Gift*," the octogenarian announced. Having possessed few things of significance in his life, this thought pleased him.

"You're crazy!" the anteater shouted.

"You belong in the Warehouse!" triple-chin spat.

"Away from society," the Juror with an oblong face exclaimed.

"I'm ready to vote," the octogenarian stated diffidently.

"You're too confused to vote," the toupee said.

"May I have a ballot?" the octogenarian asked politely.

"Here!" the anteater replied, throwing a scrap of paper in his direction.

"Thank you," the octogenarian said gratefully.

"Now vote!" the anteater shouted, handing the other Deciders ballots.

Votes were cast, collected, and announced: Six "Guilty" votes and one "Not Guilty."

"Now what?" the toupee asked.

"Another vote," said the anteater.

There was another vote, with an identical result, followed by rebukes of the octogenarian, and other votes with the same result and more rebukes. After adjourning, two more days of voting ensued, with no change in the outcome. On the fifth day, the anteater had the toupee inform Stifel (who had relocated to his chambers) that the Jury remained deadlocked due to the octogenarian's refusal to convict, despite efforts to persuade the "senile imbecile that the bastard is guilty."

Stifel was irritated by the Jury's failure to convict, but unwilling to declare a failed trial. Thus, he resorted to tactics he had utilized in the past to break deadlocks. In an *ex parte* message, he told the Jurors that they would no longer be served lunch and deliberation time would be increased from six to ten hours a day. When another day didn't produce a guilty verdict, Stifel extended deliberations through the weekend. After weekend voting didn't resolve the impasse, he quarantined the Jury in the Deliberation Room, forcing the Deciders to eat and sleep in the crowded, unventilated quarters.

Written appeals from the Jury seeking mercy brought the following reply from Stifel: "In the end, you must hand down a verdict. You and your associates hold the keys to your freedom. The Court strongly encourages you to do whatever is necessary to reclaim your lives. Should the stalemate continue, heat will be turned off in the room."

Accustomed to a spartan life — one with little food, heat or other amenities — the privations didn't trouble the octogenarian. Because he had grown used to being mocked, criticized, and rebuked, the comments of fellow Jurors didn't affect him. His adversaries, however, led somewhat less onerous lives and felt the pain Stifel had inflicted. As the days passed, they suffered while remaining deadlocked, six against one.

Awaiting the verdict, the anxiety of Leopold Plotkin, his family, and supporters mounted. Plotkin ate sparingly and prayed for the first time in decades. Jacob Plotkin said that he couldn't take much more and that his father, Shlomo, had made a terrible mistake sending him to the Republic. Plotkin's mother, worried that her son wouldn't survive imprisonment, agreed. The twin uncles became depressed, despite not knowing why. Extended family members worried that the Plotkin name would be stained in perpetuity if Leopold were convicted. Arturo Kimmelmen was too depressed to joke. Jacobi Kimmelmen was too depressed to listen to Arturo's jokes. Ana Bloom couldn't concentrate and repeatedly misfiled books at the National Library. Hinta Gelb blamed herself for being too hard on her protégé. Guda Prikash berated himself for not performing up to his normal trial standards. Bernard Talisman continued to convalesce in the hospital, wondering whether his dislodgement from the case had sealed the butcher's fate.

In an attempt to raise Plotkin's spirits, Ana Bloom took him to a performance of *A Midsummer's Night Dream*. Given the circumstances, neither was able to laugh at Puck's humor. In another effort to bolster Plotkin, she joined him and the Kimmelmen brothers at Rubenstein's Grecian Tearoom where she encouraged Arturo Kimmelmen to tell one of his hilarious jokes. The joke fell flat, however, when Arturo began to cry and said, "I can't be funny when my friend is about to be sent to prison." The next day, Bloom accompanied Plotkin to the National Zoo to visit Bruno. That effort failed when Bruno refused to come to the bars, as if sensing what was probably about to happen to Plotkin. "I hope to see you again in a few decades, if we're both still alive," the dejected butcher said as he waved farewell to the orangutan.

As Plotkin and others in his camp worried, the adversaries were relaxed and optimistic. Umberto Malatesta contemplated a bright future, perhaps appointment to the High Court of Final Supplications when one of the tribunal's relics retired or died. The Prosecutor General's minions busied themselves by writing a post-verdict speech for Malatesta to deliver from the Courthouse steps, praising the genius of the Jury system and his trial performance. Justice Stifel slept much of the time but periodically searched for ways to increase Plotkin's sentence beyond what the anti-window-covering statute permitted.

The Jury stalemate continued. Stifel's patience eventually depleted. On the ninth day of the impasse, he threatened to impose privations of unimaginable scope the next morning unless the Jurors reached a verdict. Fearing the unknown, the anteater and his compatriots grew more anxious with each six to one vote. Minutes before sunrise on the tenth day of deliberations, the anteater removed the last sheet from his notebook and distributed the scraps to his sleep-deprived allies and the octogenarian.

At first light, he informed the Bailiff that the Jury had reached a decision.

Orange smoke bellowed from a chimney of the Low Court of Criminal Transgressions to alert the public that the jury had rendered a verdict in *The Republic against Plotkin*. Within the hour, people descended on the Courthouse in motorcars, trams, subways, cabs, bicycles, wheelchairs and gurneys to attend the Reading of the Verdict. When the Pews filled to capacity, the overflow was dispersed to the edifice's hallways and grounds.

The mood was ebullient. Anticipation of a guilty verdict coupled with a National Day of Celebration scheduled to begin after the Reading, raised the excitement level to a fever pitch. Among the scheduled events were performances by the Fettig Rhapsodic Symphony, the Fettig Drama Consortium, and a reading by the Republic's Poet Laureate, Ernst Lubish. There would also be a parade from the Inner Chamber to the butcher shop, where Inner Chamber Leader Cicero Bookbinder would deliver a speech praising the genius of trial by jury. The day would end in a ritualistic cleansing of the window by High Minister Emile Threadbare and his Cabinet, with official photographers recording the historic moment for posterity.

Inner Chamber contrarian Milos Gorky denounced the National Day of Celebration. To demonstrate his displeasure, Gorky announced an unofficial Day of Mourning featuring funeral dirges and a silent procession to the butcher shop, where he would criticize the practices of trials and imprisonment.

Plotkin's parents, other family members, Ana Bloom, the chicken plucker, Magdalena, Gopnik, delegates from the Women's Association for the Prevention of Cruelty to the Truly Despised, and Hinta Gelb sat in the Pews awaiting the Reading of the Verdict. Unlike the anti-Plotkin forces around them, there was neither gleeful chatter nor happy faces among the butcher's partisans—only silence.

Plotkin sank beside Guda Prikash at the Accused's Table, braced for the conviction. Tears brimmed in his mournful eyes.

On the other side of the Well, Umberto Malatesta was radiant. Anticipating the adulation awaiting him after the Reading, he bantered with his minions, thanking them for their "minor contributions." Soon he would be speaking from the Courthouse steps, praising himself in front of an adoring crowd of citizens.

The gleeful chatter ended when a Bailiff demanded silence and ordered everyone to rise while Justice Stifel ascended the Great Bench. Once on the Perch, the judge said in a solemn tone befitting the occasion: "First and foremost, overt demonstrations of approval or disapproval are to be kept to a minimum. This includes shouts, cheers, or moans, as well as applause, frowns, winces, shrugs, and embraces. Second, and less important, the Court reluctantly thanks the Jurors for the cooperation they exhibited last night after too many days of intransigence. Third, and of least significance, after sentencing, the Jurors are invited to a brief reception in Chambers where they will receive half-hearted thanks for their less than commendable service."

Looking down at the Stall, Stifel asked, "Has a verdict been reached?"

"Yes," the anteater replied in his capacity as Chairman.

"It appears that the Jury has reached a verdict," Stifel said almost ebulliently. He could barely contain his enthusiasm over the prospect of hearing the guilty verdict. "The Courtroom Crier shall take possession of the Verdict Form and advise the Court when he has done so."

The Crier marched to the Stall, grabbed the sealed document from the anteater, positioned himself at the base of the Great Bench, looked up to the Perch, and announced gravely, "The Verdict Form has been seized, Your Honor. With the Court's indulgence, I am prepared to unseal and read it."

"The Reading being imminent," Stifel sighed, "the Court instructs prison guards to position themselves to take the accused into custody as soon as the verdict is announced."

Five meaty men in black uniforms took up stations at the entrance to the Courtroom Well and prepared to subdue the butcher as soon as the Crier uttered "Guilty."

"The Crier shall unseal the Verdict Form and commence the Reading," Stifel proclaimed.

As the Crier's fingers grasped the seal, a kaleidoscope of the most traumatic events of Plotkin's troubled life raced through the butcher's mind: the aborted bar mitzvah rehearsal; the Tree of Temptation debacle; his conscription into the shop; the termination of his studies at the Lyceum for Cerebral Children; the end of his intellectual feasting at the National Library of Pedantic Writings; cessation of his childhood friendship with Ana Bloom; his arrest and imprisonment in Purgatory; and other tribulations. A guilty verdict, he reasoned after reimagining those events, would be a fitting punctuation to his misery.

Upon unsealing the Verdict Form, the Crier opened his mouth, lowered his head, and began reciting: "We the Jury...in the case of The Republic against Plotkin...after due consideration of the evidence...and diligent deliberation...do hereby find...the accused... the accused...the accused____."

"What happened?" asked Stifel, unable to see the Crier and accustomed to the vassal reading the verdict straight through.

"He seems to be having trouble breathing," the Scrivener reported.

"In that event, the Chief Bailiff shall complete the Reading," Stifel declared impatiently.

Spectators who favored a guilty verdict were delighted when Stifel decided to move ahead without waiting for the Crier's breathing to improve. Prikash and Plotkin—too anxious to endure even a brief delay—were pleased that the torch was passed from the hyperventilating official to the Chief Bailiff, who appeared to be in excellent health.

The Chief Bailiff removed the Verdict Form from the Crier's limp hand and declaimed as loudly as he could: "We the Jury in the case of The Republic against Plotkin...after due consideration of the evidence...and diligent deliberation...do hereby find the accused...Not... Not____."

"Not *what*?" Stifel demanded.

"Not Guilty!" the shocked Bailiff managed to say incredulously.

A moment of silence followed. Stifel broke the silence with a gasp. The gasp was soon joined by gasps from the pews, as well as groaning and gagging. A few onlookers fainted. Even Leopold Plotkin—a person not easily given to gasping, groaning, or fainting—lapsed into a gasping fit, followed by a few groans and lightheadedness.

"There's been a *mistake*!" Stifel shrieked. "The verdict was either misread or miswritten! Bring the Form here—without delay!"

As the Bailiff ascended the stairs, a debate erupted in the Pews as to whether the Form had been misread or miswritten. Whatever the case, most members of the audience were confident Stifel would quickly set things right. When he received the Form, the Jurist pushed his spectacles to the end of his nose and scanned it, looking for a "Not." Apoplectic to discover there was a "Not" in the document, immediately in front of "Guilty," Stifel glared down at the anteater, waved the Form frenetically, insisted there had obviously been a transcription error, and ordered the quaking Chairman to announce the actual verdict.

"The actual verdict *is* 'Not Guilty'," the petrified Chairman mumbled sheepishly.

Shock, bewilderment, and then pandemonium erupted in the Pews. There were waves of boos, hisses, and groans, followed by demands to charge Jurors with crimes and calls for an immediate retrial. Angry dignitaries and their handlers fled; Malatesta and his minions sat stupefied; Stifel and courtroom personnel stood rigidly; and Jury members, except for the octogenarian, cowered in their Stall.

Tears flowed down Plotkin's cheeks as he struggled to come to terms with the acquittal. Prikash wrapped his arms tightly around Plotkin's upper back, kissed the moist cheeks, and pronounced the verdict the most satisfying one of his long career. Overcome by gratitude, Plotkin didn't object to Prikash's grandiose show of affection and thanked the lawyer for sparing him from re-imprisonment. The butcher turned towards family members and supporters to take in their reactions. His mother, a devout agnostic since the Bar Mitzvah debacle, was praying; his father and deranged uncles were grinning; the chicken plucker and Magdalena were kissing; Ana Bloom was smiling; Hinta Gelb was applauding; Gopnik was blinking back tears; and Myra Rabinowitz-Pritzker and her Women's Society confederates were shouting ebulliently.

Several minutes into the pandemonium, Justice Stifel called for order and disinvited Jurors from the post-verdict gathering in Chambers. Pounding his gavel, he directed Bailiffs to escort the "dishonorable idiots" from the Courtroom. He added, "Each of the imbeciles is banned for life from jury duty." After their removal, the Judge extended condolences to "the esteemed Prosecutor General, the incomparable Inner Chamber Leader, the revered High Minister, and all other patriots who tried to end the scourge visited upon us by the reprobate who, unfortunately, has been set free by seven deviants." Stifel fixed steely eyes on Plotkin as he unleashed a diatribe, in which he exposited why he would have convicted him had he been the Decider. When finished, the deflated Jurist summoned Bailiffs to carry him to his Chambers.

Once Stifel was carried away, Plotkin fled the Courtroom in the company of loyalists. In the hallway, he was met by an angry mob that waved fists and hurled invectives in his direction. As he inched down the corridor toward a bank of elevators, the chicken plucker and other allies formed a human shield around him. While hostile hands reached out for the butcher, attorneys Rogoff and Babel threatened to sue anybody who assaulted Plotkin; Magdalena threatened to kick anybody who touched him; Myra Rabinowitz-Pritzker threatened to slap anybody who came too close to him; Milos Gorky threatened to introduce legislation if anybody bothered him; and Jacob Plotkin threatened to strangle anybody who approached his beloved son. As the group managed to board an elevator and move through the Courthouse lobby without incident, the loyalists maintained a protective phalanx around the butcher until they safely arrived at the tenement building.

Early that afternoon, the Inner Chamber convened an emergency session. Without debate, the body rescinded the National Day of Celebration and replaced it with a National Year of Despondence. The scheduled events were appropriately altered to reflect the new themes of anger and despair. The parade was transformed into a funeral procession; the reading by the Poet Laureate was postponed; the speech by Cicero Bookbinder lauding the genius of the jury system was revised to question whether trial by jury had outlived its usefulness; and the cleaning of the window was cancelled.

On the evening of the acquittal, Jacob Plotkin presided over a dinner to honor his son. Seated at the head of a large dining table, on loan from Hinta Gelb, Innerchamberman Milos Gorky and seventeen other meat merchant loyalists shared a sumptuous meal. Several bottles of sacramental wine were consumed as one supporter after another toasted Plotkin's unwavering courage and adherence to principle. After those toasts, Plotkin toasted Prikash for his brilliant defense; Prikash toasted Myra Rabinowitz-Pritzker for her companionship; and Ana Bloom toasted the still hospitalized Bernard Talisman for his tireless work on the case before his collapse. Arturo Kimmelmen toasted all of the toasters with an unfunny joke that everyone cordially laughed at. Finally, Jacob Plotkin, the family patriarch, stood to say, "I have always loved my son despite appearances to the contrary." Leopold Plotkin was touched by his father's revelation and the camaraderie of those who shared in the celebration of his acquittal. The butcher would later recall that he enjoyed one of the most pleasurable evenings of his life and slept well for the first time in decades.

Epilogue

After Leopold Plotkin's acquittal, the protests soon ended. They gave way to pilgrimages to the display window by people who wanted to determine whether they possessed *The Gift* described by A. I. Gopnik at trial. At first, few claimed to see a painting. Over time, however, sightings increased to three in ten visitors, a number low enough to preserve *The Gift's* rarity but sufficiently high to avoid ridicule from those who saw only mud.

Gustave Pugachev, a prominent *avant-garde* art dealer, became intrigued by the burgeoning interest in the window. Recognizing the potential for profit, he offered to purchase the glass for a minimal fee. Although Plotkin was reluctant, for sentimental reasons, to sell the window, the chicken plucker persuaded him that his need for money trumped sentimentality. Before the butcher parted with the window, he brushed mud onto a replacement, a denser version of the original. The replacement attracted more pilgrims to the site. Pugachev was excited by the public's reaction to the new work, purchased it for another modest amount, and sold it for a sizeable profit. The process was repeated every few weeks, until Gopnik's release from the Warehouse ended the arrangement.

When Gopnik learned of Plotkin's dealings with Pugachev, the former curator told the butcher that the unscrupulous dealer was cheating him by purchasing the windows at below- market rates and selling them for exorbitant prices. "Let me be your broker," Gopnik suggested. Despite qualms about Gopnik's stability, Plotkin was grateful for his trial testimony and retained him as his exclusive agent. Under Gopnik's management, Plotkin's reputation as an artist and his income from the artwork reached new heights. With increased demand for his work, Plotkin considered closing the butcher shop to devote himself to painting full-time. Consistent with his practice, he consulted with his father before making a decision. The patriarch angrily told him that becoming a full-time artist was out of the question because butchering was the only occupation for a Plotkin. "If you become a painter, it will kill me."

Despite Jacob's dire prediction, Leopold stood up to his father for the first time in his life. "Painting is my destiny, Papa. Unless I paint, I will die." Soon thereafter, Leopold opened an art gallery to display his works. The gallery exhibited paintings on canvas rather than glass and enjoyed enormous success, catering to high-end private collectors and museums. As his reputation as an artist grew, he lectured at prestigious universities about his new School of Art, and his new works routinely received rave reviews by professional critics.

Suddenly a man of independent means, Plotkin moved with the elders to a three-story brownstone in a fashionable district of Fettig and retained a live-in caretaker to oversee and entertain them. Contrary to Jacob's prediction, the patriarch didn't die. Instead, he enjoyed the benefits of his son's success.

When not painting or arguing with his father and uncles, Plotkin read voraciously. On weekends, he met with Ana Bloom and Hinta Gelb to discuss books or attend lectures. The activities stimulated his intellectual appetite. Eventually, his psychosomatic illnesses all but disappeared. Likewise, his disappointment over not becoming a public intellectual receded into the background.

Primo Astigmatopolous had attended the post-verdict dinner in the Plotkin flat with Magdalena. Nibbling on her neck between courses, the chicken plucker confessed his love for the prostitute. Because Magdalena had heard Astigmatopolous read his journal entries at trial, the confession came as no surprise to her. She smiled knowingly, acknowledged her desire for him, placed a sliver of brisket on her fork, and fed it to the love-starved trilogist. Encouraged by her behavior, the chicken plucker launched an intense month-long courtship of the woman whose native intelligence, nurturing nature, and anatomy he found irresistible. At the end of the month, he invited her to move in with him.

Astigmatopolous continued plucking during the day and writing at night until Plotkin closed the shop to open his art gallery. He rejected Plotkin's offer of work as a porter in the gallery because portering didn't strike him as fulfilling. Magdalena saw his unemployment as an opportunity to complete the trilogy before he reached old age. She offered to support him with her brothel earnings. Astigmatopolous, too prideful to be a kept man, rejected the offer, declaring that no man of character would permit such a thing. Later, after giving the proposal more thought, he relented. With Magdalena's gentle prodding, the retired chicken plucker discontinued his incessant interviews and began to write. Three years later, he completed the first volume of the planned trilogy. The volume sold reasonably well for a book by an unknown, first-time author on the problems of the underclass. A year of uninterrupted writing culminated in publication of the second volume of his *magnum opus*. Positive reviews and impressive sales enabled Magdalena to retire while Astigmatopolous authored the final volume. At that juncture, she proposed marriage. Against Plotkin's advice, he accepted the proposal. In a church wedding conducted by Father Sagittarius, he and his radiant bride were betrothed. Soon after publication of the third volume, Magdalena bore three children, one for each book. Needing more room, the couple moved to a larger residence. There, Astigmatopolous authored several other noteworthy trilogies, and a novella that enjoyed critical acclaim and economic success. In his later years, he taught literature at a university, focusing on his *oeuvre*.

Not long after the trial, Bernard Talisman recovered from his never-diagnosed illness and was discharged from Our Lady of the Albatross Hospital. Following his release, he spent more time with Ana Bloom and less on lawyering. When not attending operas, symphonies, or lectures, Talisman and Bloom enjoyed stimulating intellectual discussions and more stimulating sexual activities. Their love reached new heights with the introduction of sex into their relationship. When it reached its apogee, Talisman proposed marriage. Bloom accepted. They married at Fettig's largest synagogue.

After the ceremony, Bloom left the National Library of Pedantic Writings to devote herself to social causes. She joined the boards of the Society for the Prevention of Cruelty to the Truly Despised, the Association for Gender Advancement, the Committee for Redemption of Prostitutes, and several suffragette brigades. Though frustrated by the slow pace of progress in those areas, she found her work fulfilling. She and Talisman held weekly dinner parties for their most intimate friends. Among the frequent guests were Plotkin, Astigmatopolous, Magdalena, Prikash, Gelb, and Gopnik.

Guda Prikash's defense of Plotkin established his reputation in the firm as an accomplished trial attorney. He enthusiastically accepted all trial-related assignments, even on short notice, and flourished as a brilliant tactician known for scrupulous attention to detail, a commanding presence, and an instinct for persuading juries to acquit guilty clients. Rarely losing, Prikash became a luminary in litigation circles.

The former recluse worked in a glass-fronted office on the firm's top floor. He leased a flat in a densely populated section of Fettig and enjoyed weekend outings with Myra Rabinowitz-Pritzker. Apprised by Dr. Bartok Golub of the calamitous effect repetitive whistles would have on Guda Prikash's innate reclusive propensity, Rabinowitz-Pritzker was careful to keep him away from train stations and other sites where whistling was likely. Although Prikash and Rabinowitz-Pritzker enjoyed their time together, they didn't form a romantic alliance in the first decade following Plotkin's acquittal. In addition to weekend outings, their relationship during that time period was limited to interesting repartee, attending cultural events, and engaging in occasional coitus to satisfy their animal lusts. Their relationship changed, however, the following decade when they engaged in unprotected sex and unexpectedly conceived. With Prikash's encouragement, Rabinowitz-Pritzker carried the child to term. A few days before the birth of their daughter, they married. Despite a lack of deep romantic feelings, their marriage was respectful and pleasant. Prikash assumed many paternal duties and, to his surprise, found them nearly as fulfilling as trialmongering, though more stressful.

After trial, Pincus Barrenblat continued his lunatic ways in Purgatory's basement. Stripped of his coveted trustee position for his dismal performance at trial, he spent his time shouting and threatening to sue prison officials for violating his constitutional rights. Plotkin visited him on weekends, out of appreciation for his generous testimony. During one visit, the Lunatic asked Plotkin to enlist Guda Prikash's services in a class action challenging the prison's horrific conditions. Intrigued, Prikash agreed to take up the cause. Nine years of litigation ultimately resulted in improvements that changed Purgatory from a profoundly overcrowded, filthy, and violent institution to a moderately overcrowded, dirty place of violence. When Barrenblat was released from prison, Plotkin hired him as a sales representative at the art gallery, where the lunatic's talents for embellishing the truth served him well. Despite continuous threats to sue Plotkin over imagined grievances, Barrenblat remained a loyal employee until retirement.

A day after Leopold Plotkin's acquittal, Justice Stifel resigned from the Judicialhood to devote his waning energy to a campaign to abolish the right to a jury trial. He traveled the Republic, accompanied by likeminded legal scholars who were enraged by Plotkin's acquittal. Stifel found it easy to stir up mobs with the proposition that feckless citizens like them could not be trusted to reliably convict criminals. Using *The Republic against Plotkin* as a case study, he and his cohorts whipped up support for a constitutional amendment to ban jury trials by stressing the innate stupidity and naïveté of laypeople and the obvious superiority of men trained in the law in ascertaining the truth. Crowds enthusiastically applauded Stifel for illuminating their deficiencies by waving placards emblazoned with the phrase LAYMEN ARE TOO STUPID TO DECIDE and chanting "No more juries!" Despite those efforts, Stifel's labors to amend the Republic's Constitution to eliminate trial by jury failed. Disappointment eventually pushed Stifel into a deep depression. Unable to eat, sleep, or engage in sex, the diminutive former Jurist died in his sleep. His last words to his frustrated wife were: "That goddam butcher destroyed me."

Umberto Malatesta, who presented a moving eulogy at Justice Stifel's funeral, continued for a few years to serve as the Prosecutor General. His stumbles at Plotkin's trial, however, permanently diminished his undeserved self-confidence and took a toll on his voice. He became timid and old before his time as well as the object of derision. He found himself in a permanent state of doubt, lost his prosecutorial edge and never regained his mediocre skills, despite his Chief Minion's best efforts. Eventually, Malatesta refused to boast about his non-accomplishments and disappeared from public view. A shell of his former self, he spent his days in solitude, holed up in his office, brooding over Plotkin's acquittal and railing against the Jury system. "Had it not been for the Jury, I would have won," he was often heard to mumble when the door was open.

After the campaign to eliminate trial by jury failed, Cicero Bookbinder resigned from the Inner Chamber to become a professional lobbyist. In that monetarily rewarding capacity, he hectored former colleagues to enact laws for the benefit of captains of industry and any organizations willing to pay his exorbitant fees. Bookbinder utilized methods lobbyists had practiced on him, became wealthy and achieved a degree of influence comparable to his time as Leader, but without the burden of standing for election every five years.

Mendel Sprem continued to function as Bookbinder's "Brain" while the lobbyist lobbied. As such, he shared some of the monetary fruits of Bookbinder's labors and remained loyal even after Bookbinder was charged with illegal influence-purchasing, arrested, and incarcerated in Purgatory. A jury trial resulted in a "Not Guilty" verdict, clearing the way for Bookbinder's return to lobbying. Following the acquittal, Bookbinder affirmed on the Courthouse steps his lifelong, unflagging confidence in the jury system and declared himself utterly vindicated. Sprem remained the source of Bookbinder's success until the former Leader was later convicted of bribery and imprisoned. While the former Leader languished in Purgatory, Sprem wrote an unauthorized biography of Bookbinder in which he exposed the vacuous politician's ineptitude. It became a best seller and enabled the former Alter Ego to retire to a life of luxury.

After Plotkin's trial, Felix I. Bleifus continued to work at the Society for the Apparent Representation of Indigent Criminal Types. Still laboring in obscurity, he grew obsessively jealous of Guda Prikash's meteoric rise from an unknown to the apogee of the Trialmongerhood on the heels of Plotkin's acquittal. As a result, he brooded over his lost opportunity to represent the butcher. Convinced, despite his severely limited litigational skills and poor study habits, that he would have prevailed at the butcher's trial, Bleifus told colleagues he could have been *somebody* were life fair, a refrain that drew laughter and other skeptical reactions.

In the years following the Mud Crisis, life in the Republic continued much as it had been before the crisis. There were other occasional crises and outbreaks of hostilities on the Republic's borders. No other matter, however, captured the public's attention as the Mud Crisis had, and it became the standard by which all other social upheavals were measured. Scholarly books, treatises and other writings about it continued to be published long after Leopold Plotkin's death—twenty years to the day he first covered the display window with mud.

After his burial, a plaque commemorating Plotkin was hung on the wall where the once infamous display window stood. It read:

> ON THIS SITE LEOPOLD PLOTKIN INVENTED A NEW SCHOOL OF ART THAT WILL INSPIRE GENERATIONS TO COME. UNFAIRLY PROSECUTED FOR HIS INNOVATION, BUT ALWAYS UNDAUNTED, THIS ARTISTIC GENIUS PRODUCED A LARGE CANON OF WORK THAT HAS BROUGHT IMMENSE AESTHETIC PLEASURE TO COUNTLESS CITIZENS. WE MOURN HIS PASSING.

These words confirmed what Hinta Gelb had prophesized years earlier, when Plotkin was a child prodigy studying at her feet. She firmly believed that he would someday be a person of prominence and command the respect of his peers. Although it had taken most of a lifetime to achieve, the erstwhile butcher did, in fact, become one of the Republic's most revered figures.

OTHER ANAPHORA LITERARY PRESS TITLES

Film Theory and Modern Art
Editor: Anna Faktorovich

Interview with Larry Niven
Editor: Anna Faktorovich

Dragonflies in the Cowburbs
Donelle Dreese

Domestic Subversive
Roberta Salper

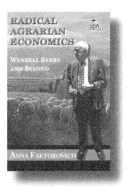

Radical Agrarian Economics
Anna Faktorovich

Fajitas and Beer Convention
Roger Rodriguez

Spirit of Tabasco
Richard Diedrichs

Skating in Concord
Jean LeBlanc

CPSIA information can be obtained at www.ICGtesting.com
Printed in the USA
BVOW08s1244240216

437877BV00002B/136/P

9 781681 141978